END

An absolutely gripping classic British whodunnit

JANET NEEL

A Wilson and McLeish Mystery Book 7

Previously published as *O Gentle Death*

JOFFE
Ostara
CLASSICS

Revised edition 2024
Joffe Books, London
www.joffebooks.com

First published as *O Gentle Death* in Great Britain in 2000

This paperback edition was first published
in Great Britain in 2024

Cover art by Dee Dee Book Designs

ISBN: 978-1-83526-454-6

For my dancer daughter, Isobel Cohen

CHAPTER 1

Monday, 17th April

> *'Me, me and none but me, dart home, O gentle death.'*

Detective Chief Superintendent John McLeish, who had just let himself into his house, glanced irritably up the stairs. He had hoped to find his wife and small son alone, but he could hear the piano.

> *'And quickly, for I draw too long this idle breath'*

—the high, clear voice continued, with passion—

> *'Oh how I long till I may flee to heaven above*
> *unto my faithful and beloved turtle dove.'*

This was the more annoying since he had brought home a new, remarkably young Detective Inspector Camberton, just arrived from Hull, so they could both pick up some clothes prior to getting to a double murder on the western edges of the Met's territory. He looked back, apologetically, but his new DI appeared to have been turned to stone, as the voice started again:

'Like to the silver swan, before my death I sing
And yet where my fatal knell I help to ring
Still I desire from earth and earthly joys to fly
He never happy lived that cannot love to die.'

'It's probably one of my brothers-in-law playing around,' McLeish said, crossly.

'One of them is a countertenor? An alto? I thought they were tenors.'

So they were, McLeish recollected. So what on earth was a countertenor? Someone who sounded more like a boy or a woman, he decided, listening to the voice. 'My wife's an alto — it must be her.'

Camberton gave him the cautious look of one dealing with a rather slow child, and he decided he probably had that wrong too. The voice was stronger and louder than his wife's. He stamped upstairs. If Francesca had adopted another child musician to add to Jamie, for whom she often had to stand *in loco parentis*, and their own William and the baby expected in three months' time, he would put his foot down.

He pushed open the door of the big first-floor living-room which, like all the houses in Francesca's family, had a piano at one end. His wife walked over to him, all smiles, the bulge of the baby already conspicuous. Her godson, the eighteen-year-old Jamie Miles Brett, who appeared to have grown again since he had last seen him, three weeks ago, rose from the piano with cries of welcome, but McLeish's attention was on the three strangers, two boys and a girl of about Jamie's age. One boy was also tall, over six feet, though he could give him a couple of inches. And a personality, dark blond with wide blue eyes, a full-lipped mouth and square cheekbones, slightly puglike if you were being perfectionist, but this boy's easy relaxed grace suggested that people did not usually exercise critical faculties in his vicinity.

'Giles Quentin. How kind of you to have us here to rehearse,' the boy said, gracefully. 'I'm one of Jamie's Faraday friends.'

'And this is Damien Fry, also at Faraday's' Francesca said, prodding forward the slight, dark boy, 'and Catriona Roberts, who is another school friend.'

Miss Roberts, dark, not pretty, very tense, with lank hair, severely bitten fingernails and, he observed, every nerve sharply alerted, bandaged wrists. He shot his wife a look of enquiry and reproach which she ignored in favour of taking them to the other end of the room, handing over a suitcase and asking if he and Inspector Camberton were honouring them for lunch.

'The children are staying,' she pointed out. 'I thought you were away. I'm rehearsing Giles and Jamie for tomorrow, and Damien and Catriona were waiting to take them off for the afternoon.'

'What is tomorrow?' Kevin Camberton asked.

'Recital. In the Wigmore Hall. The boys are doing a set of songs, mostly Dowland and some Purcell. Jamie should be playing a lute, but you can't have everything.'

'So it is Mr Quentin, who is the countertenor?' Camberton asked.

'That's right. And a very good one too. So, can you wait ten minutes while we finish, or are you starving?'

'Oh, that's very kind of you, but I have to get to my flat and pick up a bag,' Camberton said, reluctance in his voice, and she considered him.

'Do you want to wait while we do the last song?'

'I'd love to,' he said, avoiding McLeish's gaze, and she waved him to a sofa next to Catriona Roberts and Damien, placed herself by the piano at Jamie's elbow and nodded to the boys to start.

It was another Jacobean hymn to the pleasures of Death, every word audible, and to McLeish's critical ear totally implausible, coming from the lips of the self-confident Giles, who knew he was good and wasn't in the slightest bit interested in dying before everyone else had had a chance to appreciate him. But it was an extraordinary voice, in a totally different place from the lad's light baritone speaking voice. It had a flat purity, almost inhuman except for the passion with which he was infusing the unlikely sentiments of the lyric.

'Tears, sighs and ceaseless cries alone I spend
My woe wants comfort, and my sorrow end.'

The eerie, pure sound died away on the long-held last note, leaving total silence in the room.

'Well, you won't do better than that,' Francesca observed. 'Just right, keep it there. Lunch?'

McLeish looked to Camberton, but the young detective was transfixed, watching Giles Quentin.

'He is *wonderful*, isn't he?' It was the worrying Catriona who spoke, pushing back her sleeves just so they all got a good look at the bandages; a sight, he was pleased to see, not lost on his new underling.

'Extraordinary,' Kevin Camberton said, seriously. 'Has he recorded anything yet?'

'No, but there are plans,' Francesca said. 'Do you sing?'

'Yes.'

'A baritone?'

'Yes. Yes, indeed.'

They looked at each other with interest, and McLeish decided to intervene before his new DI got into the act.

'So, Kevin. You take the car and come back for me.'

'Sir.' Camberton rallied to his duty, said goodbye to Francesca and managed to get Giles's slightly sardonic attention long enough to wish him every success before taking himself off.

'Lunch then,' Francesca said. 'It's steak, so you can all come downstairs now and I'll take orders.'

Catriona followed them downstairs and sat at the top of the table, biting her fingernails, casting a pall of gloom around her. If Francesca was even thinking of taking this one under her capacious wing, he would fall on the plan from a great height. As you had to, and quickly; with the family he had married, non-intervention was always taken for consent.

He felt better, sitting down with the best and largest steak in front of him, in deference to his status as Father and Principal Breadwinner. The boys watched him hungrily until Francesca popped three plates in front of them and a fourth in front of the sulking Catriona. He had poured himself red wine which he offered around, being covertly pleased when the boys refused. Catriona, inevitably, accepted and drank it too quickly, bringing uneven smudgy patches to her pale face. Francesca, hospitable to a fault, pressed her to another but Jamie refused it for the girl and got her some Evian from the fridge, teasing her gently. Not his girlfriend though, McLeish observed with relief, no sexual element at all in the patient brotherly approach. The tiresome Catriona was not at all grateful for Jamie's kind attentions, being patently desperate for any crumb of notice from Giles Quentin, who was studiously ignoring her. And she was, in her turn, ignoring the slight, dark Damien, who was politely but distractedly answering Francesca's enquiries about his A-levels.

He finished his own steak but refused the offer of pudding. 'I have to get on. Kevin Camberton will be back with the car in ten minutes,' he said, meaningfully, hoping to extract Francesca from her teenage associates. 'He moves fast and I need to keep up with him.'

'He's gay, isn't he? I didn't realise they were acceptable in the police force,' Giles Quentin said, conversationally, badly startling him. He was, as it happened, in no doubt about Kevin Camberton's sexual orientation; the man had insisted on having the fact of his homosexuality recorded on his file when he had applied to join as a graduate entry. In Hull, five years ago, that had taken guts. But if Camberton had been trying to conceal or to suppress his sexuality then this casual statement to a senior colleague was either seriously malicious, or a near psychopathic absence of empathy with other people.

'Excellent man. And sensible not to try to hide it,' McLeish said, briskly.

'He's musical too.' Francesca was trying to keep the conversation light, but he could see that she too had been shaken by the manner if not the matter of Giles Quentin's disclosure.

'Well, I could do without that,' he said, straight-faced, and Jamie grinned at him. It was understood in the family that McLeish could do with a great deal less music and musicality than he got.

'You don't like music?' It was Catriona Roberts, sounding priggishly shocked.

'Don't mind a brass band, love,' he said, stolidly.

'Oh, John, you're not as bad as that,' his wife said, reproachfully. 'What is *your* preferred art, Catriona?'

'Well, I *love* music.'

Francesca's expression said unmistakably that this was not an answer to her question and the girl started to bite the nails on her left hand, hiding behind her lank hair.

'She's doing A-levels in art and theatre studies.' Jamie was sounding defensive while Giles Quentin's absence of comment or contribution was more eloquent than anything he could have said. So this difficult girl was also untalented. In the Faraday Foundation school, famed for the high level of its music, art, design and theatre, which all these four attended, she would be something of an outsider. McLeish found himself reluctantly beginning to sympathise; himself secure in his career he was still capable of feeling like a backward child in the company of the artistically gifted.

'Coffee?' Francesca offered.

'No time. We'll miss the movie.' Jamie got up and beamed at her. 'Smashing meal.'

'Have you got your key? Yes, all right, darling, I know you're eighteen and a great big competent lump, but you forgot it yesterday. Damien, Catriona, are you all set?'

'What about me?' Giles Quentin asked, laughing. 'I need lots of looking after.'

'*You* need to get to bed early tonight,' Francesca told him, briskly. 'And not to be in smoky atmospheres. I'll expect you all for supper.' She waved them off and came back to sit beside him and lean against him with a sigh. 'How long have we got?'

'About ten minutes — sorry, my love. You're not going to take over that droopy little girl, are you?'

'No. And I wish Jamie hadn't. The trouble *is* that what with his father he's used to dafties, and they all know that, instinctively, and rush to him.'

McLeish silently agreed with her assessment; Jamie, son of a schizophrenic father who had spent his adult life in and out of mental hospitals, had both the experience and the innate niceness to be an irresistible magnet for the disturbed.

'You saw her wrists?' he asked, just to make sure.

'Yes. And I'd heard about her from Jamie. She slashes them quite often, apparently. I can't think why the school keeps her — I mean imagine the trouble they've laid up for themselves if she actually does herself real harm. But they're very high-principled there, of course — it's in their charter — and they're trying to shelter her through her A-levels. Which are only about six weeks away for all those four . . .'

'Mm. I didn't terribly care for Jamie's musical friend either.' He considered her. 'I suppose you don't mind because of the voice. Like Kevin Camberton, who would have forgiven him anything.'

'Well, your new inspector understood what he was listening to. Giles is not just a magnificent countertenor, but a massive expressive talent, appallingly well developed for someone of eighteen. He's Sir Andrew Quentin's son, of course. Dad left Mum when Giles was about three and since Dad jet-sets around conducting about three orchestras at opposite corners of the world, Giles was largely brought up by his mother, Susie Miller, who is head of music at Faraday's. Married to someone slightly younger, called Piers, who, come to think of it, looks rather like Giles, large, blond, snub-nosed.'

McLeish, stirring himself reluctantly to check his suitcase, was reminded of his original question. 'Fran, what *is* a countertenor? No, sorry, wrong question — I know what it sounds like now, but why does it? The lad speaks perfectly ordinarily. Can anyone do it?'

His wife gave him just the ghost of the missionary-faced-with-savage-tribe look but pulled herself together. 'No. In the old days . . . well, until the late eighteenth century, promising trebles were castrated so that their voices never dropped, or not much, they just became stronger and developed a deeper tone.'

'But now that we don't do that anymore?'

'Chaps have to work very hard. It's an artificial voice for a normal man and not everyone can do it. But if you've always sung and your natural grown-up voice isn't useful and you *can* do alto, then I guess that's what you do, and work at it. Jamie now, as you know, has settled between bass and baritone which isn't useful for a soloist. But he is a superb violinist, and can make his living in music. If all he could do was sing, since he *must* express himself musically, he might have tried to develop an alto voice when his treble voice went.' She stopped to consider, 'Giles found he could do it straight away; he was a treble too and he went straight on into being a countertenor, so there must be a lot of nature as opposed to nurture.'

'Is Giles gay?'

'Indeed no. That's an assumption people tend to make about countertenors while in my experience it's the heavy-duty basses who turn out to be living with a boyfriend. Giles is very heterosexual, Jamie says. And I see your car outside, blast it.'

'Don't come out. And *don't* fuss over those kids. There are four of them, they can look after each other. Promise?'

She smiled at him and plastered herself to him so he could feel the baby kick, and he was several hundred yards away in the car before he realised she hadn't committed herself to non-intervention.

* * *

Seventy miles away in Dorset, the most senior staff of the Faraday Trust school were gathered to contemplate and plan for the summer term. The full staff, with visiting specialists, ran to eighty for four hundred teenagers between thirteen and eighteen, but this meeting contained only the headmaster, his deputy, heads of department and four housemasters and housemistresses, which kept it to a more manageable dozen, there being some overlap between the functions. The group was gathered round a large table in the dining-room, dressed eclectically and without particular regard to sex or age in anything from jeans to long cotton skirts to sports jackets. The slim man in his fifties, not much above medium height, hair receding decisively from a round patch at the crown of his head, watched them for a moment with affection, then stepped into the room, and the parrot-house noise of twelve people exchanging news and gossip quietened.

'Hello, Nick! Had a good weekend?'

The headmaster acknowledged this greeting and sat down, waiting for silence — as good teachers do — then said, without emphasis, that he had just come from a Trustees' meeting, which had not gone at all well.

'What were they worrying about this time?' Amanda Roberts, in her mid-thirties, thick, dark hair, good-looking and an extremely competent head of biology and chemistry, asked impatiently, and he looked at her sadly.

'The usual. Our patchy academic results, past and projected. Oh, and the more financially orientated members were concerned about our enrolment figures. We have had six or seven withdrawals for September.'

'Well, I suppose the two problems are interrelated, Headmaster, aren't they?' Piers Miller was one of the hawks among his staff; ambitious for himself and his pupils, he had not quite adjusted to the Faraday ethos, despite being married for the last five years to Susie, the head of music. Piers had come from Rugby, and he still looked like a conventional public school teacher, tall with dark blond hair, rather too long at the front, with regular blunt features. On all matters academic he was an ally of Amanda Roberts, and Nick found himself wondering whether they were hunting as a pack today. Amanda's husband, Louis Roberts, father of Catriona, now in her last year at school, was a substantial benefactor and had organised the last appeal with brutal efficiency. He was not on the Governing Body, the original founders of the Trust having had the sense to decree that no member of the Governing Body should be related by blood or marriage to any pupil or teacher at the school. His views were however represented there, and at least one member reported faithfully all discussions to him.

'I hope you took a robust line, Nick.' His deputy head, Roland Willis, was looking more like a farmer than usual today, a big shambling man with a thatch of dark hair. His customary outfit of cotton trousers and large chequered shirts and heavy sweaters only reinforced the impression, but he was a dedicated and able teacher. 'The school is about the whole child, not only about examination success. The terms of the Trust make that quite clear. And whenever we forget it, the school loses something. We just have to defend the line every time.'

Nick smiled at him; he was right, of course. Roland practised what he preached too. His stepdaughter, Catriona Roberts, was one of the school's most difficult and unrewarding pupils, but he never stopped trying with her.

'I hope you reminded them how staggeringly good our music is this year,' Susie Miller, a plump, energetic woman of forty, blond hair two shades darker than her talented son's said warmly. 'And this isn't all down to the staff, we've got some wonderful young musicians at the moment. And how did we get them? Not by worrying them about passing examinations.'

'Well, of course we're lucky enough to have two who can do the exams as well, with your Giles and Jamie Miles Brett,' Roland Willis observed.

'Yes, all right, they are both able, but that doesn't destroy my point. Both those two pass exams easily, *because* they are in a place where their musical talents can flower. Getting good A-levels in any subject is easy for them because they're both happy and fulfilled and going somewhere.'

Piers opened his mouth to speak, thought better of it, and started to draw little circles on the pad in front of him. He looked sideways at Amanda Roberts who shook her head.

'Yes, thank you, Susie.' Nick, who had managed a cup of tea and several biscuits during this exchange, took control, feeling better for the sugar in his bloodstream. 'The difficulty — as all heads are having to recognise — is that universities now operate on examination success at A-level. And parents want their children to go to university, partly because there are not that many credible jobs for people of eighteen.'

'But the children from here *do* go on to university.'

'Not all of them, and some not easily. And of course it is a consequence of what we teach them here that some of them take a few years to decide what to do and how to do it.'

'Instead of going mindlessly on from school to university to training as accountants,' Susie Miller agreed.

Her husband sighed and Nick considered him. Piers was five years younger than Susie — thirty-five to her forty — and he often wondered why he had chosen Susie instead of the many attractive women in their twenties who had obviously offered for him. Needed a mother perhaps. He nodded to him to speak; better to hear the opposition view stated now. 'The trouble is,' Piers said, to the meeting at large, 'and this is where our defences look feeble, that the more conventional schools — like Rugby, indeed — push ordinary, untalented children into perfectly creditable A-levels so they can go on to university. Not one of the top universities, but they get degrees and then they can get on with their lives. Here — and I know I've only seen three years' worth — we just don't seem to manage to push our more difficult or immature kids through even with C or D grades. And *that's* not acceptable to the average parent who's paid a small fortune for five years here. At a rate rather higher than Rugby.' Several people gaped at him. 'I checked with ex-colleagues. We're charging £500 a term more than they are. And any respectable boarding-school is costing parents £14,000 a year, which is £70,000 over five years, and you don't pay that to have the kid end up with A-levels which won't get them into anything except the University of Tooting.'

'Precisely the point which the governors were addressing this morning, Piers.' Nick tried another biscuit in the hope that he would feel less exhausted. 'Last year five of our eighty odd Six Senior got D or E grades which indeed, as we all know, will only secure entry to places neither they nor their parents wanted them to go to. And I have just had to tell the Trustees that while we expect exceptional success for many of this year's Six Senior, there are once more at least five for whom our hopes are very modest indeed. For various understandable reasons,' he added, belatedly conscious of his deputy.

'Catriona being one of them, I'm afraid,' Roland Willis confirmed. He looked at his big farmer's hands. 'I fear it was a mistake to have her in a school where I was teaching, but Louis wanted it, particularly of course since Amanda is here as well.'

Dear Roland, the head thought impatiently, only you would have stopped to pay a wholly unmerited tribute to Amanda Roberts, second wife to Louis and Catriona's stepmother by that marriage. Able teacher though she was, she was jealous of Catriona's mother — a very successful business woman now married to Roland — and worse, disliked Catriona with real force.

Roland smiled sadly round at his colleagues. 'We'd probably have done better to send her to Gordonstoun.'

'Oh good heavens, Roland,' Nick protested, gratefully, amid general laughter.

'No, you wouldn't,' Susie Miller said, firmly. 'Children like Catriona are precisely what this school is about. We have not made the success of her which we hoped — and that is *our* failure. Roland, it is the responsibility of us all. But she is better here, she has been happier, she has been more understood and loved than at any other school I can imagine. And the groundwork we lay will stand her in good stead one day.' She glanced across at Amanda Roberts who was looking sour.

Nick smiled at Susie. 'I could not — indeed I am afraid did not — this morning produce such an eloquent and clear statement of our principles. Thank you, Susie.' He looked down at his papers, trying to decide how to say what he had to, and around him the meeting went very quiet; all fidgeting ceased as twelve men and women realised that something was seriously wrong. He got his head up and looked into the anxious faces. 'At the end of this very difficult meeting, the Chairman made it clear that he thought I should consider my position. As headmaster, that is.' He paused but his colleagues appeared to have stopped breathing. 'I have considered. I have been here for twenty years, ten as headmaster, and I am fifty-five. It is time that someone else had a go at finding a way — which must *be* found or this school will be at risk — of reconnecting the ideals of the Trustees with the need to be able to send the children on their way able to fit into the modern world.'

'Don't do it, Nick.' It was Roland Willis, sounding genuinely appalled.

'I have done it, Roland. Subject to reasonable financial arrangements — and there is no suggestion that these will not be made — I shall leave at the end of the autumn term. Which gives them time to test the market. They do of course want to consider internal candidates, but if they have to go outside they know that anyone they find will have to give at least a term's notice.' He found himself able to raise his eyes and look round the table. Most of his colleagues were looking horrified, and Susie Miller was rooting frantically through her bag for a handkerchief. Piers on the other hand was gazing blankly out of the window; it was possible, he thought drily, to see the wheels turning. He glanced across at Amanda Roberts who had her head down, but the tension in every line of her neck and shoulders told him she was engaged in calculation every bit as feverish as Piers Miller's. Ah, well, he thought with relief, I'm out of it now, and so clear was the thought that he looked anxiously round to see he had not spoken it aloud. He saw against the light the rigid profile of Roland Willis, his deputy, who had been at the school as long as he had and who had worked even harder for it than he had. And who was now, alas, engaged in precisely the same process as Piers Miller, or Amanda Roberts, calculating his chances of the head's job. No, no, Roland, he thought alarmed, they don't want someone who has been at the school for twenty years like me and is imbued with the Trust values, they want the new broom, the shining A-level results, the glittering prizes. Well, that was not a problem for today, but he must talk to Roland. Or perhaps to his wife Vivienne; ambitious, capable, worldly, she would understand the Trustees' views and see how little her second husband conformed to the specification for a new head. The habits of a lifetime carried him forward; he tapped on the table for silence and plunged the meeting into a grimly detailed consideration of timetabling to ensure that public examinations, two school plays, three concerts, Founder's Day, and Parents' Day were all accommodated in the brief summer term without mortally exhausting pupils or staff.

* * *

'You shouldn't have come in, Peter. I'd have brought the stuff round.'

'Easier this way, Matthew. You can run round the office fetching things as I think of them. No, sit down for a moment — I've got a list.'

Matt Sutherland folded himself into a chair in the ground-floor meeting room of Graebner Associates, solicitors, and gazed anxiously at his senior partner. At the best of times Peter Graebner did not look the picture of health, with the sallow skin of his central European forebears and the habitual chain-smoker's cough. But today he was looking grey, and while the cough was still there he wasn't smoking and he appeared to have shrunk even from his normal five feet four. His office was a shambolic, smoke-filled den at the top of the terraced house which was Graebner Associates' principal headquarters, but it was clear that today the stairs would defeat him. Matt, twenty-seven years old, the red-headed, six-foot-two son of a robust Scots family that had emigrated to New Zealand, felt helplessly protective, and extremely insecure. Graebner Associates had been his home ever since Peter had taken a chance on giving him a training contract in preference to a couple of Oxbridge candidates four years ago.

'It's an ulcer, Matthew, not a death sentence,' his senior partner said, crossly. 'I am relieved, not distressed. I have been in great discomfort and have been fearing terrible things. An ulcer is nothing. Except of course that I have to give up smoking, which is making me short-tempered, but I console myself with the thought that if it had been as I feared, no one would have thought it worth asking me to stop.'

Matthew disentangled the thought and found himself feeling much better. Peter Graebner never told lies or less than the truth to his colleagues; unless the quacks (Matt's father was a surgeon) had missed something, Peter would be back.

'So what can I do?'

He spent the next two hours, as Peter had indicated, running up and down stairs with files and making notes. There were four partners as well as Peter at Graebner Associates, but as Peter observed, all had their own heavy loads and, apart from two cases which he had passed over, the rational thing was to give everything to the recently qualified Matt and get him to do it, stall it, or pass it up to one of the partners until Peter got back in four weeks' time. Not full-time of course, but he would be at the office, with his encyclopaedic memory for clients and cases and his thirty years' hard experience. Comforted by the thought, Matt finished his notes, and put the pile of files together.

'Right. You'd better go home, Peter.'

'There is one thing more.' Matt rose, poised to run up three flights of stairs, but Peter Graebner waved him back to his seat. 'This is a responsibility which I had undertaken personally. I had not intended to burden anyone else.'

'Yes?'

'It is a person.'

'A client?'

'No. A young woman who wishes to be a solicitor. Or thinks she might want to be one. In a firm like this.'

Matthew looked at him, appalled. 'Another one who's read about Law Centres and wants to try one. But Peter, we . . .' His voice tailed off.

'We refuse three a week. I know. But *this* one I owe. And the child — no, not a child anymore, she is twenty-two — is extremely clever. She might even be useful.'

'She done any law? How long do we have to have her?'

'She is reading law at Durham. But she wants to come for four months.'

'From when?'

'Well, she has, you see, no exams this year but all are required to have a few months work experience. So she is free, well, very soon.' Matthew gazed at him wordlessly. 'Indeed, Matt, my boy, I expect her at 6 p.m. to see us all, and she had hoped — I had hoped — that she would start with me this week. She was going to shadow me, personally.'

'You can't put her off?' No, of course Peter couldn't, he thought crossly, close enough in age to this unknown bloody girl to remember how terrible it would be for her, and Peter's expression said the same.

'I'll look after her,' he said, heroically. 'Though it won't be the same for her, shadowing me.'

'It will be better. She will see more of the grassroots detail with you, and will understand more from someone near her own age.'

'Her father saved your life, I take it?'

'It was her mother.'

'Oh.' Matt boggled, decided he dared not ask, then noticed that Peter had gone an even nastier colour. 'You go home. Now. I know your wife's waiting.' He walked round and helped his senior partner to his feet, over his protests. 'If this girl and I have to work together for four months the sooner she finds out what I'm like the better. Or she can decide to piss off now.' He had pushed open the door into the general reception which contained, unusually, only Peter's wife and a skinny girl who had looked up at him sharply as he spoke. The four of them stared at each other, like a Victorian tableau, both Graebners dumb with embarrassment, Matthew also embarrassed but determined not to back down, and the skinny girl, who had red hair scraped back off her face and was dressed as a marine in battle order, plainly furious. Her gaze shifted to Peter, her face changed and she started out of her chair.

'Peter, you need to go home.'

'He does.' Mrs Graebner moved to take him from Matt.

'I am very sorry about all this,' Peter said, grey and exhausted. 'Alexandra, my dear, here is Matthew Sutherland. Matthew, Alexandra Ferguson. Also, like you, in origin a Scot.' He looked hopelessly at the two set hostile faces and, leaning on his wife, turned to shuffle to the door.

Matthew, left to do the honours, under the interested gaze of Candace, an enormous, deeply efficient West Indian woman who was the receptionist, filter system and chief organiser, invited the girl back into the ground-floor conference room and asked for coffee. They sat down opposite each other; it endeared her to him not at all that her hair was only a shade lighter red than his own.

'I don't intend to piss off, you know,' the girl said, helping herself uninvited to coffee.

'No reason you should, if you can be useful.' Matt suppressed, rigidly, the blush he felt coming on and distracted himself by examining her more carefully. With her scraped back hair and round glasses she looked more like seventeen than twenty-two. She had very pale skin which nonetheless glowed with health, wide eyes, and a perfect fine-cut profile. And she wasn't so skinny after all, he thought, appreciatively watching the top pockets on the combat jacket rise and fall. The blue eyes behind the unbecoming glasses narrowed and he pulled himself together hastily. 'Sorry, I don't know anything about you. Peter told me you were coming about half an hour ago and he didn't have time to explain.'

'He was probably ducking it. He didn't really want someone for work experience, but Mum talked him into it.'

'But you really wanted to come?'

'Yes.' He waited for her to expand, but she was hunting in a small rucksack. 'My résumé. Mum says anyone interviewing you has always lost it.'

Matt took two sheets of paper from her and read them feeling his eyebrows go up. Ten GCSEs, all at A* grade, three A-levels, the top prize in the country for German, then what? 'You went to dance school?'

'I wanted to be a professional dancer.'

She had had two years there, then had gone to Durham where in her first year reading law she seemed to have been top. Presumably she had given up dancing because she wasn't top of that.

'I haven't given up dancing.' And the bloody girl was a mind-reader. 'I do it as well. But I couldn't make my living doing contemporary dance, which is what I want.'

'Why law?'

'I went to a lecture on constitutional law in my last year in school. It's interesting.'

'Why here then, where we do almost exclusively criminal, welfare rights and the odd landlord and tenant?'

'Because you can't *do* constitutional law. It's nice, it's satisfying, but you can't *do* anything with it. Except, I suppose, if you find you're President of Czechoslovakia.'

And she is sending me up, Matt thought, sulphurously. 'Can you type?'

'As in word-processing, do you mean? Yes. And do most forms of bog standard computing.'

'Spreadsheets? Databases?'

'Those are bog standard, surely?'

Snotty little whatnot, he thought. 'Our evening session starts in half an hour. People come in off the street, mostly new cases. Once we've taken them on we try and see them during the day. You could stay for two hours and watch me do the first interview. Or perhaps you have a date?'

'I do, but I can postpone it.' She reached across without asking him, got an outside line after a two second scan of the pad and waited, not looking at him. 'May I speak to Jamie? Jamie?' The austere face broke into a wide mouthy grin. 'I'm longing to see you but I've started this job. I've got two hours on then I'll be round. Where is it you're staying? Oh, with your godmother. I remember her. OK. I'll meet you at Pralettes.'

CHAPTER 2

Tuesday, 18th April

Francesca edged the big Volvo slowly into a narrow space between two other cars in the inadequate carpark at Gladstone College. I should have abandoned my principles on hierarchy and bureaucracy and got a space labelled BURSAR. And, she thought, conscience-stricken, another one for my friend and colleague Dame Sarah Murchieson, labelled PRINCIPAL. Sarah, who has arthritis, and I, who am six months pregnant, should not have to exhaust ourselves wrestling cars into awkward spaces. She collected her possessions from the passenger seat and discovered that she couldn't get out on the driver's side. She could get the door open, yes, and in normal circumstances she could have wriggled out, but the bulge of the baby had just got to the point where it could not be compressed. Nor could she scramble across the gear lever to the passenger side. She could back out, get out, and then what? *Push* the big Volvo into the space? And she couldn't even get her door shut again, the seat belt had escaped, obstructing her efforts at every corner.

'It's too much,' she heard herself whine and realised that this outburst of woe and self-pity was imperceptibly soothing and absolutely necessary. So she went on complaining aloud about Jamie, who had gone out again after supper and come in late, waking the household, lit up with excitement at having seen again the wonderful Older Woman who had mentored him through his first two terms at Faraday's. Then she moaned about her husband, who was there for about twenty minutes in any one day, and the forthcoming baby who would without doubt keep her awake all night for months just as its brother had done.

Exhausted by emotion, she stopped, found a proper ladylike clean handkerchief, blew her nose and prepared to address herself to the problem of how to get out of the car. She restored the driving-mirror to its proper angle and saw in it a slight blond man, who looked young until you saw the receding hair, standing behind her car in an attitude of polite attention. She considered him; and heaven alone knew how long he had been standing there, or how much he had heard, but in this new mood of calm she decided she did not care.

'Can I help?' It was a brisk, capable-sounding voice.

'Please. I can't get out, and I can't get my door closed again.'

He was at her side in a second, considering the tangled seat belt. 'Excuse me.' He reached above her shoulder and reeled in the belt, untangling it as he went, and held the door ready to close it. 'If you reverse straight out you can get out and I will park the car.'

That I can just about manage, she thought, grimly, and backed out with the handbrake still on, as she realised when she jerked to a halt. The man held the door open for her, handed her all her possessions and hopped into the driver's seat, releasing the handbrake and driving the car in at exactly equal distance from the two parked on either side in a position that left her and the bulge enough room to get in. She watched, exhausted, but appreciative, as he checked the inside of the car, picking up an envelope she had forgotten, and locked it. He gave her the key, and took her possessions back while she stowed it away in her handbag.

'Thank you very much,' she said, stolidly, managing to ignore the condition of her face and look him in the eye. 'That *was* kind. The Porter's Lodge is there.'

He went ahead of her to open the heavy door, and she felt him watch her out of sight — in case I fall down in a fit, she thought, resignedly.

Twenty minutes later, make-up on again and the morning's mail hastily looked at, she went over to the Principal's Lodge, pausing only to check she had the right papers. They were interviewing, with increasing desperation, for her successor as bursar. She had done her two-year secondment and should have been on maternity leave. There was still three months before the baby was due and she had offered to work until the last possible moment and to come back as soon as possible to cover until a successor had been found, but she and Sarah both knew this plan to be impracticable. She would need time and space to integrate a second child into the family structure even if it was a docile, easy baby, unlike its elder brother. At the same time they had agreed the first four bursarial candidates had all been potentially worse than useless. The present candidate came courtesy of the Armed Services Resettlement Board, which of itself put him ahead of the last two who might well have been sent by the Martian Redeployment Unit.

They settled themselves, agreed, again, who asked which questions and waited unhopefully as the secretary announced Lieutenant Commander Harrison, and Francesca found herself staring at the slight, brisk man who had saved her from imprisonment in the carpark. He blinked, and endearingly went pink over the cheekbones, but the principal was greeting him and he turned his full attention on her while she explained who she was.

'And I am the bursar,' Francesca said, feeling it necessary to get this point across fast. 'We met in the carpark.'

'Indeed we did,' he said, with equal briskness, and got himself sat down and given a coffee.

He was perfect, assuming he was not too good to be real, Francesca decided, after the first ten minutes, observing that Sarah felt the same. Which was a huge relief; the sixty-four-year-old Dame Sarah Murchieson had had a distinguished career as a civil servant and educationalist and had experience of all manners and conditions of men. Indeed, Francesca recalled, it had been she who had suggested the Armed Services Resettlement lot, on the basis that the military regularly cast on to the streets excellent, superbly trained people for whom they no longer had a particular slot.

Yes, all right, she thought, as the Commander dealt competently with a question about pay (a bursar's pay would not keep his hopeful family of three daughters, no, but he had a naval pension on top and would be fine), but is he going to be able to stand academic women instead of civil deferential men, working under military discipline? She opened her mouth to ask and realised that she already had a partial answer to that question from the morning's experience. She listened appreciatively while he explained to Sarah that (a) he had had charge of Wrens, and (b) male attacks of temperament simply took on a different form from female hysterics, usually involving violent attacks on naval property. She had not seen it that way, she thought, restored, but he was right. Any man in her state and predicament this morning would have banged his way out, scarring the car next to him, leading to damage and vast insurance claims, rather than collapsed in a harmless fit of weeping and wailing which left all expensive machinery intact.

They bade him farewell, reluctantly, after an hour, having ascertained that he was free to start at the beginning of June.

'Grab him,' Francesca suggested, a barely decent interval after the door had closed.

'I was going to. But I thought we'd better let him get home and give ourselves a chance to compare notes.'

'And check his references?'

'One offers subject to references. Except for you, my dear Francesca, where I knew exactly who you were and where you had been.'

'And I was only a secondee. You could have thrown me back. You *are* throwing me back, if God wills, and the good Commander accepts. You did like him, didn't you, Sarah? You wouldn't just take him in order to release me?'

'I would consider myself very fortunate to get him. I've always found the navy produced excellent people. It's being in sole charge of large ships with no one to go to for help if anything goes wrong. Makes them careful and resourceful. Now go away, Francesca, and I promise I will ring him before the end of the day and offer him your job. What time are you leaving today?'

'Five o'clock. I'm chaperoning Jamie Miles Brett at a recital at the Wigmore Hall.'

'*Jamie* is doing the Wigmore Hall? But he is only, what, eighteen?'

'He *is* very good, but he is there primarily to accompany another eighteen-year-old called Giles Quentin. Who is a marvellous, sensational countertenor, but would also never have got to the Wigmore Hall at this stage, were it not that his father is Andrew Quentin, who is spending the summer here apparently.'

'Leaving the Los Angeles Symphony Orchestra to an understrapper? I see. Oh well, that's going to be very exciting. Should I try for a ticket?'

'I'll get you one.'

* * *

'You didn't get to bed then, Kevin?'

John McLeish, who had had all of five hours' sleep, considered his inspector. They were sitting in the CID room of the local station, which was not a large one, and the room was barely adequate as an incident room. The routine was complicated because all the local CID had wanted the chance at least to see and perhaps to impress a real live detective chief superintendent so they were all there, desks huddled against the back wall, helping where they could. Kevin Camberton appeared to have worked all night, done a colossal amount and taken some extremely daring decisions, which he had not woken his superior to discuss or authorise. It had been a double murder, involving one known dealer in heroin and one male person who had no form at all and had led an apparently law-abiding life until his thirties when he was discovered all but dead, in a warehouse with the dealer dead beside him. The apparently blameless citizen had expired without saying another word to anyone, including his wife, in hysterics at his hospital bed. Or the local GP who had arrived in support of the wife, which the local force had universally commended as an unusual devotion to duty. John McLeish had gone about the task of causing all the dead drug dealer's known associates to be rounded up and questioned, leaving Kevin Camberton with the wife and the doctor. The result of this delegation appeared to be that somewhere between six o'clock that morning when he had gone to get his head down and twelve noon, Kevin Camberton had arrested both, bestowing the wife in one cell downstairs, and the doctor in another, and was withstanding steadily all requests for their release, jointly or severally.

'What was the charge?'

'Obstruction, sir.'

'You allowed them the phone call, I take it?'

'Yes.'

'And what has turned up?'

'A Mr Benjamin Latham from Arlington, Dowd. For the doctor.'

'Did he now?' Now that was interesting, and a considerable relief. An ordinary GP in that part of London could not afford Ben Latham and should not indeed have known he existed. 'What about the wife?'

'She rang her mother, who is downstairs calling upon the saints and giving the station sergeant hell. A Mrs McCully. Irish by origin. As is the doctor. His name is Farmer, but his mother was Mrs Eileen Garragher. Mrs McCully told us — and the whole station indeed.'

McLeish considered him thoughtfully. He was very young and much too thin, and homosexual, but he was a real detective and a bold man. Most ambitious detective inspectors would have woken up their detective chief superintendent before imprisoning two apparently innocent bystanders.

'What made you charge them?'

'Oh, I could hear the accent — it's not strong but it's there on Dr Farmer. And *she* was frightened of him. The wife.'

'You're assuming an IRA connection?'

'Yes. But I thought . . . well . . . since you were here it might be best if you were to talk to whoever it is in MI5. I had a friend there but he's moved on.'

And tactful with it, McLeish thought admiringly, and warily. 'Well, you're likely right. Ben Latham does a lot of the IRA legal work. MI5 will be pleased. I'll make the call but you deal with them — anyone in the Met needs to know those people. No, don't go.' McLeish, who was an excellent manager on the basis of Edith Cavell's dictum that you could do anything in the world provided you didn't mind who got the credit, rang his contact in MI5 in full hearing of the CID room. He heard the voice at the other end lift with excitement. 'Right, Kevin,' he said, handing over the phone. 'You wait and liaise with them.' He glanced round the room. 'Sorry, everyone, but if we have it right then the case will be taken away from the Met immediately. Thank you for your help. All of you.'

He tidied such papers as he immediately needed into one of his briefcases and called for his driver, deciding he would only get in Camberton's way and take the gilt off the gingerbread if he stayed. 'When they've come and gone, Kevin — and since you've been up all night — you can take the rest of the day off.'

There was no hope that Camberton would be free before 5 p.m. and it was a time-honoured Metropolitan Police joke, but it went down gratefully as it always did. He left the CID laughing and clambered into his car, divided between simple gratitude at having found such talented and confident help and a small anxiety about whether so enterprising a subordinate might one day involve both of them in a career-destroying mistake.

* * *

Matt Sutherland watched, with increasing impatience, as the tall, thin African behind the plastic-coated counter struggled to assemble two ham and salad rolls. The man seemed to need to gather his thoughts between each element of the process; he reached a thin brown languid hand for the butter, paused to decide its function and purpose, put it down, found a knife, thought about that, then slowly associated roll and butter. He gazed at his work for a minute before beginning the hunt for ham, lettuce, mayonnaise and the other half of the bun, all in slow motion, while Matt waited on the verge of saying something unbrotherly. Finally, the man presented him and Alexandra with the untidy fruits of his labours, lettuce seeping at all angles from roughly cut buns with a smile of ineffable peaceful goodwill. Alexandra produced the right money, shaking her head at Matt's offer to pay, and leant over the counter to help the man get it into the right parts of the till.

'No reason you should pay for my lunch,' Matt grumbled, as they sat down. She had left him at 9.30 the night before and by the time he arrived at nine this morning she had left on his desk perfectly word-processed notes of the interviews they had done. He had been secretly relieved to discover that she had missed the point altogether in one out of six and omitted a minor point in another, but it was a formidable performance. He had not yet had time to talk to her about her notes, or anything else, but had swept her off with him to West London Magistrates where he had two customers appearing.

'The man is too stoned to manage change. We'd be here all afternoon.'

I am getting *old*, Matt thought, with a pang, not to have recognised a man high on ganja. He probably thought he was floating through the trees, not fixing a ham roll. He gazed at her, sheltering behind her glasses, her hair pinned into a topknot today, above an enormous sweatshirt which fitted nowhere and camouflage trousers.

'One thing you need to remember about drugs, one strike and you're out as a lawyer.' As I very nearly was, he remembered, and but for Francesca McLeish I would have been. Which reminded him about last night. 'Did you have a good drink with your man?'

'Not my man. My prot from school.'

'Your prot?'

'Short for protégé originally. At Faraday's, where I went, everyone in the Sixth was responsible for someone in the third year — the new thirteen-year-olds. Jamie was mine.'

'But Jamie's a boy?'

'Of course. Oh, I see. The school was co-educational but there were more girls than boys in my year so a lot of us had boys to look after. And Jamie is a musician so it seemed sensible for me to have him.'

'His second name isn't Miles Brett by any chance?'

She choked on her coffee. 'How did you know?'

'And his godmother, where he's staying, is called Francesca Wilson? Francesca McLeish rather?'

She was gazing at him as if he had produced a rabbit from his ear.

'Francesca's mum is a volunteer at the Refuge — you haven't seen it yet, but we do all their cases. We go over there on Thursdays to see what's what. Also we get called out there in emergencies.'

She took off the spectacles and cleaned them on a corner of the sweatshirt, watching him disbelievingly. 'I'm meeting Mrs Wilson tonight. Jamie and Giles are at the Wigmore Hall. Francesca is Jamie's mother's third cousin. I haven't seen her since I left school which is four years ago. She's pregnant so Jamie and I went out to a coffee bar last night. But she's coming tonight.'

'I know Francesca quite well too.' A very temperate statement, he thought, considering they had had a brief but passionate affair eighteen months before. She had not meant to do that, he knew, and regretted it, but this had not dented his affection for her, or his amusement when she tried to treat him as a younger brother, from the height of her eight years' seniority. 'She's filled in several times at the Refuge for her mother,' he added, hastily. He considered Alexandra, who was still looking mildly shell-shocked. 'So this was a boarding-school. A private school.'

She blinked and put the glasses on again. 'Yes. I didn't go till the sixth form. I wanted to be out of London and I wanted to dance and I was at my mother's old school which is in the middle of the City, very academic and plays games. And is all female.'

'Ah.'

'No need to say it like that. I have older brothers and missed them and I wanted to have ordinary friends who were boys, not boyfriends.'

'And all that worked. You liked it.'

'I loved it. I still miss it. And it was great to see Jamie again.'

Matt considered his old school with some bemusement; a large all-male state school in Christchurch where, on the whole, you worked professionally and got the hell out the second the bell rang at the end of the last lesson. He hadn't disliked it but the idea of missing it was wholly foreign. But Alexandra was looking quietly happy, the wide mouth curling at the corners as she gazed out of the misted windows.

'So what time do you need to leave for this outing?'

'Oh.' He was relieved to see this formidable girl disconcerted. 'Six o'clock, if that's all right. I'm sorry, I didn't think about evening sessions.'

'Oh, that's all right,' he said, magnanimously. 'People are only expected to do two a week. And I'm only on call tonight anyway. We have one fully qualified solicitor on call during the night just in case anything serious comes in.'

'Do all solicitors work this hard? I mean such long hours?'

'We work long hours so the clients can get to us, which is often only after normal working hours. Or when they can leave the kids with someone. But all London solicitors work hard. I've got mates in the posh City offices who are working nights all the time on the big deals. They get better money.'

'Like my mother.'

'Is she a lawyer?'

'A tax barrister. Never sees a human being unless they have a problem of more than £1m.'

'Ah.'

'No, "ah" about it. I love her, I just don't want to do that or live like that.' She looked at him through the unbecoming glasses. 'What does your mother do?'

'She's a housewife. My father is a surgeon.' Did Alex have a father, or had she sprung fully armed from the head of her tax barrister mother? Had he raised a painful subject?

The beautiful face split in its wide frog grin. 'My poor old pa's an engineer, and he works all hours too.'

Matthew decided he knew better than to ask; the poor old man referred to was probably consulting engineer to the Queen, or near offer. And Alex loved him too, that was clear.

'Back to the salt mines then.' He nodded sternly to the stoned help who gave him a wide unfocused happy smile and wished them 'Peace', a kind thought but unlikely to be realised, with clients packing out the waiting-room.

* * *

'Do I have to come tonight?'

'No, you don't. Jamie's not expecting you.'

McLeish, who had left a difficult meeting to ring home and explore his options, was momentarily relieved, but something about his wife's voice alerted him. 'You all right?'

'A bit tired. We found a successor for me this morning, only now Sarah can't *find* him to offer him the job. So I'm a bit edgy.'

'And you are tired. Do *you* have to go?'

'Oh, darling. Of course I do. I wouldn't miss it for anything. Besides which I am representing Perry.'

John McLeish's enormously successful singer brother-in-law, Peregrine, was in San Francisco promoting his latest record, but why his presence would have been expected, or desired, at this concert momentarily eluded McLeish and he said so.

'He pays Jamie's fees at Faraday.' She was sounding surprised.

'I thought the lad had a scholarship.'

'So he does. It's one of those scholarships limited to choristers who also play two instruments.'

'And are called Jamie Miles Brett.'

'Something like that, yes. Jamie made quite a lot of money as a treble, but of course it ran out pretty fast, because his father only earns when he is out of the bin. And not very much then. So Perry stepped in, what, two years ago to keep Jamie at Faraday's.'

'You never told me.'

'I expect you were working too hard for us to bother you.'

A typically swift sibling response, McLeish thought, and an equally typical family arrangement which nobody had bothered to tell him about despite the fact that Jamie spent a part of every school holidays under his roof.

'Darling? I'm sorry. I didn't mean not to tell you. We were so obsessed with not telling anyone except the headmaster at Faraday's. And then I forgot you didn't know.'

The trouble was, he thought, that he probably *had* been working, and the whole thing would have been fixed by Francesca in about ten minutes when she could find Perry and his cheque book. But it did give him an uneasy feeling of several lives going on under his roof which he didn't even know about.

'I'd like to try and get to the concert,' he decided. 'And I want to get you home afterwards. So keep me a seat — end of a row.'

'Oh good.' Her voice lightened and he resolved, again, to try and get back at a reasonable hour more often.

He arrived with all of three minutes to spare, neither he nor a police driver being immediately familiar with the exact location of the Wigmore Hall. He scrambled out of the car, and stopped, dismayed, in the entrance hall; there was no sign of his wife, and a substantial queue at the small box office where she would have left his ticket.

'Detective Chief Superintendent McLeish?' He looked down at a young woman, dressed in a tight polo neck sweater that made the most of some very elegant curves and a long black velvet skirt. She was a redhead, the long hair curling on her shoulders, dark eyebrows and long eyelashes in bright contrast to a pale, fine skin.

'Yes.'

'I have your ticket. I made Francesca go in, it's too crowded here. We have to hurry.'

She was a tall girl, he saw, as she turned to lead the way, made taller by the pair of hiking-boots she seemed to be wearing under the long black velvet skirt, and by the way she moved, upright and graceful. He could see two seats waiting for them in the middle of the row and hesitated; the lights were beginning to dim but the girl in front of him was in no doubt about where they needed to be and had the whole row on its feet to let them through. She stood aside to let him sit next to his wife and sat herself on his other side.

'I thought you were keeping an end seat for me,' he whispered to his wife.

'That young woman — Alexandra — would not permit it. She said Jamie often spoke of you and that you must be next to me in the middle so that you could really see.'

With a strong feeling that he had arrived in the middle of a serial of which he had missed the earlier episodes, McLeish gazed at a stage empty of everything except a grand piano. The auditorium lights dimmed and his wife nudged him.

'Three in front of us, and to the right. Sitting by himself. Andrew Quentin. Conducts the Los Angeles Symphony and guests for the LSO. Giles's father, as you see.'

You could indeed, McLeish thought, considering the blunt profile presented to him. Like his son, Andrew Quentin was dark blond and sallow skinned with a high square forehead, high flat cheekbones and a wide full-lipped mouth. And a big chap, even sitting down you could see he was tall and took up a lot of space, both arms extended over the backs of the empty seats either side of him. He looked perfectly at home, as if he was in his own living room, plainly impatient for the performance to begin. As McLeish watched, the lights went down conclusively and Andrew Quentin sat up and firmly led the applause that greeted the two boys walking onto the stage, Jamie violin held in his left hand and a stolid plump boy with thick glasses called Will something whom he vaguely remembered from the school. He watched Jamie; the boy was nervous and no wonder, for all he had been performing as a chorister since he was eight years old — and a soloist from not that much older — this was something else, his first semi-professional date as a solo violinist. McLeish glanced at his wife, pale and biting her nails, and put a comforting hand on her knee.

Will something, looking as cheerful and stolid as if he were still at school, though surely he must be nervous too, played a chord while Jamie checked the tuning on the violin. The boys looked at each other, and nodded. Will's hands came down firmly on the piano, Jamie's elbow moved, and they were off. Mozart or near offer, McLeish thought, he would have to look it up in the programme at half time, but it didn't go on too long. And when it ended instead of the decorous clapping he had expected, piercing whistles and shouts of 'Jamie', 'Will' broke out all over the auditorium. On his right the beautiful redhead, looking about twelve years old, was stamping her feet and whistling as piercingly as the boys, two fingers stuck in the corners of her wide mouth. Andrew Quentin, clapping hesitantly, swung round to gaze at the noise-makers, and raised an eyebrow at him, acknowledging the presence of another grown up.

'You'd think the good Sir Andrew would be used to the traditional Faraday reception.' Francesca, pink with relief, was doing her share of stamping but blessedly not whistling. 'I see it must be a surprise to the rest of the audience but surely as Giles's father he must have seen it before. Half the school seems to be here — a real tribute to the boys that, not all these kids can be musical.'

No indeed, McLeish thought but then neither am I and here I am. Will and Jamie were leaving the stage, finally, and there was a pause while nothing much seemed to be happening, and the audience started to chatter.

'I expect Jamie's having a pee,' Francesca said, sotto voce. 'He's on again with Giles of course.' Indeed and of course he would be, as Giles's regular accompanist. McLeish considered Andrew Quentin who was sitting impressively still, arms stretched, head thrown back, and realised the man was rigid with tension, as strung up as Francesca had been waiting for Jamie to perform. It never got any better then, or not for the spectators.

Jamie and Giles walked onto the stage, acknowledging steady applause, and this time it was Jamie who sat at the piano, played a couple of chords and looked up at Giles, waiting for him to be ready. Neither of them, McLeish realised slowly, had any music with them, they were doing it all from memory, nothing to cue them if they fluffed from nerves. He understood suddenly that these boys — these young men — were professionals, this was their trade, and however unmusical he might be, this he could understand and take seriously.

The boys nodded to each other and Giles started to sing, the high unearthly sound reaching every corner of the hall. McLeish was expecting the minor key dirge about dying swans that he had last heard floating into the quiet street, but to his surprise and pleasure the tune was familiar. He searched his memory and then got it. It was a Kathleen Ferrier number, 'Art thou weary', a great favourite of his mother's, and he could have sung along with it if anyone had wanted him too. Except it appeared to be sung in Italian. He frowned over the small puzzle and settled to listen to the beautiful, authoritative voice. It was superbly sung, he could hear that, but for him the Kathleen Ferrier version was better. Not, he understood now, that this boy was any less of a musician than she, or that his voice was not of staggering quality, but because it was inhuman, like an instrument, a trumpet perhaps, whereas with Kathleen Ferrier you were listening to a person.

There was a respectful pause as the song ended, and McLeish thought that you could almost feel the Faraday kids remembering that you did not applaud until the end of the group. He watched Andrew Quentin; the man had relaxed perceptibly, the shoulders had flattened. Jamie and Giles grinned at each other in a moment of perfect understanding, and set off on the next song, a jolly piece about romping in the hay with some girl. Then another, rather more serious, then the dirge about the swans which was now almost familiar, then a lament. Then they stopped, and Jamie got up from the piano and stood by Giles to bow, and the same violent whistles and stamping came from the Faraday-dominated audience. More so for Jamie than for Giles he noticed and this was a musical school, they must know that Giles was a very rare talent. They just like Jamie better; well so did he.

'That lament was also from *Rodelinda*. Like "Dov'e sei",' his wife said, instructively, as the audience quietened down.

'Which was "Dov'e sei"?'

'Ah. I thought you recognised it. I expect you know it as "Art thou weary". Kathleen Ferrier.'

McLeish agreed meekly that this was his understanding and she explained that it was in fact the exiled Bertarido, King of Lombardy's, lament from a Handel opera called *Rodelinda*.

'Why is it in Italian?' McLeish asked, crossly, having once established, he thought, that Handel — very decently for a German — wrote in English.

'Because he had two or three star Italian castrati singing for him, I expect. Plus an Italian soprano. It probably seemed easier than getting them to learn English. Alexandra.'

The redhead, who had been conversing with a child five rows in front, turned round.

'Very clever to find John. Thank you.'

'I'd met him before. He's forgotten me.'

As McLeish looked at her blankly she produced a pair of battered spectacles from a pocket of the skirt, put them on and put up both hands to pull her hair back from her face. She smiled at him, the classical lines of the face vanishing in a broad monkey grin.

'I remember now. You're the dancer.'

His wife gaped at him, but he was on sure ground. 'We came down to see Jamie and he dragged me into your show while Frannie was talking to the head.'

The girl, blushing slightly, dropped her hands so the red hair fell round her face, and took the glasses off. 'I still can't see but I've got contacts in,' she said, confidingly, to McLeish.

He opened his mouth to ask her what she was doing now but was distracted by Francesca's employer.

'Dame Sarah . . . Sarah. I gather you've found a bursar.'

'I do hope so, John. In fact if you can clear the way for me, I'm going to telephone again, quickly. I think he really wanted the job, but both Francesca and I would sleep better tonight for knowing he was on board. Oh dear, why does one always lapse into metaphor — he was a lieutenant commander in the navy, that's the trouble, I expect she told you.'

McLeish helped her negotiate her way out of the row, noticing that she was stiff in both legs and hoping very much that she was about to acquire help which, if not more talented or hard-working than his wife, was not going to disappear in a few weeks' time. She was stopped in her attempt to leave by a plump, vigorous woman of perhaps forty, dark blond and faintly familiar.

'Dame Sarah? Do you remember me? Susie Miller, or no, I would have been Susie Quentin.'

'Of course I remember you. My dear, I just hadn't put the names together — that wonderful young man must be your son. Yes? This is John McLeish.' She looked round and seized on Francesca. 'And here is John's wife and Jamie's godmother, do you know each other?'

'Indeed we do. And I saw Alexandra with you just a minute ago. She was one of my German set and got the top mark in German at A-level in all the University Boards.'

'Your pupils usually do well, but you must have been particularly pleased.' Sarah Murchieson carried in her head, apparently effortlessly, the general abilities and records of an incredible number of sixth-form staff.

Susie Miller turned pink and beamed. 'I was. Mind you, Alex was a worker. Unlike my own Giles.'

'He must work at his music.'

'Sometimes.' Susie Miller, who had taught for over twenty years, was stating a fact, they all understood, and McLeish was interested, but remembered Dame Sarah's need for a telephone and escorted her to the foyer. He went back to collect Francesca and found her, leaning on a row of stalls, one hip stuck out, still in conversation with Mrs Miller and a large untidy older man.

'He is brilliant, Susie,' he heard the older man say as he arrived, scowling, because he could see that Francesca needed to get the weight off her feet. She smiled at him, the blue eyes gone darker and hollowed as they did when she was tired.

'Mr Willis, my husband John. Mr Willis is Jamie's housemaster and Catriona's stepfather. You remember her, she was there when you came home for lunch yesterday.'

The droopsy girl, he recalled, and saw her, hanging back from the group, biting her fingernails.

'I wanted to go round to see Jamie,' she said, generally, in a thin little voice.

'Oh, no, one doesn't,' Francesca said, promptly, and the girl looked miserable. 'Believe me, he'd *hate* it. I wouldn't dare and I've known him since he was born.' She saw she was not being convincing. 'I never go round at the interval for my brothers either. They'd kill me.'

The group all laughed, probably at the idea that any brother would dare to lay a glove on Francesca.

'Is your mum here, Catriona?' She was asking kindly, but Catriona simply looked even more wretched and mumbled that she was over there somewhere. McLeish could only sympathise with Roland Willis's look of momentary furious irritation.

'Does she teach at the school?' Francesca had seen it too and was trying to lighten the atmosphere.

'No, no. She's a fund manager.'

'Who with? Oh, them. They're the college advisers. Very good woman on the team, called indeed Vivienne Willis. So *that's* your mum, Catriona.'

Less than tactful, dearest wife, McLeish thought, to identify with such obvious interest a woman who was all that her daughter was not, organised, successful, presumably happy. Catriona looked at her feet, sunk even deeper into depression, and Francesca, realising her mistake, was casting around for something to offer, when they all saw Sarah Murchieson working her way slowly down the side aisle, a smile from ear to ear.

'He's accepted?' Francesca's clear voice carried effortlessly over the general hubbub, and Dame Sarah, as befitted her seniority, merely nodded vigorously. Francesca, liberated, surged up the aisle to confer with her, leaving McLeish to explain to the group the reason for their joy.

'We have an ex-navy chap as bursar too.' The head had joined them, having picked his way across through the riotous teenage audience all of whom had greeted him with pleasure and absolutely minimum deference. 'Excellent man.' The head was looking much older, McLeish thought, although it was only two years since they had last met. 'Catriona, I've just been talking to your father. He was looking for you in case you wanted a drink or something to eat. I'm afraid we may be running out of time though. Dame Sarah, I've just been hearing of your good fortune.'

'Nick, how are you?' Sarah reached over and kissed him. 'What a lovely school you have. I'm sorry we're only getting one of yours this year.'

'Yes, but such a *good* one,' the head said, with enthusiasm, his face lighting up. 'You'll enjoy Jenny. And of course, Sarah, if Gladstone were open to young men as well more of our Sixth would apply.'

Sarah and Francesca glanced at each other; this was an old sore. Both of them were in favour of mixing the college, but they had the statutes to contend with. Both of them knew that Sarah Murchieson as warden was going to seek the Governing Body's agreement for a change in the statutes, starting her campaign in the next academic year. She was being moved to this drastic and potentially upsetting reform by precisely the point Nick Lewis had just made; girls from co-educational schools were not prepared to take what they saw as the retrograde step of applying for an all-female college. With single-sex grammar schools being disestablished and, seemingly, every boys' school in the country — except Eton and Harrow — inviting girls into their sixth forms, applicants for all-female Gladstone were thinner on the ground and of decreasing quality.

The lights started to go down and teenagers scrambled back to their places to listen, with apparently ungrudging pleasure, to their talented contemporaries. Except Catriona, McLeish observed, reading her mind, who was hating every minute of it, perceiving Jamie and Giles distancing themselves from her with success. He watched, curious, as she worked her way back to her seat, drooping, and on some instinct looked up towards the balcony, where he saw Kevin Camberton, his new inspector, sitting in the second row. He was momentarily dismayed but pulled himself together; the man was evidently musical, Giles Quentin was a stunning talent, there was no reason to suppose that it was anything more, well, difficult that had brought Camberton here. He looked again, casually, and was cheered; Kevin Camberton was with a friend, another man, talking with obvious easy pleasure. They looked happy, which was more than could be said for Catriona, and he resolved again to ensure she didn't become another house familiar.

CHAPTER 3

Friday, 5th May

'Right, Mary, this is Alexandra.'

'We've *met,* Matt.' Alex was dressed today in black jeans with the bottoms slit at each side to accommodate the boots with two-inch thick soles and a battered sweatshirt which proclaimed her unalterable opposition to the demutualisation of the building societies. 'Two weeks ago, at Jamie and Giles's concert.'

'Oh right.' Matt saw his chance. 'Can I leave Mary to explain the form here — I have a call I must make.' He shot out again on to the pavement and walked a good twenty yards away from the Refuge's door, checking automatically that there were no watchers. The West London Refuge, which took in women in flight from battering partners, often accompanied by small, terrified children, was not listed in any phone book and its address was given out only under conditions of secrecy to those who needed to use it. It looked like an ordinary small terraced house in a row of identical other such, with nothing to show that the doors to the houses on either side were nailed shut and that three houses had been put together, in the cheapest way that could be devised at the time, so there were doors in places where none could have been expected and no means of access where a door should have been. But despite its careful anonymity, the men from whom the Refuge women were taking flight occasionally found out where they were and would hang around the street in desperation or terrible uncontrollable rage. There were people about on this bright May evening but the only lone men were walking briskly and preoccupied. Satisfied that the coast was clear, Matt leant against a lamppost and pulled out his mobile phone, following the unfamiliar number in his diary.

'Peter. You by yourself or surrounded by beautiful nurses?'

'I am alone. At last.'

'How are you?'

'Terrible, but they say they are pleased with me. And you? Is the Graveley case all right?'

'Yeah, yeah, all under control, don't even think about it. Look, what I need to know is, are we paying Alex? You didn't tell me.'

'Ah. Alexandra.' Matt waited, interested. 'Is she being useful?'

'Yes.' He waited again.

'Matt, I know we do not usually pay people on work experience but this child needs not to live at home, with the parents who love her.'

'So we're paying her.'

'Not very much, Matthew, her parents pay her rent and her classes.'

'Peter. How much?'

'I have promised her £50 a week.'

'That's fucking disgraceful.'

'It isn't much to eat on, Matthew.'

'To pay anyone that little is appalling. She's doing fifty hours a week.'

'Ah. She *is* useful.'

'I told you. She's covering for Louise this week and the next two. So I haven't had to get a temp.'

'It would not be proper to use her only as a secretary, Matt.'

'She does a lot of interviewing by herself now when she's with me and takes notes.'

'Indeed! And you like her?'

'She's smart as a whip. What about £150, which is about half what we pay a temp.'

'Well, Matt. Yes. But through the books.'

'How else? Get better, Graebner, we still need you.' He rang off, grinning with relief. He had been watching Alex and had begun to notice that she didn't seem to eat much and that she studied a menu with great care to pick the cheapest and most sustaining object on it, which meant that baked beans and eggs featured largely in her choices. He had been prepared to do battle with Peter Graebner to get her properly paid, and it had amused him greatly to find his senior partner so thoroughly on the wrong foot.

He was still grinning as he knocked on the inconspicuous door and gave the password. He was startled to find it was Francesca who opened it. 'Where did you come from?' He gazed at her as she stood back on her heels, bulge worn well forward, and resisted the temptation to pat it, just to see if it was as solid as it looked.

'Gladstone.' She, too, was grinning. 'I have been liberated. By a wonderful man who used to be in submarines and finds Gladstone child's play by comparison. He's the new bursar, he gets out of the navy in a couple of weeks, he is having a holiday and coming to us at the beginning of June. By July he will have the conn, which is submariners' language for being the person holding on to the conning tower and thus responsible, entirely, for not hitting anything. I came down to see Mum and then I'm going off to meet John.' She was clearly over-excited, flushed and pretty, and he smiled at her indulgently. 'Mum's downstairs, feeding Alexandra Refuge egg and chips. Are you not allowing her time to eat? The poor child was starving. We thought she'd fall over if asked to cope here on an empty stomach.' She gave him a careful look. 'What about you, Matt? Are you not eating either?'

He bit back the statement that he didn't need looking after: he *was* hungry and it would make Alex's need for food less conspicuous. He went down to the kitchen and took the pan firmly from Mary Wilson, who looked amused and left him frying bacon, cracking eggs neatly alongside it.

'Alex, Peter just rang me. We're paying you £150 a week, right, on Thursdays, like everyone else. He forgot to tell anyone, sorry about that, Caroline will do you a sub. We need your National Insurance number and we deduct tax and grads.'

She was staring up at him, fork suspended, Heinz sauce on her chin. 'He said you'd pay me £150?'

'I know it's below the minimum hourly wage, but you are getting a training,' he said, with every expression of earnest apology. The blue eyes behind the heavy glasses suddenly misted, and he hastily addressed himself to his bacon. 'Can you manage on that?' he asked the pan.

'Yes. Oh yes. That's great. It's more than I expected.'

'Never say that to any employer, Alex.' Francesca, still high with excitement, arrived through the door like a full gale. 'We need a lawyer upstairs when you've time, Matt. I'm off.'

* * *

The next morning, a warm, bright Saturday, Susie Miller was also cooking eggs, bacon, sausages, baked beans and tomatoes, looking sideways out at the Dorset countryside, flat, with fat cows and well-kept hedges like an eighteenth-century painting. She was glad to be occupied, it was not an easy party for a hostess, containing as it did her first husband, their son and her second husband.

'Andrew, did you want fried bread?' She waited while the resident conductor of the Los Angeles Symphony Orchestra considered the point. It was unkind to offer; he was a good three stone overweight but she was feeling less than charitable. Andrew had picked — that was the only possible word — at Piers until he had been pushed into an over-emphatic justification of his teaching career and his ambitions, and was now sulking, aware he had made a fool of himself. Giles was being no help at all, being in the maddening adolescent way preoccupied with some problem beyond the understanding of the three adults closest to him in the world. She flipped two half slices on to Andrew's already loaded plate, knowing he would eat the lot and hoping it would give him indigestion and put on a couple of pounds. In fact, she reflected, he must eat all the time to be overweight at all; he used his whole body to conduct and would be running with sweat half-way through any performance. She used, she remembered with a pang, to find the feel of his body, exhausted and soaked through after a performance, the most incredible turn-on. And so had several other women, when she had been pregnant or teaching, including the second Mrs Quentin who now travelled with Andrew, having pointedly deposited both her daughters at her old school, the smart academic, single-sex prep for Cheltenham, rather than at cosy, co-educational Faraday's. It was one of the most endearing things about the son sulking across the table, picking moodily at his bacon, that he had refused, promptly and with incredulity, when his father had dangled a music scholarship to Winchester before their eyes. 'Poor old man's losing it,' the twelve-year-old Giles had said, shaking his head, and gazing benevolently round Faraday's ramshackle buildings and admiring girls. There had of course always been admiring girls since he had joined the most junior part of the school at six.

She turned to look out of the window, leaning over the sink. A group of three girls and one boy caught her eye, walking across the field carrying plastic bags and giggling. They would be aiming for the clump of trees on the hill just outside her eyeshot from this window to have a smoke and a drink. Nearly all fourteen-year-olds experimented with cigarettes and alcohol and, while both were against the school rules, she was inclined to let them get it over with; most stopped of their own accord. Drugs, class A or B, and sexual affairs were another matter; after intensive and painful debate it had been agreed ten years ago that expulsion was the only — and automatic — punishment for using drugs, or having sex on the premises. While drugs in any form were not allowed, some allowance was made for sex, which could not be totally prohibited; there were always moonstruck couples holding hands in the nineteenth-century library, or outside the range of shabby prefabricated buildings that constituted most of the classrooms, but its fullest expression was treated as automatic grounds for expulsion. Had she seriously feared the little group were going to experiment with drugs or each other it would have been her plain duty to intervene but three girls to one, late-developing boy seemed a safe enough ratio and you surely did not need four plastic bags in which to carry drugs.

'Is there any more coffee?' Andrew, who had demolished his plate, looked up hopefully. He was looking pleased with himself, having upset Piers and worried her by extension. Actually, she realised, he was looking as he did after a successful excursion with yet another young woman but it was difficult to see how he had fitted *that* in.

'Susie, I want to take Giles back with me today for the night. Sam Leavis — you remember him? He's heard all about Giles from someone who was at the Wigmore Hall and he wants to meet him.'

'No,' she said, furiously, taken aback. 'No,' she said, recovering. 'And I mean that. A-levels are four weeks away and Giles needs all the time there is to prepare calmly. If Sam Leavis is so keen, he could either have got himself to the Wigmore Hall, or he can get here for the school show.'

'I cannot see myself suggesting to the head of the largest music agency in the USA that he comes to an amateur night two and a half hours from London,' Andrew said, equally furious, and she warned Piers, with a fierce glare, not to interfere; this was between her and Andrew and was an old battle.

'Then tough. He should have got himself to the Father and Son outing in the middle of London two weeks ago.'

'He wasn't here.'

'Too bad. Giles, let me remind you, has a place at Cambridge which depends on him getting two A grades and a B. Which is testing for anyone.'

'Magdalene would *never* let a few A-level grades stand between them and a countertenor of Giles's quality.'

'They can and would,' she said, stoutly, keeping any doubts on the matter to herself. 'Christ's turned John Dawson down last year when he got ABC instead of AAB, and he was the best bass they had seen in five years. The Dean was in tears on the phone.'

She had scored a point, at least with her son, she saw, gratefully, but Andrew was still intent on battle.

'He can't be going to do worse than an A in French or German. He speaks both fluently.'

'He is in Alan's set for both — and Alan says neither his written French nor his German is as good as it needs to be for safe As.'

'And Roland Willis, who teaches him English, says Giles simply hasn't done enough work on the set texts to be sure of a B.'

Piers had, finally, been unable to resist getting one back and she could hardly blame him.

'What *are* the set texts?' Andrew Quentin asked.

'*King Lear*, far too much of *Paradise Lost*, *Jude the deservedly Obscure*, and *Mrs Bloody Dalloway*,' Giles said, furiously.

'Given *that* attitude you can see he may have a problem with an A,' Piers pointed out. 'And these *are* set texts, and Giles knew what they were when he decided to do English rather than music for his third A.'

'Why didn't you do music, Giles?' his father asked, his eye on her.

'English seemed a much better choice,' she said. Her sympathies were with her son over at least two of the set texts, but Roland was a good teacher, far better than Laurence who had the other set, and Giles had agreed to all of this. 'At all events,' she said, breathing in, 'Giles cannot be confident of two As and a B; things can always go wrong on the day, and I do not want him distracted.'

'Doesn't Giles have a vote? I thought that was the point of this school. He might as well have gone to Winchester the way you're behaving. And they'd have made bloody sure he got three As.'

Piers started to speak and Giles got up and made for the door, banging it as he went out.

'Come back here,' his father shouted, scarlet and starting out of his chair, but Susie, beside herself, pushed him back.

'You can't walk in here every six months and upset Giles and all our plans. He needs to be quiet and work, not to be jerked around in London. Sam Leavis will still be interested in him after his A-levels. Leave him alone, can't you? He'll be out of school, exams finished in two months' time, then you can mess us all around.' She was scarlet, near tears, and shaking with rage; Andrew had always been able to madden her and drive her into injudicious, unteacherly behaviour, and the fact that she was now forty seemed not to have helped at all.

'He really could drop to a C for English, I'm afraid, if he doesn't put in a bit more work.' Piers meant to help, but he had the disadvantage of being both right and married to her.

Andrew opened his mouth to blast them both, but the door flew open, banging against the edge of a kitchen cupboard, and Giles, looking both enraged and hunted, strode back into the room.

'Mum. One reason I wanted to go to London is that bloody Catriona Roberts keeps following me around. She's hanging round outside. That girl is *seriously* deranged. I can't stand it.'

'That's not a reason for running off to London when you need to work. That's a problem for the staff and I will make sure we take it on.' At least, she thought, we were getting to the real reasons here.

'Any other eighteen-year-old would kill for the chance of singing for Sam Leavis,' Andrew said, stonily.

'Not if they were the son of the great Andrew Quentin,' she said, suddenly seeing it clear. 'They'd know they didn't need to, their father had only to ask to have even the grandest agent audition their son at any time.'

Andrew Quentin, faced with denying the fact of his own undoubted market power, hesitated, fatally, and his son saw it. 'So, OK,' he said, 'it's cool. I stay here, provided Mum gets Catriona off my back. You fix me up with this Leavis after A-levels. I could go wherever he is.' He spread his hands, pleased with himself, and his warring parents stared at each other.

'But if you can't get that tiresome little girl put in a bin or locked in a room, or whatever, then he might as well come to London and get a few hours' peace with me,' Andrew Quentin said, bad-temperedly, as he got to his feet and rubbed his diaphragm uneasily. Double cream in the coffee, she thought, with pleasure, on top of fried bread. 'I've got a date with the head. That's all right with you all, I suppose, I do pay the fees. You could come too, Giles, not that it's more than a courtesy call.'

'I see enough of Nick as it is, thanks, Dad. See you before you go.'

The three of them sat in the room, suddenly blessedly quiet, and she looked at them both. 'I'm going to have a coffee. Anyone else? Now, darling, Catriona. I do agree, she's clearly very depressed and a burden, and I will go over and talk to Roland.'

'She shouldn't be in this school at all.' Piers reached for the sugar, mouth set tight.

'Well, where *should* she be, Piers? All schools have problem children and this school has always — well, nearly always — been sufficient of a community to help them through. That's the point of it, we're not just an academic factory.'

'It's the same argument as with these yobs in the state schools who prevent other kids from learning anything,' her son said.

'Catriona is not disruptive in class.' She could feel herself flushing.

'Oh yes, she is. I've got friends in Piers's maths set and they say she sits there oozing misery.'

'That's perfectly true,' Piers said, judiciously. 'She casts a cloud. Very difficult for the others to concentrate.'

'You could take her individually,' Susie said, distracted.

'When had you in mind? I'm producing the third-year play, and I'm doing all Nick's current affairs teaching. This is the first hour I've had to myself in a week. *And* there are a couple more kids in my set who need a bit of individual help. I can't do it all. Catriona's in such a state she's unlikely even to scrape a pass, she's getting in the way of the others and she'll lower us a couple of places in the table all on her own if she's allowed to sit the exams. What's the point? And what are her parents doing about it? It's their responsibility.'

'Piers, I don't think we ought to be discussing all this with Giles. He ought to be working and I ought to go and talk to Roland.'

'I'm *in* this, Mum. It's me she's bugging the most.'

She looked sadly at her men and wondered what Andrew was saying, even now, to the head. 'I will do something, I promise. But in the spirit of this school, not by stamping around and shouting. Giles, why don't you work in my study here, I won't let Catriona disturb you if she turns up.'

'I have to teach.' Piers got up to go. 'But Susie, so you understand, in fairness to the rest of my maths set — and to myself — unless you can negotiate something I will have to go and see the head before Monday and say I can't go on teaching Catriona. It's a waste of time while she's in this state.' He left, on that line, and Giles took her hand.

'Sorry, Mum.'

She squeezed his hand. Her bouncing, confident boy, who looked so like his father and could behave in the same arrogant way, was looking haggard and pale, and she felt a rush of defensive love. No badly depressed contemporary was going to be allowed to threaten her only chick at this critical stage of his life. They both jumped at a knock on the door.

'Go and get started, Giles, now.' She kissed him, put his half-drunk cup of coffee in his hand, steered him along the corridor and shut the study door behind him before going to the front door. 'Yes?'

It was of course Catriona Roberts, looking miserably thin and woebegone like a stray cat, and for a moment she felt like sweeping her into the warmth of the kitchen, but remembered her promise to Giles.

'I forgot to say my father wants me to stay with him overnight. My last lesson is at eleven o'clock. Can I get the train after that? He rang last night.'

'Your father. Yes, of course, Catriona — you want to go after lunch?'

All members of the seniors were allowed to leave at 2 p.m. on Saturday provided they were back for the Sunday evening assembly at 7 p.m. and that they were staying with their parents or at a known and declared address. Any feeling of comfort this procedure gave to any house-parent was illusory, they all agreed, given that most of the Six Senior had two sets of parents, plus grandparents, aunts, uncles, godparents, and if all or any of those failed they would end up in gangs staying with each other's parents, step-parents, godparents, and so on. All the conscientious house-parent could really do was take a note of the address and hope it was the kid's real destination. After all, as they had agreed, you could not treat seventeen and eighteen-year-olds, legally able to vote and marry, as children.

She hesitated; she was housemistress and responsible for this child, but she had her own child to think of. 'I'm in a rush this morning, sorry, but of course that's all right. Have a good time, forget about the work, but try and get some sleep.' All sound, useful advice, she thought, watching Catriona trail sadly off, regretting her harsh thoughts. It was not after all Giles that the poor sad child had been hanging round to see, but herself, on the legitimate and proper duty of securing her housemistress's consent to being absent for the rest of the weekend. She decided to salve her conscience by ringing Louis Roberts just to check that Catriona was expected and to warn him that she was still depressed. Even this small, conscientious effort went unrewarded. She got an answer-phone and did not like to tell it of any of her concerns, so she confined herself to confirming that Catriona did indeed have permission to leave school premises for the night.

* * *

Alexandra Ferguson was feeling ruffled. She was sitting, knee to knee, with the sort of large braying young man she particularly disliked, at a crowded table in the Freezer, normally one of her favourite clubs. She had been invited by old friends from the fiercely academic girls' day-school she had attended before Faraday's; the girls were a bit uptight by the standards of Faraday's, but she had after all spent ten years at school with them. The men on the other hand were intolerable, mostly from the grand London boys' school where some of the girls had done their sixth-form work. She was used to her contemporaries, male and female, incautiously drinking too much, but even in their cups the Faraday boys had never been such louts. Nor had this abominable hostility to women revealed itself, welling up from a seemingly bottomless pit. The worst of it was that her female friends seemed either not to notice or to accept resignedly that this was what young men were like. She remembered the firmness with which her mother had vetoed consideration of any school which took girls only in the sixth form and blessed her silently for it. She could hear inside her head her parent saying, with her usual annoying confidence, that boys' schools who took girls only into their sixth forms were letting them in on sufferance, drawn by the girls' brains and ability, and by their parents' money. Those girls whose parents did not know better than to let them go near such an establishment would have a miserable time and have their confidence dented for ever by horrible adolescent male behaviour. She had been spot on, Alex accepted secretly, watching, horrified, one of the plump, plain but brilliant young women of her own age laugh sycophantically while her appalling escorts made loud, savagely rude remarks about the girls dancing near them.

Faraday people did not, of course, just sit, lumpen, while atrocities happened around them. They confronted awful behaviour and spoke their minds; it was all but written in the statutes. 'Do you mean what you are saying about that girl?' Alex asked the nearest young man in the controlled shout that was the only possible method of communication.

'What? 'Scuse me.' He was looking both hostile and frightened.

She repeated her question at the same pitch, but into comparative quiet, and he gaped at her. 'How would you feel if someone said that about your girlfriend, or your sister?'

'Alex . . .' It was a frightened squeak and she saw with regret that her clever, erstwhile friend was embarrassed, and that the girl she had liked least was tugging at her boyfriend to get him away from this dreadful scene.

'Jenny,' she said firmly, 'if people use language like that about women that's how they think about them, and you can't want to accept *that*.'

One of the young men started to mutter and she froze him with a look; another said something under his breath to Jenny who giggled convincingly. Alex, understanding she was outnumbered and by people she was not going to bother with ever again, considered her position. She liked the club, she was not going to walk out leaving these dreadful young men the field, but not one minute more was she going to spend in their company. She looked across at the bar where one of the barmen raised a hand to her, unhurriedly bid the group goodnight, leaving behind her a mutinous and disgruntled silence.

'Hi, Alex.' The barman, who was in his late twenties, tall, blond, superbly good-looking and gay, greeted her with real pleasure. 'Left your friends?'

'Puh-lease. The girls were friends once, but I'd never seen the men before.'

'*That's* interesting. The dark boy, *very* nice-looking, is my way inclined. In Jams the other night with an older boy. What's he doing with girls, trying to pass? Don't stare, m'dear.'

'Sorry.' Alex had swung round to look at the group and turned back, stunned. 'He's the one I ticked off for calling those girls slags.'

'Very bad manners. No need to be rude about what you don't want. If they're bothering anyone, Steve will get them to leave.'

'I don't think so. Not yet. Not enough.' Alex was considering seriously whether being invited to leave London's most sought after club would drive the lesson home and decided it might have the reverse effect. 'I suppose he *was* trying to pass — I missed that, I was just confronting appalling attitudes to women.' She considered her friend Ted, serving six people at once, not a hair out of place, and he glanced at her, neatly jerking the caps off a row of bitter lemon bottles.

'Don't wear yourself out,' he advised, looking sharply older and more tired.

She watched him as he turned, neatly, in the confined space, long arms everywhere as he opened bottles, removed glasses, exchanged ashtrays and took money, all at the same time, seeing as she had not before that he had made his choices. He was not going to take on the world; anyone in this club who said anything derogatory about Ted or any of his friends would be out on the street, exiled for ever. It was his place and that was how he got by.

She swung round to watch the dancers, sipping her tonic broodingly. The place was packed to the rafters of the low basement ceiling, with people under twenty-five, dressed to kill, dancing in groups. One or two real dancers here, she thought, watching a black girl gyrating in a tiny, confined space with every bit of herself moving, but mostly just kids. And then she realised she knew one of the kids.

'Jamie,' she shrieked, causing half the floor to look round, and he stumbled towards her, falling over his feet, all one enormous smile.

'Alex!' He beamed at her, but she pulled him to her in the warm embrace with which the Faraday kids greeted each other. 'Who are you with?'

'Nobody,' she said, cheerfully. 'Where're your friends?'

'Here.' Two boys and a sullen-looking girl, all about his own age. John, ridiculously tall and thin, well in command of himself with a grave and serious manner that sat oddly with the strobe lighting and the heaving dancers. The girl, thin with black hair in need of a wash, she half recognised; Catriona something, drippy friend of Jamie's. The other boy, introduced as Damien, not as tall, slight and dark, was high with excitement, hardly able to stand still.

'Must get some water,' he said. Alex called to Ted, who gave them a jug and five glasses, shaking his head minutely at the suggestion of payment, and the boys gazed at Alex, impressed. Damien, who was, she saw, sweating heavily, drank his glass down, then a second, and was looking hopefully into the empty jug before the rest of them had taken more than a sip. Finding Ted close to her, Alex passed the jug back, hoping for a refill, but he was not looking at her.

'What's he on?' he said, jerking his head at Damien. 'E's?'

Alex stared at him, then at Damien, who looked back earnestly, sweat pouring off him. 'I need some more water,' he said, loudly.

Ted beckoned him to the bar. 'Where did you get them? Who from?'

'What?'

'Don't mess with me. The E's.'

'He got some pills from a man,' the sullen Catriona said, brightening up, and Ted swung on her.

'Here?'

'Over there.' She pointed into the strobe-lit darkness. Ted followed her gaze, swore and signalled to a heavy man in a T-shirt, then swung back.

'Get him out of here, Alex. There was trouble night before last. He doesn't look too good. Take him to UCH casualty and remember he got them on the street. Not here.'

'Right.' She took the sweating Damien firmly by the arm, then hesitated. 'Sorry, Ted, what do you think he took?'

'Oh Christ. Ecstasy tablets. Take too many, drink too much water, you're dead. Get going!'

Jamie looked at her in appalled apology but she shook her head, grimly accepting responsibility for getting them out. 'Alex, I'm sorry,' he muttered. 'It's because . . . he's a bit upset about Catriona. They used to go out.'

'Really?' she said, crossly. 'Why, I wonder? OK, never mind now.'

The cellar was crowded, but the area around the stairs where those who had come to drink and watch were most closely clustered was almost solid with bodies, and Damien didn't want to leave, so even with John and Jamie forming a wedge it was a good ten minutes before they were anywhere near the street door, Catriona trailing behind, being less than useful, talking anxiously. Alex took a grateful breath of air and tried to push her way through a final row of bodies in the wake of the boys.

'Excuse me, miss.'

A slight young man with very short hair, dressed in combat trousers and a T-shirt, an earring in one ear, put a hand on her arm and she made to shake it off but the grip tightened. She called to the boys but there were more young men oddly similar surrounding them. 'If you'll come this way, please, miss.'

'Why should I?'

'I am a police officer.' He used the other hand to fish a leather-covered card from his back pocket and wave it at her.

'Let me look at that,' she said, peremptorily, and his hand checked. She read it, solemnly, realising she had no idea what a warrant card should look like, but this one had a picture of the young man, in suit and tie, but nonetheless recognisable and a name, DC Flight. 'Why aren't you in uniform?' she asked, severely.

'Because I am CID, miss. Not the uniformed branch at all. Now, will you and your friends please step this way?'

They found themselves in a large room, all five of them, Damien, wide-eyed, protesting incoherently, the other two boys desperately anxious, watching her for a lead, and bloody Catriona still making worried noises and massaging the bandages on her wrists. She sighed, feeling very old.

'Mr Flight. Damien here has apparently had some Ecstasy. We understand he got it outside the club.' (She crossed her fingers but she had promised Ted.) 'How much he's had we don't know, but we were on our way to UCH casualty when you stopped us. He has to see a doctor.'

DC Flight looked at her sharply, then at Damien, and spoke into the mobile phone which also appeared from a pocket of the combat trousers. That's the point of those trousers, she thought drearily, you can go to a club disguised as one of us but with all the grown-up authoritative paraphernalia of warrant cards, mobile phones, credit cards and probably a palm-top computer as well.

'This young man will go to UCH with a constable and the rest of you will come to the station with me,' DC Flight announced, and Alex felt Catriona clutch at her. She was wide-eyed with horror.

'Damien will get kicked out of school.'

'He'll still be alive,' Alex snapped, feeling terrible.

'That's a point,' the tall John said, calmly, and her head cleared.

'Mr Flight, are you arresting us?'

'No. Just asking you to help with our enquiries.'

'I'd like to ring a solicitor, please.'

He turned sharply, measuring her. 'He'll be up this time of night, will he?'

'I am with Graebner Associates. Matthew Sutherland is on call tonight.' She watched with interest, as his expression changed from one of amused patronage to something different and more wary.

'You should know better then.'

'I do not take drugs. Neither do these three,' she added, hoping that was right. 'And, as I am sure you know, the club has a no-drugs policy.'

'Oh yeah?'

'So I want to make a phone call. Now.' Alex felt her voice rise.

'There's a phone in the hall,' DC Flight said, grudgingly, but the tall John wordlessly produced a mobile. She put in Matt's number and waited for a mind-numbing fifteen rings.

'Yeah, Sutherland. Christ.'

'Which of you is it?' she asked, instantly restored by the familiar New Zealand accent.

'Alex. What the fuck?'

'I am being invited to accompany a DC Flight to his police station. I have Jamie and three Faraday kids with me. One's just gone to UCH casualty. Ecstasy, we think, but we don't know.'

'The rest of you clean?'

'Sparkling.'

'Gimme this Flight.'

'Mr Flight. Would you speak to Mr Sutherland, please?' She listened, with mounting indignation, to DC Flight telling Matthew that he was knee-deep in snotty kids who thought it was OK to take anything they liked and then call for posh lawyers. She took back the phone, tight-lipped.

'Alex, I'll meet you at the station. They want to take blood and urine from you four, but don't let them touch you or the kids till I get there. OK?' She essayed a protest on the lines that this was a waste of time. 'Bloody do as you are told. *I'm* the lawyer.'

She did, crossly, as she was told, venting her feelings by telling Catriona to shut *up*, and informed DC Flight they would be glad to join him in a van, crowded with other suspect clubbers. She sat, irritably watching Jamie comfort the tiresome Catriona, gazing into what space there was in the middle of the van between the seats, wondering how long Matthew would take to get to wherever it was. The van drew up and they climbed out and, unbelievably, there he was, leaning on the counter chatting to the duty sergeant, wearing his good suit and a clean white shirt, a bulging briefcase parked at his feet. He greeted them with a stern, reproving gaze, which effectively stopped her from throwing herself into his arms.

'Jamie, mate,' he said, ignoring her, 'will Francesca be worrying?'

'No. I have a key and I'm with a friend, and I have the house taxi number.'

Just like my own parents, she thought.

'And now you've got me.' Seeing DC Flight fully engaged with the rest of the group, he said, conversationally, 'Any reason all four of you wouldn't pass the tests? Tell me now.'

Alex answered for herself and waited while the boys and Catriona confirmed their freedom from banned substances.

'That's a relief; with one of your mates in casualty, having his stomach pumped — no, he's OK, I got the sergeant to check — I'd have been pushed to claim no reasonable grounds.'

DC Flight, who now had a leather jacket on over his clubbing outfit, walked slowly over. 'So you're picking up business again, Mr Sutherland?'

'Bunch of citizens here exercising their right to be represented is the other way you could put it.'

Oh God, men, she thought, alarmed, watching them squaring up to each other; they were of an age, Matt was much taller and heavier, but DC Flight looked capable of punching a lot more than his weight. She held her breath, but DC Flight confined himself to enquiring disagreeably whether Matt insisted on being present while samples were taken.

'I saw Doc Allen in here, didn't I? No, I don't need to be present if he's doing them. Off you go, kids, I need to have a word with the others. Alex, come back when you're done, you can take notes.'

She went, straight-backed, shepherding Catriona, and when she had been searched, given blood and, gratefully, had an enormous pee, handing over a sample in a bottle, she looked at herself in the small mirror. She took out her contact lenses carefully, washed her face clean of make-up, put on the battered glasses she always carried and pulled her hair back with one of the overstretched rubberised bands that lurked in the pockets of whatever she was wearing. There was nothing to be done about the light trousers but she buttoned her denim jacket over the skimpy top, so that her midriff and arms were covered. She was too hot in the stuffy room but she looked much more like a solicitor. Or much more like one than Catriona, who was quite unnecessarily a mess, make-up smeared, hair all over the place, having sullenly refused the loan of Alex's comb, or to wash her face. Alex gave up and went out to join Matthew, who had got through the preliminaries of names and addresses and handed her the pad and pen, watched by DC Flight and two of his confrères.

'I need a room, please,' he said, firmly. 'Client confidentiality.'

DC Flight, plainly furious, banged his way down the corridor and showed them into it with a single, startled glance at Alex. Matt waved them to chairs. 'Assume that there's a mike going straight to the CID room,' he advised, briskly, silencing his clièntele who looked anxiously round the ceiling. 'They want us to wait while they check the samples — they're making a special effort; they've got forensics people here tonight. You were with a kid who was taking drugs, so it's not unreasonable to ask you to wait. For not more than an hour,' he added, with a menacing look at the ceiling. 'Then I'll make a fuss.'

After fifty minutes DC Flight, resentful and deeply ungracious, appeared. It was a properly run police station, and they had other, bigger, more obvious, less well-advised, fish to fry, and half an hour later the group was on the streets. Catriona was all too clearly prepared to stand weeping in the street, but Jamie whistled up a black cab for her, using her father's account, in what was obviously a practised routine. He looked apologetically at Alex who managed not to comment in any way.

'Where are the rest of you going?' Matthew asked. 'Oh, Francesca's. I'll drop you. I owe Francesca one. Don't ask, she won't tell you, but take it from me.' He drove easily and fast through the silent streets and stopped outside the familiar doorway. 'In fact, Jamie, John, don't tell her anything, OK? You just had a good evening and it went on till, what, four thirty. Bloody hell. You can come in the front seat now, Alex.' He waited to see the boys through the front door then drove off. It was getting light, the brightness in the sky dimming the streetlights.

'Thank you for coming, Matt,' she said, getting out of the car. 'And for acting for my friends.'

'It's what I'm paid for. Even if I have to leave a warm friend of my own behind.'

She grinned at him, mockingly, and after a minute he laughed back, and closed the door after her.

CHAPTER 4

Sunday, 7th May

Francesca was in her kitchen with coffee and the paper, half listening to the shrieks of joy from the two-and-a-quarter-year-old William, who was assisting his father with his bath. They were probably flooding the place again, she thought, stretching her back. The phone rang and she reached out for it.

'Wendy,' she said, in pleased recognition to her cousin, Jamie's mother.

'I need some help.' Oh God, Francesca thought, without impiety, please not a crisis. She remembered how difficult Wendy's situation was and settled to listen. 'I'm not going to tell Jamie yet, not until after his exams, but I thought I ought to tell you. And Mary.'

'Is it Steve?' Wendy's husband was a schizophrenic, fine if rather dull when he was taking his pills, frighteningly, desperately mad when he wasn't.

'Yes. He's in hospital now, thank God, but I thought he was going to kill me this time. He'd been getting worse, and he went for me. I saw him coming and I ran out of the door and round to Dr Foot. Well, he wasn't there, he was out on a call, but they found him and he went straight round with a couple of policemen — you know, all the usual carry-on — and I just thought, I've had enough, it's never going to get any better and I'll never have any life, do you know what I mean?' Mercifully no, Francesca thought, soberly, as she had before. It was unimaginable; how could you live with a man who, quite unexpectedly, would perceive you as the Devil himself and attack you with whatever he had to hand? 'So I'm going to say I won't have him back when he comes out. The pills work quite quickly and they *never* keep him in if he wants to get out, 'cause they know he's got somewhere to go. Or had somewhere. Do you think I'm awful?'

'Darling, no one could blame you. You've gone on for much longer than most women would,' Francesca said, warmly, meaning it, but unable to avoid the haunting vision of Steve, back in his right dull mind, having forgotten all that had passed, confidently expecting to go home to a loving wife, and being told that that door was barred. She pulled herself together; that must be precisely the vision that had kept Wendy in this hopeless situation for twenty years of marriage. She tried for optimism. 'And you never know, darling, that might do it. If he really understood that you wouldn't have him back he might manage to force the pills down whatever the side-effects, and defy the demons.'

'It's too late.' It was a wail of despair, and Francesca was silenced. 'I'm going to go for a divorce so there's no going back. And I'm going to move and not give them my address, so no one can try and send him back. His mother or his brother can cope.'

Except, of course, that they couldn't and wouldn't, as both women knew. Steve had been a late child and his mother was nearly eighty. His brother, Ralph, hated and feared the whole situation and would decamp to Australia at the slightest threat of being involved. So it would be care in the community for Steve, God help him. Wendy might just be able to tough it out, but the tender-hearted vulnerable Jamie would be distraught.

'I know Jamie's going to try and persuade me.'

'Jamie's going to have to find his own way of dealing with all this,' Francesca said, slowly, thinking her way forward. 'He's eighteen, you've stuck it out till now, you can't go on. You've actually been lucky not to have been killed.'

'That's true, isn't it? It's just I know what Steve looks like when he's getting bad and I can usually get out of the way. And get Jamie out too, mostly by sending him to you.'

'You know we love him,' Francesca reassured her. 'But you've missed a lot of him.'

'I *know*. And I'm not going to miss more. So I'm not going to say anything about divorce, I know I mustn't. It's only, what, four weeks to the exams, so I'll just say that Steve's gone into hospital because they're trying something new. Do you think that'll work?'

'Yes. Yes, why not? They're all pretty preoccupied with themselves and their own affairs, you know. Probably wouldn't notice if you and I *both* went round the bend.' Black jokes about serious mental illness were always an effective way of cheering Wendy up and indeed this feeble effort produced the high relieved laugh of the seriously over-stressed.

'You're right, Fran. If Jamie's thinking about something he's composing I could walk around the house stark-naked.'

'Same here. I've often felt I could have a nice conversation with the banisters, dressed as a daffodil, and neither he nor his little chums would see anything amiss.'

They chatted on for a bit and Francesca found that, as usual, Wendy was feeling better, and she was feeling worse at the end of the conversation. The least I can do however, she thought, getting up to distribute towels to husband and son in the flooded bathroom.

* * *

The May sun streamed into the small room, illuminating every dusty corner. When he became headmaster, Nick Lewis had kept the small office from the days when he was a head of department, because of its view across a gentle slope to the church and the heavy cattle grazing in the field beyond. He was sitting at the small table in the corner of the room with four anxious colleagues on this bright Monday; Piers Miller and Amanda Roberts, who were between them responsible for teaching Damien Fry for his A-levels in biology, chemistry, maths and physics; Susie Miller as the boy's general tutor; and Roland Willis as his housemaster and deputy headmaster. The subject of the meeting was at home in London, with his mother and stepfather, shaken but alive.

'Headmaster, it was apparently only a designer stimulant. Not a class A drug. Indeed, it seems that it may have been an over-reaction to take Damien to hospital at all; he could have slept it off. And the police are not charging him. And it is only four weeks to the exams and it would destroy two years' work if he were not to take them.'

Amanda Roberts pushed carefully cut blond hair back behind her ears, leaning across the table to Nick Lewis to plead her case. Nor was she the only one. He had already sustained calls from Damien's mother, his stepfather, and his father, all trying to persuade him that Ecstasy did not come within the inexorable school rule that prescribed expulsion for drug use or, further and in the alternative, that Damien had not been on school premises at the time. Amanda, he noted with interest, had not made the point that Damien was a straight A candidate in biology and chemistry — her subjects — as well as physics and maths, which were Piers Miller's subjects. He watched as she kicked Piers Miller under the table; these two ambitious rivals must have agreed their approach. Piers Miller obligingly leapt into action.

'Nick, may I add my voice to the argument? I believe that Faraday's hard-line stance on drugs is absolutely right; once you get students taking class A, or cannabis, you're in trouble, and it spreads like wildfire. As we found at my last school. But Ecstasy isn't an addictive drug. And Damien isn't a druggie. Few regular users, either of class A drugs or cannabis, would bother with Ecstasy. I feel that this one, very unfortunate, outbreak — particularly since it did not happen on school premises — could be seen in the same light as one of the students getting sodden drunk to the point where medical intervention was necessary, like that lad last year.'

'And if he had made himself ill on heroin, never having tried it before?' the headmaster asked, drily.

'He won't do it again,' Amanda Roberts said, desperate for her best candidate. 'And if we don't let him back here then one of the London crammers will take him, he'll take the exams from there and *they'll* get the credit.'

Piers Miller threw her a reproachful glance, well telegraphed to the head. 'I teach him too, Nick, and while I would be sorry to lose an A grade candidate for the school, I think the point is the effect on Damien himself. I don't share Amanda's optimism about his ability to overcome this setback and do himself justice from a London crammer. As I said, he *is* young for his age.'

Susie Miller stirred. 'He's been here right through the junior school as well, since he was seven. We're his home, and he doesn't have time to find another one.'

Now there is the real truth, the Head thought, and smiled at her. 'I'm inclined to try and find a way of seeing Damien through this nonsense he has made,' he said, calmly. 'I have told John, Jamie and Catriona that they must not gossip or speculate, and that Damien is recovering from whatever it was that he incautiously took. I expect Damien can act with discretion too, since he understands that if this incident were to get round the school he could not come back.' He looked round the anxious faces. 'However, this is a decision which I believe I will have to share with the Trustees, or at least the Chairman, particularly in present circumstances. I have after all resigned with effect from the end of next term.'

'Oh Lord.' Roland Willis looked appalled. 'They could decide against — they've always been very hot on drugs.'

'They have a right to be consulted. They are committed to a draconian policy for keeping drugs out of the school and we are, at best, seeking a loophole.' He smiled serenely at Amanda Roberts; he hardly needed to remind her as Louis Roberts' wife and a candidate for head that the Trustees were quite as keen on A-level success as any anti-drug policy. A clever girl, he thought, pity I don't like her.

He watched as she decided that her husband would have to square his friends for her. She won't like that, he thought, she doesn't like any suggestion that she is not all powerful. Piers Miller, now, had played a more subtle hand; fully as ambitious as Amanda, he had emphasised the risk to young Damien. Well, in fairness he probably was as concerned for Damien as he was for his own teaching record; ambitious chap though he was, he could not really have married the tender-hearted child-loving Susie if he had not been concerned for humanity.

'Thank you, everyone,' he said, rising to indicate the meeting was over. 'I have a call booked to the Chairman in an hour, and I will let you all know as soon as possible whether he supports my view. We must put Damien out of his misery as soon as possible and I'd like to get him back here tonight if he's coming.'

'Nick, sorry, I need a word.' Piers Miller spoke without getting up, and with a sidelong look at his wife. She looked back at him, angrily. He understood he was witnessing a marital disagreement and his heart sank.

'Certainly, Piers,' he said, sitting down again.

'I will stay too, please, Nick.' Susie was flushed but determined, and the three waited in silence while Amanda and Roland left, Amanda in a hurry, Roland with obvious reluctance.

'It's about Catriona,' Piers said.

'Ah.' A known problem, not thank God a new one.

'I have to say, Nick — and as you can see Susie isn't happy about this — that I am at a stand with teaching Catriona. *She* isn't, in my view, capable of absorbing any maths in her present state and she is disrupting the rest of my set. I have the weaker maths set and I'm glad to do so, it's more of a challenge, but they need a lot of help in their final period. What they don't need is a black hole of misery and resentment sitting in the middle of the class. It's oppressive; even I find it so.'

'Her other subject teachers do not seem to be having so much difficulty.'

Piers looked affronted. 'Her other subjects are theatre studies and art, where the teaching is perhaps more diffuse, and there is more emphasis on practical work.'

'Susie, what do you feel about the situation?' She obviously had an opinion since she had insisted on staying and her view was critical, even though she did not teach the girl.

'I should make it clear, Nick, that I, too, am having a problem with her, but it doesn't have anything to do with me being her housemistress.' Her head was down and she was looking miserable. 'She seems to have become fixated on Giles.'

'And Giles is having difficulty dealing with that?' He knew he sounded incredulous; that confident, attractive, dominant personality had been surrounded by adoring girls since his first days at the school.

'Yes, I know. But he *is*, Nick. I agree it's not like him but he's tense because of the exams. And it's very difficult having Andrew here and all the excitement of the concert. I have to say — and I hate myself — that I wish Catriona would just vanish until after A-levels.'

Dear Susie, he thought with love, too honest to wrap it all up in consideration for Catriona's welfare.

'Piers and Amanda are right too. I cannot believe she is managing to take anything in in any subject. Theatre, well, a lot of it is project work, but she hasn't managed to finish the last one. She has completed her art portfolio, but Jed says it isn't any good. Of course he's never liked her work, he thinks it's constrained and derivative.'

'I hope he doesn't say that to her.'

'He doesn't need to, Nick, you know what Jed is like. Wonderful teacher for most of them, but quite awful with kids he doesn't think are talented.'

He thought about the gifted, inspirational, uncompromising Jed. A problem for my successor, he thought, having decided that he must refrain from making staff changes unless they were absolutely necessary. No one would thank him for losing the most successful teacher of art in the southern counties. He turned to Piers Miller, who was sitting in controlled stillness, cautiously watching his wife, energy barely contained.

'What are you suggesting?' he asked them both.

'Oh.' Susie ran both hands through her short hair so it stood up on end, raggedly, making her look exactly like her son. 'I've talked to Vivienne and Louis. They're neither of them much *use*, frankly, Vivienne's working on a huge presentation and is very busy. Louis is just shouting at the child, telling her to shape up.'

'What about Roland and Amanda? They may only be step-parents, but they are teaching here.'

'They are not in agreement about what to do.' There was an awkward silence, broken by Piers.

'Roland thinks we should Micawber along, hoping Catriona feels better, and get her through the exams somehow. Amanda thinks, as I do, that Catriona ought to be in a good clinic, forget A-levels for now, and maybe plan to do them in January, with a crammer. But in the end they are only step-parents. Roland, as you know, loves the child, but Amanda — well, she's got two of her own and rather feels Catriona is Louis's business.'

'I will call them in.'

'All of them, Nick?' Susie sounded respectful and incredulous.

'Why not? Catriona is a problem for all of them.'

'And we haven't made a lot of progress talking to them separately.' Piers was unoffended and interested, that sharp mind closing like a trap round an unfamiliar concept.

'It's worth trying and if it is ineffective then we will do something else. For the moment, Susie, you stop worrying about her and keep Giles calm and working. Piers, I want you to find time to work with Catriona on maths individually, today and tomorrow — I know, I know, but you might get a breakthrough, individual tuition sometimes does that. Then we must talk again. Thank you both.'

* * *

'Morning, Kevin.' John McLeish, who liked to walk about and see his people rather than summoning them to his office, walked into the small cell off the big open-plan room which Kevin Camberton, as a DI, was allowed.

'Morning, sir.'

The man was looking a bit constrained, McLeish thought. 'Good weekend?' he enquired.

'I worked most of it.'

'Oh, did you? What on?'

'The O'Brien case.' This was a difficult one; a seven-year-old girl had gone missing from her crowded home two weeks earlier, and the police view was that her stepfather was involved. He was still in the marital home, at his wife's side, apparently deeply concerned, appealing to the public for help in finding the child, appearing every day at the incident room to ask for news, but experienced policemen were uncomfortable with the case and with him.

'Anderton turned up, pissed, on Saturday night, so I asked to talk to him. *He* knows where the kid is.'

'So you charged him?' McLeish wondered how he, or the newspapers, had missed it.

'Not yet.'

McLeish nodded. 'Careful, Kevin. The detail matters here.'

The man nodded, unoffended by the reminder. He was on the trail, McLeish recognised, and Mr Anderton was going to meet his just deserts.

'We ought to review tomorrow. Put a time in my diary, will you? In the morning. I've promised my wife to get home. We've got the house to ourselves for once. We sent Jamie back yesterday.'

'Jamie all right, was he?'

'Bit of a hangover.' He had been half turned to walk across the room, but stopped, every instinct alert. 'Why wouldn't he have been?'

'Oh shit. Sorry. He was at Notting Dale nick about 4 a.m. on Sunday with a load of other kids. I came up for a break from Anderton and I stopped just to see what was going on.'

McLeish found a chair and sat down, heavily. 'Tell me.'

Kevin Camberton, flushed to the eyebrows with embarrassment, made a visible effort to marshal his story.

'Notting Dale CID had done a raid on a club called the Freezer. Behind the Gate, in the old cinema. Brought in a roomful of kids and a couple of dealers.' He caught McLeish's eye. 'I'm sorry, I should've made it clear that Jamie and the boy and the two girls with him tested clean.'

'Thank God for that. A lad called John, presumably — he was staying with us and I thought they looked a bit rough yesterday morning. Did you have to help?'

'No, they had a lawyer there, came out from the local law firm. Big red-headed lad, Scots name.'

'Matthew Sutherland.'

'You know him?' McLeish confined himself to a weary nod.

'One of the girls, the one who was with Jamie, works at the firm apparently.'

John McLeish had no difficulty putting a face on the girl; Jamie and John had both made much of the chance meeting.

'The beautiful Alexandra.'

Camberton blinked and gave him a careful look. 'This one was a tall red-haired girl with glasses and a bun, and no make-up.'

'Ah . . . you need to see her with her hair down, no glasses and little glitter spots on her cheekbones. A stunner.'

Camberton was considering him with something between amusement and alarm, and McLeish recalled that they did not share the same tastes. 'So, why had Notting Dale pulled them in? General over-conscientiousness?'

'There was another lad with them,' Camberton said, reluctantly. 'Taken to UCH. Ecstasy, apparently, but he wasn't charged — I checked. His mother took him home, good as new, yesterday. When the Notting Dale lads picked up your boy, the first thing he and this — Alexandra, is it? — told them was that their friend had taken E and that he needed a hospital. CID took him there.'

'So there's one lucky lad alive where he might not have been,' McLeish said, heavily.

'I'm sorry, sir, I assumed you'd have known.'

'Oh, I would have if Jamie himself had been charged,' he said heartily, hoping it was true. Matt Sutherland told them to keep their mouths shut, he thought, unsure whether to be grateful or not. Not, on the whole; protecting his wife from shock and distress was for him to do, not some cocky young solicitor. Camberton was keeping silent, conscious of a change in the atmosphere.

'Kids,' McLeish said at last, reminding himself that shooting the messenger was not usually profitable. 'And I'll have it all to do again in about twelve years' time when my little lad's a teenager.'

'Not to mention the one on the way,' Camberton joked.

'Oh him. Forgot for a moment.'

* * *

At first sight it was a pleasant spring scene, two men and two women grouped on comfortable sofas round a low table, drinks, tinkling ice to hand. But there was no conversation, all four were sitting tense, locked in their own thoughts. The last hour, spent in the headmaster's company, had upset all four of Catriona's parents and step-parents in different ways and for different reasons, not improved by the brief distraction afforded by getting into two cars and driving the mile to Roland and Vivienne Willis's small house in the village. It had been agreed, tacitly, that this particular discussion could not be held in the school grounds. Roland Willis finished his gin and tonic in a gulp and gave himself and Louis Roberts another one. Both women refused.

'I'm driving back to London after this,' Vivienne Willis said, glancing out of the window at the latest BMW 7 Series Saloon sitting in the driveway beside Louis Roberts' more modest BMW 5 Series Estate. She thought with pleasure that it got right up Louis's substantial nose that she should have become so valuable to her bank employers as to be given, on request, £40,000 of car and a salary which more than compensated for Roland's modest £32,000 a year and a tied cottage at Faraday's. Louis, she knew, even fourteen years after the divorce, was continuously galled by the half-admitted knowledge that the bloody fools were paying his ex-wife more every year than he drew from his engineering business. She smiled at Louis and crossed one leg over the other, the skirt of the Armani suit riding up over the expensive tights and Bruno Magli shoes. She had met him when she was on her way to a first in economics at Birmingham and he was President of the Union, a loud-mouth even then, but very successful with it. They had married immediately after graduating and she had gone on to a PhD while Louis went into his father's business and doubled its turnover. And she had been happy until Catriona had arrived and she had to abandon her research and look after the house and the fretful, difficult baby who had grown into a whiny, demanding child. She had become quite desperate but had retained the strength to find an escape from this particular hole; her PhD supervisor acted as a consultant for one of the Birmingham stockbrokers and had recommended her for a part-time analyst's job which could just be combined with running a big house and the two-year-old Catriona. She thought indeed that she had managed rather well, even as the part-time job became imperceptibly full-time. Louis, however, had not shared her view and, when Catriona was a difficult four-year-old, had left them both for Amanda, seated opposite her, looking sullen and dressed by Marks and Spencer. She watched them both, reflecting that she had done better than Louis out of the reshuffle. He had got another ambitious woman who was going to annoy him by going her own way. Indeed, the signs were already clear, with his second and third daughters away at the prep for Roedean instead of at Faraday's junior as he had wanted. And now Amanda was hoping for the head's job, and while she was not going to get it here, she'd get one somewhere else, sooner rather than later. He wasn't going to like that any better than he had liked his first wife's full-time job.

She looked with affection at Roland, his big hands folded round his drink. He was twelve years her senior and ambitious only for the kids in his charge and for this school. He was proud of her, supported her need to work, and had taken on, unhesitatingly, her tiresome daughter. He suited her, and the fact that he earned about a fifth of what she did worried her not at all. Like the first-class academic and child of comfortably-off middle-class parents she had once been, she took a detached view of her own ability to earn money; it was a useful ability like an ear for languages, or perfect pitch, but it didn't make you into a superior being or ensure lasting happiness. But Roland ought to be headmaster, in succession to Nick Lewis, he deserved it and she wasn't going to let anything stand in his way, including boring little Amanda.

It was characteristically her husband who broke the sullen silence. 'Well, I feel rather crushed by that session, I expect we all do.'

'No,' she said, promptly. 'As far as I'm concerned the answer is straightforward. We all agree Catriona is too depressed and distressed to make any sense out of A-levels. She needs proper psychiatric help, so we have to find the best way to get it for her. She can do her A-levels any time.'

'I agree.' Amanda Roberts put her glass down firmly and nodded to her in a rare moment of unity. 'The poor kid is wretched and it's even worse for her because her contemporaries are absolutely occupied in driving themselves towards the exams.' Their menfolk, united only in opposition, looked at each other.

'Well, *I* don't agree.' Louis Roberts, as Dominant Male, dived in. 'I don't want her sent away from all her mates to be messed around in a clinic and treated as if she were ill. What she needs is her mother to stay home for a change, and see her through these exams, instead of flying to Milan, or wherever.'

'Or more attention from her stepmother who is actually part of this school that she loves so much.' Vivienne had learned to get her retaliation in first in the competition for fund management commissions. 'No, sorry, Amanda, that isn't the point at all; for the moment neither of us nor the school is any use to her. She needs a calm unstressed environment and therapy.'

'Bloody nonsense,' Louis Roberts exploded. 'They charge £1000 a week at the funny farm you're thinking of and they don't hurry to get anyone better and back on their feet, I wouldn't either at that kind of money. She wants to be here, doing her exams like the other kids.'

Roland Willis pulled himself forward out of the depths of the sofa. 'Isn't there a compromise? Catriona stays here, I'll make sure I'm free as much as possible to look after her. Of course she must be put on anti-depressants — I understand they're very good and work quite quickly — but I'm really not convinced she needs to have her emotions and feelings analysed by a psychiatrist. And I'm quite, quite sure she ought not to be in a clinic thirty miles away. She would feel terrifyingly abandoned.' He looked round the assembled company. 'I know she's not my daughter but our circumstances — all our circumstances — have meant that for most of her life I have had as much contact with her as any of you.'

'And what's her mother going to do in all this? Bugger off to Milan.'

'Yes,' Vivienne said crisply. 'Roland is much better with her than I am — sorry, but that's the truth. In any case I don't believe it is any of us that she needs. Or the school. She is in breakdown — and if none of you've seen one before,

I have — and that means a good hospital with expensive psychiatric help. And Milan means I'll be able to pay for it.'

'You've never had to ask twice for money for her,' Louis said, stung.

Vivienne ignored him and turned to her husband. 'Roland, I'm sorry, but I have to get to Milan tomorrow. I'll be back late Friday and I'll take over then. But you know my view, she shouldn't be here, not now, not in her state. I'll take her to Dr Wright if that's what's wanted, but I can't do more, not till Saturday.'

'Bugger that,' Louis Roberts said, furiously. 'I don't want her being messed around by psychiatrists. She can stay with us while you're gone.'

Amanda Roberts just managed not to look horrified, and Roland Willis held up a hand, commandingly. 'It's good of you both but if we're deciding to keep her in school, she is much better in her own house, even if Vivienne is away. She can get to her classes in two minutes, I see her several times a day and she's got friends and company.'

Louis Roberts made to protest but caught his wife's eye.

'Look,' Amanda said, uneasily, 'it's very good of you, Roland, but we haven't actually solved the problem, have we? Nick was quite clear that some solution had to be found that got Catriona help and kept her from being a burden on the rest of Six Senior who've got their own problems. We haven't *done* that; if she stays here, she's going to go on being miserable, go on following Giles Quentin about and spending hours talking about herself to Jamie Miles Brett. Giles has got a mother to protect him and he's a tough customer anyway; Jamie is second only to Damien in both my subjects, but he's a tender-hearted boy and she's eating up his revision time. That is not a position Nick will accept. Nor will I. Nor should any of us.'

Roland Willis got up, looking much too big for the small room. 'Look,' he said, forcefully, 'it's only two weeks till half-term. I will personally guarantee that Catriona stays with us — with me — and either works or not from 5 p.m.

every day and Wednesday afternoons; I can't do much better because I teach the rest of the hours but then she is in class. Or, as I understand the arrangement, being coached personally in her subjects — Nick has asked Piers and Jed to help. I'm sure he'll accept it just for two weeks.' He looked at Vivienne, who nodded agreement, knowing she was in no position to oppose. Amanda was also silent, feeling she had shot her bolt, and it was left to Louis Roberts to express, between his teeth, his sense of obligation for Roland's offer.

CHAPTER 5

Saturday, 1st July

Alexandra Ferguson strode into the dance centre, hefting easily in her right hand the large bag containing her dancer's kit, the towels, the mineral water and the spare shoes which went everywhere with her. She raised her hand in greeting to the big man at the reception desk as she passed, but he called to her to stop.

'Message for you. Young man sounding very upset. You been giving him a hard time?'

'No,' she said, looking at the pleading message. Not only would she never give Jamie Miles Brett a hard time, she had taken particular trouble to ring him and wish him good luck at the start of his A-levels four weeks ago, *and* she had spoken to him twice during the exams. Jamie was extremely capable academically and had been experiencing no particular difficulty. Then he had gone off on the Six Senior journey perfectly happily. She was expecting to see him that evening at the very grand party Sir Andrew Quentin was giving, in order to show off Giles, and at which Jamie would also be playing. She could not imagine why he needed to see her so urgently.

'You told him I had a class?'

'He said he'd come straight afterwards. You could get out the back, if you want.'

'He's a friend. But I really didn't want to miss class. You are clever.'

The man grinned at her. 'I was looking after the poor lad's interests. You'd have eaten him if he'd made you miss it.'

'I have to get to class on Saturdays,' she said, defensively. 'I can't do the weekdays, I'm working.'

'How's that going?'

'It's hard work.' But it was going well, she acknowledged. Matt Sutherland was a brilliant if impatient teacher and had let her try her hand at everything in the eleven weeks she had been working at the Centre. Of course, being allowed a go at everything that was going on meant there was very little free time in the week. She was doing two evening shifts at the Centre and one at the Refuge, as substitute for Francesca McLeish whose advancing pregnancy was felt to make her unsuitable for a long shift dealing with violent and disturbed people. This initially reflected Matthew's view of the matter rather than Francesca's, but John McLeish had apparently agreed and insisted she give up. Alex had been glad to take her place, but it did mean that she relied on doing three or four hours' dancing on both days at the weekend on top of two evenings to keep herself in training. Hopefully whatever Jamie needed could be fitted into the forty-five-minute break between the two professional classes.

An hour and a half later, red hair sticking damply to her neck, muffled in a track suit over leotard and tights, and uneasily conscious that she smelled of sweat, she stopped, taken aback by the number of people crammed into the large, shabby, badly lit café. The room had been grudgingly set aside by the management of the studios to provide sustenance for their customers, and their conviction that expensive studio space was being gratuitously wasted was reflected in the furnishings. These comprised six battered tables of varying sizes, an inadequate and temperamental coffee machine, a small, cramped old electric stove and one awkwardly shaped display case, featuring discouraged sandwiches. Cigarette smoke hung in a thick cloud — one of the minor miracles is how dancers work, for hours, on a diet of Coca Cola, white bread sandwiches, chocolate bars and cigarettes. She peered anxiously through the throng and saw Jamie Miles Brett, awkward and cramped in a corner, wedged between a wall and the back of a young woman in a sweat-stained leotard and the grubby grey cardigan and trousers, apparently made of bin liners, which are virtually a dancer's uniform. She hesitated, anguished, there was no space beside Jamie, or anywhere else, and she only had half an hour before she needed to warm up for her next class; she really could not go out of the building, even for Jamie.

'Boys and girls!' It was an authoritative female voice from behind her. 'Two minutes.'

There was a universal groan, but all the bodies disentangled themselves and rose, winding improbable garments around long elegant, perfectly muscled limbs. She stood aside as the company, eyes fixed on a distant objective, pushed past her, taking a last drag of a cigarette or mouthful of doughnut.

'Jamie. Sorry. Let's get a window open.' She did that, then kissed him, looking at him carefully. He had just come back from the Six Senior journey, traditionally undertaken to a centre in Wales immediately after A-levels. It had been decided many years ago that rather than have eighty odd liberated eighteen-year-olds roaming the school and disrupting fellow pupils who were still working, the Trustees would fund this annual outing. Despite his holiday Jamie was looking rough; very tired and dishevelled. And he was smoking, she observed, horrified. 'Stay there,' she said, automatically delivering the coffee machine a smart blow low down on its right-hand side. She carried over the two cups and sat down opposite him. 'I've only got twenty minutes,' she said, apologetically. 'I'm sorry, but I can't do enough classes during the week even to keep supple.'

'You still want to be a dancer? Not a lawyer?'

She had no time for idle chat, but perhaps Jamie needed to work himself up to tell her whatever the trouble was. 'I like law. And I decided I couldn't make a living as a dancer, not when I think about it. But if I were offered a real job with a good contemporary company . . .' She let the sentence trail away; it was not the moment to try to describe the continual tension between dance and the need to be independent and respected. 'But how's you?'

The familiar greeting cracked Jamie's composure and his face started to crumple. She seized a handful of the cheap, tiny paper napkins (stolen in bulk from some other establishment, it had always been assumed), placed them in his hand and sat drinking the over-sweetened coffee her whole system craved after an hour and a half of intensive exercise.

'Is it the exams?' she asked, as Jamie seemed unable to start.

'No. They were OK. Well, you know.'

'Friends? Catriona OK? Did she manage the exams?'

He blinked at her, roused from whatever was troubling him. 'Actually she did. Perfectly well. But then . . . well, she's got much worse.'

'How worse?'

'Mad. Well, not mad,' he corrected himself, conscientiously. 'But much more ill and distressed. She was awful on the Six Senior trip.'

'Did she have another go at her wrists?'

'Yes, but only once. She was with me — in my tent — and when I got her up in the morning the sleeping bag was covered with blood. She wouldn't let me tell anyone, she was desperate not to be sent home.'

'Oh, Jamie.'

'Yeah, well, so I didn't. I just helped her clean up and told her next time I would tell Roland.'

'But he is her home, isn't he? I mean, where would she have gone?'

'To her father. He's OK, but she can't stand Amanda, and I see why. She's awful to her.'

'Well, Catriona's pretty difficult,' Alex said, feeling that a note of reality might help.

'Yes, she is,' Jamie said, soberly. 'She's really ill. She ought to be in hospital.'

Coming from Jamie this had real authority. Unlike his contemporaries, Jamie knew what mental illness looked like.

'What else was she doing?'

He blushed scarlet. 'Sex things.'

Alex, out of her depth, gazed at him and he went on, reluctantly. 'Hanging round Giles, trying to sit on his lap, saying she could . . . could do things for him, and it would be better than him wanking all the time.'

'Does he?'

'He doesn't need to. He's going out with Jenny Fairbrooks, and she was there too.'

'Actually on the journey?'

'Going out' in Faraday parlance presumably still meant 'going to bed with', forbidden on school grounds.

'Yeh. I think even Roland knew, but he didn't let on. We'll all be gone in two weeks, after all.'

'So what did Giles do?'

'Well, he was quite good with her, spent a lot of time talking to her and jollying her on. So did I, but old Giles made an effort too, for once. And Damien did his bit, but she just gets annoyed with him.'

'Why didn't the staff do something?'

'They tried. I know Piers wanted her sent home — she'd said something awful to him too — but, of course, old Roland's her father really, so he wouldn't. You know what he's like, the caring and sharing type. So he just ignored it all — she slept in my tent most nights and he pretended not to notice.'

Sharing tents was also not permitted, on the basis that it would lead exactly where anyone might think. At the same time she thought Roland had been right to ignore this particular breach; Jamie would never have taken advantage of a sick friend. She considered him, he was trying to tell her something and she had got in his way.

'What else is wrong?'

'It's Mum and Dad. They're splitting up.'

'She's leaving him?'

'Yes.' He had gone very red and was struggling not to cry. 'I know Mum's had a hard time with him, but Dad can't manage. He's got nowhere to go. I don't have a home. Of my own, I mean.'

'But Jamie . . . but you wouldn't manage any better than your mum. Your father is ill.'

'Not if he takes his pills.'

'But he mostly doesn't.'

'Where is he going to go?'

Her heart was wrung, as she tried to imagine her parents in this predicament. How could she in the same situation let her father come out to nowhere? 'Your mum — I mean, she surely won't leave him until he's got somewhere fixed up?'

'No, of course not. But he'll hate it; and then he won't take his pills and he'll be back in hospital and he won't have anything to try for.' He started to cry again and she held his hand.

'Or he might decide, once and for all, to take the pills so that your mum could have him back.'

'She says they've been through that. She tells him she'd have to leave him, he takes his pills for a bit, but then decides not to. *He* says they are horrible and make him feel sick and stupid all the time.'

Alex looked desperately at her watch. 'Have you told Francesca?'

'She knew. Mum told her but no one was going to tell me till after the exams and the Six Senior journey. She says she's very sorry, but she thinks it's best for Mum.'

Everybody did, Alex understood, except for her weeping Jamie.

'Wait for me,' she said, sadly abandoning her next class. 'I'll get changed and we'll go and have lunch. Something decent — I'll buy, I'm a rich lawyer right now. We'll never get enough to eat at the party tonight.'

He was gazing at her, not too drowned in misery to understand that he was being indulged. 'You don't mind? About your class.'

'Of course not,' she lied, stoutly. 'This way I'll enjoy the party and won't just want to go to sleep. There's going to be lots of useful people there — Giles's old father knows everyone — and I'll be better off fresh. And you're my prot after all.'

She got a watery, shamefaced smile and a huge, relieved sigh, as she patted his hand and made for the cluttered, airless basement dressing-rooms smelling of talcum powder and stale sweat, none of which worried her any more than they had when she was a skinny, entranced ten-year-old.

* * *

In the big kitchen in the sixth-form house at Faraday's, Susie Miller was trying to cook lunch, and iron her dress for the party at the same time, handicapped by the presence of her son, mooching aimlessly about the room.

'Why did Dad have to invite Catriona for tonight?' he demanded, tripping over a trailing shoelace and steadying himself on the ironing board which jolted the iron so that she narrowly avoided scorching a seam. 'He knows I don't want her.'

'He wanted to invite Louis and Amanda and could hardly not ask Catriona. He couldn't say it was only an oldies' party, because lots of your age are coming.' She had offered versions of this explanation twice to her son and her husband since the night before when Catriona Roberts, roused to animation, had consulted her on what to wear. 'Besides which, darling, it's a huge party, over a hundred people, you ought to be able to avoid her if you need to. Lots of other people there will want to talk to you.'

'You know I'm singing tonight.' He was carefully not looking at her, and she banged the iron down in loving exasperation.

'Darling, I'm happy for you to sing, for anyone, now you have A-levels behind you. I just didn't want you careering off to London being distracted when you needed to be calm and revise.' She considered her son. 'Not nervous, are you?'

'No.' He had always been perfectly confident in his gift. 'I'm rehearsing with Jamie just before the party kicks off.'

'So we have to get you there early.' She looked anxiously at the clock.

'I'll get the train, Ma, don't *fuss.*' He flung away crossly just as Piers walked in, also looking harassed.

'Darling, have you seen my blue jacket?'

'Oh Lord,' she said, heart sinking, 'it's at the cleaners'.'

'I'll go and get it. The grey one's got a mark on it.'

'I'm very sorry.' She gathered her forces. 'I've been so busy I only managed to take the cleaning yesterday. It won't be ready.'

'Oh *Christ.*' She looked at him, startled; he was not usually so readily exasperated. 'I suppose we have to go tonight.'

'I'm singing,' Giles said, shocked.

'Why?'

'My *father* asked me to.'

The emphasis was not accidental she understood and wished her menfolk would be less touchy with each other. 'I expect he wants to show Giles off to someone,' she offered, wearily.

'He does. This American agent he bangs on about.'

'Oh well, that settles it.' Piers was all too obviously looking for trouble. 'We'll all have to go, me in a dirty jacket so that Andrew can treat me even more like the hired help than he already does. And in Roland Willis's awful Volvo because, as I have not had a chance to tell you, Susie, the silencer has finally fallen off your car. I thought you were having it serviced last week.'

'I ran out of time,' she said, bleakly. And cash, she thought, what with new shoes and a new haircut for her ex-husband's party at which she was not prepared to feature as a sad, mousy, discarded ex-wife.

'Well, you and I are going in the back with Catriona,' Piers said, evilly, to Giles.

'No way. I'm going up by train.'

'Using what for cash?'

'My allowance, which Dad pays.'

'That must be why you took a tenner off me last night.'

And me, Susie thought, alarmed by the hostility sparking between them, as well as the rate at which Giles seemed to be getting through cash.

Giles, furious, glanced at his watch, and she read his mind. He had no cash on him and had been hoping to borrow more from her. Now he would have to raid his Post Office account and would miss a train. 'You haven't had lunch,' she said, loyalties and affections torn.

'I'll get some at Dad's place,' he said, giving Piers a dirty look, returned with interest. He hesitated as he passed her, stopped and awkwardly kissed the side of her head. 'Catch you later.'

He left a thunderous silence behind him in which she tried not to look at Piers. 'I'm sorry about the domestic chaos,' she said, head down over the ironing. 'I had a difficult week too — you and Giles were away but I had all the GCSE children.'

'I know, I know. It's always like this towards the end of term. They're intolerable, all these kids.'

She lifted her head in surprise. 'Darling, not a very teacherly sentiment.'

'Not one I'd use to anyone but you. Do you want to stop ironing and have a cuddle?'

She did that, thankfully.

'Shall we go upstairs? We've got at least two hours before we have to make a start.'

'Let me turn the oven down. Oh dear, I'm sure Giles won't get a stew where he's going.'

'Serve him right. Though I don't blame him for not wanting to go in the back seat of Roland's Volvo.' She felt him hesitate. 'Would you mind very much if you sat in the back rather than me? I know you're never car-sick.'

'Of course,' she said, happy to have found something she could do for him. 'But what about Vivienne?'

'Taking her own car, apparently. Has to go on tomorrow to Geneva. Or Amsterdam. Or Paris.'

'Or somewhere busy and fashionable,' she agreed, as they headed upstairs, holding each other.

* * *

'So the Six Senior trip wasn't much good?'

'Not to Catriona, apparently. Roland had a very difficult time.' Amanda Roberts tried not to sound smug.

'He said so?' her husband asked, sharply.

'Not in so many words, no. But I met the bus and Jamie Miles Brett said she had not been very happy. Giles Quentin rushed off, looking like a thundercloud, and Roland was looking absolutely washed-out.'

'A week shut up with eighty kids in a bunkhouse would leave *me* washed-out.'

'There were four other staff with him. And it was very good weather — I asked. No, the problem was Catriona. She moped about and *clung* apparently. To anyone who would put up with it, which didn't include Giles Quentin.' She watched her husband push open one of the big windows in their immaculate living-room, with its view of manicured green hills. 'She needs professional help, Louis, there's no way round it. Roland is the next thing to a saint but he's worn thin. And it's the end of term in twelve days.'

'And you're not going to help.' He banged the window shut again.

She gritted her teeth. 'I — we — have two daughters due back from Porterfield in twelve days, hoping for a peaceful holiday with their parents. Which they're not going to get with Catriona drooping around, threatening suicide. Very frightening for them, even if it's only an idle threat.'

'She got through the exams, didn't she? And didn't threaten anything or anyone?' Louis Roberts was looking stubbornly miserable in a way she recognised; he was going to stand fast on untenable ground, even if it meant sinking up to his neck.

'I'm afraid that's not true,' she said, carefully. 'She had fresh bandages on her wrists and she meant us all to see them, believe me. I asked Roland, who had to say that yes, she had had another episode.'

'But he coped.'

'Yes . . . but he won't be around the next time this happens.'

'How do you *know* it'll happen again? You've written her off, haven't you? Put her away is what you're saying.'

'I'm saying she is past the ability of well-meaning people to help. Louis, for God's sake, if she had a broken leg, or was covered with spots, you'd have her at the best doctor you know, inside the day.' She saw that she was making ground. 'I don't understand why you won't find the help for her. It costs money, of course.'

'And I've got that,' he shouted, as she had known he would. 'Look,' he said, banging his palm against the wall. 'I don't want her being messed around by some quack, telling him . . .'

'Telling him what? Terrible things about us? That's par for the course. And probably nothing to what the kids tell each other.'

'I don't want to send her away,' her husband said, sullenly, and she sighed.

'You sent her away, as you put it, to Faraday's, long before you met me. And we send away our two, so they can get a good education. It's no different; in a residential place she would get more time and space to find help. She wouldn't have to cope with us as well.'

'I don't want to go on talking about it.' He turned at bay. 'Look, I know we have to do something. But can we just go to this party and enjoy ourselves together, as a family, just for once.' He looked at her, mutinous and pleading, and she sighed.

'Of course. See how she seems to you tonight.'

'Right.' He was looking tired and angry, but she knew she had made progress and hastened to find a change of subject.

'Nick is going to tell the kids on Monday that he is going.'

'Not before time.' Louis leapt at the chance of talking about something new. 'The Trustees wanted to advertise last week, or so I understand,' he added, catching her eye.

'I'm going to apply.'

'Oh, I knew that, my dear. You, and Piers Miller, and Roland Willis.'

'How do you know about them?' She was disconcerted and saw that he had intended that result.

'Little birds.' He was looking smug and hostile but she was too agitated to leave the subject.

'But Piers is a year younger than I am. And he's only just arrived from Rugby.'

'Three years come September, I understand. Long enough. And you can't discount Roland Willis. Lot of the Trustees think very highly of his pastoral qualities — they feel the school needs someone like him.' He looked at her sideways.

'Indeed,' she said, calming down, recognising that her husband needed to score a few points. 'But the Trustees are also concerned about academic standards, particularly in the sciences. And if I were blocked here I might want to apply somewhere else. Lots of schools within fifty miles.' And let him pass that back to the little birdies, she thought, savagely.

'I expect Piers Miller would say the same,' her husband said, with a pleased smile. 'We'd better get into our glad rags for this party, hadn't we?'

* * *

Vivienne Willis pulled on a floating white dress, looked at herself in the awkward mirror and considered her image, doubtfully. Perhaps a little *jeune fille* for this rather grand gathering.

'Roland, what do you think?' She could see her husband, slumped on the bed.

'You look very nice,' he said, and she turned round, amazed.

'You didn't even look,' she said, ready to be amused, but he was not looking at her even now, the dark eyes under the mop of greying dark hair looking past her, unseeing.

'Darling? Never mind me, I'll wear the green silk, but what are you wearing?'

He had come back from the Six Senior journey twenty-four hours ago, exhausted and depressed, and despite three square meals, a rousing fuck and a night's sleep he was still unreachably low and miserable.

'Roland? Darling, we do have to go to this party, and it will be smart.'

He groaned and swung his feet in huge badly worn leather slippers on to the bed. 'I really am exhausted. Could we . . . well, could we not go?' He was looking utterly hangdog and she was exasperated.

'We have to go. Catriona would never forgive us if she missed it. And I want to go — it'll be a very good party. We don't get many invitations like this.'

He rolled over on his side and buried his face in the pillows in silent protest and she stared at the back of his head, angry and worried.

'Darling.' She sat beside him and rubbed the back of his neck. 'Talk to me. What went so wrong on the journey?'

'I *have* told you. Catriona behaved very badly, and I'm very worried about her. I don't think she ought to go out tonight.'

'What do you think she'll do?' He groaned and she tried again.

'Well, what did she do that was so awful on the journey? You said she hung round Giles — well, I've seen her do *that* and I agree it's embarrassing, but it's not abnormal, is it?'

He sighed. 'Well, it was not only embarrassing but totally inappropriate. That devil Giles has . . . well, transferred whatever affections he is capable of feeling.'

'To whom?' she asked, startled.

'Jenny Fairbrooks. You may not know her.'

'That very pretty blonde who was Juliet in the play?'

'That's the one. Well, Catriona . . . everyone else knew, but she wouldn't get the message as the kids say, and then, apparently, on the Wednesday night she tried to invade Giles's tent and of course found Jenny. Quite against the rules, but we can't police everything, these are eighteen-year-old adults, or supposed to be, and in two weeks' time they will be right out of our control.'

Vivienne gazed at him; he was not looking at her and picking at the counterpane. 'What happened?'

'She made *the* most frightful scene. The good Jamie did his best, and I got into it too. I had to tell her I would send her home if she could not control herself. So she was very angry with me and we had a row.'

'Oh, darling.' She was very sorry for him, he looked wretched, but she was not going to commiserate; all this could have been expected, as she just managed not to say.

'Worse than a row,' he said, miserably. 'She accused me of all sorts of things.'

'She's ill, darling.'

'Yes. I couldn't . . . well, it was as if she'd become a different person.'

'She has,' she said, stonily. 'Could we not — should we not — consider getting help now the exams are over? I mean, even if she does get three Cs she can't go up to university in her present state. Even you think she's getting worse.'

'She is. Wholly irrational and a danger to herself.' He was sounding absolutely exhausted.

She clasped her hands together, hoping her timing was right. 'I think I should talk to Louis again. Really, we aren't helping her. A couple of weeks even, in a clinic, with a really good therapist—'

'No,' he said, sharply. 'There must be a better answer. She'll be better away, quietly, with us.' His face was shuttered and miserable and she decided not to challenge him for the moment.

'Well, why don't we tell her we are none of us going to this party?'

'No, I can't. Or rather I daren't.' She stared at him, and he bent his head, so she could see the flecks of grey and the thinning patch at the crown. 'I'd rather just try and get through till tomorrow. I wish we weren't staying with the Quentins, kind though it was to invite us — but, I promise, on Monday we'll all go and see Dr Martin and perhaps get something to calm her down.' He got up and looked, unseeingly, at his clothes in the wardrobe. 'She *was* better, wasn't she, while the exams were on?'

'Yes, she was. Much.' She watched impatiently as her husband slowly got out his only respectable tie, his movements alarmingly lethargic, and tried for optimism. 'She'll be all right tonight, I'm sure, she'll be on her best behaviour, surely, for Giles's parents. She probably hopes to get him back — one always does.'

'I hope so.' He sounded totally unhopeful and she hesitated, but he was slowly organising a clean shirt. She glanced at the mirror. 'Let's go and see how she's doing,' she said, and they crossed the corridor to her daughter's bedroom, and knocked on the door.

'Are you organised for tonight?' she called, trying to keep the exasperation out of her voice but aware she was sounding shrill. 'Do you need any help?' And of all the stupid rhetorical questions, that must take the biscuit, she thought, furiously. I should never have had a child, or not this child, and yes, you would have to say that I was the worst mother for her, with the possible exception of her stepmother Amanda. But I have at least presented her with a devoted stepfather who has more patience with her than her own father ever summoned.

'Sweetie? Trina? You need to be ready in an hour. Don't leave yourself short of time.'

'I'm *dressed*.' It came out as a whine and Vivienne wanted to scream at her to cheer up for God's sake, they were going to a party, where she would have all the attention she could want.

The door opened, slowly, and Catriona crept round it, head lowered. 'I hate this dress,' she said, by way of greeting.

'You look very pretty,' her stepfather said, warmly. Catriona didn't, but then she wasn't giving the dress a chance, letting it hang off her. And she had done something new and experimental with her eye make-up which was a mistake.

'Then wear something else,' Vivienne said, in a moment of practical feminine sympathy. 'It's never any good wearing something you don't feel right in for a party. What else have you got?'

'Only jeans. And my school skirt.'

Faraday's did not have a uniform, but ties for the boys and skirts for the girls were prescribed for the school meeting on Sunday evenings with the result that all Faraday girls possessed a skirt, usually very tight and very short. Catriona's, typically, was long, very woollen, moth-eaten tartan, wholly unsuitable for a London party, or indeed for anything; it was another way of making a protest.

'Clean jeans?' Vivienne asked, deciding to make the best of it; far better that Catriona should be happy and unsuitably dressed than wretched but correct.

'Fairly.'

'Get into the best pair and you can have one of my shirts if you like.'

'Your new white one?'

'Yes, of course.' It was a white linen tunic, bought in Paris at hideous expense, but she was cheered beyond measure at this sign of life and animation. She went and got the shirt out of her wardrobe, while Catriona changed into jeans. Vivienne popped the shirt over Catriona's head and they both gazed into the long mirror. Catriona had washed her hair for once and it floated to her shoulders, over the beautifully cut linen tunic in a subtle off-white that flattered Catriona's sallow skin. It fell to just below her hips, eliminating a bit of puppy fat, and the low collar flattered a slightly short neck.

She stared at herself in the mirror, cautiously pleased, turning to get a view of the back.

'It looks terrific on you. You'd better keep it,' Vivienne said, overwhelmingly pleased. 'Would you like a necklace or a chain, or something? Here.' She handed her a thick gold chain and they both gazed at the result.

'No, it's better by itself,' Catriona said, just like anyone's daughter, and delighted, Vivienne agreed that her eye had failed her.

'And I've got too much eye stuff on,' Catriona said, critically.

'A bit perhaps.'

She waited, not daring to offer help, while her daughter took the lot off her eyelids and put on very much less in a different colour.

'Perfect,' she said, meaning it, and they went down together to find Roland.

'Ta ra,' she said, standing aside so that he could see his stepdaughter. He hauled himself out of a chair, putting down the newspaper and stared at Catriona, amazed.

'You look lovely.'

She looked at him, seriously, then suddenly smiled and twirled, provocatively, so that he could get the full benefit, flirting a bit like any teenage daughter, and Vivienne sighed with relief.

'Now, am *I* smart enough for you two good-looking women?' he asked, and they walked round him, considering him carefully, for a blessed moment like any ordinary family going to a party.

* * *

For once William McLeish had gone to sleep without protest, but his father was not at all reconciled to going out. As usual he seemed to be going because one of the family was performing, Jamie Miles Brett in this case. Francesca had pressed him into it by saying it might be her last outing before the new baby, due in three weeks.

Why does one say 'new' baby, he wondered, looking for a tie, as if less fortunate people had old or second-hand babies. This apparently idle musing plunged him back into the black hole of worry which had plagued him all through his wife's pregnancy; a totally irrational but uncontrollable conviction that there was something wrong with this baby. He had not felt it fair to share this worry with Francesca, who had no concerns at all about the physical and mental health of the expected child, but was instead fretting obsessively about how William, and his nanny, were going to receive the newcomer.

'*Where* are we going?' he called, irritably.

'Giant palace in Highgate, headquarters of the Quentin empire. Andrew Quentin keeps threatening to sell it and to go and be a tax exile in Dublin, but Giles says it'll never happen.'

'Have you been there?'

'No. I look forward. It has an indoor swimming-pool — a real one, proper length.'

'Surely we aren't going to do that?'

'No, but I want to look at it.'

'And Jamie is playing?'

'Yes. They're doing a selection of the things they did at the Wigmore Hall. Not more than thirty minutes' worth, in order not to bore the audience.'

'I thought all Sir Andrew's mates would be musical.'

'Well, they are, but they're professionals. They won't mind listening to their host's gifted son and his gifted friend for half an hour, but more would be pushing it.' She shot him an amused glance. 'So it won't go on very long, and you can probably even creep away and do something else while it's happening. No, come to think of it, you can't — Jamie knows your views but the poor kid loves you and he keeps hoping you'll improve.'

He laughed and promised to attend faithfully and prominently. 'But we mustn't stay too late.'

'Not past eleven, I promise. I don't think I could take much more.'

He helped her into her dress. As she observed, it was not a question of making a selection from a vast wardrobe, she had precisely three garments that she could get into at all: a pair of maternity trousers, a smock, and one vast capacious evening dress which only just went on over the bulge. They gazed together in the mirror as he did up the hook at the back. 'Ah well. Nobody's going to be looking at me.'

McLeish mentally disagreed; she was a sight to fill the eye, majestic in her blue silk tent and shining dark hair. It might not be the image she wished to cultivate but it was a remarkable vision. And it was a remarkable party. They were received by a butler and taken through a substantial reception room occupied by several young women and an array of drinks, catering to all tastes, so that McLeish was gratefully able to find a good single malt, and Francesca something soft but delicious. They were then led through to a huge double-room full of very elegant people. He found Francesca a chair — with three weeks to go she could stand for about five minutes. He settled her in it, noticing anxiously that she had gone rather pale, but she waved him away and leaned over to talk to Lady Quentin, a languid but determined blonde.

He went, obediently, not wanting to worry her. He had never quite taken the music world seriously but found himself nodding and even conversing with half-familiar famous faces, who seemed to have known Francesca or one of her brothers for *ever*. One of the half-familiar faces was Sir Andrew Quentin, who had, alarmingly, been looking for him and cut him, expertly, out from the crowd, took him to a table by the window and poured him a sizeable refill.

'You're a policeman, I understand.'

McLeish agreed that this was so and nursed his drink.

'Your wife is a very gifted voice teacher. Well, of course, there are those brothers . . . And young Miles Brett. I suppose she's always done it. How . . .'

'How did I get involved with this lot?'

Andrew Quentin coughed on his drink. 'Yes. That was what I was wondering.' Both of them were watching

Francesca, dragonfly bright in turquoise silk if hardly dragonfly agile, conferring with Giles and Jamie. 'When is the baby due? Very soon, I take it.'

'Not quite as soon as you might think. Three weeks.' McLeish realised he was holding his glass very tightly.

'Let me fill that up for you. It's your second child, isn't it? And the first was . . . well . . . free of problems?'

Yes, McLeish agreed, grateful to be reminded, all that was true. There was no cause to fear trouble, he reminded himself, Francesca was so obviously well, if tired. Perceptive of Andrew Quentin to have noticed that he was worried, he thought.

'I'm glad to hear this because there are one or two rather important people who can't be here tonight, who are coming to the Faraday school concert on the 12th. I had very much hoped that Francesca would be able to go on coaching Giles. He has great confidence in her, which is half the battle.'

Of course, Andrew Quentin had not been interested in his worries — or even noticed them, McLeish thought, amused. He had been concerned only that Francesca wouldn't be well enough to go on coaching his treasured son. 'She can, of course, but only if Giles can get to London.' Andrew Quentin's face fell. 'I'm not risking her having the baby in some cottage hospital in Dorset. She needs to be within reach of UCH.'

It must have come out more forcefully than he had intended, because Andrew Quentin was looking just faintly alarmed as well as disappointed. 'But, she — you — are coming to the concert?'

Yes, McLeish conceded, knowing that teams of wild horses would not keep his wife away. 'But just for the day. I'll be driving her.'

'Well.' Andrew Quentin, however chagrined, was a professional. 'Of course, the baby is the most important . . . But if I can get Giles to London, she'll work with him? And you could get down in the morning of the show so she could just loosen the voice up? We'd be most grateful.' He was watching the other side of the room and waved in answer to a signal from Lady Quentin. 'Very nice to have met you at last.'

He went, leaving McLeish with the bottle and two loudly arguing musicians bearing down on him. He looked round and with relief saw Alexandra through the crowd, herself the centre of a good deal of attention, looking ravishing in conventional black velvet, the red hair up and with elaborately curled tendrils. She was on the hunt too, he recognised; there must be some dance celebrities among the half-recognised faces here tonight.

'*That* was Antony Williams,' she confirmed, arriving bright-eyed at his side. 'He was at Pineapple the other day, rehearsing the ENB, but I didn't quite dare bounce up to him there. He's very nice.'

'You'll break Matt Sutherland's heart if you jack in the law,' McLeish pointed out, suppressing a mean pleasure. 'He's putting in a lot of effort for you.'

He got a stern look from the beautiful blue eyes. 'I'm very effective cheap labour.'

This one had always known her own value, he understood. 'Useful for you to be invited here.'

'Indeed. All done by Jamie.' Her face sobered. 'My poor little prot. I had lunch with him, he's desperate about his dad.'

'That's an old trouble of course.'

'New to Jamie.'

'True,' he conceded, gazing pleasurably at her supple, elegant back, most of which was on display.

'The bodice of this dress is boned.'

'I wasn't going to ask.' He was only just old enough for this, he thought, alarmed, and became aware that there was a general shift going on, and people were being marshalled towards the music room. He followed Alex, very conscious of the attention she was attracting, and feeling like a harassed uncle.

The original programme had been rejigged, so that Jamie came on first to do his solo. This was familiar ground even to McLeish; he had heard it practised many times, complete with repeats. But the lad was an impressive performer, no question, calm, deeply absorbed and getting a wonderful sound out of his instrument. The applause, from this knowledgeable audience, was temperate but solid, and he looked across at his wife who was beaming, well pleased with her godson. She shook her head imperceptibly in answer to Jamie's look of enquiry, and he put his violin down and moved to the piano, displacing Andrew Quentin, and sat waiting for Giles who bounced on to the little stage, nodded to Jamie and his father and went straight in with a brisk paean to kind Amaryllis, so much nicer and more accommodating than grander ladies. McLeish remembered the lyrics from his own living-room, together with his wife observing that men everywhere went on like that, which was why all the dear kind Amaryllises ended up in the pudding club. The boys had laughed uneasily, he remembered, but Giles was giving it all he had, the graceful, flexible, disconcerting voice effortless, with every word clear. He went straight on to 'O Gentle Death', in sharp contrast, but the beauty of the voice was such as to make the sad lyrics a graceful conceit. There was a silence at the end, and experienced musicians all over the room turned to each other in recognition and nodded, clapping soberly. Jamie played again and McLeish saw a couple of people write notes on their programmes, but everyone was really waiting for Giles to sing again. He silenced the big room absolutely with what McLeish would always think of as 'Art thou weary'.

'Thank you, Jamie, Giles.' Andrew Quentin allowed the heartfelt applause but spoke over any suggestion of an encore. 'And many thanks to Francesca Wilson, who has done such a good job of coaching Giles. The next thing is supper in the dining-room; do just sit anywhere.'

McLeish, who was hungry, looked round for his wife, while Alexandra darted across to kiss Jamie. Francesca came over, her smile warming the room.

'Went well. Lots of people wanting to get hold of Jamie.'

'And Giles.'

'Ah, well, he's a one-off. But it is Jamie who will go the distance. I wouldn't be absolutely sure about Giles.'

They both looked across to the throng gathered round Giles Quentin, virtually invisible except for his distinctive blond hair.

'Look at that tiresome girl, sulking at the edge,' Francesca said, crossly, nodding towards Catriona Roberts.

'Pity that,' McLeish said, judiciously. 'I noticed her earlier — I thought she was looking rather pretty. White suits her.'

'Not as pretty as Alex, I note,' his wife said, drily. 'Oops.' He followed the line of her gaze and saw, in cameo, Giles Quentin who had emerged from the group being clutched at by Catriona and was shaking her off with something approaching a snarl.

'A theatrical air kiss followed by a smart exit is the correct response to a fan you don't want,' Francesca said, disapprovingly.

'He's a bit young maybe,' McLeish said, watching a blond man — Piers Miller, Giles's stepfather, he remembered — step on to the scene and try to remove Catriona.

'No.' All heads turned as she struck out at Piers. 'Take your hands off me — I'm sick of you pawing me.'

The man drew back as if he had been bitten and looked wildly round.

'Catriona.' A pretty plump blond woman bore down on the girl.

'Susie Miller, remember. Wife to Piers. Oh dear, oh dear, what a bitch. The child, I mean. Oh blast, Jamie's got into it.'

And indeed, McLeish observed, that kindly boy was trying to pour oil on troubled waters and was getting nowhere; Catriona had turned on him and was shouting something unintelligible. McLeish put a heavy arm round his wife's shoulders to prevent her going over and saw out of the corner of his eye a flash of red hair and long legs in fishnet tights, and then Catriona somehow vanishing out of the french windows in the grip of a furious Alexandra, who banged the door shut behind her, indicating unmistakably to Jamie that he should rejoin his admirers.

'She ought to be on the stage,' Francesca said, awed, 'I've never seen anything put so clearly without a word spoken. *Now* may I rescue Jamie?'

'No need,' McLeish said. 'There's an old gent bearing down on him — I sort of know his face.'

'Michael Hordern, conductor of the LSO. Yes. More I could not ask.'

He allowed her a minute of pleasurable contemplation; Mr Hordern had a notebook out and he and Jamie were in animated negotiation. Then he swept her into the dining-room, reminding her that it was now 9.30 and under the terms of their agreement she had precisely an hour and a half to get supper down her, find her coat and bid her host a civil farewell.

CHAPTER 6

Saturday 1st July — Later

Ten thirty, McLeish thought, looking at his watch, and fidgeting. Half an hour until he could take his wife and the baby home. He looked across the table with some misgiving; flushed with excitement and mineral water Francesca was deep in conversation with some man who had worked with Tristram, one of her twin brothers now blessedly absent in Verona. He must stretch his legs, he decided, as he had been sitting on a small gilt chair not constructed for a man of six foot four inches veering uncomfortably close to fifteen stone. Through the wide arch which separated the enormous dining-room from the vast living-room some of the younger members of the party were dancing, and he went towards them. He blinked as a pair of fish netted legs cartwheeled through the air, followed by a fall of red hair. There was Alex, in mid-flow, only just wearing the velvet dress which was now revealed to have a wraparound skirt that fell away from her long legs at every step. She was dancing with a much older man with dark springy hair and they were both extremely pleased with themselves, flinging themselves around in what he recognised as an apache routine. Alex cast herself in one exquisite fluid movement at the man, plastering herself to his side, and he, head disdainfully averted, flicked her over his head. McLeish gaped; the man was slight and Alex, elegant though she was, had curves in all the right places. She dropped to the floor, in a perfect split, and allowed herself to be pulled up in one single movement to the man's chest and bent right back, the heavy red hair falling clear of her neck, eyes fixed in mock submission on the man's face. He cast her from him and the dance ended with Alex in a composed exquisite heap of black velvet, long legs and red hair on the parquet floor, and the man, also a sight to fill the eye, totally commanding as he stood over her, arm extended, back drawn up. The Faraday kids were greeting this performance with their customary shrieks and whistles as the man bent to give Alex a hand so that she came up off the floor in one piece and bowed, laughing, red hair falling into her eyes.

'Do it again. Encore!' Francesca had arrived by his side. 'I missed the start of that,' she confided, sadly. 'Do you think he can be persuaded to do it again?'

'Who he?'

'Darling, that is Antony Williams. *Surely* . . . Oh well, perhaps not. He doesn't dance much these days, but isn't he wonderful?'

'I was watching Alex,' he said feebly.

'Of course you were. A comedienne. On the edge of sending it up.'

Yes, he thought, recognising the quality that had eluded him. But the man, now he saw him with Francesca's eyes, took it all absolutely seriously, including being the star he evidently was. Alex was thanking him, prettily, for the honour done her and he was bowing over her hands as the Faraday kids shouted for an encore. Williams laughed, obviously amused, and said something interrogative to Alex and went over to the piano. It was Jamie, of course, who nodded, hunting through a pile of music. He and Williams could have been father and son in terms of age, but what they both demonstrably were, McLeish understood, were craftsmen professionals, dedicated to the same end. Whatever happened to Jamie's family, that was him settled; at just eighteen he was a professional musician, being in the LSO, or conducting, or whatever, that was his life. Fortunate man, for all his family worries. He looked back to Alex who had recovered her breath and was carefully stretching her back. It wasn't exactly unselfconscious, she knew every other eye in the room was on her, but she was concentrated on being ready for Williams. Jamie played a few bars and Williams nodded, going back towards Alex — and she pushed her hair out of her face and stood ready.

'Twyla Tharp. A display piece,' Francesca said, quietly, and he realised she was still standing, set back on her heels, hands at her back. He looked round and seized a chair from a Faraday boy and settled her in it, she never having taken her eyes off the dancers. Alex was tiring, he could see, missing the occasional step, but Williams was carrying her. There was more for the man to do, presumably the reason for this choice, and Alex, with sense beyond her years, was acting as background, not throwing herself into it but sketching elegantly some of the movements. At the end, with a glint in her eye, she led Williams to centre stage and presented him to the audience, gravely standing behind him, bowing one hand crossed on her chest in the traditional posture of the supporting man. The man laughed and embraced her and stretched an arm to bring Jamie into the circle.

'Well, that's a night she'll never forget,' Francesca said, beaming and applauding. 'Oops.'

'What?'

She had gone pale. 'No, it's all right. The creature just kicked me.'

'You need to go home. It's just eleven.'

It took a frustrating fifteen minutes to find her coat and to establish that the mini cab service had misunderstood or not believed his instructions and was not expected for another fifteen minutes. Crossly he sat her down to see her recover instantly talking to some musical person. He looked at his watch to discover that it was actually now 11.40 and rose in wrath, but Jamie, wild-eyed, appeared at his elbow.

'John, could you come?' He was some colour paler than white, the dark brown eyes enormous, all elation and pleasure gone.

'What is it, Jamie?'

'It's Catriona. She's . . . she's . . .' His eyes turned up and his arms went up and McLeish caught him as he went crashing down. He held him and looked frantically at his wife, who was struggling from her chair. He lowered him to the floor, and looked round for help; there was Alex, as white as Jamie, and for some reason with hair and face and the front of her dress soaking wet.

'I have to go to direct the ambulance.'

'Alex, what is it?' Francesca asked.

'Catriona,' she said, over her shoulder, slipping past them.

'Whatever it is,' McLeish said, 'I will stay and you will go home. Your mum's there, after all.' He looked round, agonised, as he located the apologetic cabdriver, taking a careful look at him to make quite certain he hadn't been drinking anything alcoholic and, satisfied, urged his wife into the car. 'It's not starting, is it?'

'No. Remember, I've done this before. I'm just kippered.' She touched his face. 'Bring Jamie home when you come. I expect the wretched girl's had another go at her wrists. She *would* when they were all having such a good time.'

McLeish banged the car door and made a swift savage indication to the driver that he should stop gawping at the lights flashing down the street and get out of it. The car leapt away from the kerb, the ambulance pulled into its space and the crew poured out, Alex shivering and frenzied, shouting that it was the *third* floor, there was a lift and people would be waiting. McLeish pushed her gently aside, noticing that Jamie had been helped up and was sitting, head between his knees, two Faraday colleagues arranged round him in anxious tableau. He rushed to help two paramedics into the lift. There was no more room, what with them and their kit, and

Alex had already taken off up the stairs, so he raced up after her, catching up with her just as they reached the third floor.

'Please hurry.' It was Susie Miller, also unexplainedly wet, and near hysterical, and McLeish left her to Alex while he disentangled the paramedics and their equipment from the lift. He followed them into a bedroom and over their shoulders got his first sight of tragedy: a hunched back bent over, then moving aside in an undignified scramble to let the medical help through.

Catriona Roberts was briefly visible on the floor, then the medics closed in with oxygen masks and tubes. He looked over their heads, a door was open and there was brightly coloured liquid everywhere, the colour of blood, but far too thin and wet. One of the medics was speaking urgently into a mobile phone.

'We need a doctor. Casualty cut her wrists and got in the bath. No. No. No, I don't think so. Yes, we are.' He hunched himself back to Catriona's side, taking over smoothly from his colleague who was steadily and rhythmically beating on the breastbone to try to restart the heart. McLeish, deciding there was no doubt about where his duty lay, knelt beside them.

'I'm a police officer. I was a guest here. Anything I can do? Clear the room?'

'That'd help,' the second man agreed, two fingers laid on the pulse point in Catriona's neck. McLeish looked round, for the first time conscious of hysterical weeping. Not Susie Miller, but Vivienne Willis whom she was cradling in her arms, awkwardly crushed between the oblivious paramedics and the bed. Roland Willis was sitting on the bed, head in hands, praying. Louis Roberts, also wet through, was kneeling at Catriona's head, Amanda beside him.

'Can we give these lads some space?' McLeish said, sounding over-hearty in the confined room. 'Everyone please. We may need the bed.' Susie Miller nodded to him gratefully and stretched a hand to be helped up, pulling the weeping Vivienne with her, and Louis Roberts turned, blindly, into his wife's arms. Roland Willis did not move and McLeish leaned over to touch his shoulder.

'Oh God, is she going to be all right? She was in the bath, it was all red.'

'And you pulled her out?' His jacket lay by his side and the white shirt was sopping and blotched with pink. 'Was her mouth under water?'

'Yes, I told them.' He made a helpless gesture at the paramedics, working, oblivious of him.

'You need something sweet.'

Roland Willis started to shiver convulsively, and McLeish looked round for help, finding it in Alex, herself pale and shivery, but there, on her feet.

'Tea and biscuits. No alcohol,' he instructed and handed over the shaking, white-faced Roland Willis. 'You too, Alex. Get something down you. And I want Sir Andrew, please. Get someone to find him.' He closed the door firmly behind them and went to kneel by the medics; a chap of his age and a younger assistant. Catriona's face was all but invisible under an oxygen mask. Her elegant shirt was stained with blood and the paramedics had slashed it to get at her heart. The wide sleeves were rolled back over wrist bandages, pure white against the pallid flesh. They'd stopped the bleeding at least, he thought, then his heart thudded as he understood what he was seeing. He glanced up at the drip; it had a bottle of plasma and a saline solution, and he looked again at the limp arms. The older man at her head, fingers laid on the jugular vein at the neck, looked up at him and shook his head. 'We'll keep going till the doc gets here,' he said quietly, and returned his attention to his colleague. 'Two more, George, and I'll take over.'

McLeish watched them, there being nothing else useful to do, for a long ten minutes, while they changed hands twice, then he heard a knock on the door and opened it a crack. 'Doctor. From the Whittington.' She was not much older than Alex, fair hair tucked into a cap, and dark shadows under the blue eyes. He held the door for her and she bumped a bag on to the bed and went to kneel beside her colleagues.

'Not a flicker,' the older man said quietly. 'Found under water with her wrists cut.'

She picked up a flaccid arm and looked at the bandages still pristine. 'Can we have the blanket pulled back? Carry on.'

The older man was now patiently continuing the rhythmic thump on the breastbone and the younger one helped to pull back the blanket.

'How long?' she asked.

George looked at his watch. 'We've been here twenty minutes. Took us fourteen minutes from the call, and people here worked on her. Say thirty-four minutes.'

The young doctor nodded, gently turning a lifeless arm to look at the inside of the elbow. 'Lost a lot of blood. Stop a minute, Kevin.' She pushed the stethoscope into her ears and went quickly over the girl's chest, then laid her fingers again on the pulse, signalling them to carry on. 'I'm sorry,' she said, directly to McLeish, sitting back on her heels, looking about sixteen.

'Are you sure?' he asked, stupidly, but the young woman was unperturbed by this slur on her professional competence.

'Yes. We could carry on and take her into hospital but she's dead. She's lost a lot of blood and may have had a heart attack. That may be how she died rather than by drowning. The autopsy will show.'

'She was gone when we got here,' the older man confirmed, and George nodded.

'Which is why they called me,' the young doctor explained. 'I couldn't do anything, none of us could, but with me here we can agree to stop.'

'Right.' He pulled himself together, wishing that this had not been a night when the drink had been of a particularly high quality, and he had expected to be driven home.

'We'd better take her to the mortuary.' The young woman was packing her bag, tears in her eyes, and McLeish reassured himself at this evidence of humanity.

'No. Sorry.' He looked at three blank faces. 'I'll call out the police doctor. It'll save time and trouble. I am Detective Chief Superintendent McLeish — I was a guest here.' He produced a warrant card which the doctor examined solemnly, then she looked up at him, wide-eyed.

'Poor girl . . .'

'I'll find the parents.'

* * *

'She's dead.'

'Yes, Jamie. Everyone tried but she's dead. I heard the medics say she was probably dead when Roland got her out of the bath.'

Alex, still wrapped in the coat she had snatched up, reached out to cuddle him. He was looking very young and pale in an armchair. 'God, you're *freezing*,' she said, appalled, as she pressed her cheek against his.

'You're pretty cold yourself. They're bringing me tea.'

'Good, I'll have some of yours.' He looked at her pathetically, and she remembered her four years' seniority. 'Well, it's not a surprise, is it, Jamie? I mean, it's awful, but not totally unexpected.'

Tears started to pour down his cheeks, but mercifully tea and sandwiches on a tray arrived, brought by one of the caterers. She folded his hands round a cup and herself stuffed a sandwich inelegantly into her mouth, along with a gulp of hot, sweet tea. She was shivering convulsively still, and chilled right to her bones; her dress was wet and she dabbed at it. The wodge of Kleenex turned pink and she looked at it in slow realisation, the sandwich and tea sour on her stomach. Made frantic by the marks on her dress she found herself wanting her parents, here, now. But they, she remembered, were in India on the sort of non-holiday they always took, her mother interfering in some piece of fiscal administration and her father advising on a dam or a road, or something. She took a deep breath; she wanted to go home, but John McLeish had made it clear she wasn't to do that until he had had a chance to talk to her. There was only one other person she wanted, and he would hardly be sitting at home at something past midnight on a Saturday night, unless . . . Pausing only to make sure that Jamie was getting some food down him, she unearthed the telephone she had noticed earlier.

'Sutherland.' Gratitude overwhelmed her at the familiar New Zealand accent.

'Me. Alex.'

'You're not in bother *again?*'

She took a huge breath, restored by the simple abrasiveness.

'Not personally. But Catriona — Jamie's little friend — just killed herself. In a bath.'

'Oh Jesus. Is Jamie OK?'

'No. And nor am I . . .'

'You called the police?'

'They were here. John McLeish is in charge.'

'You're at this posh party, right? Well, McLeish is much too grand for a suicide. He'll just be waiting for the local nick to take over.' There was a pause while she snuffled. 'You're not *involved*, Alex, are you? Or Jamie?'

'No.'

'But you rang me.'

'Yes.'

'So you'd like me to come round and hold your hand?'

'Yes,' she said, baldly, and listened to the silence at the other end.

'I'll be there. Give me the address. I'm on call, so I may have to go again,' he added warningly.

In case I should think he's a total push-over, she thought, nursing a new warm glow. 'Matt? You couldn't bring a couple of spare sweaters . . . or something, could you? For me and Jamie.'

'My wardrobe is at your disposal. See you soon.'

* * *

'Giles, you have to talk to us.' Andrew Quentin, pale with worry, gazed at his son who was standing looking out over the magnificent view of the London skyline, the whole panoply of the City and the dome of St Paul's laid before him. 'You had a row with her and that very grand policeman knows it.'

'I've had plenty of rows with her. She was bugging me. She's never felt badly enough to kill herself before.'

For all his brave words, his mother thought, with sinking heart, her boy was badly rattled, looking much as he had as a twelve-year-old. 'She was very unstable,' she said, wearily. 'And I blame myself — so does poor Roland — for keeping her in the Faraday community, rather than letting her mother sweep her into a hospital. With hindsight, Vivienne was absolutely right. Rotten mother though she is and was,' she added, finally allowing some relief to her feelings, but finding herself immediately conscience-stricken. 'I shouldn't say that, her child is dead, how must she feel.' Her son made an instinctive move to comfort her, but thought better of it and stayed, scowling and rigid by the window.

'She had a row with Piers as well,' he observed, to the starlit scenery.

'At the end of the show? Didn't hear the words, just the music.' Andrew Quentin had perked up.

'She said he groped her, if not worse,' Giles said, with one miserable, malicious glance at his mother.

'And I was very cross with her. In fact it made me realise she was much more ill than I'd understood. It's very hard on Piers, who put so much work into her maths when he had no time at all.'

'So you all had a row with her. Or several rows? Not just Giles.' Andrew Quentin was looking considerably heartened.

'I suppose that's true,' she acknowledged, wearily. 'So however bad it was, Giles, you weren't alone, she was just — poor girl — attacking everyone and we were *all* cross with her. Including Roland, for once. He was very angry that she tried to spoil yours and Jamie's triumph. I suppose she saw you all going on and away to greater things and just couldn't bear it, oh *dear*.' She felt tears rising and scuffled in her bag for a handkerchief. She blew her nose, becoming aware that her ex-husband was watching her steadily.

'The other thing,' he said, getting out of his chair and joining their son by the window, 'the thing is, I understand — well, John McLeish told me, that's why we are stuck here, that the police will take an interest. They assume it's suicide, just as we do.'

'Did she say why she was so unhappy? Of course she didn't, I mean there wasn't a note, was there?'

'Not that anyone's found. Or not yet.' He turned to face her so that he was outlined against the lighted panorama. 'But I think we need to be prepared.' He turned his head towards his son, with the easy authoritative movement of a man who has been the undisputed centre of attention for whole armies of musicians since he was an undergraduate.

'She was having a baby. Mine, she said,' Giles mumbled, head down, and Susie felt the shock down to her stomach.

'But *Giles* . . .'

'I know it's against the rules, Mum, but we weren't at school. We were in London, at the beginning of the Easter holidays.'

'That's not the point,' she said, appalled. 'You knew what a state she was in. You shouldn't — well, have taken advantage, God damn it, whatever way it happened.' She stared at him, feeling herself going scarlet. 'And *then* you got me to protect you from her. You said she was bugging you. Well, she had every right, didn't she?' Her fingers itched to slap the sullen look off his face.

'He may not have been the only candidate.' Andrew, she saw bitterly, was not shocked.

Giles looked at him sharply, in a flare of hope, and she understood how trapped he felt, mired in a situation well beyond his eighteen-year-old capacity. Andrew moved to put an arm round his son and she saw, with a pang of jealousy, how easily Giles moved into his arms, shoulders heaving.

She'd not been any use to him either, she had failed both the children, the dead girl and her own son, blessedly alive. She bowed her head but Andrew had reached over for her and was pulling her into a communal embrace so that she too ended up snuffling into his shoulder.

* * *

'Sorry to call you out, Doc.' He looked at his watch; it was one o'clock in the morning.

'Glad to oblige.' It was Doc Jamieson whom he had worked with often before and had been lucky to find on call.

'Poor lass.' Doc Jamieson was sitting on his heels, looking at the dead, drained face.

'The casualty doctor thought she was probably dead by the time the crew got here.'

'That'll probably be right. Looks as if she drowned — there's water in the lungs. Lost enough blood to pass out and just slid under the water. Nothing to grip on to.'

They both turned to look at the bath, an elegant, free-standing cast-iron imitation of a Victorian bath. It was deep, and the only grip was afforded by the sides; there were no anachronistic useful devices like handles set in the side.

'She may even have had a heart attack — lose enough blood and that happens. But I'd take a guess that she drowned — that's what killed her. Lots of old scars on the wrists too.' They looked at each other, Dr Jamieson's blue eyes in the wrinkled face narrowed.

'Oh yes, she'd tried before,' McLeish said. 'But not this seriously. I understand she used to make cuts in her wrist and arms but little ones. Self-mutilation rather than a serious suicide attempt. That's what's worrying me.'

'It needn't. A lot of suicides have a history of self-mutilation. In various forms, including anorexia.' He got to his feet. 'Nothing left really in here.'

They both gazed round the bathroom; Roland Willis had said he thought that someone had pulled out the plug.

A natural and sensible reaction if you were trying to get out a water-logged body, but it had left, as Doc observed, not a lot to see. Little pools of bloodstained water, and stained white towels and bath-mat lay everywhere in mute witness of the struggle.

'She got into a bath this time, Doc. Gave herself a real chance of dying. She hasn't done that before.'

Doc Jamieson leaned heavily against the door. 'Why is it your case at all?'

'Oh, I was here. No, that's not entirely the point. The girl lives in London like a lot of the kids here. And it happened in Sir Andrew Quentin's house.'

'So your lot were going to get it anyway.'

'Yes. I thought so. And we'd need to do a good job just because I was here and know a lot of them. So there's a forensic squad behind you and I've got one of my DIs coming over. A lot of manpower for a potential suicide, but . . .'

'But you need to cover your backside?' Doc Jamieson asked. 'Doesn't sound like you.'

'It's Francesca's backside as well.'

'You should hand the case over then.'

'That's partly why I've got a DI coming.'

'Partly?' Doc Jamieson had known him a long time.

'And partly my bones hurt,' he confirmed. 'The girl — Catriona — was a nuisance and an exhibitionist, but I'm very surprised she went the whole way.'

'I'm a simple medical person, John. I'll bear your views in mind when I do the autopsy early on Monday. Right now I'm away to my bed, for tomorrow I have the grandchildren. Evening, gentlemen.'

An incoming forensic squad, immaculately overalled, booted and hatted, had arrived and its leader was gazing at the chaos in the bathroom.

'Just print and photograph everything,' McLeish instructed, looking the man firmly in the eye. The man gave him a look on the thoughtful side of incredulity.

'Door locked, was it?'

They both looked at the marks on the frame and then at the key in the door.

'Looks as if it was. I haven't taken statements yet. They had a go at the door before they found a key.'

'Should be another key around then. In here somewhere.'

They both looked round; there was superficially nowhere for a key to be, but McLeish knew the squad would make a careful search. He stood up. If the dead girl had locked the door from the inside then this had been for real, she had meant not to be interrupted. He backed out of the door and turned to see Kevin Camberton, a sergeant and a couple of DCs. Camberton was wide-eyed and looking actively pleased to be among those present; an emotion McLeish understood as having less to do with the honour of working with his detective chief superintendent than the fact that he was in the house of the great Andrew Quentin. Another damned musical person, he thought, sourly; well, at least it would keep his promising DI civil about being called out to what was on the face of it a sadly commonplace suicide. He reflected; as usual he needed to be in two places at once, but the forensic team was experienced, they could get on by themselves.

'Right. Kevin, will you stay here with the squad and give me a DC. I need to talk to the parents and the people who found her.'

'They do know she's dead, sir?'

'Yes, I did that. They're divorced. I'll take the mother first.'

Camberton nodded and turned to watch the squad. McLeish and a DC went down to the first floor, which was as palatial as the ground floor. A door open to their right revealed a vast bedroom, furnished only with a regally large bed; rich, successful men like Andrew Quentin obviously kept their clothes, hairbrushes and general clutter somewhere completely different. Upon this thought the man himself appeared.

'My wife's gone to bed in her dressing-room. I hope that's all right, she was rather shocked and she didn't see anything.'

'We can talk to Lady Quentin in the morning. Are the Willis family still where they were?'

'In my office. I've had food and drink sent up and we lent them some clothes. Do you want . . . sorry, of course you do. Will you have anything yourselves?'

'No, we'll wait,' McLeish said. 'We'll need a word with the Roberts family, and could someone see that Jamie Miles Brett is all right? We will take a statement from him and Alexandra Ferguson. Everyone else I think can go as soon as they've given their addresses to my people.'

'Is that usual, with a suicide? All this?'

'It is a crime. And a bit of attention to procedure now may save trouble later. None of us would want to go to an inquest without having done all reasonable investigations.'

'Mm.' Andrew Quentin was not moving from his position between them and the study door. 'I'd assumed that this was an accident; the poor girl was trying to make a point and went too far. For the parents' sake . . . well, I'd hoped that that was a possible verdict.'

'And so it may be, but we don't know enough of the background yet.'

Andrew Quentin moved aside, reluctantly. 'They're very distressed,' he warned, but something in McLeish's face stopped him. 'Oh, you broke the news.'

'Yes,' McLeish agreed patiently, and the man nodded distractedly but did finally get out of their way.

Andrew Quentin's office was as minimalist as his bedroom, all the normal clutter of an office locked away in the walls somehow, and only a huge glass table and an enormous, detailed wall calendar covering several years in evidence. On the edges of this austere splendour sat Roland and Vivienne Willis slumped in stylish dark brown leather chairs. They looked, both of them, utterly worn out. Vivienne Willis's eye make-up had run and her short blond, beautifully cut hair hung limply plastered to her head. She was dressed in a skirt and sweater which were rather too big for her. Roland Willis's face was swollen, and his shaggy dark hair seemed to have become greyer since McLeish had seen him forty minutes before. He was wearing a sweatshirt, rather too small, under his jacket, and no shirt. They both looked like refugees, shabby, uprooted and defensive. McLeish pulled up another of the smart leather chairs and explained that he needed a brief description of what had happened.

'I don't know,' Roland Willis said, hopelessly.

'You found her, I understand.'

'Yes. Oh God, yes.' He pushed his fingers through his hair. 'She — Catriona — was in distress and picking quarrels with her friends and she'd flung off. But she had someone with her. So we left her alone — well, we thought she'd recover herself better if we did. About 11.30 I thought I'd better see she was all right. We were — we are — staying the night.'

'You'd last seen her where?' McLeish glanced at his DC who, lacking a chair, was sitting on the edge of the magnificent desk, taking notes.

'I can't quite remember. We had had a little episode earlier in the evening, and Alex Ferguson had whisked her out on the terrace to get her to cool off.' He hesitated. 'I thought it perhaps better to leave her to her own generation. I shouldn't have.'

'Oh Roland.' Vivienne Willis had started to weep again. 'She meant to do it, you couldn't have stopped her. It's my fault, if anyone's, it's my failure.'

Roland Willis reached blindly for her hand. 'I should have listened to you. I should have let her go to a hospital.'

McLeish waited for them to compose themselves.

'That was before supper, wasn't it?'

'Yes,' Vivienne Willis said. 'Then I realised I hadn't seen her for sometime — this must have been about 11.30 or so. I started to look for her and I met Giles . . . He said, very crossly, that he hadn't seen her recently and that he thought she had gone off to her own room, so I went up and looked. The whole house was full of people, having a good look round. It's all arranged as a showplace. Anyway, she wasn't in her room, but I decided to check the bathroom in case she'd locked herself in to have a sulk — it's the sort of house where all the bedrooms have bathrooms, so I thought I'd look.' She paused again. 'The door was locked, so I hammered on it and called her. I couldn't hear anyone.' She put her face in her hands. 'Then I panicked. I thought — well, yes, — I *did* think that she might be having a go at her wrists, so I went to find one of the Quentins, but I couldn't. Then I met Jamie and, well, I told him, of course I did, and he found Alex, who found Giles.'

'Who found me,' Roland Willis said, 'and we all rushed up there. There wasn't a key in the lock — Alex looked through the keyhole but when she . . . when she stood up she found her knees were wet and then . . . then we all saw that there was — well — red water coming from under the door.' He drew breath, looking wretched. 'So I tried to break it down. I was frantic by then, but it wouldn't budge.'

'Then Louis, who had arrived by then, yelled at everyone until they found a key,' Vivienne Willis said, with dislike.

'Who unlocked the door?'

'I did,' Roland Willis said. 'There was water coming through all the time and it was — you could see, it was staining the carpet.' He stared at his hands. 'And all I saw was this bath full of red water and something floating in it. It felt like a long time before I worked out what it was and then I rushed to pull her out.' He paused, keeping his eyes on his hands. 'She was so heavy I couldn't do it.'

'I let the water out,' Vivienne said into the silence. 'It looked so awful. And Giles and Jamie and Louis and Amanda and the Millers, who had arrived by then, all helped to get her out and we put her on the carpet in the bedroom.'

'We started artificial respiration,' Roland Willis said, drearily. 'Amanda Roberts is trained and she started, then Louis, then I had a go. And then the ambulance men came.' He looked up at McLeish. 'Then you came and turned us all out. Was she dead then? When you came?'

'The ambulance men thought so,' McLeish said gently. 'That doesn't mean they didn't do their damnedest to save her but they never had much hope.' He hesitated but the question had to be put. 'Do you know why she would have wanted to commit suicide? Now, I mean?'

They both jerked and stared at him.

'She has been very depressed,' Roland Willis said, at last.

'That I had understood, from her friends. But was there anything specific?'

Vivienne Willis started to weep again and Roland put an arm round her, pulling her to his side. 'Couldn't this wait? No, I suppose it couldn't, but . . . Well, she had a spat tonight with Giles Quentin — oh, you saw. Yes, it was a pretty conclusive rejection, and of course that is terrible at that age. She has had a crush on Giles for some time and I think hoped that . . . that there might be . . . that he might . . . The teenage boy can be very unkind.'

'We'll have to talk to Giles Quentin as well. You're staying here? I'll ask you both to make statements in the morning.'

'I can't stay here,' Vivienne Willis said, through tears. 'Not with . . . not with . . .'

'Catriona will be taken to the mortuary inside the next hour,' McLeish said, gently.

'I must see her — I must say goodbye.' Roland Willis was struggling out of his chair.

McLeish stood up. 'Can you wait just a minute while DI Camberton clears the room for you?'

They nodded, wordlessly, and when the signal came they went, together, holding hands against the awful reality. McLeish followed them to the door, closed it gently behind him and waited with Camberton, and the forensic squad who were leaning against the walls, shuffling their feet.

'Sir,' Camberton said, softly, 'no key found in the bathroom.'

McLeish turned to look at him. 'You sure?'

Camberton indicated, wordlessly, the leader of the scene of crime squad, who nodded in confirmation.

'We need to find it,' McLeish said, redundantly.

'Search everyone?' Kevin Camberton was absolutely right; if someone had locked the door on the drowning girl then the key was most likely still in their pocket and no time should be lost. McLeish hesitated, trying to decide what to do first, but Kevin Camberton, he noticed with pleasure, had arrived at the same point, and as the Willises trailed downstairs he signalled the squad into the bedroom. Both senior policemen watched as they took it apart, discreetly and carefully.

'Try the bed,' Kevin Camberton said, urgently, and two of the squad started at the bottom, working round the shrouded package lying on it, moving the edges of the sheets.

'No key.'

McLeish stood, grim-faced, calculating his next move, and headed out on the small landing. Camberton was ahead of him and was crouched on the stairs, working methodically down them.

'Got it,' he reported, somewhere between triumph and disbelief, as heads popped out of the bedroom above.

'Don't touch it,' McLeish said, involuntarily, and apologised hastily. They heard footsteps on the stairs and looked down to see a small man, encumbered by a heavy case, looking up. 'You from Forensic? Quick.'

They stood, motionless, while the envoy from Forensic liberated his kit and tested the key, turning it over delicately. They could all see the answer before he shook his head.

'Nothing?'

'It's been wiped.'

'Right.'

They were all watching McLeish. The first rule was to preserve the evidence. He thought of the crowd in Catriona's bedroom and the Willises' description of the scene, people tumbling over each other to get the dead girl out of the bath, all of them getting blood and water over their clothes.

'Clothes,' he said, aloud, remembering the strange array of garments the Willises had been wearing, and Kevin Camberton nodded.

'Anyone gone home, sir?'

'Oh, I'm afraid so. The parents are here — both sets. We'd better see the girl's father now and collect clothes.'

'Superintendent.' They all started, but it was Andrew Quentin, looking worn out. 'I've put the Roberts — Louis and Amanda — to bed. He was hysterical and my own man's given him a sedative. Amanda doesn't want to leave him of course.'

'I'll need to take statements tonight, Sir Andrew, and I'd like a word with you now.' No point in delaying telling his host the news that it seemed likely that a murder had taken place under his roof and that any guests remaining would have to be searched and their clothes confiscated.

Much, much later, feeling infinitely old and tired, the initial adrenalin drained, he came downstairs. He had talked to the Roberts parents and taken a brief statement from Andrew Quentin, leaving Kevin Camberton to do the lion's share of the work, including taking statements from Alex and Jamie. He arrived and blinked at the sight of a dark red head visible over the back of a chair.

'Matthew.'

'Chief Superintendent.' Matthew Sutherland swung his chair round, got to his feet and gravely shook hands.

'Are you here professionally, Matt?'

'No. I'm on call for the Centre, but Alex asked me to come. I can be on call here as well as anywhere else.'

Alex had acquired a huge sweater, nearly as long as the black velvet dress, had tied her hair back behind her head and put on battered spectacles. She was looking, he saw with a pang, transparent with exhaustion, and was still shivering despite the sweater.

'Where's Jamie?' he asked her.

'Over there. Asleep, worn out by emotion and whisky. Matt brought him a sweater and I've covered him with a rug.'

'Mm. Wake him up, there's a good girl. We've done with you both, so I'm sending him back in a cab. With you, unless you've made other arrangements,' he added awkwardly.

'I'm her arrangements,' Matt Sutherland confirmed amicably, standing up and shrugging himself into several of the jackets piled on the floor. 'I'm going back to my cot and she lives quite close.' He beamed at McLeish who suppressed an unexpected urge to hit him. He looked away, across the room to where Alex was bent, all black fish netted legs, trying to coax the recumbent bundle of clothes that was Jamie. He went over, hauled Jamie up and strode to the door, carrying him like a baby to lay him in the back of Matthew's car, wishing that it had been Alex who had needed carrying.

CHAPTER 7

Sunday, 2nd July

'Morning, sir.'

'Morning, Kevin.' McLeish, himself feeling groggy, observed that Kevin Camberton was looking less than rested. He looked round him; there were four DCs in the big room and a good deal of paper. Camberton had been busy. 'You got some sleep, I take it?'

'Not yet. I went round to Forensic.'

'Any joy?'

'None at all. They're going on of course, but everyone's clothes were wet.'

'Mm.' He was getting old, McLeish reflected. 'I got my head down in the end. Had breakfast with Jamie.'

'How is he?'

'Not in good shape. Francesca's got him playing with William, but his heart's not in it. They're all due back at school tomorrow — all the Faraday kids, I mean. I'm not sure Jamie's going to make it.'

'He's taking the death hard?'

McLeish thought about Jamie, pale and hag-ridden, trying to enter into a game where he built a tower of bricks, and

Will, with a cry of joy, indefatigably demolished it. 'That's not his main problem. As Francesca says, he was unfailingly decent to the girl so he doesn't feel that guilty. He's shocked of course, but I think his main worry is that his parents are divorcing.'

'Mm.' Camberton was not sounding convinced, but McLeish was not concerned to pursue the matter. They were sitting in the music room, with coffee provided by one of the Australian housekeepers, less brisk this morning, her hair hanging limp and having had two shots at getting coffee into the cup rather than the saucer.

'Sir, John. Am I . . . are you . . . sorry, are you in charge of this one? At working level, I mean.'

'No, no. Or I hope not. I'm trying to hand it over to you, and it's *your* report that will go up to the Commander. It's just well . . . there are difficulties.'

'Sir.' There was an offended pause through which McLeish drank coffee. 'I've talked to Doc Jamieson again this morning,' Camberton offered, 'I was trying to establish the time of death. He says it could have taken only about twenty minutes to exsanguinate to the point where she might have lost consciousness. But he doesn't think that's what happened. He thinks she drowned.'

'He's doing the autopsy tomorrow. She was found at 11.30, already drowned. The hospital troops were clear about that. So the latest she could have got into the bath was, say, 11 p.m.'

Kevin Camberton nodded. 'Alexandra Ferguson says she took Catriona upstairs at about 9.45 and left her there.'

'Alex was doing a showpiece dance by 10.30 or so,' McLeish said, sharply.

'Indeed. And Mrs Miller saw Alex come down again at about 10.00.'

'Too early, from the medical evidence,' Kevin Camberton agreed.

McLeish, remembering Alex on top of her sparkling form in the apache dance, could not believe she had done other than deposit the tiresome Catriona with a few well-chosen words to wash her face and comb her hair. But that argued that Catriona must have been in a stable state at 10.00; so what could have happened to cause her to be found dead with her wrists slit an hour and a half later?

'You need to talk to Alexandra again, I suppose,' McLeish said, reluctantly.

'I do. Her flatmate says she is at the dance studios. She found me the number.'

McLeish was instantly, guiltily, pleased to hear that it had not been Matt Sutherland who had picked up the phone. The good girl had obviously said goodbye to Matthew at the door, gone to bed and got up early to work in a studio.

'No reason for Alex to want to drown Miss Roberts, no matter how tiresome she was being.'

'She's not a good candidate,' Kevin Camberton agreed. 'Isn't that Peter Graebner just come in?'

McLeish peered round through the door which the dazed Australian help had left open to see the familiar greying profile.

'Would he be coming on business, I wonder?' Camberton had turned into a living question-mark, tiredness gone, eyes bright with interest.

Both policemen watched as Andrew Quentin appeared and shook hands with the small man before taking him away somewhere. Sir Andrew Quentin had summoned one of London's best known criminal solicitors. He re-examined that thought; Peter Graebner was a feared opponent, but he acted normally for the huddled masses, on legal aid, not for the likes of Andrew Quentin — a small mystery, which would elucidate itself. He turned his attention to Camberton. 'Who have you seen this morning?'

'Lady Quentin, but she hadn't noticed any of the kids and was in the dining-room with a lot of distinguished musicians from 9.45 to . . . well, 11.20 or so. We can check of course, but . . .'

'What *happened* to all the guests in fact? I was upstairs from 11.40 and by the time I got down they'd all gone.'

'I understand Lady Quentin sent them home. Told them there'd been an accident. She had everyone's addresses and nobody brought anyone she didn't know. They all ran, my guess is, busy people, not involved, no need of more excitement in their lives.'

'We need to see Giles Quentin,' McLeish said soberly. 'Yes, I did mean "we",' he said, in answer to Kevin Camberton's delicately raised eyebrows. 'Both of us. Where's your DC?'

Camberton opened his mouth but the Australian housekeeper, who had managed to comb her hair and get both eyes open, appeared with the information that Sir Andrew Quentin was now ready and where would they like to be? McLeish, mindful of the shortage of chairs in the study, suggested Sir Andrew join them in the music room. They sent three of the DCs away, kept one to take the notes and gingerly moved piles of music up to the other end of the table.

'He'll be coming mob-handed?' the DC enquired, gazing at the space.

McLeish was saved a reply by the entry of a silent, anxious group. Sir Andrew was in the lead, followed by Peter Graebner, Giles Quentin and Susie Miller. The policemen got to their feet but Susie Miller waved them down; she was pale and tired and staying very close to her son, putting a hand on his arm as she passed him a coffee.

'Mr Graebner?' McLeish said, encouragingly, as the party arranged itself.

'I am representing Giles Quentin, Chief Superintendent.'

Alex had told him that Peter Graebner, although now back for three days a week, still looked half dead. That was the young for you, McLeish reflected heavily from the heights of his thirty-nine years; Peter Graebner had always looked like that. He might be a bit thinner but there would be nothing wrong with his brains. He was however still an odd choice as advocate for the rich and powerful Quentin family.

'Alexandra was good enough to recommend me,' Peter Graebner said, extracting a pad covered with hieroglyphics from an ancient briefcase with a broken strap, and McLeish kept his face straight with an effort. 'You have had, I understand from Giles here, an account of his movements last night. He wishes now to make a further statement about the background to this sad business.'

'Yes, Giles?' Whatever the conventions, it would dry young Quentin's throat still further to be called 'Mr'.

'I wanted to . . .' Giles stopped. 'Sorry. I saw her — Catriona — around 10.25 in her room where Alex had left her. I went up well . . . because people said I'd been a bit rude before. She was, well, awful, so I told her I wouldn't let her mess up my evening and went down again. And that was it, I never saw her again until Alex came and found me — I was in the music room by then.' He stopped, and visibly tried to remember what he had come to say, and Susie reached forward and stroked his arm. 'What it is . . . I mean, what I must tell you is that she had told me she was pregnant, but she said it was my fault and it could have been. We went out for, oh, a couple of weeks in the Easter holidays.'

'When did she tell you?'

'Oh, a long time ago. When she was three weeks late.' The boy looked desperately tired, and McLeish remembered his own A-level term; he could not imagine how he would have coped.

'So that would have been when?'

'A couple of weeks before half-term,' Giles said, bitterly, to the piece of table in front of him.

'What were her expectations of you? What did she want you to do?'

Giles considered the question. 'Different things. Sometimes she wanted me to marry her, but . . . well, I told her I couldn't. Then she wanted me to acknowledge that I was the father and support them, and I told her that was mad.'

'Did she, or both of you, consider a termination?'

'She wouldn't. She got hysterical. She said she couldn't do that, it would be murder, she'd have the baby and look after it herself.'

'Had she told anyone else? Her mother for instance?'

'No. I wanted her to. I mean, I knew I — we — needed help. But she wouldn't, she wanted to wait until it was too late. She said her mother would make her have an abortion, she'd drug her and drag her to a clinic if necessary.' He looked up and said helplessly, 'She couldn't have, could she? I mean, I don't know Mrs Willis very well, but even if she'd wanted to, she couldn't. But Trina was well . . .' His voice trailed away.

'You didn't tell your parents?'

'I wish he had,' Susie Miller said, miserably. 'I was trying to support Catriona and keep her in the school environment. I had no idea that . . . that she was so ill.' Or such a threat to her son, she might as well have said.

'I told Dad.' Giles was staring at a spot on the table.

'When?' Susie Miller pounced.

'Before his exams,' Andrew Quentin said, trying to make it sound matter-of-fact.

Susie Miller stared at him and turned scarlet, the colour rising from her neck, garish against the blond hair. 'How could you do that? Not tell me. I am Giles's *mother*. I was Catriona's housemistress. I was responsible for her. Andrew, I cannot believe it. Even of you.'

'Mum.' Giles was agonised.

'Oh, one doesn't expect children to tell us anything, but you're not a child, Andrew, in some idiotic adolescent conspiracy. What possessed you? This is all your fault.'

'Look, Susie, hang on. Giles asked me not to tell. We had a plan — OK, with hindsight it seems a less good idea than it did — but we were going to wait till after the exams. Don't look at me like that, Susie — would it have helped if the young woman and Giles had not taken their exams? The school would have had to suspend them both. And there would still have been time to do something sensible — she was only twelve weeks pregnant then.'

'And what *were* you going to do?'

'Tell you. And her parents. Today, after the party, that's why everyone's *staying* with us, for Christ's sake. And then get her to be sensible, to see she couldn't go on with this . . . this fantasy.'

'Mum. Please, I'm sorry.'

Susie Miller burst into tears and Giles put his arm round her awkwardly. Andrew Quentin swung round in his chair and gazed out of the window.

'Giles.' McLeish waited till he had the boy's full attention. 'What do you think Catriona would have done? When you had all talked about it.'

'I hoped, see, that everyone would agree she was too ill and that . . . somehow . . . it wouldn't happen. I don't want a baby.'

'Most young men of eighteen would feel the same,' Peter Graebner pointed out, without looking at anyone. Indeed, and in spades, McLeish silently agreed but it left them all with a problem. It was more than convenient that Catriona Roberts had removed herself and the problem.

'She could have had the baby adopted,' Susie Miller said, blowing her nose.

'She wasn't going to do that, Mum. That's one of the reasons I didn't tell you. That, and I couldn't really think about it. I'm sorry I told Dad now, but I did, well, feel better because, you know, someone knew, and he said he could fix it. It's just that when I think . . . well, I don't think anyone was going to be able to fix it.'

'It might not even have been your baby,' his father said.

'I hoped, but you know . . . well, she had a crush on me, I knew that.' He stared at his hands. 'It wasn't the first time for her, I did ask that, but she didn't have anyone else, I'm sure. I wish she had.' His face went rigid and he started to cry, his neck bending slowly under some invisible weight.

'For Christ's sake, Giles,' his father said, voice husky, leaning over to clasp a hand. 'Oh God. This is why condoms were invented, to stop girls with their own agenda creating this kind of havoc.' His son looked at him, appalled, and he winced. 'I really didn't mean to say that, I'm sorry. I know she was ill, but you were a *chump*.'

Curiously enough this cleared the air. Giles blew his nose and Susie gave her ex-husband a look of reproach, but her heart was not in it; clearly somebody had needed to say exactly what Andrew Quentin just had.

'Giles.' McLeish decided to take advantage of the shift of mood. 'Why do you think she despaired at this point?'

'We had a row.'

'When?'

'I *told* you, about half ten last night. I'd gone up for a pee and she was lurking on the stairs when I came out.'

'What sort of row?'

'I told her Dad knew. I told her that my parents wouldn't let me be married this young and that whatever happened she'd be on her own.'

'What was her reaction?'

'She said she'd sell the story to the newspapers.'

The present-day remedy of course. 'What did you say?'

'That she could do what she liked, it wouldn't make any difference to my career. Well, Dad had said that to me, you see.'

'And he would know.'

'Susie, please.'

'Andrew, you are *intolerable*. Where did all this masculine solidarity leave Catriona? Or her parents? Or me? Or the school which has tried so hard?'

'It was Giles she was trying to blackmail, my dear, not the oldies.'

Susie Miller, scarlet with rage, turned and slapped his face, hard enough that he rocked on his chair.

'Mum!'

Andrew Quentin, fingermarks clear on his cheek, got up to go.

'Dad!' It was a cry of painful distress and the man hesitated. McLeish sat tight, waiting to see what would happen.

'We should take a break.' Quentin had himself in hand and was in great conductor faced with difficult orchestra mode. 'Ten minutes,' he added, without interrogative inflection.

'That would be fine,' McLeish said, reaching over to switch off the tape recorder, glancing at his watch to get the time right. 'We need in any case to get longer statements from each of you individually about last night; Inspector Camberton will take you through those. I'll talk to the Roberts parents.'

'Right.' Andrew Quentin was disconcerted. 'Yes. Well, I'll see if Louis is on his feet this morning.' He swept out, looking at no one.

Susie Miller blew her nose, and tucked her handkerchief back into the sleeve of her heavy cardigan. 'I'll go and see where Piers is and come back.' She avoided looking at her son, or anyone else, and they watched as she all but ran from the room.

'Tell me, my boy, what A-levels you were taking. And come and have coffee so that the police can get on.' Peter Graebner, sounding as if he was in his own kitchen, had taken charge, and they watched him go, looking very small beside the gangling Giles.

* * *

Louis and Amanda Roberts were having breakfast at the end of a long table in the dining-room. McLeish, who had last seen the room lit and decorated with flowers in every corner, stopped, startled. Stripped of most of the flowers and the heavy curtains pulled back, it had turned into a breakfast room in a very grand country house with lawns and birds singing outside. Well, that was why people lived in Highgate; several miles from the very centre of London there was space and green. And plenty of room to park cars, he thought, remembering the wide drive littered with expensive motors and a rank of garages no doubt housing even more. He blinked in the noon sun as he walked along one side of the long table; Andrew Quentin was pouring coffee, head bent towards Amanda Roberts, who was responding to whatever he was offering. Louis Roberts was hunched over a plate, next to them, but completely separated, away somewhere else. He looked unseeingly at McLeish through a thick fog of misery. Amanda Roberts gave him an anxious look and suggested that he might talk to them both together.

'We need to take individual statements,' he said, civilly, but without compromise.

'But. . . .' She looked at her husband who put his head in his hands, withdrawing from the scene. 'Well, of course, yes . . . where would you . . . ?' She got up, looked at McLeish who was doing nothing other than stand, bent over her husband and kissed his totally unresponsive cheek, and followed McLeish out of the room.

'I'm sorry. Louis is . . . well, he's full of tranquillisers. He collapsed last night when we . . . when they said she — Catriona — was dead. He helped pull her out of the bath; it was terrible for him. I wasn't *there*, I was downstairs and by the time they found me she was on the floor and Louis had collapsed. I thought it was his heart.'

She, too, had had a terrible shock last night but it was over her husband, not her unsatisfactory stepdaughter, McLeish thought. Louis Roberts did look like a heart attack candidate; in his fifties, overweight, high colour, probably high blood pressure. He got her sat down in a secondary office, with three blank computer screens gazing at them and a DC to watch the tape. She had not been upstairs at all last night before 11 p.m.; after supper she had used one of the guest cloakrooms on the ground floor. Yes, she had seen Catriona make a scene at the end of Jamie and Giles's performance but had taken the view that a respected near contemporary like Alexandra Ferguson would deal with the situation far more efficaciously than a member of the despised older generation. And she had not seen her after supper until she had been part of the chaotic scene in the bathroom.

'And of course I was fed up with her,' she added, pink but resolute. 'And I didn't — and never have — felt I was any good with her, though I tried, I really, really did try when I married Louis.'

'Did you see a lot of her at that time?'

'Not at first.' Amanda Roberts was looking back to a time long ago, eyebrows pulled together, mouth tight. 'She was, what, four when Louis and I were first living together, and Vivienne, who was trying to get a settlement, wouldn't let her come when I was there. *That* changed fast enough, of course, when Vivienne got her divorce and wanted to pick up her social life again. So yes, from when she was about six, she came to us every other weekend. I had Sarah by then — that's our elder daughter — so it was really hard. Catriona was very difficult even then. A whinger. She never took to me at all.'

Nor you to her, McLeish understood and thought with pity of a difficult, anxious six-year-old trying to get to her father through the thicket hedge of the determined Amanda and a new, treasured baby.

'And when Joanna came, it actually became impossible. I just couldn't manage a baby and a toddler, and Catriona. She must have been eight, and I certainly didn't expect her to help very much, but it was worse than that, you couldn't leave her with the little ones, even for a few minutes. She was spiteful with them.' Her voice had risen and her neck was scarlet and blotchy, and McLeish understood that this speech had been running like a tape in her mind all night and probably for many years before that. 'So we agreed . . . we *all* agreed that it would be better if Louis went to see her for a day every other weekend and she came to us perhaps once a month and a bit in the holidays.' She sighed, deeply. 'Well, that didn't work very well either, Louis hated taking her out to restaurants and places and she was worse than ever when she came to stay. It can't have been easy for her either, but I was desperate. Joanna's asthmatic, she never slept and I was teaching. I could have given up, Louis wanted me to, but . . .' He and his DC, frozen into position, might as well not have been there, he understood, this was a conversation being held entirely with herself. 'Then Vivienne married Roland

— Catriona was six — and that was wonderful. Roland loved Catriona immediately, there weren't any new babies — well, we held our breath, because Vivienne was only, what, thirty-five but she didn't want any more presumably. She's not the maternal type — I mean, I may not have been much of a stepmother, but she certainly wasn't much of a mother.' She ran down suddenly and stared at one of the blank computer screens, her face reddening, and tears threatening.

'So Catriona was happier then?' McLeish asked, after a couple of minutes.

'Yes.' She was back with them, looking at him when she spoke. 'Yes, she really was. Well, life got a bit easier all round for her. She went to the junior — that's the preparatory for Faraday's, it's next door to the main school and she liked that, and she had Roland who's taught at Faraday's for ever. And I came to teach biology when she was eleven — not that she liked me any better than she ever did but it meant Louis was here a lot and it was easier to have her to stay because our two were older and she was better with them. She was still no help, but we didn't really need any. And sometimes it all worked quite well. Until she was about thirteen or fourteen, when she changed to the senior school — Faraday's.'

'What happened then?'

'Nothing *happened* in the sense that none of us did anything in particular. We were all there, Roland was actually teaching her. I wasn't because. I was doing sixth form by then. But she'd been used to the junior school, which is quite small, and then she found herself with, what, nearly fifty new children — about twenty-five to thirty came up with her from the junior and about fifty joined from other schools, and it wasn't so easy for her. There was a lot of competition from *very* talented kids.' She paused, searching for fairness. 'That particular year, who are now the Six Senior group, had an unusual number of very gifted children coming in at thirteen, all from established artistic families who *know* how good they are. And she's never really been in with them, the cool people as the kids say, and she wanted that. Catriona isn't — wasn't — artistically talented. And she was nowhere near getting into a reputable university. She wasn't stupid, in fact her IQ is *very* respectable. But . . .' She stopped, biting her lips.

But, what with all of you and a difficult temperament, and probably the wrong school, Catriona was in no shape to perform to her IQ. McLeish silently filled in for her.

'Louis is devastated,' Amanda Roberts said, flatly. 'He may not tell you why, apart from the obvious, so I'd better — he just isn't making sense. We — that is Vivienne and I and a few people like Piers Miller, who actually had to teach Catriona — knew she was very ill and were pushing for her to go into a clinic. Louis — and Roland indeed — were opposed. And of course, you can't do anything unless all the parents agree in this sort of thing — I've seen it time and time again with divorced parents and children who are playing up. So Louis feels it is his fault that she wasn't in a place of safety. Which it is. I'm just telling you. And I'd like to get back to him, if that's all.'

McLeish, refusing to be rushed, considered his notes. The key point was that Amanda Roberts, who had disliked the dead girl, had not apparently been anywhere physically close enough to do harm or to prevent it at the operative time. He checked to make sure who she had been with, or had spoken to, after Catriona's exit to the balcony with Alex. It would need corroboration, and Kevin Camberton could do that, but it was likely to be right. He looked up.

'Thank you, Mrs Roberts. We will need to talk to your husband but we'll try not to distress him further.'

'You . . . are sure it was . . . well . . . murder? It couldn't have been an accident?'

'We are keeping an open mind at this stage,' McLeish said, calmly, and she went slowly, turning back once as if to speak, then thinking better of it.

'Didn't like her much, did she? The deceased, I mean.'

'Felt guilty about her, didn't you think?' McLeish always treated even the newest DC as a colleague; it was not a matter of policy to do so but nuggets of pure gold revealed themselves in unexpected places.

'Not particularly.' The DC — Michael Harter — was another Scot from the Borders. He struggled for expression. 'Pretty, well, detached. As in I inherited this difficult child and I didn't do very well and she's dead but there you are, that's life.' McLeish considered him thoughtfully, and he blushed. 'Only it wasn't *her* life, was it?'

A very shrewd observation, McLeish thought, and realised the man was being made anxious by his expression. 'I agree. A very cool view. Better with her own children perhaps.'

'They aren't usually. Women like that.'

Now that was true too, McLeish agreed, trying and failing to imagine the deeply family-oriented Francesca taking as cool a view of a failure relating to a child as Mrs Roberts. 'Better see Mr Roberts. Ten minutes?'

* * *

Kevin Camberton was feeling mildly miffed. He had just finished getting signed statements from Andrew Quentin, Susie Miller and their son Giles, and he had hoped to be either summoned to McLeish's side or put in charge of the whole investigation. But his boss did not seem to be disposed to hand over and he had left no instructions.

The door opened and McLeish put his head in. 'I've done Amanda Roberts and I'm moving on to Louis. Will you take a statement from Piers Miller so that we can let the Miller family go? Things to do at the school, I understand.'

'Piers Miller. The stepfather.'

'One of them.'

There were, Camberton conceded mentally, a lot of stepfathers in this case. 'Sorry, I should have said Giles Quentin's stepfather.'

'That's right.' His boss had obviously remembered something and came through the door properly, closing it behind him. 'This scene last night that everyone talks about.

The deceased was hanging round Giles Quentin who made it plain that he didn't want her. Well, Piers Miller tried to get her away. She told him to keep his hands off her, she was sick of being pawed.'

'I'd been told.' By Susie Miller, who had been seemingly cross with the girl rather than worried about the truth of her accusation. In his experience kids usually were telling the truth in these affairs, even if no one believed them.

'Good.' McLeish said. 'Ask him about it.'

'Did you think there was anything in it? You were there.'

'I couldn't tell. The girl was in a rage and knew she was making a fool of herself. His wife — Mrs Miller didn't seem worried.'

His boss knew as well as — better than — he did that the wives usually didn't know in these cases. 'I'll ask him. Any other background?'

'Only been at the school three years.'

'I'll get the history.'

And I could take over the case too, as you said at the beginning, Camberton thought, angrily. He went in search of Piers Miller and met him on the stairs, and asked him to come and make his statement, explaining carefully that Chief Superintendent McLeish was busy with Mrs Roberts and they knew the Millers wanted to get home. He was interested but not surprised to see Piers Miller's shoulders relax, following without effort the man's conclusion that he was being left to an understrapper and could not therefore be an object of serious questioning.

He started slowly, with coffee, and an explanation of the necessity for the tape machine and a DC who he had co-opted from answering the telephone. He listened with mounting interest; Piers Miller too, it transpired, had been outside in the garden from about 10.35, wandering about looking at the house.

'And before 10.35, how did you spend the evening?'

'We arrived about 7.30 and drank and talked to people. Catriona was there — I think they arrived just after we did but I didn't particularly notice what she was doing. I was rather hungry so I was snacking off the cocktail bits. Very classy cocktail bits. Then Giles and Jamie did their bit. It was a great success.'

'Was Catriona Roberts there?'

'Yes.'

Camberton paused to see what the man would do. He was sitting, tense, waiting to be asked the next question.

'Did you speak to her?'

'Yes, of course.'

'Before or after the concert?'

'It wasn't really a concert, more a set of turns so that Andrew Quentin could show Giles off to an agent. I certainly spoke to her before it started.'

Camberton waited, and silence worked its usual miracle. 'I expect people will tell you if they haven't already. She tried to monopolise Giles — who is — was — rather tired of her, so I went over to distract her and save a scene. She was furious.'

'With you or with Giles?'

'Giles of course, but she didn't dare take it out on him. So she attacked me.'

'What form would that attack have taken?'

'She screamed at me to let her go and said something to the effect that she was sick of being pawed.'

'What did you do?'

'Let go of her of course. Then Alex Ferguson — whom let the Almighty continue to smile upon — appeared from nowhere to bustle her out into the garden to cool her head.'

'Distressing for you.'

'Well, yes, but that sort of intemperate nonsense goes with the territory these days if you're a teacher. In boys' schools as well, believe me. I've seen it.' He sneaked a look to see how this was being received but Camberton presented a face devoid of expression. 'Actually I was pissed off. I never liked her, either as a person or a pupil — I teach . . . taught . . . her maths — and she's been the most frightful nuisance to me and my wife, who was her housemistress and has bust a gut to help her. I recently put several hours I really didn't have into coaching her for A-level.'

'That would be individual tuition, I take it?' He kept his tone level, but Piers Miller gave him a long careful look.

'Inspector, no child at this school would tolerate any . . . inappropriate . . . advances from a member of staff. Everything is discussed at form meetings, and I mean *everything*. The week a pathetic cleaner put a hairy hand on one of our Fourths in the boiler-room I never will forget. The whole event was discussed as if it had been a set text. I thought the cleaner needed trauma counselling rather than the kid.'

'What was the young woman's reaction?'

'Young *man's*. Delivered the wretched cleaner a lecture on grown-ups abusing dependants. In my view the whole lecture was based on a failure of analysis; the power lay and lies squarely with the articulate fourteen-year-old child of privilege rather than a forty-year-old semi-literate countryman. Sorry, I digress, but you get the point. You would be out of your mind to attempt sexual harassment — anything that could be construed as such — at Faraday's.'

'So Miss Roberts' allegation was without foundation.'

'Entirely. And no one took her seriously, which would have made her even more furious.'

Not much observance of the convention that decreed speaking well of the dead. The young woman must have caused him rather more trouble than he was letting on.

'Is it a problem you've met before? Yourself?' Camberton asked, not quite knowing where he was going with the question but understanding immediately that he had struck gold. Piers Miller's hands, which he had been using freely to illustrate his statements, stilled, frozen in mid-air, and a red flush crept up from his neck.

'Not really,' he said, lamely, far too late, and tried to look boldly into their interested faces. 'Oh *shit*. *That* was another neurotic adolescent and it only blew up into a fuss because the head at Melton was so wet you could shoot snipe off him. But yes, an eighteen-year-old who I was trying to help *did* suggest I'd tried to get her knickers off. I had to accept a reprimand for incautious behaviour. I've been very, very cautious around young women ever since, *and* I thought twice about Catriona. Well of course, I'd never have been able to persuade anyone in Faraday's that I needed a chaperone to teach a young woman of eighteen, so I got another girl from the same set to come too. The trouble was that Catriona was so far behind that it was a waste of the other girl's time, and you don't ask *children* facing A-level to waste time. Just teachers.' He made to get up, thought better of it, and turned in his chair, nervous energy barely held in. 'But I was still careful. I taught with the door open *except* the one day when the Junior Chess Club could only find the corridor to practise in.'

'Was she directing her accusations to that particular day?'

'I've no idea. She wasn't specific, and I certainly wasn't going to pursue it at that moment. Susie intended to have a word when we were all back at school — she didn't think it right to beat the child up at a party. More's the pity. Now there's a dirty taste and nothing to be done.'

'You say that none of your colleagues — or your wife — believed the accusations?'

'They didn't. They all knew too much about her. Oh, what's the point. Are we done?'

Camberton checked his notes and agreed they were done, left the DC to type up a statement and tried not to rush with unseemly haste to find McLeish. The big man listened with all the interest he could have hoped.

'Check exactly, will you, what happened the last time. You got the school? Good, saves asking Mr Miller.'

Are we colleagues or are we not? Camberton wondered.

'What did Alex Ferguson do when she whisked Miss Roberts outside, by the way?' McLeish asked, a little too casually, and Camberton looked for his notes.

'According to her, she told Catriona that there ought to be a law against the Teenage Boy and that she should find somebody older and more sensible. Catriona did not tell her anything about being pregnant. So she took her to her room to cool down. At about 10.15, as near as she can guess.' He considered his superior who was grinning. 'How did you get on with Louis Roberts, John?'

'Not well — I've got a statement, but I wouldn't depend on it. His wife told me he was paralysed with guilt at not putting Catriona into a suitable place for treatment and certainly something's got to him. He said he went upstairs with the aim of seeing Catriona at about ten minutes past ten, couldn't find her, got talking to some other guests, had a few drinks and at 11.30 p.m. started out again to look for her — he wasn't particularly worried, he said, he just wanted to see she was all right. And then he heard yells and screams and noises of a door being battered down. He got Andrew Quentin to find a key and then tried to get Catriona out of the bath. Ties in with Roland Willis's statement which I got him to sign this morning. He's going home with the wife driving.'

CHAPTER 8

Monday, 3rd July

'She *was* pregnant, then.' John McLeish had telephoned Doc Jamieson immediately after the interview with Giles Quentin the day before.

'Yes, yes, she was telling the truth there. About thirteen weeks.'

'Takes us back to April, then.' And the school holidays, as Giles had said.

'Yes. You'll want DNA samples, I take it?'

It was not of course a foregone conclusion that Giles Quentin was the father, even though the boy himself had accepted responsibility. 'Yes. I'll get Giles Quentin to give a sample.' He waited for Doc Jamieson to acknowledge, but he had always been economical with words. 'So, how did she die, Doc?'

'She drowned.'

'Well, Doc, I thought I'd understood that.' John McLeish put his cup of coffee down. It was 10 a.m. but he had only just left the AC's office. Doc Jamieson must have been working since dawn.

'The point is, John, that it wasn't a heart attack, she was drowned. It was murder, as you had cause to fear.'

'Tell.'

'She didn't lose enough blood, you see. Oh, I know the room looked like a chain-saw massacre, but blood does that. She'd only lost about four pints, not enough to make her unconscious. You stop losing after the heart stops.'

McLeish, never one to mind a silence, thought about it. Of course you did, the heart stopped pumping and blood stopped going round, or out.

'So I looked for signs that someone had helped, do you see?'

'And?'

'I found them. I thought I'd seen something on the Saturday night, but now I'm sure. Bruising on the shoulders. Someone pushed her under — from behind — and held her with sufficient force to drown her. She'd not have been able to put up much of a fight, with four pints of blood gone and attacked from behind, but whoever it was used force — the marks of the fingers are clear.'

'Fingers. Not gloves?'

'Could be. But thin ones. And so I shall say at the inquest.'

John McLeish drew in a long breath and stared down the path laid before him. He pressed the buzzer for his secretary and scribbled a note to tell her to assemble the team in twenty minutes' time, while listening to Doc Jamieson particularising the details of the bruising not visible on the Saturday night but there to be seen today early when Doc had got to the corpse.

'Doc. He or she — the person who pushed her — would have got wet.'

'Up to the elbows, indeed. And bloodstained from the water.'

John McLeish remembered wearily the scene on Saturday night. Everyone there had got wet, and bloodstained, to the elbows and beyond, including himself and Alexandra. Everyone present had rushed to get Catriona out of the water and save her life, and somewhere among the ranks of the innocent was a murderer, mucking in with the rest, covering any possible traces. But whoever it was must have been wet already, to the elbows at least. Someone who lived in the house and could change his shirt. Someone who more likely just put a jacket or sweater over a wet shirt?

Both men sat unspeaking at opposite ends of the telephone. Doc Jamieson broke the silence. 'Lots of people pushed in and helped get her out of the bath, I suppose. I haven't had time to talk to Forensic, but I doubt we'd learn much from clothing, John.'

'Anything you can tell us from the bruising?' he asked, unhopefully. 'Large hands? Small hands?'

'The spacing of the marks suggests large rather than small. I'll give you everything I can in the report, but . . .'

'But forensic science isn't going to be what will catch this one.'

'That's right. Old-fashioned police methods, as they say.'

'Well,' McLeish said, heavily, 'we ought to find this one — there can't have been any planning gone into it, someone just seized their chance and locked the door after them so that they had time to get away.' A thought struck him. 'The murderer couldn't have put her *in* the bath, could he — she — they? And cut her wrists, before or after?'

'The slashes to the wrists are characteristic — she did them herself. The angle and the inclination of the cut tells you. And the cuts are deeper on the left wrist — she was right-handed, so she couldn't make as good a job on her right wrist. So he didn't do *that.* He could of course have dropped her in the bath and sat chatting to her for a bit then pushed her under.'

'Sat chatting?'

'The cuts are too small to have caused her to lose four pints of blood. In the air, the blood would have clotted quite quickly. It's the water that prevented it clotting and kept it flowing. That's why people do it. So she was in the bath . . . oh, for fifteen to twenty minutes to lose that amount of blood.'

'Yes. So the murderer found her in the bath in a weakened state, wrists cut, and rather than remonstrating with her and calling for help as she would have hoped and expected — she didn't lock the door — he (or she) pushed her under, then went off and waited for someone to raise the alarm . . .'

'That would fit.'

'And he locked the door to gain time to get clear, wiped the key and dropped it because he couldn't have it found on him. We discovered the key on the stairs, remember?'

'Yes. I'm sorry, John, I don't envy you.'

'Thanks, Doc.' He thought of the dead girl, feeling her terror as firm hands held her below the water. She would have tried to scream of course. What had the murderer done about that? Or had he got her under water quickly enough? Or had the sound of revelry by night covered any other noise? The thud of multiple feet in the corridor told him his meeting was assembling and he moved stiffly to join them in the big team conference room.

* * *

Two hours later, another meeting was convened in the headmaster's room at Faraday's. Nick Lewis was feeling sick after the call from McLeish, which had told him the grim news that one of his pupils had been murdered, and by someone who had been of the crowd at Andrew Quentin's party.

'I am sorry to tell you that I cannot guarantee the contents of the autopsy report will remain confidential,' the deep voice with the slight Scots accent had said. 'Not in a case like this, where the death happened in the house of a celebrity like Sir Andrew Quentin. We're knee-deep in reporters as it is. So I need to hurry to get those most closely involved informed.'

Put like that Nick had felt it his plain duty to go round immediately to both the Millers, Roland Willis and Amanda Roberts. No one's reactions had been in any way untoward or unexpected, all four had been warned that this conclusion was likely, but the detail had distressed them; Roland Willis and Susie Miller had both wept, and Susie Miller's second thought had been for her son. Nor, naturally, had she been reassured to hear that John McLeish had told Giles personally, along with his father and his newly acquired solicitor, and had asked for a blood sample from Giles. So Nick had given Roland Willis and Amanda Roberts an hour to talk to their spouses and asked them to join a brief meeting stated to be dedicated entirely to practicalities. Only the Millers, Roland Willis and Amanda Roberts were present; Giles had elected to stay in London with his father and lawyer, Vivienne Willis was in her office and would arrive much later, and Louis Roberts was back home but still under heavy sedation. The four of them sat, heavy-eyed, to right and to left of him and he looked out briefly to the country beyond, at its most beautiful, with the wheat heavy and pale brown, ready to be gathered in in this warm, southerly place. It was perfectly true, he thought, drearily, that life went on regardless of tragedy and loss; the sun shone, the harvesters crawled across the fields, the evening came, the darkness fell, then came dawn and the whole process started again without reference to suffering human beings. But people and the things they built could be utterly changed by disaster; no one in this room would be untouched and the school itself was under threat. A suicide — well, it was a tragedy, but all establishments housing volatile teenagers ran that risk and a sizeable minority had had the awful experience of losing a child whose parents had confided them to you for safekeeping. A murder, however, was in a different category. Please God, he thought, obsessively, as he had ever since he had talked to John McLeish, let it not be another child in my keeping who is involved. It was impossible not to look at Susie Miller at this point; she was all too clearly occupied with the same obsessive, anxious churning as he was.

'If only we'd not gone to that party.' Roland Willis, head down, was digging holes with his pen, and Susie came back from where she had been and covered his hand with hers.

'You didn't go, Nick. Lucky you.' It was Piers who spoke.

'Not entirely.' He seized his chance. 'I was intending to go but had to cancel the day before because I was needed here.'

All four of them stared at him. It had been agreed that at this stage of the term, with all the exams behind them and the pupils mostly away for the weekend, a skeleton group of teachers could look after the place.

'I was needed to show the headmaster of another school discreetly around the premises and to have a long talk with him — and the Chairman of Governors — about the needs of this school.'

'But they only advertised, what, last week.'

'I expect he would have been made to fill up the form, Piers.'

'They haven't *appointed*, have they?' Amanda Roberts had gone very pink.

'No. For the very good reason that this particular man indicated this morning that, much though he had liked the school, he did not feel it was the right place for him.' He raised a hand to quell Amanda. 'He was the second person — the other was also already a headteacher — to take this view.'

'But they haven't even asked . . . I mean . . .' Amanda looked wildly at Piers.

'No, they didn't and they haven't, Amanda. And don't worry, I'm out of it. I'm withdrawing my application, Nick.'

'Do you feel able to tell us why?'

'Oh yes. No trouble. You all heard Catriona accuse me of sexual abuse. And now she's dead, murdered, and I'm probably high on the police list as a suspect. They know all about it. It's going to be some time, if ever, that anyone is prepared to consider me for a headship. So I'm withdrawing from this competition and I'm thinking of getting out of teaching altogether.'

'I hope you'll reconsider that, Piers. You're a good teacher, and all this will pass.' Nick had a migraine starting, in addition to feeling sick; there was a suspicious set of lines just at the edge of his vision, but he exerted himself to reassure.

'I feel I should withdraw too,' Roland Willis said, heavily. 'I failed with Catriona in every possible way; I neither managed to make her life tolerable nor got her to a place of safety.'

'Roland, the child was murdered.' Roland was going to need a great deal of help and coaxing; the man had aged ten years since Saturday, he was stooped, slow-moving and haggard, and his hair seemed to have gone much greyer. No interviewing committee would do other than treat him very, very kindly and put him out of their minds as soon as he left the room.

'Yes,' Lewis's deputy said, to the table, 'but she was trying to kill herself, wasn't she? She . . . well, she would never — could never — have been a victim of . . . well, whoever . . . unless she had been unhappy enough to try to die. I failed her, Nick.'

'We all did.'

'I'm not going to withdraw,' Amanda Roberts, still rather pink, said, defiantly. 'I don't see why I should.' She leaned towards him, forcing him to pay attention. 'Although I can't see them taking me. They don't want any of us, do they, Headmaster? Or they wouldn't have been sneaking people in here to have a look. People they *must* have contacted before they put in an advertisement to keep the rest of us quiet.'

He tried to ignore the increasing pressure over his right eye. 'I am sure it is fair to say they wanted a change . . . well, a change of approach. And it isn't unreasonable for the Trustees to think that an outsider might be the best person to bring about that change. It is, moreover, wholly understandable that, in what the Trustees perceive to be a difficult time for the school, they should initially prefer experience. Someone who has already done the job. The responsibilities of a head are very different from anything else.' He must have spoken with more force than he had intended; his audience was watching him very carefully.

'But whatever the Trustees might have wanted, it seems they can't get it.' Susie Miller, deeply distressed for her son, was displaying her well-known ability to keep her eye on the facts, and he looked at her with respect.

'That is indeed correct. Or, at the very least, it is going to take them time to find someone who is already a head.'

'Because the candidates — the prospective heads — think we are in too much of a mess?' And Piers Miller, even angry as he was, remained able to think.

'That too, I'm afraid. I know that the Trustees hope — or hoped — that many of our Six Senior would perform sufficiently well at A-level to tempt candidates. Six Junior is also very strong academically which ought to translate into some excellent A-levels next year and be a bonus for an incoming head.'

'Not many artists or musicians in that year,' Susie Miller observed.

'Artistic talent, Susie, is notoriously difficult to direct, look after or persuade into the A-level structure. As we all know.'

'So the Trustees' two favourites wouldn't come,' Amanda said, hauling the discussion back to where her interests lay. 'What, pray, do they intend to do? Ask you to stay on, Nick?'

'They did. And I can't beyond Christmas.' He had managed to say it and that was what mattered. His colleagues gaped at him.

'Ah. You've got something else.' It was Piers, typically, who got there.

'Yes, Piers. I'm sorry I cannot tell you all where. It will be announced next week, but there are people who have not been told yet.'

'Somewhere nice?'

'I'm very pleased with it, Susie.'

'Oh, well *done*, Nick. That'll show those bastards.' Typically she had been roused from grief and anxiety by pleasure in a friend's success.

'The Trustees were a little taken aback,' he agreed, with his first smile of the day.

'They thought that you'd still be hanging around, waiting at their beck and call. It's . . . it's disgraceful. A man of your quality and experience.'

'Well, Roland, that's Trustees for you.' He stretched his back, feeling a weight lift, and smiled kindly on Roland Willis, who was sitting up properly and looking very much better, roused from his misery by indignation on behalf of his profession.

'So what *do* they plan to do, Nick?' It was of course the persistent Amanda Roberts.

'I believe they will seek to make an interim appointment. They won't put it that way — you couldn't and still expect someone to take the job. But that's their calculation: find someone who will keep the ship steady while they look round for the real head as it were.' He looked round him and met Susie Miller's considering eye.

'But it would be a great opportunity for the interim appointee. If they made a good job of it no one would want to dispossess them. The children would make a terrible row.'

'That is quite true.'

Another of the revolutionary concepts squarely embodied in the Faraday charter was that the pupils were involved in the choice. Any proposed new head or deputy head had to have the approval of a majority of the top two years.

'Well,' he said, into a silence full of calculation, 'I know no more than I have told you. No doubt the summer holidays will be busy. Now, can we move on to the rest of the very difficult problems that face us on our way to the end of term? Which is going to be more than ordinarily welcome this year.' All agreed, fervently, that this was the case and the meeting changed gear. 'The show,' he said, flatly, feeling the headache come back with reinforcements. He avoided looking at Susie Miller, but three of his colleagues did the job for him.

'Giles,' she said, dully. 'He is doing two solos, and he's in the chamber choir and the orchestra. The orchestra doesn't matter.'

The head agreed silently; Giles was also a respectable violinist, but the school was rich in them.

'You're assuming he won't be there.' Amanda Roberts strode in where angels would have turned and gone in the opposite direction.

'Yes. No. I really don't know.'

'Jamie Miles Brett is also a doubtful starter.' There was no doubt of it, Roland Willis was managing to rally; there was colour in his cheeks and he was sitting up straight.

'Oh, Roland.' Susie Miller stared at him. 'Why?'

'Well . . . Catriona. He's taken her death very badly — well, why wouldn't he? He had made huge efforts with her. And . . .' Roland Willis stopped abruptly.

'*What*, Roland?'

'He blames us all, Susie.'

'You mean he blames Giles. He doesn't think that . . . that he killed her, Roland, surely . . .' She looked round them wild-eyed.

'You know that everybody who wasn't surrounded by other people after about 10.30 is under suspicion,' Piers Miller said, firmly placing an arm round his wife.

'I'm afraid that's right, Piers.'

The flickering yellow lights just at the edge of Lewis's vision were a warning that time was running out. 'The school show.'

'Without Giles and Jamie.' Susie Miller was looking old too, her plump, pleasant face pale and drawn, so that the age gap between her and Piers became suddenly noticeable. She spread large capable hands before her as an aid to thought. 'The orchestra will be all over the place without Jamie as leader. The choir will be all right.'

'What about the solo turns?' Roland Willis asked.

'Giles is irreplaceable. We have no other countertenor. Nor do we have a violinist anywhere near Jamie's quality.'

No one was going to argue with the head of music. Without Giles and Jamie the concert was going to fall to the level of the average school.

'I can play in the orchestra, though I wasn't going to. And Susannah Evans will have to substitute as leader,' Susie Miller said, without confidence. 'There's very little rehearsal time now, of course . . .' Her voice trailed away and everyone understood that her mind was a long way from the plight of the orchestra.

He bestirred himself to speak. 'Well, we have over a week and much can change in that time. Thank you all, particularly Susie, since I can see where the work is going to fall.' He touched her hand. 'You will tell me when I can be useful? I must ring up Andrew tonight and talk to Giles, but just now . . .'

'You've got a migraine coming.' She looked into his eyes, roused from her own worries. 'I can see it. Let me walk you back.'

* * *

Peter Graebner also had a headache, but he hoped it would subside when he had got rid of the two young men in his office and this telephone call.

'Yes, Sir Andrew, Giles and I have been together for much of the morning. Yes, he has given a sample of blood to the police. No, it may tell them nothing new but this is the procedure.' He listened for a minute. 'Excuse me.' He covered the mouthpiece. 'Giles, your father will pick you up?' The boy shook his head violently. 'Very well, I will tell him we are having lunch and you will telephone afterwards.'

'Yes.'

Peter turned an imploring eye on Matthew Sutherland, who was lounging in the opposite corner of the office, red hair glinting in the sun.

'I'll buy him lunch, sure,' Matt said, obligingly, and Giles Quentin smiled in relief.

'Sir Andrew? All is arranged; Giles will have lunch with my associate, Matthew Sutherland — I have to be in court — and he will ring you afterwards. You have a rehearsal? After that then. Goodbye. Thank you.' He put the phone down and gazed severely at Giles. 'You will ring your father in good time after his rehearsal, yes? And now I need five minutes with Matthew — can you wait downstairs?'

Yes, Giles had said gratefully, and the two lawyers listened as he clattered down the awkward staircase that separated Peter as senior partner from the rest of the office.

'I'll keep the file,' his associate said, hastily, and Peter gave it to him, absently, because he had something more important that needed saying.

'Matthew, I bear in mind always . . .'

'That our customer may be guilty. *I* know.'

'And that if we were to be told that this were the case . . .'

'We are respectable solicitors and would have to give the case up. Jesus, Peter, you trained me and I've been qualified a year.'

'Sorry, my boy.'

'Besides, I'm going to ask Alex to join us, make sure it's social.'

'Indeed.' Peter Graebner considered his associate who was conscientiously bolting loose papers into the file. 'She is not too much of a nuisance to you then? I hear you were called out to rescue her on Saturday.'

The bright blue eyes set in the pale, freckled skin looked up at him, warily. 'That was OK. She's a good kid.'

'Will she make a lawyer?'

'Standing on her head if she wants it. Very smart. But . . .'

'But?'

'She'd rather be a dancer. She met this chap, somebody Williams, at the party and danced with him. She was lit up like a Christmas tree.'

'We speak here of Antony Williams? The greatest male British dancer we have?'

'I suppose.'

'And he danced with her?'

Matt scowled. 'I assumed that was sex.'

'Matthew, my dear boy. His preferences lie elsewhere, like many of our finest dancers.'

'Oh, right.'

Badly disconcerted, Peter observed, his headache lightening by the minute. 'So you take her to lunch,' he suggested, benevolently.

'Yeh. Assuming that's all you wanted to say to me, Graebner. Nothing else I didn't know?' He hauled himself out of the chair and gazed uncertainly at his boss. 'I'll be back,' he said, menacingly, and clattered off downstairs, leaving Peter Graebner to the morning's only moment of amusement.

* * *

Matthew, running downstairs, stopping to put the Quentin file, loose papers anchored to it, on his own desk, was aware that he was affording his senior partner a certain amount of simple pleasure. He reminded himself of his status as Graebner Associates' most promising Associate and descended the next two floors slowly, putting his full weight on the treads. He nodded to Giles Quentin who was sitting staring into space, next to a large Jamaican with his hair in plaits and went into the dark back room on the ground floor that Alex was sharing with a secretary. She looked up and his heart lifted; the red hair was down, freshly washed and curled, her eyes were carefully made up and she had her contact lenses in. And she was wearing the short tight jacket he and every other man in the office particularly liked over black jeans, which followed every contour of her hips and long legs. He asked her briskly if she could spare the time to have lunch with them, since Giles Quentin had had a difficult morning and there was neither benefit nor pleasure in going over, yet again, the events of Saturday evening.

'I'm meeting Jamie,' she said, gazing past him, a pink flush over the pale skin.

'The kid?' He knew he was sounding incredulous. 'For lunch?'

'No. Later.' Unlike many of the women in his life this one told the truth however inconvenient, he realised fondly, and was brought up short by the memory of the other lady who always told him the odds. 'Isn't he going back to school?'

'Well, not *just* now, Matt. He's only just heard.'

'He can come too, keep Giles company.'

She gave him a look of simple exasperation and he woke up from his immediate preoccupation. 'Oh. He's gone off Giles?'

'He blames him for Catriona's death and has done ever since he heard about the affair. Oh yes, it'll be round Faraday's by now, I can't imagine how Giles kept it quiet in the first place. Jamie feels it was the final step — the affair and Giles then not wanting to know — that wrecked her.'

'You think that too?'

'I think Giles behaved no worse than the average Teenage Boy who can't wait to get a girl into bed, then wakes up embarrassed and wants to go back to playing footie with his mates. Which is why my girlfriends at Faraday's and I stuck to the rules and never went to bed with any of the boys there.'

'Mm. At what age does Teenage Boy turn into something more reliable?'

He got a single, nail-sharp glance. 'My mother says a lot of men retain that basic pattern — obsessive pursuit followed by desire to escape back to the lads or have a crack at the next pretty flower — all their lives. She says you have to look carefully to make sure you've got one of the ones who want *you*, not just a fuck.' He was aware that something had happened to his expression and the glint in her eyes confirmed it.

'Your ma's experience must be very valuable to you,' he said, heavily. 'You coming to lunch or not?'

She hesitated. 'Did he . . . ?'

'Kill the girl? I don't know, but he didn't have much time. He says he went upstairs about 11 p.m. because he was bursting for a pee and all the downstairs loos were full. He went to his own room, he says, used the bathroom and combed his hair, and rushed downstairs in order to be fussed over some more by all his pa's posh friends.'

'So he could have . . .'

He sat down and looked at her carefully. 'You've heard what they think happened? Someone pushed her under water while she was still alive and conscious and held her there. It wouldn't have taken long. Five minutes perhaps.' She was looking stricken, the pale skin without a vestige of colour, so that the spattering of freckles showed brown. 'But Giles had already confessed the affair *and* the fact that she was pregnant, to his father.'

'Ah.' Her face eased and colour came back, so she looked quite different. 'He'd got organised to face the trouble. It's not just dad covering up.'

'Giles had told him. Before the A-levels.'

'Then he didn't do it. I'll tell Jamie.'

'Hang on. *Why* didn't he?'

'Because . . .' She thought, looking out of the window, and he saw that her hair had streaks of near blond among the red. 'Because he'd handed the problem to his dad; it would still be a hassle of course, but dad would fix it.' She looked at him seriously. '*Think* about Sir Andrew Quentin, and what he must have fixed in his time. And Giles knows he is the heir, the next generation's musical star doing everything his dad would have hoped.' She caught his expression. 'No, I wouldn't think like that now but at eighteen,' her tone suggested some immeasurable distance in the past, 'I did think my parents could fix anything.'

'I hope the police are going to see it like that.'

'John McLeish is very clever, don't worry. *Are* we having lunch?'

'Yes,' he said, startled, recovered to ask if she was sure she had time before meeting her toy boy. He got the wide, amused grin which told him that he had not fooled her for a minute. He trooped after her into the hall, reconsidering his strategy, the other half of his brain occupied with a vision of Sir Andrew Quentin, whose house it was, who knew where all the keys were, disposing of a threat to his treasured son, then changing his shirt and going blithely back to join his guests.

* * *

Francesca felt as if she had been stuck at her kitchen table forever; she had missed the afternoon's rest, her back was hurting and shortly, come what may, she was going to *have* to run to the lavatory since the baby seemed to be sitting on her bladder. She reminded herself again that the trouble the other two people in the room were facing dwarfed any minor physical concerns of her own. It was also possible that they could only manage the agonising conversation they were having in the presence of a third party, so she exerted herself to endure.

'Mum, he'll top himself.' Jamie had finally managed to state his worst fears.

'Darling.' Her cousin Wendy had been in tears for the last hour, and this had elicited another spurt. Francesca, resolutely silent, passed the box of Kleenex along the table. 'I'm *sorry* but I cannot go on.'

'But if he promised . . . And if I were there — it's the holidays, I'm free, I'd make sure he took the pills. Mum?'

'Oh Jamie, if you *knew* how many times he'd promised he'd take his pills.' She scrubbed her eyes with a fresh wodge of Kleenex and blew her nose on the result. She looked at them both exhausted, pale blond fine hair clinging unbecomingly to her scalp, looking as if she had been dredged from a river. 'I can't.'

'You mean you won't.' Jamie was as pale as she, but he had his father's brown curly hair and olive skin and the advantage of youth so he looked ill, not half dead. His mother's hands stopped bunching the Kleenex. 'Yes, I do mean I won't. I've had *enough*, Jamie. You know as well as I do that the minute he feels better he'll stop taking the pills, he'll say he doesn't need them, whatever. And then it'll all start again, he'll just become a little odd, nothing you could describe to anyone else, and if you ask him, he'll say of course he's taking his pills, he may even take a set in front of me, but I *know*, and so does he, that he's going to get rid of them, make himself sick, *anything*. And then, one day, he won't look much different but if I'm not quick he'll come after me. Yes, it's always me, so far, but next time it'll be you or someone in the street. I'm not going to have it, any of it, anymore.'

Francesca had heard segments of this speech many times, but strung together, delivered in tones of utter exhaustion, it carried total conviction and the three of them sat in drained silence. Truth does that, she thought disjointedly, it has a ring like nothing else, and this time Steve would not be allowed to come home. She hitched her chair forward and put her hand over Wendy's. 'What shall you do?' she asked, and Wendy turned to her gratefully.

'Divorce him.' She snatched a sideways glance at her son. 'I've already got an order that he's not to come to the house, or indeed within a mile. I'm going to sell the house, put Steve's share in trust, and go back to Edinburgh. I can work there.'

'Indeed.'

Wendy was a theatre designer on and off and her skills were always in demand. Francesca looked cautiously at Jamie, sitting hunched at the end of the table, too far for her to reach out and touch him.

'You're ditching him,' he said, furiously to his mother.

'Jamie,' Francesca protested. 'After fifteen years and some very narrow escapes, *we* can all tell you.' Many — no, most — women would have left before now, as she decided not to say.

'That's how he'll see it. And he'll top himself.'

Back round full circle, Francesca thought, between exhaustion and pity. Jamie is never going to accept this decision, we'll be here all night and Wendy, for all she has taken legal advice and got the injunction, will in the end probably weaken and it will all start again. She glanced surreptitiously at her watch — she dared not look at the kitchen clock — and saw that it was 3.30, and she had about half an hour to get her feet up before William and his nanny came back, and her own child would need her attention.

'We've worn you out, Fran. You're looking green. I'll take Jamie away with me — we'll have a walk and decide when he is going back to school.'

Francesca glanced involuntarily at Jamie who had stated several times his unalterable opposition to going anywhere where he might meet Giles Quentin, but his head was down, fought to exhaustion. 'I *am* kippered,' she confessed. 'So much for the bloom of pregnancy.' She pushed back the chair and rose effortfully to her feet to kiss her cousin and touch Jamie's bent head before going upstairs, clinging to the banister, dragging herself up to lie blessedly alone on the big double-bed.

* * *

John McLeish had stopped on his way home by the incident room, which was organised like a well-run factory. Kevin Camberton picked five sheets off a neat pile and handed him Piers Miller's statement to read. It was 7.30 p.m., and he was clearly settled in for the night.

'Did you find anything more about his earlier trouble?' McLeish asked, skimming the pages.

'Indeed yes. It wasn't the sort of minor-remark-taken-the-wrong-way episode he's tried to sell us. It was a full-blown affair with a sixth-former. Raged all the way through the school trip and everybody knew about it apparently. He got away without being sacked because the girl left that summer, after her A-levels.'

'What happened to the girl?'

'I'm just finding out. She'll be twenty-seven now and I'm getting an address out of the school.' Camberton looked up at him, sideways. 'I reckon we're going to find a story that looks very like the one we've got here. Only *this* time he couldn't afford a rebuke; he's married and he wants to be headmaster.'

'At Faraday's?' McLeish sat down; this he had to hear however late he was for supper. Kevin Camberton had done a staggering amount of work since the morning. Including, as it turned out, talking to the secretary to the Trustees at Faraday's.

'The Trustees had twelve applications for the job, three from within the school: Amanda Roberts, Roland Willis and Piers Miller. Nine from outsiders, two of which have now been withdrawn.'

'They'll want to appoint an outsider, surely.'

'They might have. But the two they wanted — the suggestion was that they were actually *asked* to apply — turned them down after they'd seen the school. Too much of a challenge.'

'I've seen the school,' McLeish objected. 'Nice kids.'

'Dodgy A-level results. *Stroppy* kids, lots of artists there.' He caught McLeish's thoughtful glance. 'I have an acquaintance who went there. He was very helpful on the background. And now of course you've got a murder and a scandal.'

'Alex Ferguson was there too,' McLeish was thinking aloud.

'I'd not forgotten. But she works for Graebner.'

'Indeed.' McLeish had been sorry not to see that pretty face this morning when he had interviewed Giles Quentin. Peter Graebner and Matthew Sutherland had been no substitute. He remembered that Kevin Camberton was owed an explanation which there had been no time to make, in the press of events. 'I would have asked you to take charge, Kevin, in any normal circumstance. But I am under orders.' Camberton looked at him, doubtfully. 'The facts that Francesca and I were there and that Francesca is informally a coach to both the boys might not by themselves have mattered. The final straw was Sir Andrew Quentin.' He sighed, as heartfeltly as he had on hearing all this at 9.30 that morning. 'You have to keep this to yourself, Kevin, but he is about to undertake a Public Office — no, they didn't tell me, could be anything, King? Chairman of the BBC? — and this case has to be cleared up, and by the most senior officer they can properly ask to do it. Which is me. So, sorry,' he added, since Camberton was frowning.

'But Sir Andrew conducts the Los Angeles Symphony.'

'Ah. This is the bit that you really have not to know. He's prepared to give that up, apparently, in favour of what he's being offered here, but you don't know that or they'll hang me. Next case is yours alone, but on this one you're stuck with me. *But* I've got a few other things to do so I'm relying on you to do most of this one, without getting the credit for it. All right?'

'Absolutely all right, sir. I don't think it's going to be that difficult.'

'Be careful with that. Don't make your mind up too early.' McLeish saw a clock and got up to go, hastily, then paused. 'And don't think good musicians can't get into beds they shouldn't be in or won't kill to get out of a mess.' He got a guarded, acknowledging smile and turned for home.

CHAPTER 9

Tuesday, 4th July

Another hot day, McLeish thought, looking longingly out of the window. He was, like everyone else in the office, wearing a jacket to combat the unnatural chill of a modern air-conditioning system. He pulled himself up; he had sweltered in offices without air-conditioning in his time and *that* was worse. It was a difficult day, that was what was getting him down. At the team meeting, which he had just left, he had established that the time of death was between 10.30 p.m. when Giles had left Catriona in her bedroom after a row and 11.30 p.m. when she had been found drowned. Given this unusually precise timing, there was a startling number of people who could not account for their movements for some or all of that hour. The size of the Quentin house, that was the problem. It boasted three substantial floors with nine bedrooms and matching bathrooms plus two staircases, one of which was accessible via a pantry from the garden. This left a lot of scope for people to move around. And even worse, the Willises, the Roberts, the Millers, Catriona herself were guests for the night and had rooms on the second floor to which they had retired at various points. Piers Miller, for example, after the spat with Catriona, had eaten his supper with his wife and then disappeared from human sight until 11.15 p.m. when he had appeared downstairs, this time being witnessed by his wife, Amanda Roberts and Andrew Quentin. From his own account he was walking in the gardens, to cool down, physically and spiritually. Giles Quentin, housed on the first floor, had been missing for twenty minutes at the most, but it was the twenty minutes between 11 p.m. and 11.20 p.m. which could have been the critical time; the half-hour would have left Catriona just time to slash her wrists and bleed four pints of blood into the bath. The earliest time she could have been drowned would be about 10.45 p.m. according to the best medical evidence, so the real time of the murder was more likely to have been between 11 p.m. and 11.30 p.m. Piers therefore certainly, and Giles possibly, could have done it. Roland Willis was unaccounted for between 10.30 p.m. and 11.30 p.m., when he had been among the party in the bathroom. He had been, he had said apologetically, having a quiet read in the bedroom allotted to him and Vivienne. Louis Roberts had also been having a break in his and Amanda's bedroom. He had not yet made a statement, but it had been agreed that he would, to John McLeish, later that day. In the intricate map that now covered the wall of the incident room, however, his name appeared within the critical period. 'The murderer could have been a woman,' McLeish had said, neutrally, but the clever female Detective Sergeant Black had, unsmilingly, taken him to the wall chart to show him where the Principal Women had been at the time. Susie Miller had been in plain sight of several people until 11 p.m. when she had gone to look for Piers in the garden, but had missed him, returning ten minutes after he had returned. In ten minutes it was of course not impossible for her to have gone up the back stairs and drowned Catriona, and come down again, re-entering through the garden. The timing was very tight and McLeish was not disposed to the theory, but there was no denying that Susie had a motive. She claimed not to have learned that Catriona was pregnant by Giles until after the girl's death, but if she had known or suspected it before then, there was the motive and a strong one. Vivienne Willis was also without an independent alibi; she had been expecting a call from Japan at 10.45 p.m. (it being 7.45 a.m. the next day in Tokyo) and had closeted herself in Andrew Quentin's study to receive it. She had spoken for ten minutes and written her notes up afterwards and had then rejoined the party at about twenty past eleven, and shortly afterwards had set out to look for Catriona. It was difficult but not at all impossible to envisage her coolly going to hunt for a daughter she knew to be dead. Only Amanda Roberts was in the clear; she had not left the ground floor between 10.30 p.m. and 11.30 p.m. All this needed cross-checking and the team had dispersed to do that. Kevin Camberton, having done sterling work all night and overseen the production of the wall chart, had asked to see him afterwards. McLeish intended to send him home to get some sleep.

'Sir?'

'Come in, Kevin. Excellent work on the chart.'

'Thank you. I've arranged to see Yvette Simpson.'

'Who?'

'The girl Piers Miller seduced at his last school but one.'

'You found her?'

'It wasn't that difficult. The school knew where she was.'

'And she's willing to talk to you?'

'Not particularly, but people usually behave when you tell them it's murder.'

'They do, don't they?' McLeish agreed, struck afresh by this fact. The non-criminal classes anyway. They may lie their socks off but they do accept that they can't refuse to be involved.

'It's one of the examples of a universally agreed standard. In Western societies of course,' Camberton observed.

'Did you read *sociology*, Kevin?' McLeish asked, in the tones of his first boss in the Flying Squad who had enquired what use a *graduate* could possibly be to the squad.

'No. It was a lecture at Bramshill.'

'Place has gone to the dogs since I was there,' McLeish growled, obligingly. 'But you need some sleep. Easy to make a mistake with a delicate interview when you're overtired. Get a few hours in before you go off. Where does she live?'

'In Islington. She's at work till six, anyway.'

'Off you go then, leave Sergeant Black in charge. Competent girl.'

'Better than that. Well, I will get my head down, but not till a bit later.'

'Go now,' McLeish said, and the man looked at him, startled.

'Oh. Right. See you later.'

'No, you won't. I'm going home at six unless something breaks. Call me there if you need anything before tomorrow morning. I'm interviewing Louis Roberts next and I'll make quite sure DS Black gets a transcript straight away for the chart.' He rose and escorted Kevin Camberton to his own office and waited, placidly, until his DI had got himself into his jacket and out of the door.

* * *

An hour later he was being driven to the depths of Dorset, deciding that it was extraordinary how rural the place looked, despite being so close to London. Rotten train service, his driver, with whom he shared this view, said cheerfully.

This small mystery solved, McLeish buried himself in the contents of his in-tray, making phone calls as bits of it appeared from the submerged depths which could have done with an answer yesterday. He managed to get right to the bottom of it, giving occupation to an excellent secretary for the rest of the day. He stretched, feeling virtuously in control of his life, as the car swung through wide gateposts and up the hill to a substantial eighteenth-century building, set well below the brow of the hill, but commanding a wide view of rounded hills. He ran the window down to identify the noise of machinery and saw a huge combine harvester tipped well over as it clambered slowly and noisily up the side of a field in a haze of golden dust, leaving tidy bales of straw behind it.

'Early to harvest,' he observed.

'You're on the chalk here. Drains easily, so you can get the seed in early. And that slope faces south.'

A country boy then, this driver, trapped in the maw of the Metropolitan Police. He asked a question and the man confirmed; he was a farmer's son, but there was no living to be had from the small family farm for more than one man, and that man was his father.

'I'm there every weekend to help out. When the old man retires the idea was I'd take over, but I'm not sure that's going to work. My dad barely makes an income. It's not a life unless you've got some way of bringing in the cash. Like selling a bit of land for housing. See those.' He nodded to the left of the drive where men could be seen, half hidden by trees. 'That'll have fetched a bit; they're getting, what, four big houses down there. Shall I pull up in the front?'

'Yes. I'm expected. When you've seen me in get yourself something to eat and pick up a sandwich for me. Come back in an hour and a half.' He rang the bell and waited, but the door was answered quickly by a middle-aged woman. Not Mrs Roberts of course, who would be away at Faraday's, no doubt involved in the feverish conversations about the school show, which seemed to be haunting his own home.

'Mr Roberts is in the study.'

The study was a room which would have made a hugely generous living-room for any London house, with a view across lawns and trees. It was also uncomfortably warm and he saw that all the windows were closed.

'Hello.' Louis Roberts was in shirt-sleeves, looking ill, seated in a big armchair. 'I'm sorry not to get up but I seem to turn dizzy — it's these bloody drugs. Thank you, nurse.' He managed a tight smile for the middle-aged woman, who had come in with coffee. 'And I'm sorry to drag you all the way down here. They won't let me drive. Or do anything much.' His face crumpled but the nurse gave him some Kleenex and a cup of coffee without making a fuss. Roberts blew his nose and drank his coffee. 'Sorry,' he said, bleakly. 'Where were we? You by yourself? I thought you always come in pairs.'

'We would, but the whole team is usefully otherwise occupied.'

'I'm sorry I couldn't talk on Sunday. You were there, weren't you?'

'Initially as a guest, yes. My wife is Jamie Miles Brett's godmother. He had brought Catriona to lunch with us in London.' It was possible that Louis Roberts had never been aware of any of this information, and if he had it was better to assume he had forgotten it all.

'Oh, Catriona didn't say. But then she doesn't seem to have said very much about anything to me. Oh Christ, sorry. I should have let her mother do what she wanted, but I didn't want Catriona away in a loony bin — I thought it would make her worse. What gets *into* these kids? What can be that bad, when you're eighteen and your life's in front of you?'

'I can only suppose that teenagers don't see it that way.'

'I can't remember being that miserable as a teenager. A bit, maybe, over girls who wouldn't look at you, you know, and you wondered if anyone ever would.' The man was dark, like his daughter, but otherwise did not resemble her. A good-looking man beneath the misery, hair only just beginning to go back, a square face with well-opened blue eyes, good regular features and, he remembered, well above average height. Perhaps he had not had very much to be miserable about as a boy, but then Catriona had been quite pretty when she was relaxed and hopeful, it was just that mostly she had looked wretched and unkempt, her obvious misery repellent in itself.

'This is a splendid view.' McLeish decided to chat over coffee, in order to relax the man a little before eliciting precisely what he had been doing for that key hour on Saturday night.

'I bought the house for it and it cost me too much.'

'You have your own company, I think I remember.'

'Yes. Not doing well this year. Or last for that matter. We've got products people want, but they can't afford them, with sterling as high as it is. We make valves and closures for the oil business — most of our stuff goes to the USA. Or did. The fucking exchange rate is killing us, and nobody seems to give a damn.' Louis Roberts was showing signs of over-excitement, his coffee spilling into his saucer, and McLeish sought for a calmer topic of conversation.

'I see you are to have neighbours. The houses to the left as we came up.'

'Oh. Them. That was my land. Well, we were lucky to get planning consent — the chap who's building them saw to that, he's got good contacts on the council. I won't see or hear them up here, not once they've finished building, but of course the access to the houses is off my drive. Couldn't be helped; I've hardly taken anything out of the business the last three years.' Tears suddenly glittered in his eyes. 'And yes, I have to say that being asked for £1000 a week to keep Catriona in some nursing home wasn't favourite at the moment, and that's another reason I didn't want her to go. Oh God, I wish I'd agreed and found the cash.' There was a long pause. 'I don't usually go on like this, it's all just been too bloody much. You'd better ask what you want to know before nurse comes back with the next lot of pills.'

'Right.' McLeish agreed mentally that Louis Roberts probably didn't have that much more endurance. 'We are still trying to establish everyone's movements on Saturday evening. After Giles Quentin saw her, which we have established was about 10.30 p.m.'

'Giles. Yes. She'd started a row with him much earlier and been swept away by the lovely red-haired girl. Alex something. The dancer.'

'Alexandra Ferguson. She said that Catriona was still angry at what she felt was cavalier treatment by Giles Quentin.'

Louis Roberts winced. 'I saw the whole thing. Of course I didn't know then that the bastard had got her pregnant, but I still thought that he was bloody ungracious.'

'So did I,' McLeish agreed.

'You were there? Of course you were, I'm just not with it, it's the drugs.' He snuffled into the Kleenex and recovered himself, looking exhausted. 'Your wife's godson was there too of course. Actually there's one who was always kind to Catriona.'

'Yes. He is a kind lad.'

'His father's in a bin, Catriona says . . . said.'

'His father's a schizophrenic and a danger to himself and others if he doesn't take his medication. Mr Roberts, I can see you're getting tired; can I just try and get an account of your movements after 10.15 p.m.? So, you were in the music room at 10.15 p.m. With your wife?'

'Yes, and a group. Susie Miller was there, I can't remember all the others.'

McLeish could have named every member of that group after the morning's briefing but wanted to hear a full account from Louis Roberts. You never knew what you were going to get, you had to approach each witness with an open mind. 'And then?'

'I watched Alexandra and that chap dance, then I had another drink, or a coffee or something about, what, 10.45. Then I needed a pee so I thought I'd go up to our room — we were staying the night. Took me a little while to find it again but I did, and . . . oh, I sat down for a while, I think, then I was just thinking of going downstairs again when I heard everyone yelling and screaming. Our room was on the second floor and I couldn't work out where the noise was coming from, then I realised it was coming sideways from the same floor, then it was still going on so I thought perhaps I ought to go and see what was happening and I — well, you know the rest.'

'I need to hear it, please.'

'The noise was all coming from the back bedroom — I didn't even realise it was Catriona's, the housekeeper had showed us our room and then taken her off. I was just, well, deciding whether to go in when Alex came out, more or less carrying Jamie. They were both soaking wet and I thought it was a game of some sort. She just looked at me and went absolutely white — I wondered what I'd done, left my flies undone, you know how it is, and then she just pulled Jamie past me and carted him into the lift and they vanished. I still thought it was some kind of kid's game. But I went in and there was Roland Willis, kneeling on the floor of the little room — well, I could see it was a bathroom — reaching into the bath and he was calling for help. Vivienne was there too and there was this gurgling noise.'

Vivienne Willis had kept her head and run out the water to facilitate the task of getting Catriona out of the bath. McLeish looked anxiously at Louis Roberts who was visibly shying from the next part.

'Roland and Vivienne lifted her out and I saw then . . . who it was. So I rushed over and tried to help and tried to . . . to bring her back. I got soaked . . . oh God . . . in her blood, it was everywhere. Then the doctors came and asked me to move.' His voice was dreary with remembered pain. His eyes focused. 'Then *you* came, didn't you, or have I got that wrong?'

'Yes, I came up just after the paramedics — Alex had found me but she had already called for medical help.' He eyed his customer anxiously. 'Can we just go over the period from when you came upstairs to your room. Did you use the lift?'

'Yes. I have a heart condition — a murmur only — but I'm not supposed to climb stairs.'

'And when you'd used the bathroom, what time would that be?'

'Eleven o'clock.'

Now that was suspiciously precise. 'You looked at your watch? Or a clock?'

'Yes, my watch.' There was a pause in which McLeish heard the man collect himself to go carefully. 'Then I sat down for a minute, picked up a book and had a little break. I find these late parties very tiring and to be honest I was hoping the other guests would go and Amanda and I could get to bed.' He wasn't looking at McLeish and was shredding a Kleenex. 'It's about time for the next set of dope, I'm sorry,' he said, looking past McLeish to the door.

'Mr Roberts, you know that the autopsy report suggests that Catriona was held under the water and drowned.'

'Amanda told me.'

'The most likely time given when she was last seen would have been between 10.45 p.m. and 11.15 p.m. So we need to be clear where everyone was at that point. You were in your room?'

'I was, yes.'

'By yourself?'

'Yes.'

McLeish let the silence fall and watched as it did its usual work. Roberts was shredding a second Kleenex in his hands, his head bent over his task. 'I was making a telephone call,' he said, finally.

'To whom?'

'To a woman friend.'

'May I have her name and address?'

'You have to talk to her, I suppose?'

'Yes.'

'Oh Christ. You don't believe I was where I said I was. In our room.'

'We do not deal in belief where evidence is available.'

'That sounds very pompous.'

'Being a policeman often necessitates a bit of that.' This welcome irritability meant he could safely push on. 'For how long do you think you spoke?'

'Probably twenty minutes. She's . . . she's a single woman and she was expecting me to call.'

'We can find out how long the call took.'

Both of them heard the soft tap on the door.

'Will you write down the name and address and phone number for me?'

'Yes. Yes, of course. Come in, Nurse.'

She padded in quietly, eyes only for her patient, and she sat and took his wrist, watching his face. 'I would say you've had enough, Mr Roberts.'

'Oh I have, I have.' McLeish switched off his tape, looking at his watch to get the time right. He waited while Louis Roberts wrote and gave him a folded piece of paper.

'I'll need to talk to you again, Mr Roberts.'

'I'm not going anywhere just yet. Can you let yourself out?' He was gulping pills, shoulders hunched, the nurse's hand on his wrist, the bright day outside offering him no warmth.

* * *

'Jamie!' Francesca, out of breath after three flights of stairs, subsided onto the pile of clothes on the chair, rising again sharply to remove from the chair a pair of jeans with belt still slotted in and a pair of underpants which had seen better days. 'Jamie. Darling. It's twelve o'clock. You need to get up. And Tina needs to get into your room.'

It was unreasonable to expect a teenage boy to be interested in the needs of a cleaner, but Jamie had always been a good kind boy who understood about the hopeless feminine need for order. He grunted, and turned convulsively in his bed, and she looked with love at the long foot which emerged from a corner of the heap of blankets. There was something about boys that reduced the most neatly made bed to a heap of decaying textiles.

'Mm. I will. I am.' The blankets heaved and a wild, disordered mop of dark hair emerged. 'You'll have to go.'

'I'm leaving but I'm taking some of the pile on this chair with me to the wash.'

'Not the jeans. Nor the shirt. My other one's in the wash.'

'Your other shirt is clean. Hanging up downstairs.'

A disaffected grunt greeted this information and she bent with difficulty to pick up as many dirty garments as she could conveniently reach before heaving herself to her feet, clutching her booty. She headed downstairs, one hand clinging to the banisters, the other clutching the dirty clothes to her, murmuring under her breath a little litany. 'Oh thank you, Francesca. How kind to have organised a clean shirt. And clean pants and T-shirts and many clean if unmatching socks, so at least I can get up. It is a comfort to me.' No, it wasn't, of course, Jamie was beyond comfort, the trouble with his father had weighed him down to the point where the ordinary easements of life availed him not at all, and his only escape was to the deathlike sleep of the adolescent. She stopped, stabbed by this understanding as Susannah emerged from a bathroom. 'Francesca. Give me those. If you fall on the stairs, now . . .'

'I was holding on with the other hand,' she said, defensively, surrendering the bundle to Susannah who cast her eyes to heaven.

'His Lordship up?' Susannah had no time at all for boys over the age of five.

'Almost. I'm going to get him out for lunch.'

'When does he go back to school?'

'I'm trying, I'm trying. But I agree, he needs to go back.'

They both heard sounds from above them and dispersed, guiltily. Francesca arrived in the kitchen and made for the telephone. Two years as a bursar in the all-female Gladstone College had introduced her to the concept of sisterhood, which she had missed out on in a childhood as the only girl among four brothers.

'Alexandra. It's Francesca McLeish, and I need help. You couldn't take Jamie to lunch? I'll pay. He must go back to school.'

'Of course.' The clear voice was very assured, and Francesca waited patiently while the young woman at the other end thought.

'Right. Well, there're two problems about going back. His father . . .'

'In hospital still,' Francesca said, trying to match her economy of speech. 'Discussions going on about placement in a suitable hostel.'

'Mm. Giles Quentin. Do you know if he's gone back to school?'

'No. I could ask. I owe Lady Quentin a thank-you letter for the party but I really couldn't work out what to write. Thank you for a lovely party, such fun, sorry about the unfortunateness and that I had to leave my husband behind.'

Alex went into fits of giggles, and Francesca remembered that this infinitely competent young woman was only twenty-two. 'It would be useful to know, if you can find out. Giles was here yesterday — at the office — and I had lunch with him. I think Peter Graebner got all he wanted for the moment, so there's no reason he shouldn't have gone back. Can Jamie pick me up here? Any time, really.'

It remained only to get Jamie round to the Law Centre, clothed and in his right mind. If the influence of dear Alexandra could not get him back to school, then John would have to be asked to come the heavy, usurping the role of the useless, absent Steve. She looked up and saw, refreshingly, her godson dressed in vest and jeans, his hair more or less combed, groping his way to the laundry room. He hadn't shaved but then Alex would be used to that among her contemporaries.

'Darling,' she said, resolutely, to his back, 'that was Alex. Can you have lunch, she says.' She watched his back, right arm stuck at an impossible angle as he fought to get into the denim shirt. He wheeled round and looked at her suspiciously.

'I saw her yesterday.'

'I'm sorry if you're bored by the idea.'

'I'm never bored by Alex. I love her.' He did up a cuff, broodingly.

'That's what I thought, I must say.'

'But she didn't *say* yesterday. I wonder what she wants?'

'Maybe just lunch? Have you got any cash?'

He looked at her, worried, and searched his pockets. 'A fiver. But we usually go Dutch.'

'Poor starving Alex. Let me give you a tenner so she can have two lots of baked beans, or whatever. Consider it my contribution to the arts. I'll drop you there, it's an awkward journey.'

'Should you be driving?'

'I'm only pregnant, even if I have been for about a hundred years. While I can still fit under the steering wheel, I drive.'

He finished doing up his shirt and she watched him under her eyelashes. He was suspicious, but prepared not to examine his doubts, because of the pleasure of lunch with Alex. Now it was up to that clever girl.

'She said yesterday she was sure Giles hadn't . . . hadn't . . . wasn't . . .'

'Ah. She doesn't think Giles had anything to do with Catriona's death?' A policeman's wife had to be able to speak without euphemism of death and destruction.

'In the sense that it wasn't him who . . . who drowned her perhaps. He *was* bloody responsible for her being miserable enough to put herself in the bath, the bastard. Went out with her, got her pregnant and ditched her when she needed help.'

She would have to deal with this, and now, she understood, feeling the baby kick in response to the clenching of her stomach muscles. 'It wasn't good. But Jamie, are you not importing what you feel about how your mum — and we indeed — are behaving towards your father?'

He stood, frozen, then sat down abruptly and she watched with pity as the whole misery came back to get him. His back bent and his head went into his hands. She paid him the respect due to a fellow grown-up by not moving to embrace him.

'It's not fair to Giles, who was a friend, no matter how stupidly he has behaved,' she said, steadily, after a minute or so. 'Or to Faraday's where you have been so happy, to blame them for what is happening with your father.'

He reached for a tea-towel and scrubbed it over his face, then looked at it. 'Oh, sorry.

'No, no, darling. Feel free. Blow your nose on it.'

He snorted, explosively, and got up to find a handful of kitchen towel on which he did blow his nose.

'Better?'

'A bit. You're right, I am mixing the two.' He was sloshing water over his face. 'You — you and John — think Mum's right, don't you?'

'It's not about right and wrong. It's what she can cope with. Which I have to say, over the years, is a lot more than I could have.' She watched him, thoughtfully. 'After all, Jamie, this isn't the worst that could happen. Your father, when the disease is raging, could easily kill your mother, or you, because he thinks he must, and where would that leave everyone? This way, well, he may really decide to live on medication and your parents may — I only say may — be able to live together again. Or they may each be able to live with someone else.'

'I feel so helpless.'

'Hard for a young man. But we *are* all helpless; no one can make your pa take his pills unless he wants to — they have trouble even in hospital, don't they? He hides them or spits them out.'

'Yes, he does.'

'He'll need you to do what you can. To visit faithfully.'

He gave her a long, searching look which she met, steadily.

'I'd better get over there for lunch,' he said, resolutely. 'I know what Alex wants; she thinks I should go back to school, and do the concert because they'll be short in several places without me, and the school needs a triumph.' She was not surprised to find that her godson spoke without any kind of boastfulness; like the musicians in her own family he knew to a hair how good he was. '*And* she thinks Giles and I should perform together, same as . . . as we always did.'

'Yes, I expect she does.' She felt herself turn pink at the neck and Jamie saw it too.

'You rang her?'

In the teeth of the direct question, she never lied. 'I did. I thought she would cheer you up.'

'You're a pair of conniving women.'

And nothing could have given him greater pleasure even in the depth of his trouble, she saw, than that his godmother and his adored mentor should conspire for his good. He peered at himself in the battered mirror that hung by the refrigerator. 'Can you wait two minutes — I need to shave.'

She indicated gravely that this was possible and sat slumped with relief, listening to the heavy feet thundering upstairs.

* * *

John McLeish had eaten his sandwich in the car and captured four biscuits and a cup of coffee from the machine back at the station. It wasn't good coffee but he was used to it; indeed he sometimes thought he had forgotten what real coffee tasted like. It had been all but abandoned at his home, because Francesca, when pregnant, was nauseated by the smell, and when not pregnant apologetically preferred instant.

The competent DS Black appeared at his elbow and he handed her his tape recorder.

'Tape's not run back.' He stood in front of the wall chart, scratching his chin. The trouble was that six of those closest to Catriona were wholly or partially unaccounted for at the critical time. Both the Millers, Louis Roberts, both Willises, and Giles Quentin. Only Jamie and Amanda Roberts, having been in plain sight of several people for the critical time, were in the clear, as was Alexandra. He thought about Andrew Quentin, who had assembled the Millers, the Willises and Roberts, allegedly in order to spend a gruelling Sunday morning in discussion with all parents and step-parents about the mess that two of the children had got themselves into. No better smokescreen for murder could have been devised, and yet how could anyone have known that Catriona would so obligingly arrange herself as a victim? This is not a Jacobean play, this murder must have been opportunistic and unplanned, he reminded himself, and followed

Andrew Quentin's recorded movements carefully through the chart. On the face of it, it was unlikely that the host could have been missing for very long. It was clear that the man had been downstairs from the beginning of Giles and Jamie's little concert all the way through to about 10.30 p.m. after Alexandra's performance. It was much less clear how he had spent the time between 10.30 p.m. and 11.30 p.m. Some of the distinguished guests had by now proved helpful in filling in the gaps, and those of them sophisticated enough to understand that they were also providing their host with an alibi had not commented on the point. But it wasn't a complete alibi. By that stage of the party the timings were beginning to get a bit hazy. One distinguished guest had been clear that he had bidden farewell to Lady Quentin at 11 p.m. but when pressed could not be positive that Sir Andrew had also been present. Various people, including Lady Quentin and Giles, had been sure they had seen him but not at all sure of the precise timing. So Sir Andrew could be in the frame as well: he had known that Catriona represented a threat to his son, had known where she was quartered and could easily have gone looking for her and found his opportunity.

'Sir, it's Doc Jamieson. I thought you'd want to speak.'

He seized a phone. 'Yes?'

'You're not going to like this at all. Giles Quentin could not have been the father. He may have slept with her but he didn't put her in the club. He has Group AB blood, so did the young woman, and the foetus is Group O.'

'So it's not possible?'

'Absolutely not. The father has to be Group O.'

'Damn, damn, damn.' He bent a hostile gaze on DS Black, who was openly listening, and she bent hastily to some paperwork. 'I ought to have been ready for this,' he said, recovering his equilibrium. 'But I wasn't.'

'You'll have to test a lot more people.'

'Thank you, Doc. Don't call us . . .' He put the phone down, and recovered himself. If Giles Quentin, an admitted lover, was not the father then the case opened up. There was another man who would have been threatened by Catriona's pregnancy, now all he had to do was find him.

He called his team together, regretting the absence of Kevin Camberton, but vetoing firmly the idea of waking him from his first sound sleep for thirty-six hours.

'Who are we going to test, sir?' DS Black as usual on to the point, and not afraid to ask the obvious question.

'Well, we can forget about anyone who isn't Group O. That gets us down to 40% of the population. Where do you think we should start?' No one was going to learn just by listening to him tell them.

'The boys at her school. The ones who aren't Giles Quentin,' DS Black said, promptly.

'Well, yes, but there are a lot of them.'

'The men at the party,' a young DC said, diffidently. 'Not all of them, but the ones who were around in the bathroom.'

'I think that's the place to start. The male suspects.'

They moved to look at the wall chart.

'Piers Miller and Roland Willis,' Michelle Black observed.

'What about Louis Roberts?'

'But he's her *father*,' Michelle Black said, horrified.

'Not impossible.'

'No, sir,' she said, blushing.

'And Andrew Quentin. We haven't cleared him.'

There was a slight pause.

'Sir, and the other boy, Jamie. He seemed to be close to her, even though he is accounted for. The father needn't be the murderer.' It was the young DC who spoke.

Oh, yes, and indeed Jamie, no matter how unlikely he might find him as a lover of Catriona's. 'Certainly Jamie,' he said, calmly. 'That makes five. Have we missed anyone? Right, good.' And now, he thought, all that remains is for me to ask the girl's father, and stepfather, as well as her distinguished host, her housemistress's husband, and her best male friend to provide the proof that they did not father her child. He dismissed his team and went off to make the necessary arrangements, including the despatch of an officer to Faraday's for Piers Miller and to his own home to catch Jamie just before he went back to school. Francesca had been less distressed by the news than he had expected, opining that it would help Jamie to know Giles had not been the father and that she did not believe for one moment that Jamie, who knew what madness looked like, would ever have slept with Catriona. It was to be hoped she was right.

* * *

Kevin Camberton rolled over and decided to get up. He had slept soundly for a couple of hours and fitfully for three; even in this side street off Islington Green the traffic was relentless, becoming quiet only between midnight and about five in the morning. He needed to organise double-glazing, at least for the bedroom, but the job left him very little time to do any of that. In any case he preferred to spend his free time entertaining and being entertained. London in general and Islington had been a revelation to him. The gay scene in Hull had tended to the rough, but here there was a fully-fledged and cultured society, pleasantly non-exclusive. He had been introduced to as many straight as gay at some of the parties locally. In blessed London people seemed to be relaxed about those who did not share their sexual tastes, unlike Hull where there had always been an undertone of unease and patronage when straight met gay. He looked at his watch. Four o'clock and he was seeing the Simpson girl at 6.30, which gave him time to get some food inside him, check up by phone on the rest of the investigation and bath and shave. Despite John McLeish's warning he had no doubt he was engaged in the only definitive piece of detective work. All the rest needed doing, to make quite sure that the case against Piers Miller could not be muddled or made to look doubtful in the hands of a clever barrister, but it was he who was going to nail the man.

He finished shaving and dressing, made a swift efficient foray to the supermarket, then headed for Yvette Simpson's flat. Where he got a surprise: it was a small house rather than a flat and had, impressively, a dining area off the kitchen and separate from the living-room. And the girl was unexpected too, tall, slim, beautifully cut straight blond hair framing a face not exactly pretty, the jaw was too strong and the nose had a bump in it. A lot of style, he concluded, interested, as she hitched up the elegant long skirt that all the smartest women were wearing that season. Her shoes were original too, Manolo Blahnik he recognised. She served them both coffee in thick pottery mugs, with elegant thin ginger biscuits, which she didn't eat. He stopped, embarrassed, when he found he had somehow eaten half a dozen of them.

'What is your work, Miss Simpson?' he asked, hastily, to cover up his lapse.

'I have my own PR firm.'

'You're, what, twenty-seven now?'

'And I've been running my own firm since I left Cambridge.'

'Oh, you were there.' The school had not specified which university she had attended.

'At King's. Dad's college. He's a judge. My pa.'

This went some way to explain why she was receiving a visit from the police with such unconcerned civility. She gave him a faint mischievous sidelong look as he realised he had straightened convulsively in his chair. Simpson. Yes. Well, it wasn't an uncommon name, not stupid of him not to have thought of it. He took a deep breath and embarked on his carefully prepared explanation, and she heard him out without comment or exclamation, a circumstance rare in itself.

'So,' he said, having got himself where he meant to be, 'at the party where Miss Roberts died, there had been a little scene — very public — where she accused Mr Miller of pawing her. Now, we have to follow up all these things, you understand.'

'Well, it won't have been Piers killed her. I can tell you that. Not his style.'

He breathed out. 'I'd be very grateful for anything you can tell me.'

'Well, you're here because you know I had an affair with Piers when I was at school. They were very cross with both of us. I was asked not to join the Old Meltonians.' She was absolutely straight-faced and he did not dare to comment.

'And Piers was reprimanded by the school and in fact left for another job a year later.'

'Yes.' She lit a cigarette and offered him one. 'Sensible of him, I thought, no point in staying to be shat on. Rugby, wasn't it, where he went? And now he's at Faraday's.'

'You didn't stay in touch with him after . . .'

'After school, as it were? No.' She looked at him consideringly. 'I fancied him. I thought he'd be a good fuck, and I have to say I was fed up with the school, all of it, couldn't wait to get out, so I seduced him.'

'You seduced him?'

'You have met *Piers*? Yes? Well, that's what happened to him. I bet it still does.'

Yes, he thought, that rang a bell. And the reason he had not seen it for himself was that these people were straight and he didn't recognise the exact parallels with gay society. Piers was recognisably a seducee, straight or gay, liked sex, loved admiration, but would always wait to be asked. Susie Miller must have done just that. 'Mm,' he said, that being temporarily the only suitable reaction he could find and got another slyly amused look from the brown eyes.

'He's a good teacher. Not particularly good at sex though, but quite good enough for what I knew then. But a *great* maths teacher. I was never taught as well again at Cambridge. I got four Grade As at A-level, including two maths. And of course I had two languages.'

'Both of you must have been pretty good.'

'No, that's the point. I read maths but in fact I had to give up after a year at Cambridge. That happens to people who aren't real mathematicians, which I wasn't. He was just a bloody good maths teacher. Another biscuit? Finish them, do.'

She had understood that he was gay, he realised, and had relaxed with him, as if he was one of her girlfriends. He gave himself time to think, in unconscious imitation of John McLeish.

'In this case, the girl was also in her last year but not — not anything like you. Unconfident and depressed.'

'He probably felt sorry for her. Was she a mathematician?'

'Yes, but by all accounts not very clever.'

'But he taught her? Yes, then I can see it. Maths wasn't your subject? There's something about it, when you see the answer. It's beautiful. You feel like kissing the person who showed it to you, but of course in a school situation you usually can't. Not with six other people in the set.'

'He gave her some individual tuition because she was struggling.' There was not much he did not know about Piers Miller's recent career.

'And it happened then?'

'No one had time to ask her. But she accused him of pawing her.'

'And he says he didn't.'

'Yes.' He watched her, while she poured more coffee for them both unhurriedly.

'Well, the last time — with me — Piers got into *really* bad trouble. He was nearly sacked. *I* didn't care what the school said, I went off to Greece, then to King's. Poor old Piers got the trouble. I wouldn't think he'd want all *that* again. I mean, where do you go after three schools?'

'To a head's job, perhaps.'

Her head went up. 'Ah. One of my clients did happen to say Faraday's were advertising, only it didn't really click till now. He's up for that?'

He wasn't going to tell this confident communicative witness that Piers Miller had withdrawn his candidature; the withdrawal itself could be a red herring, and it was fair enough to treat it as that.

'Well, I imagine he'd not make the short list with *two* blots on the escutcheon,' she said, thoughtfully.

'No.'

'So, you, the police, wonder whether he might have killed her to silence her? It sounds sort of sensible, but I just don't believe it. Not Piers.'

'When did you last see him?'

'Two years ago. Ran into him at a party and we had lunch for old times' sake. I like him. And I'm sure you're barking up the wrong tree.' She studied his face. 'I'm not convincing you, am I? Well, I was only eighteen when I knew him best, and my poor old dad is always telling me about the things that go on, but *I* can't see Piers as a killer. He might lash out if he was pissed off. It wasn't like that?'

'Miss Roberts was drowned. Held under water in a bath.'

'Oh no. Not Piers.' She was distressed, he saw, her hands moving restlessly. 'Coffee? No.' She took a deep breath. 'Is there anything else I can tell you?'

'No, thank you. You've been most helpful.' He left, sad to be leaving her distressed, but with his conviction of Piers Miller's guilt undiminished. It fitted quite well, better in fact than the vision of a Piers as a cynical abuser. He was a victim not a predator, the girl had seduced him and then threatened to tell on him, as the children say. Piers, with everything to lose, wife, the good opinion of his fellows, his hopes of advancement, indeed probably his whole teaching career, had seen his chance and the victim had hit back. He could see it in his mind's eye, Piers Miller going up the back stairs in search of Catriona to try and reason with her, then finding her in her own bathroom, in the course of a suicide attempt. A short step surely to the realisation that one decisive act would finish the job she had started, put her out of her all too evident misery, and save his life and his career.

He called a taxi; he needed to go to the office. He would not be able to see John McLeish but he would be able to make sure the team was working smoothly.

CHAPTER 10

Wednesday, 5th July

The Chairman of the Faraday Trust was counting his fellow Trustees. The terms of the Trust provided for twelve Trustees, but for routine business six or seven was the most he could get, given that two of them were major industrialists, and among the rest were numbered the Vice Chancellor of the local university, a woman QC, and a senior woman gynaecologist and obstetrician. For this discussion, however, he had moved the meeting to a room in his London club to suit the majority and secured the attendance of eleven out of twelve; the QC was at a torture trial in South Africa. He got the group sat round a table and to bend their minds to the papers before them.

'Michael Muirhead from Waters Prior has kindly come down to brief us. He has talked either face to face, or on the telephone, with the candidates.'

Conscientious heads bent to the papers and several people fell simultaneously on the same point.

'Two candidates and both internal,' the obstetrician said, dismayed. 'I thought — well, did no one appropriate apply from outside?'

The Chairman, who had got the head-hunter to the meeting to deal with precisely this issue, signalled wordlessly to the man that the floor was his in order that he might justify the substantial fee he was receiving for having produced two candidates the Trustees could effortlessly have proposed themselves.

'In our search for a new head for Faraday's we have been able,' Michael Muirhead began, smoothly, 'to identify and to attract twelve candidates, ten of whom were external. In consultation with your Chairman and the selection committee we reduced that list to a short list of six, four external and two internal candidates. The only two internal candidates who had applied.' He took a deep breath and slowed, in order to get a clear run at the hill. 'Two of the external candidates dropped out at an early stage, having both been offered head's jobs elsewhere. Both the other external candidates asked to see the school before going forward, and visits were duly arranged. Both candidates subsequently withdrew.'

'Were the students stroppy with them? More so than usual, I mean?' The obstetrician, herself a Faraday alumna, had been in her time a particularly difficult pupil.

'One candidate — Dr Williams — took a deputy post at his existing school — Uppingham — evidently feeling that it would suit him better. The other, David Jerrold, simply felt that he was not the man for the school, once he had seen it. And, no, he did not seem to have difficulty with the students. There were very few of them there that weekend in any case.'

'But why . . . ? No, it doesn't matter, does it? It's water under the bridge.' The obstetrician was experienced and worldly enough to rise above the implied insult to the school. 'It just didn't fit. But we had only *two* internal candidates, you said.'

'That is correct. Mrs Roberts and Mr Willis.'

'Why did Piers Miller withdraw his application, do we know?'

'He had been very unsettled and unnerved by the death of Miss Roberts, whom he had taught.'

'Hardly as unsettled as Mr Willis who was her stepfather, or Mrs Roberts who was her stepmother, one would have thought,' the consultant obstetrician objected.

The Chairman raised his hand to stop Michael Muirhead trying to take this one. 'That's quite right, but the young woman — who had been causing major problems for all her family and associates — had also publicly accused Mr Miller of making sexual advances to her.'

'When did all this happen? And where?'

'The accusation came at a party at Sir Andrew Quentin's house. The night she died. Miller felt he ought to withdraw his candidature, even though he maintained and maintains the accusation was hysterical and totally untrue.'

'He thought she'd bitched his chances,' one of the industrialists observed.

'Yes,' Michael Muirhead agreed. 'But I talked to him, because he seemed to us to be a good candidate, who had behaved . . . well, with some delicacy, and who perhaps ought to be encouraged to apply.'

There was a pause while everyone in the room remembered the background against which they would be taking this decision.

'Have the police — are they making any progress?'

'It's very early days.'

'Mm. What does Nick think of the candidates, Chairman? Or must we not ask?'

'His view is that if you want radical change, Mrs Roberts, or Mr Miller if he were a candidate, both have the capacity to deliver it. Along with a few broken eggs, he made that clear. Not that much experience, either of them.'

'And what does he think about Roland Willis?'

'That he probably lacked the capacity to make radical change, after twenty years in the school, but that he was innovative in many ways, infinitely experienced, and would certainly not be overawed by finding himself as a head rather than a second-in-command.'

'Nick didn't want to interview with us, Chairman?'

'No. He said we were going to get the grief if it went wrong, so we had better take the full weight of the decision. He is of course happy to answer any questions we forget to put to the candidates.'

There was a general pause.

'Well,' the consultant obstetrician said, doubtfully, 'it's not much of a field to choose from.'

'But we do have to make a choice,' the industrialist said, impatiently. 'Chairman, I think you should try to widen the field for us by persuading Miller to put his name forward. After all, we're not interviewing till next week, there may be developments in this sad case. And we have to have a head for the school.'

The Chairman nodded. 'Thank you, everyone, very much. See you next week.'

* * *

Kevin Camberton was sitting in the CID room of the Dorset regional crime squad, trying to carry on a conversation with a DI and his DC. Both men were perfectly civil to him but he was being uneasily reminded of Hull, and young DC Harter, whom he had brought with him, was not carrying much of the conversational load. The surroundings were quite different from Hull of course. The unit was newly built and featureless, out of the window the green flat fields sparkled in the sun, and there were stolid cows in the distance, but it still felt like Hull. It was, he understood, the CID force here deployed that reminded him. There must be people of his persuasion in this quiet country backwater, but if they attempted to declare themselves these policemen would be uncomprehending and hostile. Real tolerance and understanding was going to take weary years, out here, in places like this.

Roland Willis was late. It had been difficult to fix an interview with him at all, and Camberton had had to insist. The man had yielded, with poor grace, explaining that the life of a teacher in the penultimate week of term was so tightly scheduled as to make finding two hours impossibly difficult. He had however refused Camberton's offer to come to the school and use an office there, preferring to drive the twenty minutes each way to the regional crime squad office. Camberton had some sympathy with his objections; John McLeish had interviewed him at length the day after the murder, but orders were orders and he was here with instructions to ask very specifically for details of everything that had happened on the school trip, which had been the last time Catriona had been in close contact with her contemporaries. He had asked McLeish what he was looking for and the man had said, vaguely, that he had not felt they had really understood enough about Catriona's relationships. Well, *that* was probably true and he would do anything to make sure they got a solid case. Piers Miller had been on the trip as well, and it would always be useful to know more about him.

Noises off indicated that Willis had arrived, and Camberton collected DC Harter and thanked the local force. The interview room they gave him was small and soundproof, but the light was good and revealed how worn and haggard Willis was looking.

'Sorry to trouble you again,' he said, the introductions made.

'I just cannot see how I can help any further, but of course anything I can do . . .'

'We are talking to everyone involved with Miss Roberts,' Camberton said, meaning to reassure. 'And, of course, the events of the last week of her life could be critically important. When she — you — were all on the school journey.' He looked at Willis, and was startled; the man had frozen and was staring at him as if he were a snake. 'I understand that it did not go very easily.'

'Who told you? Oh, anyone, I suppose.' He paused and Camberton waited, as he had seen John McLeish do. A heavy, burdened sigh. 'Yes. Yes. She was very difficult.'

The man was so sunk in despondency that he feared they might spend the next hour in silence unless he asked a question.

'Was she cutting her wrists?'

'Yes, yes, she did have a go. But only when other students were about, you know.' He fell silent again, and this time Kevin Camberton remembered his training, and the two policemen sat, watching, while Roland Willis wrestled with his problem. 'She . . . she had become very demanding.' He looked across at two professionally stone faces and visibly despaired. 'She seemed to need . . . reassurance all the time.' He looked at the table, then heaved a sigh. 'Reassurance of her own . . . that she was . . . well, sexually attractive.' He let out a long breath, his shoulders sagging, evidently feeling that he had managed a major and painful step forward.

'What form did these demands for reassurance take?' Silence was a powerful weapon, but Roland Willis had got over the first hurdle and now needed to be kept moving.

'I'm sorry, it's very difficult . . . Look, if she had been, well, eight instead of eighteen one would just have said it was an anxious and clinging child. You must have seen one of those kids clinging to their mother, or to anyone who looks like a mother. Other children get absolutely fed-up with them.'

'And Catriona behaved like this?'

'Well, yes, but worse, I mean it was much more difficult to deal with because . . . because she was eighteen and there was a strong — indeed an aggressive sexual element.' He looked at them pleadingly. 'It was very unattractive, I could see that, poor child. Even I found it very difficult.'

'Mr Willis. What, precisely, did she do that worried you so much?'

'She . . . she . . .' He took a breath. 'For example, she kept trying to sit next to Giles Quentin and more or less climbed on to his knee. Of course he had been her lover, though I didn't know that at the time, so I suppose . . .' His voice trailed away and he stared out of the window. 'Dear God, I am making a meal of this, but I can hardly bear the whole thing. I should have *known* how desperate she was. She, well, she made sexual advances to several of the boys, including Jamie who was embarrassed.' He paused, head down, gripping the table, then went on painfully. 'And, worse, she started doing it with me — I simply cannot tell you how difficult that was. I didn't want to repel her because she was in such a state, but . . . I can't understand why, seeing her in that state, I didn't see the need to get her to a safe haven as it were.' He found a handkerchief and blew his nose. 'I thought, I suppose, that her school and her home were a safe haven, but all of it must have been making her more and more anxious.' He reflected, gazing miserably out of the window. 'I think — I hope — I would have got her to hospital when we got back — we were in Wales which is a long way from home and where I don't know any of the medical establishment — but there was the Quentin party the day afterwards, and she was very keen to go, so I just . . . well, procrastinated.'

Camberton murmured something vaguely consoling, and Roland Willis turned on him. 'You can have no idea, Inspector. You've never lost a child, and I *did* feel she was my child. I've had her since she was six.' He glared at them both. 'Do you think you're ever going to find out who killed her?'

'We are pursuing several lines of enquiry. I'm sorry that this is painful, but can I just pursue your description of Catriona's behaviour on the trip? She embarrassed you and Giles Quentin, and Jamie Miles Brett.'

'And Piers Miller. Gravely.'

'You mean apart from the scene at the party?' He felt his heart thump and looked to see that the tape was running.

Roland Willis looked surprised. 'You asked about Catriona's behaviour in Wales. I'm afraid she treated Piers to some of her most embarrassing approaches. Worse than embarrassing in truth, because she also implied he was — or had been — willing to respond.' He sighed. 'Piers always said that she needed professional help — that makes another person whose advice I would not heed.'

Camberton felt the hunter's pure excitement. 'How precisely did she embarrass Mr Miller?'

'Oh. Hugging him, kissing him in a very unsuitable way.' He looked up, alarmed. 'Look, I'm not suggesting he encouraged her in any way. Any more than any of us did. No, indeed. He made certain he was with one or both of our female colleagues for as much of the day as was humanly possible.'

'But?' Camberton could hear the reservation and realised he had been too eager; the man was retreating.

'But she pursued him. And there was a very unfortunate scene when she had been, well, conclusively rebuffed by Giles Quentin, and Piers, out of the kindness of his heart, sought to reassure her.'

'What happened exactly, Mr Willis?'

The man looked down, the grey forelock falling into his eyes. 'She wanted him to spend the night with her, saying that way he would get what he wanted. He refused, of course, Inspector. But it *was* very unpleasant. I could do nothing with her and that kind boy Jamie Miles Brett had to take her away.'

Camberton made a note; why had Jamie not told them all this? He looked up and met Willis's eyes, bright now and observant.

'I should make it quite clear that poor Piers was very much distressed *and* that he spent that night in our caravan. With me.'

But Piers Miller was involved all right, Camberton thought, grimly. He'd been there or thereabouts and there was something between him and the girl. Maybe nothing much on his side but the consequences could have been devastating for him. 'You did not tell Chief Superintendent McLeish about all this,' he observed as neutrally as he could.

The man blushed a slow flush that worked its way up. 'I know. I should have, but it was so painful. And . . . and, I suppose, I didn't want to . . . to speak ill of the dead. Poor Catriona.' His voice broke and they waited in respectful silence before asking one or two routine uninspired questions and winding up the interview.

'Poor bloke,' DC Harter said as they walked out to the waiting car, saying civil farewells to the local force.

'Indeed.'

'You don't think he had done . . . well, anything he shouldn't?'

'He's her stepfather. Sorry, stupid thing to say.' He considered the point, but without particular interest. 'But you heard what he had to say about Miller?'

'Oh yes. That was new, wasn't it? No one else told us that. Including Mr Miller.'

A lively one, this Michael Harter. Camberton considered him suddenly, with a sharp stab, realising something about him. Not a good-looking boy, doughy skin, overweight, but undeniably sexual. He walked on to the car, thinking hard.

'Inspector.'

He stopped and turned. 'Yes, Mike?'

'I am of your persuasion,' the lad said, formally and seriously, the Scots accent very obvious.

'So I have just understood.' Camberton decided to meet whatever trouble this was going to cause head on. He wasn't attracted at all, but you could not repel this sort of straightforwardness.

'You've come out, haven't you? In the force, I mean.'

'Yes. From the day I joined. Everyone knows who wants to.' They shared a small, wry smile.

'Have you had any bother?' Mike asked, tentatively.

'Some. Nothing too bad, but you don't get any of that with the Chief Super's squad.' He waited while Mike struggled with himself.

'See, I've got a partner. He thinks I ought to come out.'

'Mm.' He wasn't going to encourage this lad to take a stand; everyone had to make their own decision on this and it wasn't easy either way.

'Does it . . . do you think it holds you back? Having people know.'

'It's been OK so far,' he said, temperately, thinking that the lad could have worked *that* out for himself; twenty-seven was very young to have been a DI for twelve months.

'You were a graduate entry?'

'OK,' he conceded, 'so it's probably been a bit easier. And I may not get through to the very top. Who knows? But I decided I had to live as . . . as I am.' He paused. 'You don't have to, I'll keep schtum.' Mike Harter blushed, unbecomingly, and he gave him a small, tight smile. 'We'd better get on, the driver will be wondering.'

* * *

'Matt. Matthew.'

He looked up, startled. He was painstakingly tidying up files and had heard nothing on the stairs. 'Alex, you OK?'

'Yes, yes.' She was pale with excitement, the red hair standing away from her face. 'I've just . . . Matt, would it . . . I must . . .'

'Here. Sit down. Get your breath.'

She sank into the other chair and gazed at him, wide-eyed. 'Antony Williams' assistant rang.'

'The dancer bloke?'

'Yes. He wants me to come to class with his company.' On the face of it this invitation should not have turned the self-possessed Alex into this incoherent, shiny-eyed daftie.

'Why?'

'Oh, *Matt*. It's the way he recruits for the company. He invites people to class to see if — well, I suppose to see if they can keep up. And can pick up instructions.' She looked at him, twisting her hands with excitement.

'So when is this class?'

It was as if a light had been switched off. She stopped fidgeting and her hair fell into straight lines round her face. 'Well, you see . . .'

'Alex. When?'

'Tomorrow morning. At 9.30.'

He considered her severely. 'It'd better be a dentist.'

'What? Oh, Matt. Oh yes, could it be? Won't Peter be furious? I mean you're paying me such a lot.'

Feeling about sixty years old, he patted her shoulder. 'You go and give it a try. Wait a minute.' He sat on the edge of his desk. 'What happens if he offers you a job? This Williams?'

She looked up at him, eyes wide, mouth turned down.

'I see. You'd cast Graebner Associates aside like a worn-out glove.'

'It doesn't work like that. He's got a very small company and he takes on extra people for tours or particular performances. If . . . if everything went right and they liked me, I might get on a list of people he might ask. If I could manage to keep fit enough . . .'

'Lots of ifs.'

'That's why I went to university. Too many of them. But if . . .'

'You'd be off with the raggle-taggle gypsies, oh.' He gazed at her, baffled. 'What would you be paid?'

'Much less than here, and no job security.' She got up from the chair and discharged energy by reordering his careful arrangement of chair, plant and waste-paper basket. 'And rotten places to stay and not enough to eat,' she added, in the tones of one reporting a sighting of the Holy Grail. He sat still, watching her, ravishingly pretty, high as a kite with a joy he could recognise but not share.

'Matt, be pleased for me.'

'I am,' he lied, stolidly. 'It's six o'clock, and you need to eat if you've got all this tomorrow. Come on, I'll buy.'

She stopped in a patch of evening sun. 'I have to go to the studio. I haven't danced today, I have to do a class.'

He gritted his teeth. 'What time's the class? 6.30. Right. I'll pick you up afterwards and we'll eat. Go on, get off.'

* * *

'Francesca. It's Giles's father on the phone.'

'Ah. Oh.' Francesca was dismayed. This is too difficult, she thought resentfully, I'm pregnant — then pulled herself together. Life — and other people's worries — did not stop because she was going to have a baby. She bent to William who was playing under the table but remembered that picking him up had abruptly become beyond her and opened her mouth to call to Susannah and suggest that an early bath would be a good idea. On second thoughts she left her son where he was and reached for the phone extension; this conversation could be awkward and William could reliably be expected to break it up, seeing his mother's attention distracted.

'Mrs McLeish, I need help.'

A plea to which women of every nationality had no doubt responded eagerly, she thought, and made a non-committal noise. There was a slight, discommoded pause, but the pressure of need drove him on. 'You are . . . you do know, I think, that it turns out Giles was not the father — could not have been the father of Miss Roberts' child.'

'I do. My husband would not normally have discussed details of any case,' she added conscientiously, 'but what with Jamie's involvement . . .'

'Of course. I'm very relieved, of course, and so is Giles.'

'Yes,' she said, reaching out a hand to help William perch awkwardly on her non-existent lap. 'Well, you must be.'

'But I can't get him to go back to school. And I think he ought to go, he loves that place and I really don't think he needs to feel . . . well . . . shut out of paradise.'

William rose precariously and, standing on her knees, clasped her warmly round the neck. She was all too clearly on borrowed time.

'Why won't he go?'

'He thinks everybody hates him, because . . . well, because of the young woman. Apparently everyone now knows about the affair and his closest associates apparently blame him for her death.'

'If we're talking about Jamie I believe he has now seen that it is not reasonable to put the blame on Giles. Jamie is back at school by the way, went yesterday.'

'Ah.' There was a pause in which she could feel him trying to formulate an unreasonable request, probably involving her coaxing Giles to be brave and sensible. Her own son, a wild glint in his eye, reached for the phone, unbalancing himself and threatening to tip both of them over.

'Sir Andrew,' she said, transferring Will's grip to her hair, 'Giles is going to have to resign himself to accepting some censure for getting sexually involved with a vulnerable girl and then not being able to cope. But he wasn't the father. He must go back. Tell you why,' she said, suddenly seeing it, 'the school actually needs him, they're in trouble all the way round, a really good end of term show with a star like him could only help.'

Will was trampling steadily, determined to get her attention, and she decided he really was entitled to it. 'Ring the headmaster,' she urged, her natural authority returning in a rush, 'and see indeed if there is anything you can offer to make everyone feel better. No, not cash. Go and help them yourself. Take all your musical friends down for the concert. Some show of support?' She listened to the silence at the end of the phone and understood that well-meant and sound advice was not quite hitting the spot.

'The trouble is,' Andrew Quentin said, heavily, 'the trouble *is* that he doesn't seem to . . . can't . . . well, can't manage to sing. I tried to rehearse with him, to take our minds off the whole thing, you know, and he just blew up. He started and just couldn't go on.'

'Mm.' Francesca relented, unable to ignore the problems of a boy she had taught. 'He's not ill? It's not something simple like a cold?'

'No. I got our doctor to have a look at him, with his consent. He's very upset about not being able to sing.' There was a pause, charged with impatience. 'Could I bring him round to you? I know your husband's . . . but now we know Giles wasn't the father.'

'He thought he was,' she said, before she had thought.

'You don't think . . . your husband doesn't . . . ?'

'I have no views on any of my husband's cases,' she said, cursing herself for speaking her thoughts aloud. 'I am thinking about what to do about a boy who is unable to do what he always found so easy.'

'Have you had any previous experience? Sorry, I'm used to grown-up singers who have ways of getting over anxiety or whatever this is. Does this happen to young singers?'

'One of my brothers suffers from stage fright and always has. Which is of course only acute anxiety. But these days Tristram can sing his way through it.' She considered the point. 'Tris is an opera singer, so he has a lot of support from a whole cast. And he's twenty-nine.' She thought about Giles Quentin, who had always been an absolutely confident machine, like her other singer brother Perry. If Giles was now silenced the cause was emotional and the problem was unlikely to be improved by banging on at it. She said as much to Andrew Quentin, who assented, doubtfully. She could feel him drawing breath to persuade her to do something, anything, and sighed. This vastly experienced topflight musician would never have got so worked up about any other young singer, no matter what depended on his abilities. 'Sir Andrew,' she said, mustering her strength. 'I don't think pushing Giles is going to work, and I'm sure he's miserable with nothing to do but worry about his voice. Get him back to school. He's in the choir, isn't he? He'll probably find he can sing with other people — Tristram always could, no matter how anxious he was — and that will help him sing solo again.' She listened to the unconvinced silence. 'Try it, Sir Andrew. Give Giles my love and tell him I'm a bit immovable, but he can come up any day if he thinks it will help. He'll be better at school.' Her own son was pulling her hair harder than ever. 'I'm sorry, I have to bath a child.'

She rang off, firmly, and escorted William to accompany her for a joint bath which was one of their favourite activities and from which they emerged, pink and cheerful, after forty minutes.

CHAPTER 11

Thursday, 6th July

'Sir? Mr Louis Roberts' solicitor on the telephone for you. His name is Jackson.'

McLeish, on his first cup of coffee, and with the daily meeting due to start in two minutes, decided it was less trouble to take this call.

'Detective Chief Superintendent McLeish,' he said, and listened patiently while the man introduced himself and his firm and fished for mutual acquaintances.

'What can I do for you, Mr Jackson?' he asked as soon as he reasonably could.

'Well. Well, I understand you took a sample of blood from my client.'

'Indeed. With his consent.'

'As you know — well, you saw him earlier in the week, I understand — he is heavily sedated and not at all himself.'

'Yes.' The monosyllable spurred the other man to get to the point, as it was meant to.

'Neither of us can now understand why a blood sample was required.'

'As I explained at the time, it is for DNA testing. We have taken samples so far from all the men, family and outsiders, known to be close to the deceased. She was about three months pregnant, as I am sure Mr Roberts will have told you.'

'But . . . but he's her father. You cannot — well, not really have thought . . .' The man's voice trailed away, and McLeish remembered that the distinguished firm in which he was a partner were primarily commercial lawyers.

'It is routine for us to test all men in the immediate family in a case like this.'

There was a long, thoughtful pause. 'Yes, well, I seem to have been leading a sheltered life, Chief Superintendent. When do you expect . . . well, when do you expect to know who fathered the baby? I'm sorry, I assumed it was the young man she had been seeing . . .' Another pause. 'I wish Mr Roberts had asked me to be present when you saw him. But since I wasn't, is it possible to have a transcript of your conversation? You do tape them?'

'We do, and you shall, with Mr Roberts' consent.'

'Thank you. Thank you indeed.'

The man had sounded surprised, McLeish reflected as he put the phone down, as if he had expected no co-operation at all from the police. A real criminal lawyer would have known how tied by the rules the police now were, and how careful not to prejudice their chances of success in court.

He rose to go through to the team meeting just as the phone rang again.

'Dr Jamieson, sir.'

He seized the phone. 'You got the test, Doc?'

'Yes.'

'And?'

'None of the people we've tested so far is the father. Not — hang on — the Messrs Willis, Miles Brett, Quentin père, or fils, nor Mr Miller. Nor Mr Roberts.'

'That's a relief. He was her father after all.' And, as he did not say, it was a huge relief that Jamie was not involved.

'Now there's another reason I wanted to talk to you. Mr Roberts cannot possibly have been the father of the young woman I have in my mortuary. We tested her DNA, of course, as well as the foetus's. Mr Roberts wasn't her father or the foetus's grandfather.'

'What? Doc, sorry, but you — we — couldn't have got the samples mixed, could we?'

'I thought of that. And none of the men who provided the other samples could possibly have been her father either. Quite different patterns.'

McLeish stared out of his window, thinking hard. 'I've missed something,' he said. 'She must have been adopted and I've just not picked it up. Wait a minute. Does she have her mother's DNA — oh no, we didn't take tests from any of the women because we were looking for a father. I'll just have to ask.'

'Mm. Did you know that in *all* medical investigations about eleven per cent of the population surveyed turn out not to be the children of the fathers who registered them as theirs?'

'There's a sobering thought.'

'Just bear it in mind. The women are the only ones who really know. *We're* the underprivileged sex, John.'

Just for a moment, as he put the phone down, McLeish looked at the photograph of Francesca and William on his desk. His wife's face, eyes deep-set, long-nosed, needing only a helmet to place it in the Bayeux Tapestry, looked seriously back, while Wills strained out of her arms towards the photographer, blond, hefty and, even he could see, the image of himself as a baby, nothing like Francesca at all. He laughed back at his son and went off to the meeting to share the latest disconcerting news.

* * *

The Chairman of Trustees sat back, not so much ashen as a strange greenish colour, and Nick Lewis wondered about his heart. Another death would be all they needed, he thought, rising to offer a second cup of tea. The man seized it, drank, spluttered, recovered his colour and gazed at him.

'They wanted to do these tests on the whole school, Headmaster?'

'Only the boys. And only those who have reached puberty.' He gazed at his Chairman, unkindly pleased to see the man distressed, then relented. 'Then they remembered that the only possible candidates for the murder had to have been guests at the Quentin party.'

'Thank God for small mercies. How many does *that* make?'

'I need to check, but I believe only six of the Six Senior young men were there and none of the Six Junior. Two of those were Jamie Miles Brett and Giles Quentin, leaving only four to test. And I intend to talk to them when I've checked with Andrew Quentin that these were the only Faraday boys at the party.'

The Chairman finished his tea, colour slowly returning to normal. 'Keep me posted, won't you? And if you feel that . . . that I could be useful with kids or parents . . . well, just call on me.'

Nick rose, courteously, to see him out, and the man turned at the door. 'I'm very sorry you decided to resign. I should have controlled that particular meeting better.'

'It's time I went,' he said steadily. 'I'll miss the kids but I am — well, someone is — needed where I'm going.'

'Can you tell me?'

'I can now, but in confidence. South Africa. A school for orphans. Mostly children whose parents died in the townships. They are eleven-year-olds, but a lot can't read or write.'

The Chairman looked at him soberly. 'Nice quiet job for your retirement.'

'That's it. But first I must see us through this.' He glanced out of the window; the real heat had gone out of the sun and it was a perfect summer evening, with birds singing in the bushes round the window. 'I've just got time to see the boys before assembly this evening.'

* * *

Finding Vivienne Willis had proved difficult and John McLeish finally caught up with her at 6.30 in her office. He had been surprised to find her at work, rather than with her husband at Faraday's, only four days after the death of her only child. It was, however, useful to be able to talk to her on his way home rather than making the journey to Dorset.

He and Kevin Camberton waited for ten minutes in the reception area on the fifteenth floor, cheered only marginally by a spectacular view along the river to St Paul's. It was the sort of place that could only leave two hard-working policemen dissatisfied with their cramped, utilitarian working surroundings. Everything here was new and designed. The tea, brought by a quiet man in uniform, was served in bone china cups, and the newspapers were fresh and plentiful, topped off with three copies of the *Evening Standard*.

'I'm sorry.' Vivienne Willis appeared in the doorway, immaculate in a pale grey suit, her black hair newly set, and both policemen considered her. She looked worn, and not wholly at ease, but not reduced by grief or dazed, or lost in her own world, or any of the reactions they had seen from parents who had suffered the loss of a child. She led them to another expensive room, this time with a long table which could have accommodated twenty. Mineral water and orange juice were brought by the same quiet uniformed man and the party settled itself awkwardly in the middle of the table, Vivienne Willis facing across to the two of them. The man serving the drinks arranged the blinds so that the slanting evening sun did not dazzle them, and left silently.

'How can I help you?'

McLeish and Camberton had agreed that Mrs Willis would have had time to commit the murder. BT had confirmed that her Japanese call had taken twelve minutes, terminating at 10.58 p.m. She had not reappeared until 11.20, because she had been writing up notes, which indeed she had produced, but it would have been difficult to judge whether she had written them as she listened on the phone, or hours afterwards. But equally there was no apparent reason why this cool, self-contained woman should have wished to eliminate her own daughter.

'We have found a rather puzzling anomaly, which we hoped you could explain,' McLeish said, stolidly. Nothing in Vivienne Willis's face moved, but there was suddenly tension in the room between them, and he waited a beat before going on. 'You know that we have taken blood samples from family and male friends of Catriona's to try to determine the father of the child she was carrying.'

Vivienne Willis nodded, lips tightening. 'Have you the results?' She was very pale, and McLeish let a beat elapse.

'No one tested so far could have been the father of the child.'

The blood rushed back to her face and her shoulders sagged. '*What* a relief.' She looked at him. 'I didn't mean . . .' He waited for her to explain what she had not meant, but she had herself in hand. 'What a relief for the school; Roland says the atmosphere is absolutely terrible.' She coughed, and found a handkerchief. 'Have you told him? I haven't looked at my messages.'

'Someone is doing that now. For all the men we tested.'

'Well, of course he won't have been worried personally.' She was still flushed. 'But he is deputy head and . . .' She stopped, visibly deciding to calm down, and reached for some more coffee, forgetting to offer them any.

'We will have now to test more widely.'

'Ah. Of course you will. Oh. At the school?'

'Yes. Can you suggest which of her friends or acquaintance it might have been?'

'She spent a lot of time with Jamie Miles Brett. I never thought it was him. I thought it was Giles of course. Well, so did he . . . ? They go round in flocks, like starlings,' she said, staring out of the window, thinking about it. 'I'm not . . . not very good at all at this, but Roland — my husband — is infinitely hospitable. There are always lumpen teenagers in the kitchen — he's a housemaster and while I'm not much use as a housemaster's wife, I keep the place stocked up so they can eat the rubbish they prefer. Deep frozen pizza and awful hamburgers.' She looked bleakly into her memories. 'No. I couldn't suggest anyone in particular — well, I certainly didn't know at the time that she had slept with Giles Quentin, who has always been much courted. She stays with her father — with Louis — in the holidays and God alone knows what she gets up to. I'm sorry, I'm afraid that's not very helpful.' She looked at them helplessly, and McLeish let the silence stretch.

'I said that the tests had thrown up an anomaly.' She knows what's coming, he thought, watching her flinch, and she's been hoping it would go away if she talked enough. 'We tested Mr Louis Roberts as a matter of routine.'

'And you found that he isn't — wasn't — Catriona's father.'

'Yes.'

She heaved a long, painful sigh. 'I didn't know for years and years. Well, I never wanted to know, I always hoped she would . . . It was an affair, of course, with someone who was rather the same physical type as Louis. When I realised I was pregnant I panicked, then I decided that it had — well, at least a fifty-fifty chance of being Louis's baby. We'd been married for a couple of years and I was going to assume it was and not get in a state about it.'

'When did you find out . . . that Catriona wasn't? Was it a DNA test?'

'No, it was . . . easier than that. She needed blood after one of these wrist-cutting episodes, and they were short of her group. She is AB. I am O, so that wasn't going to help. They asked about her father and I remembered . . . I always knew of course, but I'd not — well, put two and two together . . . that he is O too. It was like getting kicked in the stomach. I knew, of course I knew that it isn't possible for two Group O people to have a child with AB. Louis, thank God, was out of the country, so they got some of the right blood from the next county and that was OK.' She had gone very red with remembered pain and was scrabbling in her bag.

'Does Mr Roberts know?'

'No.' There was a long pause. 'And I hope he needn't. It would be the final . . . well, the worst news for him.'

The two policemen had thought their way through this one and had agreed that no undertakings could be offered, and McLeish said as much.

'Does Catriona's biological father know? That he is or might be her father.'

'I never told him. He was married himself. The affair broke up. He was going to Australia and he went before I needed to tell anyone I was pregnant. Anyway, I thought — I hoped — that she was Louis's daughter. It was a stupid affair.' Her face crumpled and they waited while she got herself under control. 'Oh God, you make one insane mistake and it never leaves you, it just haunts you.'

That is only true, McLeish thought, if the mistake you made has physical consequences, like a baby. Anything else really, you can fix or outgrow, or emigrate away from, but it was not the moment to share this perception with the weeping woman in front of him.

'We're not in the business of making people's grief gratuitously worse.'

'He — Louis — has got other children.'

And this woman had none; he understood that although the child she had had been a worry and a burden, she saw what might have been and felt the loss.

'Roland is distraught. He loved her, at least she had *that* even if I wasn't . . . if I didn't . . .' She abandoned any attempt to finish that sentence and started to weep in earnest, so that he terminated the interview, sent Camberton off to telephone Roland Willis and left her in the custody of a colleague, who was grimly prepared either to take her back to her husband or to drive her home to Dorset, whichever seemed most useful.

* * *

'She was relieved,' McLeish said to his assistant. He and Kevin Camberton were in the back of a police car being whisked back to New Scotland Yard.

'Sorry?'

'That the tests had exonerated her husband.'

'Oh that, yes.' Camberton drew a careful breath. 'Wouldn't anyone be?'

A useful reminder, McLeish agreed, mentally. Contented married men, as he was, were in danger of forgetting that sex was a primal force, kept in check only by a pretty clear understanding among grown-ups of its consequences. He considered his DI; Kevin Camberton was probably in a better position to take a detached view of all this than he was.

'You don't think she had cause to worry?'

'She's very nervy, isn't she?'

'Yes, that's true. Up and down.'

'The sort, I thought, who would work herself into a state about — well — things she needn't. Also, John, she had something real to worry about. She knew we'd get on to the fact that Louis Roberts wasn't the kid's father.'

Yes, McLeish conceded; that trouble was real. 'We need to talk to Mr Roberts again,' he said.

* * *

Nick Lewis ate his way silently through overboiled bits of chicken and watery vegetables, followed by rhubarb and custard. Institutional food was always variable, but this evening the cuisine seemed to have reached a new low. He glanced round him; there was of course no staff table, pupils and teachers queued together and ate together, but on this difficult day his most senior staff had clustered around him for protection, though whether for him or for themselves was not clear. The four boys he had talked to, collectively, just before dinner were sitting at a neighbouring table, silent, picking at their food, and looking anywhere but at each other. It had not been an easy meeting. He had explained that the father of Catriona's child had not been identified from the tests so far carried out, and that the police would want to test more widely, starting for obvious reasons with those of Catriona's school friends who had been at the party. He had confirmed, in answer to a tentative question, that both Giles Quentin and Jamie Miles Brett had been tested.

He watched the four boys, sipping a much too strong Nescafé as he did so. Nothing could look more downcast than the Teenage Boy struggling with some unpalatable piece of Real Life. The Faraday boys did not strive for sartorial elegance at the best of times, but this group was particularly unkempt, hair apparently uncombed for months, far too many large feet, inert in huge, stuffed-looking trainers. They had all four looked guilty and anxious and sullen throughout his painstaking explanation, but that was standard Teenage Boy and it was impossible to tell whether one of them was concealing anything. Damien Fry had looked particularly uneasy and suddenly very young and thin, but it was his second scare this term; Nick himself, Damien's housemaster and year tutor had all, necessarily, taken a very heavy-handed approach to the boy's earlier experiment with drugs.

Contrary to practice, when he arrived back at his house, he allowed himself a stiff whisky, and the comforting warmth was still with him as the telephone shrilled in his study, indicating school rather than personal business. In the whisky-induced glow he forgot to be apprehensive and picked it up, being immediately made anxious by Andrew Quentin's voice. 'Giles is a bit subdued, naturally, but he seems to be all right. Yes, he was at choir rehearsal.' He listened to the authoritative voice, sounding uncharacteristically tentative. 'Well, Andrew, we should be delighted to have you. A great treat for us.' And one that he might well not have postponed till Giles's last week at school but looking at gift horses too closely was not useful in these circumstances. The presence of the great Andrew Quentin could only add lustre to the school show.

'There might be some publicity . . . of the sort that you would not welcome, I have to say,' Andrew Quentin warned, sounding anxious. 'Because of the tragedy — I mean you might rather, well, not draw attention to the show.' There was an uneasy pause. 'I'm trying to help, Nick, and support my boy and the school, but I do see it could be counter-productive, so . . .'

'I'd like very much to have you, Andrew. And Giles is a member of this school and I want him in the show, whatever the situation. I agree it would be sensible to see where we are again in a day or so? It seems to be one new shock per day at the moment.'

'And you don't feel we are at the end yet? Well, we can't be, can we? Until the police find who . . . who did this. We'll talk again soon. Thank you for understanding. I'm sorry we didn't meet yesterday. I drove Giles back but you weren't around.'

The first time *that* had ever happened too, he reflected, putting the phone down. Giles Quentin had hitherto been returned to school by a variety of secretaries, drivers, assistants, or chauffeur-driven car services, but never by his father. Still, that was true of many of the children; there were many busy and distinguished parents who delegated the routine tasks of child-rearing. And in many cases some of the most important bits as well, not necessarily out of malice but because the pressures of being rich and successful left not enough room for the children they had all presumably wanted so much. It was a conundrum with which all boarding-school heads were familiar.

Ten minutes later, he walked across the sunny gardens to the hall for assembly. This was to be a special event; normally the whole school attended but he had specified that only Six Junior and Six Senior boys and girls be present. He had decided that thirteen- to fifteen-year-olds were not an appropriate audience for what he had to say. He sat down and looked at his children with affection. He had changed into a decent jacket; it wasn't in the statutes, but from time immemorial the tradition at Faraday's required that for formal assembly teachers and pupils got into shirts and ties for the men and boys and skirts for the women and girls. The pupils adhered to the letter rather than the spirit. The boys would start out in the Thirds, at thirteen, with a proper tie conscientiously provided by parents in accordance with the school list. By the time they reached the heights of the Sixths, they wore ancient bow ties, rescued from under beds and tied insecurely, or stringy mutilated prep-school ties. The girls' skirts were equally diverse; two German girls, sent to improve their English to Eurocrat standard, had started out wearing the decent grey flannel skirts their middle-class German mothers had known would be appropriate for an English school in the country. After a couple of weeks, Gertrud had taken eighteen inches off hers and was now wearing a grey flannel bandage around the hips while Silke had quite transformed her grey flannel pleats by slicing the length of every third pleat, converting it into a grass skirt suitable for the English weather.

The tradition was that staff sat with the students and all were at the same level. His staff were there in force as he had asked, leaving only just enough people to look after the other three year groups racketing about in the summer evening. He nodded to Roland Willis and Susie Miller, who were close to him on either side. He stood up and waited for silence, which he got within seconds. The whole group, a hundred and sixty give or take the odd child, were on edge, but there was no way of dispersing tension without ploughing on. He nodded to Giles Quentin and Jamie Miles Brett, both unexpectedly formally attired in respectable jackets and real ties. They were sitting in a group with the four boys he had seen before supper and looked sombre.

'I have spoken to you all before about Catriona's death.' About half his audience looked covertly over to the little group round Giles and Jamie. The news had got round, evidently. Well, that was inevitable. 'I have to tell you that the police believe that Catriona did not commit suicide but was killed, by someone else.' A girl gave a little hastily suppressed scream, and her nearest neighbours patted her protectively. He ploughed on, over a buzz. 'Catriona, when she died, was pregnant, probably about three months.' This elicited less reaction; that news had obviously been well disseminated on the school's gossip net. 'In a case like this, the police need to know who might have been the father and have therefore sought blood tests from some of the men closest to her. So far none of the men tested could have been the father.' There was a murmur of sound, and heads turned to Jamie's group. He waited, letting them think about it. 'As the next step, the police want to take blood tests from all other male Faraday students who were at the party Catriona attended last Saturday.' That did get a reaction; students of seventeen and eighteen had mostly reached a level where they perceived that people could act out of character, that things could go spectacularly and unexpectedly wrong, where sex was involved. Nick waited for them to settle down.

'Giles and Jamie have already been tested.' A rustle of surprise, and everyone tried not to look at the group. 'Damien, Francis, Alex and John B., who were also at Sir Andrew Quentin's party, have now been asked to give samples.' No one quite knew how to react to this and they all looked at him hopefully for guidance. 'Other young men here may also be asked as this investigation goes on.' Every boy in the room shifted uneasily; such is the level of sexual anxiety among teenagers, he thought, with pity. He wasn't going to invite questions or urge co-operation with the police; if one of his boys was a murderer he must pay the price, but it was not possible for him to push a pupil of his on to his doom. He let a pause elapse and changed gear. 'In the middle of all this there is the school show.' A small eruption of nervous giggles, which he acknowledged with a smile, attended this pronouncement. 'And I have very pleasant news for the musicians among you. Sir Andrew Quentin will be coming to help with rehearsals.' He glanced at Jamie and saw from his face that he had not known, although he had accepted that Giles would sing if he could get his voice back. 'What I need to discuss with all of you, however, are the arrangements surrounding the show without which no one will get tea, and there will be disgruntled parents everywhere. The success of the show has always depended very heavily on the sixth form; for Six Senior it is your final chore for the school.' This raised a laugh, and he was able to take the meeting through a subdued but workmanlike discussion of arrangements for notices, lavatories, and staffing of enquiry points. The group warmed up as it got going and so did he. After half an hour he had difficulty not laughing aloud as the beautiful sixteen-year-old Jason, by popular vote the most troublesome child ever as a thirteen-year-old, observed disapprovingly that the little Thirds could not be relied on to control the flow of parents through Sculpture without the supervision of some responsible person such as himself. Ah well, a success there anyway, he thought, trying to catch Roland Willis's eye. Poor Roland, he thought, not even able to rejoice in the result of the work he put in on Jason, now converted to a cheerful, responsible sixth-former.

He looked at his watch and glanced out of the window. It was 9.15 and as instructed the Thirds, Fourths and Fifths had been swept off to their boarding-houses so that they could not fall on friends or mentors in the Sixth and keep them all awake half the night. It was time to go and he said as much. While the kids collected themselves and their possessions his staff lined up beside him; it was another Faraday rule that staff shook hands with every child after assembly. When you had the full four hundred you could sympathise with the Queen, but all agreed that this ceremony was an invaluable diagnostic tool, enabling staff to take the general temperature of each child. A distressed or anxious kid simply could not manage to shake hands with all thirty of the sixth-form staff without revealing their state by the end of the routine.

He had stationed himself at the end of the row of staff, as he did when no one else was claiming that spot. Giles passed, managing to say a calm goodnight, then Jamie, worn, unhappy, but in control, looking him in the eye and wishing him goodnight, then several girls, bursting to get away from the adults and share their conclusions. Next were the four boys he had seen before supper. John B., a cheerful musician, passed him, seeming only momentarily sobered. Alex and Francis looked at him rather carefully, but seemed not to want to speak. Then, hustling close to them came Damien, head bent, hand outstretched, trying to brush through quickly. He closed both hands on Damien's and felt the boy pull away.

'Damien.'

The boy's shoulders heaved and he could not look up.

'We'll talk afterwards. Go over to my house and ask Alice to give you coffee — I'll be along soon.' His housekeeper, he knew, would keep Damien by her until he got home, having discharged his duty to the other children, and he forced his concentration back to having a careful look at the rest of his flock. Fifteen minutes later he pushed open his own back door and found Damien, pale and looking about twelve years old, but head up and able to meet his eyes. Alice nodded to him and left the room quietly, shutting the door after her. He sat down, trying not to exhale in relief; Damien had never been likely casting for a murderer and it was now clear that whatever was worrying him it was not that.

'Sir. Nick. I did . . . well . . . go out with Catriona.' He blushed scarlet. 'Just once. In the holidays.'

'Just once,' he said neutrally.

'It was at a party.' The boy looked at his cup, the pale child's face still scarlet.

'Had you ever before? Been with a girl?'

'Yes. No. Not properly. Just . . . well, not properly.'

'Not getting inside.'

'No.'

'Why only just the once, with Catriona? Was it not a success? It sometimes isn't, of course.'

The boy was drinking coffee in order not to look at him, flushed with embarrassment, 'It was a success for me. I . . . well, I felt . . .' He put his cup down. 'I rang her up the next day but she wasn't there, or that's what her mother said. I did try again, but . . . but I thought perhaps she didn't . . . hadn't . . .'

'Hadn't meant to start a relationship. Very possible, sort of mistake women make as well as men. Bad luck.' He pushed a box of Kleenex towards the boy; no Faraday child carried a handkerchief despite staff urgings.

'I was . . . well, a bit upset.'

'That happens. Don't be distressed, wait a bit. You'll find girls at Oxford who will want to go out with you.'

'But I could . . . I mean, the baby.'

'Oh yes, I'm afraid you could. It's happened to lots of people on their first shot. Now you know why we expel for it.'

He got a watery embarrassed grin. 'What do I do?'

'Tell the police, take the test, then we'll know.'

'I didn't . . . I mean I wouldn't . . . have hurt her. She never even told me she was pregnant.'

She had hoped, poor child, that it was Giles Quentin's, he thought, sadly.

'Tell the police, Damien. The innocent have nothing to fear. We'll ring them up now.'

CHAPTER 12

Friday, 7th July

Kevin Camberton was deeply annoyed with life and was only just managing not to take it out on DS Black. At the team meeting that morning he had made an impassioned case for Piers Miller as Catriona's murderer but failed completely to get John McLeish's endorsement for his preferred course of action, which was to get Piers Miller in and sweat him till he broke. Within the rules of evidence of course. McLeish had done nothing to justify his formidable reputation; he had looked uncomfortable and said he thought they didn't know enough yet about everyone in the case, and new facts kept coming to light. *That* was true, of course, he reflected, as the car swept them towards the Mrs Janie Hopkins with whom Louis Roberts had deposed he had been talking on the phone from sometime before eleven to sometime after it on the Saturday night. It was certainly important to make sure that all the loose ends got tied up so that no clever counsel could deflect the case by throwing suspicion on other members of the group surrounding Catriona Roberts. So he would go doggedly on until there was no one left but Mr Miller, and then John McLeish would have to agree to Miller being arrested.

With his mind cleared, Camberton thought about the forthcoming interview.

'Michelle, did you get the stuff from BT?'

'It's Friday, Kevin, thank God,' she said, holding the phone to her ear in case anyone at BT was at home, and he understood he had been letting his feelings show.

'I know,' he said. 'And Miller'll have the weekend to recoup himself and get himself together.'

'Or to worry himself silly,' she pointed out. 'Ah. Yes, thank you.' She listened. 'That was quick — I'm sorry, I was called away and didn't check my fax. Would you . . . ? Thank you. From 10.50 p.m. to 11.01. And no second call? Nothing else that night. Thank you.' She put the phone down and they looked at each other. 'Leaves him in the frame. Just. He could have done it after eleven.'

'Just after talking to his mistress?'

'Maybe we're going to find she's Lady Macbeth. Urged him on.'

The woman who opened the door to them was not a very likely candidate for Lady Macbeth. Mrs Hopkins was pleasant looking with elegantly streaked blond hair, a figure well under control, and a brisk manner. She bade them come in but not before inspecting both their warrant cards.

'Now, you don't think Louis had anything to do with this, surely?' she said, sitting down on a well-stuffed sofa.

There'd been money spent, Camberton thought. It was a neat small house but expensively furnished, with a lot of photographs around but no pictures. And their hostess had invested carefully in her own appearance; immaculate hair, careful make-up and short polished nails, the whole encased in an expensive and flattering beige suit in which she looked cool and elegant on this hot day. What he had not expected was that she was in her fifties, probably older than Louis Roberts, and a great deal older than Amanda Roberts. More poised too; the one time he had seen Amanda Roberts, with John McLeish, he had found her an uncomfortable personality, forceful but not at ease with herself. This woman, by contrast, knew exactly who she was and what she was doing.

'I divorced my husband fifteen years ago,' she was saying, placidly. 'I had just the one shop then — hairdressing shop — and I've got six now. The kids are all grown up and living away.'

Leaving Mum to have her hair done, or at least brushed through, every day at one of her shops and, no doubt, to look for other properties. Had she hoped, perhaps, to take Louis Roberts from his wife? He hesitated, but she forestalled him.

'You want to know about me and Louis? Well, we met, what, two years ago, took to each other and we meet once or twice a week. What? Here usually, yes. No, I don't know what his wife knows about it and I'm not going to ask. I like living on my own, no one to answer to, and if I want a holiday I go with Louis for a few days, or otherwise there's usually some company to find on a cruise.'

He paused, remembering he had issued a conscientious invitation to DS Black to jump in if she wanted to, as she did evidently.

'You know that Mr Roberts was very worried about his daughter?'

'Catriona, you mean? Yes, I did. She worried him silly, little madam.'

'I'm sorry?'

'Well, I'm sorry too, and of course I never met her, but I thought she was pulling all their strings. I had two teenage daughters once and they wouldn't have been allowed to get away with that sort of nonsense.'

Refreshing in a way as an antidote to the universally sympathetic view of the dead girl they had encountered up till now, and he decided to take back the questioning. 'Did Mr Roberts blame himself for her troubles?'

'All the time. Always on about how he shouldn't have left her like that with her mother, and shouldn't have let himself be kept away from her for a year when she was small.'

'Mrs Hopkins,' he said, deciding to get to the main point of the interview, 'Mr Roberts told us he had a telephone conversation with you on Saturday night.'

'Oh, every night when we hadn't seen each other. Unless he couldn't, of course.'

Now that was love or at least dependence. Every night?

'Can you remember at what time this was?'

'Just before eleven. He rings usually just after 10.30.'

'From his house?'

'If she — Amanda — is there, which is little enough during term, he rings on the mobile when he's walking the dog.'

'How long do you think you spoke for, this time? On Saturday.'

'Perhaps ten minutes. He was in someone else's house and using their phone, he didn't want to run up their bills.' He recognised, wryly, his own mother's protective approach to the telephone. 'But BT keep records, surely?'

'Indeed they do, but we needed to make sure . . .'

'That someone hadn't come into my house to use the telephone at eleven o'clock at night?'

'That's right,' he confirmed, with a quick smile, and the atmosphere in the room eased.

'Well, now you know. You can check with BT and stop wondering about Louis, so he can get back to his business. He didn't ring on Sunday night so I rang him at his business on Monday and got what had happened from his secretary. She knows who I am. I didn't want to call him at home, but by, what, Wednesday I was wondering . . . But then he rang, he couldn't talk long but he did tell me you'd be round.'

'And last night?'

'He didn't ring. And I haven't rung him today, before you ask. I'm not getting tangled up with the nurse he's got there.' The cheekbones were scarlet under the careful make-up and her voice had gone up.

'As you said, he probably feels guilty about, well, everything.'

'Bugger that,' Mrs Hopkins' poised calm shattered, and her voice rose to fighting pitch. 'He had nothing to feel guilty about, the bloody kid wasn't even his daughter.' She stopped abruptly and they gazed back at her.

'How do you know?'

'She couldn't have been. Louis found out about two years ago. Her blood group meant she wasn't.' She looked into his face carefully. 'You knew it already. You're tricky, you coppers.'

It would not be appropriate to confirm that, indeed, Catriona had not been Louis Roberts' daughter. But he could not just stop; this woman had a view of Louis Roberts and his family relationships unique in this investigation.

'How did Mr Roberts feel when he . . . Did you discuss it?' DS Black got her mouth open, and he sat back to let her get on with it.

'I met him just after he found out, but we — he didn't tell me till, what, a year ago.' Janie Hopkins was thinking about what she said. 'I know it would have been a shock. But he's a good man, and he couldn't blame Amanda, could he, she was only the kid's stepmother.'

'He must have felt some resentment about his ex-wife, Mrs Willis. Did he talk to her about it?'

'Now there's a funny thing.' Janie Hopkins leant forward, looking, beneath the smart clothes and the immaculate hair, just like one of her own aunties. 'He wouldn't. He said they'd both been playing away at the time and she probably didn't know either. In any case, he thought Catriona had difficulties enough with her mother without throwing all *that* in for her to get in a fuss about.' She paused and thought, hands on her knees. 'And of course he'd always *been* her father, he said he was her father for all purposes and that was that.'

'Did you agree with him? Did you think he was right?' They were suddenly just two women, talking.

'I could see he didn't want to upset her. He was frightened of what she might do. But . . .'

'But?' he asked, sharply, and she looked at him.

'But the kid was such a mess by all accounts, I thought it would be better to have the whole thing out in the open. Kiddies pick things up, you know, without being told and it seemed to me — when I wasn't fed up with hearing about her nonsense — that she knew something wasn't right.' There was a pause while Janie Hopkins stared into the vast bouquet of marguerites that occupied the fireplace space. 'Louis was frightened that she'd top herself or start a hunt for her real father — it could be a bloke who's now in Australia — and upset two families. He's a good man, Louis, I told you. A lot of blokes would have lost it and gone straight round to even an ex-wife and given her a thumping, not thinking about the kid or how everyone was going to get on.' She shifted her gaze from the fireplace. 'But maybe it'd have been better if he had done all of that.'

She made them tea while they got their notes in order, and she shook hands with both of them, holding Michelle's hand for an extra few seconds. 'You married? No? Don't leave it too late.'

He waited stolidly for her to ask him the same question, but she didn't, just looked at him carefully, and wished him well in the investigation.

'She'll be on the dog and bone to Mr Roberts,' he said, holding open the car door for DS Black, a courtesy extended by no other member of the team.

'Yes. Do you want to get to him first?'

'We couldn't. She'll be calling now. But I'll call the Chief — he saw him, he can have another go at him.'

* * *

Susie Miller rounded the corner of the girls' boarding-house, nodding to a mixed lot of Thirds lounging on the grass, and passed thankfully into the private part of the house, and her own kitchen. As head of music she was carrying a heavy load of the work of preparation for the concert, but freed by Jamie's return from the necessity of playing in the orchestra, she now had a two-hour break. Nearly all the singers also played an instrument so it was blessedly impractical to have choir rehearsals at the same time as the orchestra. She stopped, surprised and pleased, to find her husband drinking coffee and writing at the kitchen table. He looked up at her, startled, and she had a brief, disconcerting impression that he did not share her pleasure. She looked at the table for guidance, and his arm moved defensively to cover the papers he was working on.

'Hello. I wasn't expecting you.'

'I can't rehearse the choir or the soloists — they're all in the orchestra,' she said, mechanically reaching for the kettle and opening the fridge in search of the material for an omelette. 'I wasn't quite expecting you either.'

'Too many of my kids are in the orchestra to rehearse Act 3. I really don't know how good this play is going to be.' It was a familiar problem; in a small school all the most talented children were in everything: choir, orchestra, and the Six Senior play. She clattered in the kitchen, breaking eggs into a bowl, waiting for the atmosphere to become less tense, and was rewarded with a heavy sigh.

'Susie, I *am* going to apply after all.'

There was no need to ask what for; every conversation not having to do with music had been on the same subject for several days.

'But you told Nick you'd withdrawn.'

'Well, I've un-withdrawn. They rang me — the search people — and we talked, and I'm doing the full forms. I'm faxing them this afternoon and they're interviewing on Monday.'

'Why did they ring you?'

'The Trustees asked them to. They thought they had better see as many of us as possible, was how they put it.' He looked across the table. 'So I told him all about my past at Melton, I thought I'd better since it is all over a police file by now, and he said he thought they might take a view.'

'A view?'

'He thought the Trustees — or anyone else — might be inclined to feel that an idiocy ten years ago did not disqualify me for ever in the teaching profession.'

'Of course it doesn't,' she said, warmly. She had received an edited version of the story well before they had married but had not been unduly surprised that her handsome husband had indeed engaged in a brief affair with an eighteen-year-old under his charge, being himself only twenty-seven at the time.

'Because — and it only really came to me today — if that stupid affair does mean I'll never get a head's job then I'm going to go off and do something else with my life.'

'What?' she asked, anxiously, seeing herself uprooted.

'I talked about that too — he's a good bloke and he specialises in education. There are jobs in the Inspectorate — I like teaching but wouldn't mind telling someone else how to do it for a change. Or in the teacher training colleges.'

She considered him carefully and recognised that he had made up his mind. He was, she knew, inclined to be headstrong, but he was looking less harassed. He was waiting for her approval, but she could not quite overcome her anxieties. 'Piers . . . you don't think that the . . . that . . .'

'Catriona, you mean?'

'Yes.'

'You don't think I did, do you?'

'No. No, of course not,' she said, hastily. 'I should have seen how much trouble she was in, but . . .'

'But you wonder if I didn't do something silly, like respond to her advances when I was meant to be cramming her Maths A.' He had gone scarlet with rage and she wanted to backtrack, but could not find the words. They waited in silence, looking at each other.

'*Anyone* might have,' she said, baldly, when the silence became intolerable.

'Anyone might have, but I didn't. And if you don't believe me I can't think why I'm still here.' He gathered up his papers with shaking hands and banged out into the sunlight, leaving her with a bowl full of whipped-up eggs.

* * *

Three hundred yards away, Roland Willis was also beating eggs. His wife had managed to get out of bed half an hour before and was sitting, dull-eyed, hair uncombed and dressing-gown carelessly bundled around her. He looked anxiously at the bottles of pills; he had been instructed to make sure she took the prescribed tranquillisers. He would get her to take them with lunch, he decided, and that would be easier.

'Two eggs or three?' he asked, breaking them into a bowl, but she did not rouse herself to answer; he hesitated and cracked three. She had not eaten that day, nor the day before when she had been brought down in a chauffeur-driven car with a harassed colleague in attendance. It was worth doing three eggs for her on the chance that she was hungry and if not he could no doubt finish them. Like most of the rest of the staff he had had a difficult morning, teaching three lessons with Thirds and Fourths, whose education had to continue, then going straight on to a play with the Fives who had just done GCSEs and had to be occupied somehow. Heaven bless the orchestra rehearsal, he thought, without impiety, that took three of his principal actors to play in the violins and the oboes respectively.

He watched as his wife picked at her eggs, then relaxed as he observed that she was actually getting through them, albeit without enthusiasm. He handed her a pill and a glass of water without comment and she took them. By the time she had managed a banana and a small piece of cake, he felt emboldened to speak. 'Darling, I am bidden to interview on Monday.'

'What for?'

'For the head's job.'

She stared at him, colour suddenly flooding back into her face. 'Oh, *Roland*, you didn't withdraw then, after all?'

'No,' he said. 'No, I decided that however . . . however awful I felt over Catriona, it was my last chance to be a head, and I owed it to you to give it a try.' He sat down, clasping her hand and looking earnestly into her face. 'Of course the Trustees could have decided not even to interview me, after this dreadful failure, but . . .'

'Of *course* they were going to interview you.'

'You mean as a courtesy?'

'*No*, don't be silly. If they can't get some flashy outsider you're the obvious person. The kids love you, you know where . . . where everything is and what to do. We must talk about the interview.' She sat up, reaching for her glasses.

'I did — I do — wonder about whether I should be applying. After . . .'

'Catriona. I know. But you *were* good to her. Better than I was.'

He took her in his arms as she wept, messily, down his sweater. After a bit she stopped and found a handkerchief and blew her nose; devoid of make-up, hair all over the place, she looked very different from the bright, impatient, elegant thirty-something person she normally presented to the world.

'Poor Catriona. I should never have had a child, I'm just the opposite of a natural mother. And I'd have been the world's worst granny.' She sniffed wrenchingly. 'And it's very bad luck on you who were a natural father.'

'Oh, I wouldn't say that.' He held her, overwhelmed by tenderness. 'I'm never . . . well, never sure . . .' He wept too, suddenly and it was she who comforted him.

'Well,' she said, suddenly brisk, and getting up to put the kettle on, 'Monday, you said.' She turned and considered him. 'Is your suit clean?' There was a long pause while they stared at each other. 'Oh, I . . . sent it to the cleaners, but . . .'

'I couldn't bear to wear it ever again.'

'Darling, no . . . of course. Your other suit . . . no, well.' They both contemplated his other suit which had done sterling duty for twenty years, winter and summer. 'We need to go out and get you one, and a couple of shirts and ties,' she said, sitting up and pushing a hand through her hair. 'And you don't have time to go to London, *I* know.' She reached for the telephone and he watched as she assembled a client who was going to arrange for them to be received, as royalty, in the Shaftesbury branch of Just Men at 9 a.m. on Saturday, at which, yes indeed, several suits in the correct size would be available. She turned a smiling face to him, pleased with herself, and he kissed her, marvelling at the speed of her recovery.

'I must have a shower and a hair wash,' she said, busily, gazing at her reflection in the small kitchen mirror. She caught his eye. 'It isn't going to help anything to have me drooping about, is it? And you deserve this job. It's something about turning a tragedy into a new beginning, isn't it?'

'Yes,' he agreed, painfully. 'Yes. We must try to do that.' He looked at his watch. 'I've got an hour, then there's the rehearsal, but . . .'

'I'm absolutely fine now.'

This meant he need not impose further on the wife of a colleague in the junior school, he thought gratefully, waiting until his wife had gone upstairs to the bathroom, before ringing up to pass on the good news.

* * *

Matt Sutherland was finding he could not settle to his work. He had, conscientiously, tidied the Quentin file so that he could lay his hands instantly on copies of Giles's statements to the police. His client was not in the clear, but the police had been content that he went back to school and had asked only that he not go abroad. That could become a problem, because Andrew Quentin had plans to take his son to Berlin for a concert and the Millers had planned a holiday after that in France, but there was no point in seeking police consent until the school term had ended the following week.

None of this of course was critical, but it was the only work he could manage to do. He needed, he told himself, to know whether he had a proper assistant for the next four weeks, or part of a dance troupe. And Alex was late; this triple-damned class/audition had been due to last from nine to 10.30 and it was now 12.30, and it should not have taken two hours for the girl to have a shower and get the Tube back to her legal duties. He heard light feet on the stairs, seized a file and stared at it sternly, feeling the draft of cool air as his door opened.

'Matt?'

He turned to her, trying to look as if he had been interrupted in a major legal task, and blinked. In the shaft of dusty sun stood a red-haired boy, who on second blink turned into Alex with totally different hair. She walked towards him, faltering in the teeth of his transfixed stare, and turned self-consciously to show him her profile.

'I needed a change,' she said, turning to look him in the eye. 'It's too difficult washing long hair every day.'

He sat, stunned into silence, looking at her. Cut short, her hair sprang up from her forehead, thicker and wavier than when it was long. It was sleek and tidy at the sides and, cut short, revealed fully the delicacy of the features and the elegant freckled pallor of her skin.

'Do you like it?' she asked, obviously unnerved by his unmoving gaze.

'Yes.' He couldn't seem to say anything else, and she looked at him anxiously. 'Yes, I love it. But I thought you'd be back earlier.'

'I would have, but . . . but . . .' She took a deep breath. 'All the girls had short hair and, just . . . looked different, so I asked one of them and she told me . . . well, this chap — Laurent, he's French . . . in the West End. He said he'd fit me in, so he cut my hair.' She wanted for him to speak, but he was watching the wide mouth which looked delicate and gamine under the new haircut. 'He said to leave the colour for the moment.'

'Good God, what was he going to do with it?' She was relieved, he saw, to find him able to speak.

'Put streaks in it. Or put something on it to make it redder.'

'No.'

'That's what I thought.' She looked at him under her eyelashes, and he managed to take a grip.

'So what happened? Before your haircut.'

'At the audition?'

'Yes. Do they want you?'

'They didn't say. There were four of us from outside the regular group.'

He gazed at her ready to sympathise, but that didn't seem to be required. He went on watching her, fascinated by the newly revealed angles of the face under the little-boy haircut. She was, he saw, thinking about how to communicate with him and he found himself sharply reminded of a conversation with Francesca about music.

'Some of them — the people in the group — are just wonderful. I would . . . well, I'd rather be able to do that . . . than anything. But some of them — well, they weren't better than me. Well, better at some things, not as good at others. I thought they'd *all* be better.' He waited, unmoving, for her to get wherever she was going. 'There's one girl there — Sarah — whose spins and turns are just better than anything I've seen, and then there's Michael whose line is wonderful. Whatever he does looks right.' She relapsed into silence, looking out of the small high window behind him. She was still in another world, and he sought crossly for specifics.

'Did they say anything to you? Like good or not good.'

She considered him, from her irritating perch in another place. 'It wasn't like that. They don't say things like that. But I did some *pas de deux* work with Michael and that was . . . well, I've never danced with anyone like that.'

'Not even your mate Williams?'

'He's wonderful, of course, but it's a very classical style. Michael now . . . well, he's quite different.'

'Michael?'

'Michael Jefferson Fairbrother. He's American. Black.'

'And gay, I suppose.' I hope is what I mean, he thought helplessly.

'Oh yes.' She looked at him surprised.

'Alex.' He took a deep breath. 'Are you going to have to leave us? Because I'd better know. I need to plan the work.'

'I'm not good enough for the core company. Not yet. But . . . but if they needed extras . . .'

'You'd be in with a chance.'

'Yes. That's right.'

That's why she had her hair cut, he saw painfully, to make her look more like the chosen group, where her heart had been given.

'We could consider doing some work this afternoon then? Even though it's Friday.'

He saw her take him in properly for the first time that day and fought not to blush or look away, as the wide monkey grin spread over her face.

'I brought a sandwich.' She fished in a carrier and offered a damp brown bag, and he recovered himself.

'Oh come on. Not every day you do an audition with a top company *and* get a haircut. We'll go out.'

* * *

As John McLeish pushed open the door of his house he could hear his wife's voice, talking on the phone. He called to tell her he was back and bent to receive the onslaught of his son and heir. He was followed by his nanny, carrying a jacket and a suitcase. She went home most weekends, which gave the family more privacy and her a proper break, but in the late stages of Francesca's pregnancy this arrangement left the household vulnerable if William had to be scooped up from the floor. Francesca had found herself, a week ago, totally unable to carry William in the throws of a tantrum. Indeed, she could only pick him up at this stage if he could be persuaded to clamber on to a chair and cling to her neck while she arranged his weight on top of the baby. Over William's excited shouts and farewells to his Susannah, McLeish heard the phone go down and his wife appeared, looking just perceptibly shifty. He kissed her, settled his son on the floor, straightened the Nicola Hicks drawing which had been knocked squint by William's exuberant greeting, and let her make him a cup of tea before he asked, casually, who had rung.

'Oh, only Andrew Quentin.'

'To talk about Giles?'

'Not about the case, darling, don't worry, you know I wouldn't let him.' She gave William a biscuit and ate one herself, avoiding his eye.

'What did he want?'

'It wasn't a want,' she said, carefully, still not looking at him. 'It was an *offer*. He was offering me a lift if I could come down the day before the concert. He thought I wouldn't be able to do the double journey in a day.' She smiled at him, wide-eyed, and he watched her with the deepest suspicion.

'You really can't do that, you know that the baby's due, what, in two weeks' time.'

'That's the *earliest* date.'

'It's too far. And you might not be able to get back to London if the baby started. You've heard Jamie and Giles perform lots of times.'

'I thought you were allowed to use the Metropolitan Police helicopter.'

He breathed out carefully. 'Not for frivolous purposes. The Met wouldn't think it reasonable to get you back to a posh London hospital and your own gynaecologist. They'd take the line you'd be fine in the local hospital.' This was of course the official and rational view, and in theory he agreed with it. In practice he was anxious enough about this baby that he was not prepared for Francesca to be anywhere other than the private wing at UCH with a pricey obstetrician in attendance.

'Don't worry, darling, I don't terribly want to have a baby in Shaftesbury hospital without Dame Ruth and where nobody can come and see me.' There was a careful pause while he waited for the other shoe to drop. 'But Will was two weeks late — you can't have forgotten — and I'm sure this one is going to do that too. The head isn't engaged — the baby's still roaming around, having a nice time and kicking me in the bladder.'

'You do not need to go. Jamie's got Wendy this time, and Giles has got his father.'

'I told Sir Andrew I didn't think I could go,' she said, sounding virtuous and ill-used, and he decided not to press further. They were together and the house was empty of teenage boys. He sat, slowly relaxing with his tea, watching his wife plod round the kitchen, back arched against the weight of the baby.

'Darling?'

'Yes,' he said, warily.

'I don't think it'll necessarily happen, but I did say I'd coach Giles if he were brought here this weekend.' She met his horrified look. 'I couldn't say otherwise, he is one of mine even if only temporarily.'

He thought about it, fair-mindedly. 'He won't take all that long, will he?'

'Couple of hours both days. *If* he comes.'

He agreed that this was not unreasonable, particularly since he already knew he would have to work on Saturday. He reached for a newspaper and a second cup of tea.

'Are we making progress?'

'What on?'

'Catriona.'

'Oh. No. The picture isn't getting any clearer. Lot of . . . well, red herrings, leads that look promising then go nowhere.'

She bent cautiously to see what her son was doing and found him absorbed. 'Did you find the father?'

He looked at her, appalled. 'I was so keen to get home, I clear forgot to check.' He reached for the phone. 'Kevin. Any luck on the DNA test?' He listened attentively. 'Bugger me.' He glanced apologetically at Francesca; they had agreed that the intelligent and imitative William would unhesitatingly absorb any unsuitable words or expressions and reproduce them at exactly the wrong moment. 'So another lead that isn't going anywhere.' He sighed and put down the phone and caught his wife's enquiring eye. The news would no doubt be round the school quickly, he decided, and Francesca would get it from Jamie anyway. 'One of the Faraday lads, Damien Fry, came forward to confess that he was a possibility as the putative dad. The tests aren't back, but he's the right blood group. His first and only shot according to him, poor little rabbit.'

'*Not* that daft boy who was here for lunch and who got Jamie and Alex into such trouble by experimenting with Ecstasy?'

'That's the one. Hang on, how did you know about all that?' I will murder Matthew Sutherland one day, he thought.

'Jamie. We've been having rather long conversations recently. Sorry if he shouldn't have told me, and I must say I was grateful to Alex and Matt telling him not to wake me at the time. *You* weren't supposed to know either. I suppose your spies were everywhere, as usual.'

'Yes. I do get to hear.' It was important that Francesca should not think anything on his vast patch could be kept from him. He remembered where he had been going. 'That particular lad — Damien — was at the party but he was downstairs all the time from 9.30 till his parents fetched him at 11.15. He's out of it as a murderer and never even suspected he might be the father, he said. He didn't think he could be . . .'

'Because it was the first time. Do *boys* think like that too? Deary me. Poor boy must feel terrible — lost a girl *and* a baby without knowing he had one. How *does* he feel?'

'I'm afraid I didn't ask. Kevin saw him. The parents have been told.'

'There's *another* kid who's not going to be on top form for the school show.'

'Who are the others? Oh, sorry, Jamie.'

'And Giles Quentin. His dad's really worried about him.'

And with cause, McLeish thought, privately. Giles Quentin had assumed he was the father of an unwanted child *and* he had been missing for a critical half-hour on Saturday night.

'Well, I'm sorry, my love, but he's not getting you to help at the expense of my second son. Hello, Will.'

His first son had popped up from under the table, eyes wide with suspicion, and he pulled him on to his knee, hastily distracting him with a wooden spoon and an empty saucepan while Francesca got their supper on to the table.

CHAPTER 13

Saturday, 8th July

'Well, it's quite simple.' John McLeish, in the big, badly lit, conference room at Scotland Yard, had managed to recover his temper after a bad start. 'We're not getting anywhere with this case, with a team of thirty, and I'm seeing the AC on Monday morning. And everyone we might want to interview, with the exception of Louis Roberts, is at that bloody school rehearsing for a show.'

There were only fifteen people gathered, this being Saturday morning and those who could be spared were at home, but they all relaxed at this brisk summation of their joint efforts. The big wall chart had got bigger, but no more illuminating. The position remained, unequivocally, that Giles Quentin, Roland Willis, Vivienne Willis, Piers Miller, Susie Miller and Louis Roberts could all have seized an opportunity and murdered Catriona. Moreover, despite the team's best efforts, Andrew Quentin was still just in the picture. As befitted a host he had been everywhere — indeed had been reported in three different places at once around 10.45 — and must still be regarded as a candidate; a host can go anywhere, or disappear for ten minutes unobserved, and it was his house and he knew the way.

'Good work, Kevin, with Janie Hopkins,' McLeish went on, remembering his staff's morale. 'And all of you, to get the chart so clear. Damien Fry really was where he said he was, Michelle? Good. Well, he didn't look likely but, as my wife is always saying, the Teenage Boy is always capable of surprising you.' He sat and thought, his staff watching him. 'Well. All right. Better bite the bullet. Mr Roberts is here and I must see him. With you, Kevin. And after that, since everyone else I'd like to talk to is at Faraday's, me, Kevin, Michelle and a volunteer DC who doesn't mind losing the rest of today will go down to Faraday's. Michelle, get a local man to help if you need one, and get somewhere set up so we can interview Mr Willis and Mr Miller. And I'll find my own way of having a word with Sir Andrew and Giles when I get there.'

'You could interview them in the library, sir,' Kevin Camberton offered, and he only just managed a smile.

'Thank you for that, Kevin. Will you go and get Mr Roberts and meet me downstairs?'

He paused to sign a chit for Michelle Black. She, he was amused to see, was pleased at the idea of a day in the country, and all four DCs present that morning had volunteered to come. He left her to sort out who should receive her favours.

Louis Roberts and Kevin Camberton were already in a dark interview room on the first floor, accompanied by Louis Roberts' solicitor, drinking coffee and engaged in stilted conversation when he arrived. He sat and considered his man; he was still sedated, his movements slow and languid, but he had recovered himself, and was on his guard. McLeish signalled for the tape to be switched on. 'Mr Roberts, I need to remind you that you will be asked to sign a sworn statement as a result of this interview.' He waited, but the man nodded, looking past his ear. 'You discovered, I understand, some time ago that Catriona was not your biological daughter.'

'I did, yes.'

The solicitor was sitting very still, he saw. 'Would you tell us how you discovered this?'

'Catriona needed a transfusion after one of these incidents.' The man had been ready for this and had the story clear. 'She was in hospital of course, and I was away on business, so I didn't get there until the next day when she was better. I got talking to one of the young nurses and she told me they'd had some difficulty finding AB blood and would have asked me if I'd been there.' He paused and shifted position. 'Well, I'm Group O. I knew that because I carry a tag for allergies. Round my neck.' He clawed at his collar and produced a metal chain with an oval disc. '"Allergic to penicillin and sulphonamide", it says, and they put your blood group on as well.' McLeish nodded, more warmly than he had meant. Francesca carried just such a disc in her handbag and two of his brothers-in-law, who also refused to wear them round their necks, were frequently engaged in agitated searches through their pockets for them. 'So I said, well, I'd not have been any use, I'm Group O, not thinking, you know, and the little girl turned green and vanished off somewhere. So I got thinking; Viv had been there, they could have used her blood for Catriona, but they hadn't. Then I remembered. She's Group O too — I know from when she was pregnant, Group O, Rhesus Positive. This was afterwards, you know, at the time I was just worried about Catriona.' He stopped, abruptly.

'What did you do then?' McLeish asked.

'Looked it all up in a library. Then I knew. Two Group O parents cannot have a Group AB child, so one of us wasn't, and it had to be me. I was there when she was born, she's Viv's daughter all right. Well, I thought about a mix-up at the hospital, but Catriona is . . . was . . . very like Viv. So I had to accept that . . . that I'd brought up — well, tried to . . . someone else's kid.' He compressed his lips, staring out of the window, and everyone in the room saw how he had felt. He came back to them slowly and considered McLeish. 'I told Janie not to feel bad about telling you. You found out anyway, didn't you? Through the DNA test — I realised when

I thought about it. I read about them when I was looking up about the blood groups. It was in the same chapter.'

'The DNA tests did indeed tell us you were not her father. I didn't have the results when I last interviewed you.' This last was for the benefit of the record and Louis Roberts' solicitor.

'I felt bad for a bit — I felt I'd been conned.' He sat and thought, looking tired and old in the harsh overhead light. 'Then I thought, well, she is my child, I've had her since she was born, whoever her father is — she's mine.' He looked at the policeman. 'People feel like that about adopted children, don't they? A child's a child, and if you bring it up it's yours. Or anyway that's what I found.'

'You didn't discuss it with your ex-wife?'

'Viv? No.' He heaved a sigh. 'I hoped she wouldn't find out.' McLeish waited in the painful silence. 'I thought, well, I thought she'd . . . well, look, Catriona was very . . . She loved her mother and I thought if she got to know I wasn't her father . . .' The voice trailed away, but they could all finish the sentence for him. He bowed his head and reached for a handkerchief. 'And *that's* why,' he said, huskily, '*that's* why I didn't want Catriona in a hospital. I thought they'd find out somehow . . . and I'd lose her for ever. So I wouldn't agree to what she . . . what she needed and now she's gone.' He stared out of the window stonily while the two policemen waited, stolid in the face of someone else's tragedy.

'I wonder . . . Chief Superintendent . . .' The solicitor was gesturing at the tape. 'Perhaps we could have a pause?'

McLeish nodded and reached over but Louis Roberts forestalled him. 'No, I want to get it over. That's the worst. That's what I did to help her to her death, but I didn't kill her, I loved her. I didn't know how to help or what to do about her, I was about as much use as a fart in a thunderstorm, but I didn't kill her.'

They went over the events of Saturday night again, patiently, impeded by the solicitor, but at the end they were back where they had started with the fact that a telephone conversation between their interviewee and Janie Hopkins had ended at 11.01 p.m. and he had not been seen again until 11.30 p.m. when the hue and cry for the child who was not his daughter had brought them to the locked bathroom.

McLeish decided to wind up the interview and said as much, but Louis Roberts stopped him. 'Wait. Look, does Viv know? She must now, mustn't she? Because of the tests. Or did you not feel able to tell her?'

'She knows, yes.' They had discussed this question before the interview and had agreed it must be answered truthfully even if Vivienne Willis would have preferred never to acknowledge the facts of her daughter's paternity.

'I'll try and talk to her about it. It's time — well, past time, we did.'

And on that note they ended the interview and gave Louis Roberts, limp and exhausted, into the hands of his solicitor who was sensibly going to get a second breakfast into him while the statement was typed up.

* * *

'Are we doing Willis or Miller first?' Kevin Camberton asked. They were squashed into one car with a police driver, and the journey was dragging.

'Willis,' McLeish said. He was aware that Kevin Camberton, while doing a decent conscientious job, had picked his man. And indeed he must look again very carefully at Piers Miller. A thought occurred to him. 'When do they choose a new headmaster, do you know?'

'Interviews Monday. Decision to be announced to candidates that evening. School to be told on Tuesday, so all the parents know before the show.'

The show, of course, and after that the school broke up and staff and children scattered to the four winds. And that was why he was driving his team to get at every detail; the school had been the dead girl's home, literally as well as figuratively for twelve years, ever since her mother had married

Roland Willis. Other children at the school had substituted for her siblings, and she had met her death when pregnant by a fellow pupil, in the house of another fellow pupil with whom she had also slept, surrounded by their parents and step-parents. The answer had to be involved with the school and there were only four days to get at it.

They were met at the school gates by the local DI and a DC, both of whom Kevin Camberton greeted. In practice they had not a lot to offer, except warm commendation of Susie Miller who, in addition to a heavy schedule at Faraday's, also organised and trained a well-regarded local choir.

A big classroom had been set aside for their use, in one of the temporary buildings one grade up from a Portakabin in which most of the school was taught. There was, McLeish knew from previous visits, a magnificent small theatre in a field at the back of the school, with state of the art lighting, an up-to-the-minute sound kit and a revolving stage, and another building wholly given over to music, with practice and rehearsal rooms. Parents had also at some stage subscribed for a modest science block, but all other teaching took place in one-storey shacks with gaps round the windows. Jamie, as well as his contemporaries, loved the place with such passion that they never noticed any discomfort or inconvenience. On his last visit here, in the dead of winter, the sheltered, pampered children of rich media households had been trudging, uncomplainingly, in the wind that always blew on this escarpment, dressed in a wild collection of jeans, sweaters, earmuffs, sub-arctic expeditionary jackets and very long scarves. On entry to one of the draughty classrooms they would remove or loosen the scarf and the earmuffs. It had been like the photographs of Russian students working under handicap in Siberia. This was July however, the chrysalises had been discarded, and the students were in skimpy shorts and sleeveless T-shirts for the boys, very short skirts, bikini tops, or even skimpier shorts and the inevitable T-shirts for the girls. The head emerged, soberly dressed in khaki trousers and a white shirt, from one of the butterfly groups to greet them, the smile for the children fading as he came towards them. 'No news?' he asked, and McLeish shook his head. 'Not yet. Is young Mr Fry all right?'

'A bit off form but that's only to be expected. Now you wanted to see Piers Miller, who is still rehearsing, but Roland Willis is free.'

'Could you ask him to come over?'

'Of course.' He turned and surveyed the crowds of children, sprawled under trees, huddled in little groups, or just walking about purposefully. 'Alex.' His voice pitched itself effortlessly over the noise of young voices.

McLeish blinked and looked again, as a thin red-haired figure detached itself from a group and loped obligingly over. He got his jaw back up just in time to greet Alexandra Ferguson, in black clinging leggings, ballet shoes and an oversize white T-shirt and very short hair, flattened to her head by sweat. She greeted him and he saw that the T-shirt was sticking to her and sweat was running down her nose by the glasses.

'What are *you* doing here?' he asked, watching fascinated as a bead of sweat ran down from her hairline.

'Helping with the dance bits of the show. No one's had much time to practise.'

He gazed at her, as she stood, straight, toes turned out, and was reminded of his wife who, like this girl, got into everything, out of a combination of vitality and raw ability. Alex was working a full week as a trainee lawyer, going to dance classes three nights a week and here she was passing a restful weekend putting some polish on the Faraday performers.

'Alex, my dear, could you tell Roland that . . . that Chief Superintendent McLeish is here.'

Didn't want to send a child, McLeish saw, watching as Alex pattered off across a field with the dancer's out-turned walk, the ridiculous T-shirt almost down to the back of her knees. Perhaps she would have lunch with them? She had to eat sometime. He watched as she turned the corner of a building.

Roland Willis emerged minutes later and made his way over to them, looking to left and right, stopping to deal with questions from a darting, harassed child, completely at home. But he, too, was on his guard; well, that was natural enough, faced with policemen, on a Saturday, having been interviewed extensively only three days ago. As they settled themselves he remembered Louis Roberts; this was another father who was not a father, another man having difficulty with an ambivalent relationship. They went over the timing again, adding nothing at all to their previous knowledge, and McLeish sat back, considering his man.

'Chief Superintendent, have you any idea . . . I mean . . .'

'No.' The monosyllable fell bleakly between them, but McLeish did not feel like expanding it. 'Looking back, could you see any sign that Catriona was more unhappy, more likely to attempt suicide than at other times when she threatened to do so?'

'Oh.' It was a sound of pure pain. 'Yes. I did. I should have . . . I ought to have been prepared to agree that she should go to a hospital, but I just . . . I didn't believe that she wouldn't get worse shut away from everyone she knew, exiled from her school. It was her last year and I thought she would feel so . . . so deprived, so cheated. So unhappy.' He shook his head, the thick dark brown hair, flecked with grey, flopping over his face.

'What do you feel specifically you should have noticed, as a danger signal?'

Roland Willis looked up in sudden alarm, the frozen rabbit expression sitting oddly on the good, regular features. 'Well,' he said, cautiously. 'Well, I suppose the . . . the untoward sexual advances to boys and staff. That was new.' He had gained confidence, once embarked. 'We all knew she had a crush on Giles Quentin, but she never . . . well, she was never all over him in public even though . . . even though they had been lovers.'

'This all started on the school trip?'

'Well, I *think* so. I've been thinking about it since we talked on Wednesday,' he said, nodding to Kevin Camberton.

'It was the first time . . . the first time she . . . she acted . . . she attempted to involve *me* in this behaviour.'

'But she might have been doing it with others.'

'I really don't know. I was terribly busy of course, but I . . .' He reached for a handkerchief. 'But it was her behaviour on the school trip which should have . . . should have made me agree that she needed help and immediately. Particularly the way she flung herself at Piers Miller, who had been so good about coaching her maths.'

'It sounds like a nightmare.'

'In patches.' Roland Willis returned the handkerchief to his pocket and sighed. 'Sometimes, you know, the interest of what we were doing and the — well — the kids' spirits made it all right. But it was a strain, and now, of course . . .'

'You have applied for the head's post, I understand.'

'Yes, I have. It wasn't an easy decision and I don't know . . . how . . . how the Trustees will . . . It was a dreadful failure with Catriona, both personal and professional.' He looked at them, the wide brown eyes anxious. 'I still felt I ought not . . . Well, I have, and that's all there is to it and I am being interviewed on Monday.' He gazed at them. 'If you — if we have finished, I have a rehearsal in ten minutes. They can start without me, of course, but . . .'

They let him go and set Michelle Black to getting the tape typed into statement form.

'I need a break,' McLeish said, firmly, to Kevin Camberton who wanted to find Piers Miller and sweat him immediately. 'And I'd like to find Jamie before we see Piers Miller. *He* didn't tell us about Catriona's behaviour on the school trip, did he? Any more than Mr Miller did.'

'Maybe *he* was embarrassed too?'

'Well, he didn't kill her and he wasn't the father, so I assume that's all it was. But I'd like to find him.'

They walked out in the warmth of the sun and the smell of the flowers and McLeish felt a great smile spreading across his face as he looked at the brightly coloured ant heap that met his eyes. The big lawn-covered campus was patterned with art, laid out on its backs waiting to be hung, and a continual stream of well-informed juvenile critics were viewing, occasionally falling to their knees to get a better look. In another patch, the craft output waited to go on display; all students did six hours craft and design work a week minimum until they were in the sixth form and there were some staggeringly ambitious projects on view: a small boat, a double bed and a wall-hanging that would have graced a palace.

'Did you do things like this at your school?' he said, generally.

'Of course not,' Kevin Camberton said, dead pan. 'I was in the scholarship stream.'

'We did art but I couldn't draw. I could — well — I might have done something like that,' Michelle Black said, gazing at the wall-hanging, while DC Harter, blushing, said he had definitely made a box for his mother in woodwork.

Just beyond the craft was a pile of musical instruments, the sun glinting off the cymbals; the orchestra was evidently on a break. A shrimp-like boy, presumably a Third, who had not yet grown, was gazing awe-struck at a double-bass and McLeish watched him, indulgently. The boy's head went up in response to some signal and he stood listening. The high plangent voice that McLeish had first heard in his own living-room, three months ago, floated from a window in the music block, every word clear. *Me, me, and none but me, dart home, O gentle death, And quickly, for I draw too long this idle breath.*

He felt the hairs lift on his neck, then the voice faltered, and the piano sounded louder, but the voice died away and the piano halted on a discord. 'I can't . . .' a husky baritone announced, then something banged, and voices rose. Giles Quentin. And presumably Jamie on the piano, whom he needed to see. He was in the building and up the stairs, Camberton and Michelle at his back, before he had worked out what he was doing, but he barely hesitated before opening the door of the room on the second floor.

'Jamie? Are you having a break?' he enquired, blandly. The boy was seated on the piano stool with Giles Quentin behind him, seemingly sheltering him from Andrew Quentin, who was in a state of terminal frustration, a big man, looking even bigger with the blond hair dishevelled. The room was much too small with the addition of three policemen, but McLeish was not disposed to try and lower the tension. Jamie looked at him with a small, apologetic shrug, indicating that he was at the mercy of powerful forces.

'We weren't having a break, Chief Superintendent, but we might as well. We're all wasting our time.' Andrew Quentin started ill-temperedly to move the stand holding the music but, in the way of collapsible objects approached in anger, it folded itself up with a clatter catching his finger, so that he cursed aloud and his son giggled nervously.

'I wanted to talk to Giles and Jamie about the school trip,' McLeish said, when order had been restored.

'Not without his solicitor here.' Andrew Quentin reacted instantly, removing his painful finger from his mouth.

'As Giles wishes, of course, Sir Andrew, but what I want to talk about is Catriona's behaviour on that trip.'

'Well, I'll tell you about that,' Jamie said. 'You never asked me.'

'I think we did, old son, but you didn't tell us a lot, other than that she was a pain. We'd find it useful to know exactly what she did to be a pain.'

'Dad, I don't mind telling them that either.' Giles came out from behind Jamie. 'You could get some lunch — it's over there, see, on the tables.'

'I'm staying.' Andrew Quentin said, flatly. 'Can we at least sit down?'

They sat on windowsills, piano stools and two chairs commandeered from a neighbouring room, and McLeish took charge of the meeting.

'I understand that Catriona's behaviour became even more difficult for everyone when she was on the school trip.' He looked at the two shuttered, defensive faces. 'To be specific, I understand that she made overt and public sexual advances to both of you, to Roland Willis and to Piers Miller.'

'And to anyone else who sat down long enough.' Giles Quentin had gone scarlet to the roots of the blond hair, and his father's eyebrows went right up, but he kept silent.

'That's not fair, Giles.' It was Jamie, looking miserable, who got his mouth open.

'What is fair, Jamie?' McLeish asked.

'All she wanted was a cuddle, John. She felt awful, you could see, and it helped . . . well, to have a cuddle. It wasn't sex.'

'That's balls,' Giles said, furiously. 'If you . . . if anyone . . . tried to tell her to bugger off she . . . she, well, groped them.'

'Like you'd groped her, you stupid sod.'

Jamie had a point there, McLeish thought, and saw that Andrew Quentin agreed with him.

'Jamie,' he said, gently to the angry face opposite him. '*You* found her content with a cuddle. What happened with other people — not Giles — but other boys, or male staff?'

'She was . . . yeah, well, it was different with them. Because they — they were embarrassed, even Roland.'

'And Piers?'

'She was really bad with him. She was trying to get a rise out of him.' He stopped, horrified, replaying his own words while McLeish reflected that the disturbed Catriona had been trying for exactly that effect.

'Are you saying that she pestered him?'

'Yes. That's what she did. And Giles, though . . .' He cast one black look at his colleague who gritted his teeth. 'And even *Roland*, although he's her stepfather. You could see it made him miserable.'

'Did you . . . any of you . . . manage to talk about it?'

'No, we didn't,' Jamie said, slowly. 'It was . . .' He looked across, and McLeish saw the thoughtful twelve-year-old he had met before he and Francesca had even become lovers. 'The staff — Roland and Piers — were too embarrassed, I suppose. And — this sounds stupid, I know — I thought somehow she'd stop, that the next day it would be OK.'

'But it wasn't.'

'Not then, but we got back to school and there were lots of other people, and Catriona's mother was here and she sort of . . . well, it was OK again.' He thought, painfully. 'No, I'm afraid that's not true. It was better, but I went to London early — well, to your house, John, to get away from her.'

'And I hid behind my mother,' Giles said, unexpectedly. 'Piers knew what she was like, of course, and he helped.'

McLeish sat, trying to formulate his question, but Kevin Camberton could restrain himself no longer. 'You did see her — Catriona — making advances to your stepfather?'

'To Piers. Oh yes. The full frontal.' He looked at them, defensively. 'I told you she was being a pain.'

But she had not been worse than that as far as Jamie was concerned. Giles Quentin had felt sufficiently guilty about his own behaviour not to feel able to tell, as his downcast look and the scarlet flush on his neck said more eloquently than words. But Piers Miller had said nothing either, kept silent perhaps through guilt, like Giles. Kevin Camberton, straining at the leash by his side, might have the right man. Well, Piers Miller was here, tied down by a rehearsal, and he would wait. He glanced round and caught Andrew Quentin off guard, watching his son with painful anxiety.

'I'm sorry to have interrupted the rehearsal,' he said, rising to leave.

'It wasn't going well,' Andrew Quentin said, heavily. 'Lunch, and go on afterwards?'

'Can't,' his son said, restored to equanimity. 'Choir rehearsal at two. I did *tell* you, Dad.'

McLeish, riveted, watched the great Sir Andrew receive the news that he was being postponed for a school choir rehearsal; the mouth opened, the strong, blunt-featured head came up, a tinge of pink appeared on the cheekbones, and then the disciplined mind took over, and the man relaxed.

'I shall go and lie in the grass until it's over, then,' he said, pleasantly. 'Come on, chaps, food.' He glanced out of the window. 'I can see the lovely Alex leading her troupe out.'

Jamie hung back, but McLeish told him to go. 'Do you know where Piers Miller will be?'

'Finishing a rehearsal in the barn, I think.'

He followed Jamie's pointing finger and saw the barn and, in sharp relief, Susie Miller almost running, carrying a pile of papers. 'Head her off,' he said, urgently, to Camberton, and followed at a pace more fitting to his seniority. Susie Miller, held in play, favoured him with the glare of an animal at bay.

'I've got twenty minutes to get these lists to the office and have lunch,' she stated, uncompromisingly.

McLeish took the pile from her and posted Michelle Black off with them, and Susie Miller reluctantly stood still. 'It's only a small question. We're on our way to talk to your husband but we've been hearing a lot about how . . . unsuitably Catriona behaved on the school journey. Was this discussed with you, as her housemistress?'

'Not while she was alive. I know this sounds awful but there just wasn't *time*. They all came back on the Friday and we had to get ourselves together to go to that damned party — no, I mean that. If it hadn't been for the party she would still be alive, wouldn't she? Anyway, Piers said they had all had a difficult time with her, but I don't suppose it was any worse for him than for anyone else. Roland was the senior teacher present, after all. And he's her stepfather.' She paused and considered him. 'Why do you ask?'

'Just to get as complete a picture as we can.'

'Are you . . . ? Do you . . . ? Well, I suppose you're not going to tell me, but it is terrible to have this . . . this awfulness hanging over us. And having you here reminds us all.'

'I'm afraid it was either have us here or ask three key people to leave the school to be interviewed.'

'I'm not sure which would have been worse,' she said, a spot of pink in both cheeks. 'If you must see Piers, well, I suppose you must, but he needs some lunch. Tell him I'll bring him a sandwich.' She turned and left them without further farewells and they gazed after her.

'She's pretty ratty today,' Kevin Camberton said, eyes narrowed. 'Worried about her husband.'

They found Piers Miller, talking to two Fifths, and got rid of them, then put the question direct.

'Why didn't I tell you she'd been all over me like a plaster on the summer trip?' He was looking exhausted, but not downcast. 'Because she was all over everyone, that's why. Starting with Jamie, who deserves canonisation. And even poor Roland, yes. It was all appallingly embarrassing and he was wretched. I don't know whether it was worse for him to watch her assaulting the rest of us or trying to keep her out of our caravan. We shared it, you see, and I came back one afternoon just in time to save him from rape. Poor Roland was at his wit's end. He's such a decent bloke he wouldn't believe the worst.'

'He is applying for the head's job, I understand.'

'He and others. And I didn't say he was the best candidate for a head's job, just that no one could fault him in the decency and charity stakes.'

They went over the timetable on the night of the party again but nothing had changed; Piers Miller had been in the garden, cooling off, for the critical half-hour.

'You must have been particularly upset to be accused of sexual misbehaviour,' McLeish said, 'given your affair with Miss Simpson. To whom we have talked.'

Piers Miller turned slowly scarlet. 'You've talked to her?'

'As part of our enquiries, yes. She says the affair between you started on a school journey, after her A-levels.'

'Just like *this* school journey, you're saying? Jesus Christ!' He looked into their unmoving faces and his mouth set in a thin line. 'I see how you would think — well — what you're thinking,' he said, steadily. 'And all I can do is tell you you're way off. For a start, the walkout with Yvette caused me so much trouble — and still does, for that matter — I'd kick Claudia Schiffer out of my bed if she were in the school here. And secondly, there *is* a difference. Yvette was a stunner — well, you've seen her — and very grown-up and together.

Catriona, poor little wretch, was a neurotic, babyish mess and even ten years ago I'd have had more sense.' He looked at them wearily. 'If you haven't got anything more sensible to ask do you mind if I get some food? I've been on the go since 6.30 and we don't stop till eight, and then we do it all over again tomorrow.'

'Ah. Your wife's bringing you a sandwich.'

'Which I wouldn't mind eating in peace.'

McLeish looked sideways at Camberton to see if he wanted to do anything else but he was sitting, steadily regarding Piers Miller, not seeming to need to speak. 'You'll still be around if we think of anything else?'

'I am stuck here twenty-four hours a day until Thursday.'

They left him and went out into the grounds. It had been arranged that they would have their lunch in the room allocated for their use, with the local DI who was putting himself out to be helpful, but McLeish looked longingly at the groups scattered all over the lawns. He was hunting for a bright red head; he could not see her, but a loud persistent thumping was coming from somewhere close, together with a high clear voice raised to drill sergeant pitch, calling 'Six, seven, eight and . . .'

He made his way to another of the old barns that reminded you that the place had once been a farm, and as he advanced the noise stopped and Alex's voice allowed as how that was *better* but it was one and a half, Julie, after the stop. Grinning to himself, he pushed open the door, his two colleagues at his back, and peered in. He pushed the door a little wider as it became clear that no one in the room was looking at anything except Alex, in conventional black leotard and tights, embellished with thick grey woollen legwarmers, a decaying brown cardigan and what looked like an old pair of tights round her head.

'Again,' she ordered, putting on her appalling glasses, and the piano started up and a line of girls kicked their way across the stage. A mixed bag, he thought, all shapes and sizes, two or three who were moving easily and neatly, but the others were obviously well-intentioned young women who had been rescued from the games field. But Alex, he saw with respect, made no distinctions, this was her company and they were going to be wielded into one moving part. He sent the others on, and watched fascinated for another five minutes, aware that he was on borrowed time with a visiting DI waiting upon his arrival, then tore himself away and walked over to the main block, understanding that he had just seen another damned artist at work.

CHAPTER 14

Monday, 10th July

The man with the curly brown hair smiled at a young woman as he turned sharply into the alcove where the cash machine for the Royal Bank of Scotland lurked. He fed in his card, which he had managed to preserve all these weeks hidden in a packet of tissues, punched in the number and a demand for £250 and waited, hands clenched, while the machine contemplated his request. 'Remove your card and take your cash promptly', it instructed, and he let out a held breath. His wife had not taken all the cash out as she could readily have done. He looked round him for a workmen's cafe where he could eat a large, cheap breakfast and get some change for the phone. He struck lucky; the establishment he found, in a side street between a hairdresser's and a launderette, also had a pay-phone. When he had finished his breakfast — bolting it because he wanted to make the phone call — he fed in coins as the machine demanded and waited hungrily for an answer. He held on for nearly a minute, listening to the phone ring, seeing the bedroom, cool and fresh with the phone by the side of the bed, and the living-room, a bit small perhaps, but comfortable and the phone on the coffee table. Or was she in the kitchen, where the phone hung on the wall beside the sink, so that her hands would be wet when she picked up the phone.

The BT answering service cut in and he put down his handset instantly. They were most likely there, his wife and that Other who would be telling her not to answer. But if she was really out he couldn't afford to hang round the house waiting for her to come back; if a neighbour saw him he might be betrayed. He would get a bit nearer to the house and wait somewhere until she answered the phone. The Other had his keys, of course, but he could wait.

* * *

Francesca, looking and feeling like a seriously over-canvassed frigate, leaned flat-footedly on the handles of the rocking push-chair. William wanted to get out and was making his preference clear, but she was not confident of hanging on to him as they crossed the busy road. They were on the crossing outside the Refuge and were coming to pick up her mother, so that she could come back and have lunch, and look after her grandson while Francesca had her afternoon sleep and Susannah shopped for vests, nappies and assorted necessities for the new baby. Francesca had maintained there was no hurry, but her entourage had ignored her and so here she was, wheeling William across a difficult road rather than sitting comfortably at home on the sofa. She pressed the bell at the door and waited to be recognised and admitted. She pushed through the door but the bag hung on the side of the push-chair caught and she swore.

'Francesca. *Not* a good example.'

'Matthew.' She watched, gratefully, as he bent to release the chair and to liberate William, pointing him firmly towards his grandmother. 'I forgot it was your morning here.'

'It isn't. It's usually Thursday, but . . . well, Alex will be out tomorrow, so we thought we'd do it today.'

'I didn't know the poor girl was allowed any time off.' Francesca had found a reasonably upright chair and sank into it, gratefully.

'She's got an audition.'

'An audition?' She sat up, interested, and considered Matthew's stony expression. 'For a part?'

'For a tour. Dancers don't get parts apparently. She'll tell you.' He indicated an open door with a jerk of his head, and Alex walked through it, eyes going apprehensively to Matt.

'You've had your hair cut,' Francesca said, jealously.

'Yes.'

'It's lovely,' Francesca said, recovering her manners sharply. 'Who did it? I've heard of him. If ever I get out of all this, I must go to someone good. Only I won't be able to, not with two children.'

'And a nanny. And a maternity nurse. And me.' Her mother, William at her side, had arrived to deflate a promising line in complaint and Francesca joined, reluctantly, in the general amusement. 'I think we'd better take William away, darling,' Mrs Wilson said, briskly. 'They have chickenpox here and you could do without that just now. Oh damn. That's my phone and I have been waiting for Mrs Brick at Social Services. May I just take it?' She disappeared and William came and leant on his mother, his eyes wide as he gazed at Alex.

'I've cut my hair,' she said, dropping to his side with a dancer's elegance, while he contemplated her seriously. Francesca looked over her head to Matthew and got a small shock; he was watching Alex, his expression unguarded. Footsteps and voices sounded in the corridor, and Mary Wilson came through the door flustered and short of breath.

'Fran. It's Wendy. She couldn't find you so she rang me and Margot directed her here.'

'What is it, Mum?'

'Oh dear.' Mrs Wilson sank on to a chair. 'It's Steve.'

'But he's in hospital.'

'He was. He escaped — walked out — sometime early this morning. They think.'

'Jamie's father,' Francesca said, aside, to Alex. She heaved herself to her feet. 'I'll talk to Wendy. She mustn't go home.'

'No, indeed, I asked her to stay with me.'

'Mum, don't be daft. You and Margot are no match for Steve when he's out of his mind. Well, none of us are, but if she comes to us . . . well, we can cope.'

'John would be furious.'

'Well, possibly, but he'd make sure the house was guarded, with me and Will there.'

'What about Jamie?' Alex had got up, William in her arms, investigating her new hair.

'He's at school.'

'I know. I was down there over the weekend, helping with the dance group. But would — could — his father go there?'

'Probably not,' Mrs Wilson said, considering the point. 'It is Wendy who is rejecting him. He's never attacked Jamie, has he?'

'Once, but only when he was trying to protect his mother,' Francesca said. 'Why, oh why, can these useless establishments not keep their customers safely locked away. He was sectioned this time, he wasn't a volunteer.'

Matthew, looking very tall in the small room, frowned at them. 'Look. He's been in, what, nine weeks, being treated. He may want to go home but he's been on the pills and they've always worked before, haven't they?'

Francesca and her mother looked at each other, momentarily abashed. 'No,' Francesca said. 'That ought to be true, but it isn't. It's all gone wrong before, three years ago. He managed somehow not to take the pills, even in hospital. I don't know how he does it, or why they can't just hold him down, night and morning, and inject the stuff, but the mad are very smart, and these hospitals tend to be staffed by a few very good people and a lot who are too idle or too stupid for the rest of the NHS.' She leant forward, talking to Matt's unconvinced expression. 'We're not going OTT, Matt. We've been here before. I'll talk to Wendy.'

'Sit there. I'll bring the phone.'

They all sat round her, including William, while she offered the shelter of the McLeish roof and the protection of the Metropolitan Police Force such as would be extended to the house of a detective chief superintendent, and finally gained reluctant agreement.

'She's coming for tonight,' she reported, putting down the phone, 'but I haven't convinced her to stay tomorrow. She wants to go down to Faraday's the night before the show so she doesn't miss any of it. She says she's missed so much . . .'

'She has, poor girl.'

'Anyway, that's tonight. We'd better get back and get a bed made.'

'And ring John,' her mother pointed out.

'Indeed.' She took a deep breath. 'I'll do *that* from home.'

* * *

'Tea, I think.' The Chairman of Trustees had presided over many meetings of this nature and knew that you had to give the participants space to get their breath and let their first, intemperate thoughts settle. It had been a heavy day; they had seen Amanda Roberts and Piers Miller before lunch in order to be able to make comparisons between the two young Turks, as one of the businessmen had observed. The school kitchen had produced ham salad followed on this hot July day by rice pudding. Elisabeth Brice, the consultant obstetrician, and the male members of the group had eaten it in loyalty to their own faraway schooldays, but the four other women had eaten about a teaspoonful each.

They had followed this slightly strange repast with coffee, and Roland Willis at 2 p.m. They had interviewed him for an hour, slightly longer than they had given the highly articulate Amanda Roberts and Piers Miller, but it had been worth it, the Chairman thought. Roland Willis had been nervous at the beginning but had warmed to the interview and had revealed an unexpected sense of humour as well as a deep and knowledgeable passion for the school, and an uncompromising support for its more difficult principles.

'Elisabeth, would you like to kick off?' the Chairman asked.

She put her cup down. 'Yes. I must say, I found all three extraordinarily interesting.' She reflected, fiddling with her teaspoon. 'I've done a lot of interviewing of course, and I am always reminded that it is a very partial method of assessment. You did very well, Chairman, to help Roland Willis to show us some of his real qualities.' She looked past him, out of the window; the sound of the orchestra repeating a difficult passage came on the summer breeze. 'All three are capable people, but in very different ways. It depends, as we have all said at different times, on what we want.' She turned squarely to face her fellow Trustees. 'And I want what this school does. The Faraday philosophy — well, I have to call it *something* — is not anti-academic. It insists rather that the kids themselves find the goals they want or need, rather than having them imposed by an adult world. A revolutionary idea in its time which is now accepted everywhere, that people who have found what they want to do work much better than those who are doing, sullenly, what they are told to do.'

There was a thoughtful silence and John Devon caught the Chairman's eye. 'Yes. I'd like to support Elisabeth on this. Almost all my problems have to do with people. Not their brains, we don't hire less than an Upper Second degree and a lot of our graduate intake have Firsts these days. But in the airline business, it's customers and regulators and engineers and all sorts, and you have to be able to work with them. Now the young people here, they learn that. Well, they breathe it in with the air, don't they? And they're good at it. Bit more emotional perhaps than we find appropriate.' He cast his eyes to heaven as a chorus of screams rose from the field outside and everyone laughed. 'But I'd be — I am — happy to employ a kid from this school.'

Well, the Chairman thought, a warm glow somewhere beneath his heart. I have not been wasting my time, we are doing something right here. He looked benevolently down the table to catch the signalling hand of his least favourite Trustee, a local solicitor, Peter Williams.

'This is all very fine,' the man said, querulously, 'but they've got to pass the exams, or no one will send their children here, no matter how good a time they have. It's not what they're paying for, and we've got parents who are making great sacrifices to send children here, you know.'

He'd have been far better off as a farmer, but he was made to train as a solicitor, because it was thought to be a solid respectable profession, the Chairman understood in a flash of illumination, and looked on him kindly. 'Of course they must, Peter.'

'Including the artistic ones. What's the use of A-level in art or crafts, unless you're going to be a designer of some sort?'

'The arts and crafts programme is part of it,' Elisabeth Brice said, impatiently, ignoring her Chairman's scowl. '*I* found my craft training of the greatest practical use as a medical student.'

'I'd like to be able to build a boat,' Tom Farmer, the other industrialist said, wistfully.

His fellow Trustees gazed at him, lost for words, and the Chairman decided the discussion had better be moved on.

'So we are in general agreement that the principles on which the school was founded — centred on the child, a strong emphasis on personal relationships and a great emphasis on arts and crafts — remain important.'

'Fundamental,' Elisabeth Brice said, firmly.

'But if anyone's going to be here to hold this debate in ten years, more of the kids have to pass exams. With better grades.' It was John Devon who stated the bottom line with his customary clarity, and the Chairman decided to move on to specifics.

'Thank you, everybody. So, against that background, who do we think best fits the bill? Is it profitable to consider the younger ones — Mr Miller and Mrs Roberts — together? Good. Anyone want to start? Elisabeth?'

'Mrs Roberts has very impressive qualifications and seems extremely capable. And the biology and chemistry results have improved enormously since she came. She will be a head somewhere, without doubt, but I don't think she's right for this school. I think we risk losing a lot of what makes the school special in a drive for results.'

'She'd drive for results all right,' John Devon, the senior industrialist, said reflectively. 'Good teacher, and you could see she was simply impatient with some of the nonsense you read in the education supplements. But I agree, Elisabeth, she'd break some irreplaceable eggs.'

The Chairman looked enquiringly down the table.

'I don't agree with you,' Peter Williams said, crossly. 'Much the best candidate. Stands out a mile. Knows what she wants and how to get it. There's far more in the school doing biology and chemistry than there were five years ago.'

'Would we lose her if we didn't make her head?' asked Jean Dalwinnie, who had been a Trustee longer than he.

'Bound to, Jean, in a year or so if not now. She wants a head's job.' Tom Farmer was a good judge of ambition.

The Chairman went on straight to consideration of Piers Miller, without revealing his own views of Mrs Roberts.

'This is the chap who was fiddling with the girl who died.' It was not difficult to tell who was last on Peter Williams' list.

'Mr Miller taught Catriona for A-level maths and did some last-minute coaching this term to try and get her to a respectable grade. Nick assures me that anyone who had had dealings with the young woman during the last few months thought her accusation was just another hysterical outburst.'

'Sounds suspicious to me,' Peter Williams grumbled. 'He's moved around a bit too. May have a history. I just don't think he's the strongest candidate.'

'Tom?'

The younger industrialist had stuck up a finger to indicate he wanted to speak. 'I liked him. Lot of scope, I thought, spoke very interestingly about the students. And he's an outstanding teacher. I would put him at the top of the list.'

So, evidently, would Elisabeth Brice and a couple of others, but there were three more strongly dissentient voices to add to Peter Williams'. No clear candidate so far, so he went on to seek the feeling of the meeting about Roland Willis's candidature and was not surprised to find that some Trustees, who had not been particularly keen on either Amanda Roberts or Piers Miller, waxed enthusiastic about Roland, his long service, his real devotion to the children and his contribution to the life of the school and the community. He raised an eyebrow at Elisabeth Brice, who was fidgeting.

'Oh, he's an excellent man. And he works all the hours God sends, and all the kids go to him with their worries, and he does the play, and so on. But, there are reasons why he's never got a head's post — and he has applied elsewhere. He lacks some essential spark, I think.' She shook her head in puzzlement. 'Anyway, Chairman, much though I like him, I think we'd be making a mistake; we wouldn't get the change the school needs.'

As an experienced Chairman, he had prepared for total disagreement, unwelcome though it was. 'Could I have some indication of preference, not a final vote, just so we can be clear where we stand. Could those who think Mrs Roberts is the best candidate please tell us?'

Three hands went up, then a fourth.

'I should not wish to continue as a Trustee were we to come to that conclusion,' Elisabeth Brice said, pleasantly, and John Devon nodded in agreement.

'Piers Miller?' Four hands went up and he looked at Peter Williams.

'*I* would resign. Even if he didn't . . . interfere with the young woman, there's a smell left. We don't need that.'

'Roland Willis.' Two hands went up and he glanced at John Devon.

'He'd do for the short term, but I'd want a time-limited appointment, and him told that we had to get the results up, whoever's feelings get hurt.'

'I couldn't say he'd do the school harm. He just isn't the best candidate,' Elisabeth Brice said, reluctantly.

He waited, but no one else seemed to have anything to say, so he proposed the appointment of Roland Willis as headmaster, his term to end five years hence. There was a pause, filled with calculation, then everyone made noises of agreement. 'I would like to ask Nick in now and tell him our decision.'

All agreed and Nick Lewis was summoned, his eyebrows lifting just perceptibly when he heard the name.

'Will the others be greatly disappointed?' the Chairman asked.

'They will need some managing, yes. But Roland will be overjoyed. We don't need to consult students where the appointee has been in the school for three years, but I can tell you they'll be pleased. So, shall I stay or go?'

He was asked to stay and a messenger sent for Roland Willis, who only just managed not to weep when he was told. The Chairman left to tell Piers Miller and Amanda Roberts that they had been unsuccessful, and, this duty discharged, went off to the Gents, feeling old and exhausted, and found John Devon beside him.

'Best I could do,' he said, defensively.

'Oh, I saw. Well, he knows the school and he's a decent bloke. We'll just have to stiffen him up.'

He would have to be content with this limited acceptance, he saw, but he knew that the right decision would have been Piers Miller. He sighed and went out into the sun, still hot at 5.30, past the chattering, indefatigable children.

* * *

'But Sir Andrew, the problem is that he hears the *words*. He was finding it impossible even with me on Sunday to sing about fair Amaryllis who never refused comfort in . . . well, in the circumstances of the death of a pregnant fellow student.' Francesca, fresh from an afternoon rest, was feeling well up to coping with the great Andrew Quentin. 'Nor indeed can the lyrics of "O Gentle Death" be entirely appropriate. That's the problem.' She listened to the furious silence at the other end of the phone. 'Well, what else can he do? What else has he rehearsed? "*Dov'e sei*" oh . . . well, I suppose not. What about the Handel aria, the famous one, Aeneas before Troy? And the Purcell thing, perhaps. Harmless words.'

'It's not really . . . yes, you're right. Of course, it's the bloody words, he has to do something else. And it's me, we've got across each other, but I can't leave him, can I, not now?'

Francesca, judging the question to be rhetorical, made no answer but signalled greetings to Wendy Miles Brett who came into the kitchen, looking exhausted, with a DC carrying her suitcase.

'Sir Andrew, I'm sorry, but visitors have just—

'Wait. Mrs McLeish. Look, I . . . well, the baby isn't due just yet. Two weeks? If we drove you down tomorrow and put you in a suite in the Fairleigh, could you possibly come down? I am literally at my wit's end. It's miserable for Giles and I really need to decide whether to tell the German I want to hear him to stay away.'

Francesca opened her mouth to refuse, but her eye checked on her cousin, slumped exhaustedly at the table, and the outlines of an idea started to take shape. 'Sir Andrew. Would your offer also extend to my cousin Wendy, Jamie's mother, and a policeman? No, not my husband who may well veto the whole scheme.' She summoned her energies to explain Wendy's position, feeling like a programme note for *Macbeth*, and watched her cousin, broodingly, as Andrew Quentin assured her, frantically, that any number of cars and suites should be hers if only she would come and use her magic touch on Giles. She promised to let him know, put the phone down and met her cousin's wondering gaze.

'I'm dying to go, Wendy. I couldn't bear to miss this show.'

'But Fran, I'd love to stay in a suite, but . . . John won't like it.'

'He won't but on the other hand he would have both of us where the Met can see us — he was worried about Steve feeling hostile to me, you know, as well as you. This way we'd only need one set of guards. And if the baby starts, the Quentin limousine can just turn itself into an ambulance and rush me back to UCH.'

'Darling, you're *not* to get too keen — he's a good man, your John.'

'I'm sure he'll see reason. I'll only be away for a night.'

'And two days.'

'Oh well, yes. I'd better go and square Susannah, but come with me and I'll show you your room. I know you know it but the good hostess does that just to make sure you've got sheets and towels. I read it somewhere.'

CHAPTER 15

Wednesday, 12th July

It was a beautiful day for the concert, Francesca thought, sitting at a rough table outside the school pottery. She was feeling guilty; she was here in the sun, having left husband, child and nanny in order to stand by her cousin and godson in a time of trouble, and to act as a mentor to Giles Quentin, and she wasn't at the moment doing any of it. Wendy, away from home, full of a magnificent breakfast provided at the local palace where they were staying, courtesy of Andrew Quentin, and in the company of her son, seemed to have forgotten her worries. Jamie, roosting briefly for coffee, was working so hard he barely had time to worry; he was leader of the orchestra, doing two solos, coached by Andrew Quentin, and singing in the choir and the chamber choir. On top of all this his adored Alex had arrived last night in order to take a final morning rehearsal of the dance group.

Nor, Francesca reflected, could she feel she was succeeding with Giles Quentin. They had put in two new arias, which was difficult but necessary, and he wasn't managing to get through either of them, or 'O Gentle Death' which he had been adamant about keeping in the programme. She badly needed to talk to Andrew Quentin and was waiting to catch his eye; he was drinking coffee and flirting with Alex. Andrew Quentin had been, she acknowledged, a revelation. He had cancelled whatever it was an internationally famous conductor was supposed to be doing that week and had stayed after the weekend, helping where he could. He had abandoned rehearsing his own son and had good-temperedly taken Jamie under his wing with an entirely new piece for violin and piano, teaching him — as Jamie had observed — more of real value in three days than he could have learned elsewhere in a year. And he had, in passing, transformed the school orchestra; he had listened to a rehearsal of the difficult Mendelssohn symphony they were attempting and spotted instantly the weakness in the second violins. He had sent a minion to London for his own instrument and joined the second violins as leader and coach. In four days, he had transformed the seven fourteen- and fifteen-year-olds from a struggling group there for practice into a powerful unit which gave real support to the rest of the orchestra. He was also contributing a much-needed tenor to both choirs and, endearingly, was enjoying it all. It would have been even nicer for everyone if he had done all this before Giles's last week at his much-loved school, but undoubtedly it was Better Late than Never. Much, much better. Just then he looked up and waved the boys off to their orchestra rehearsal and Alex to her dance, then came across to her, anxiety replacing his easy smile.

'How is it going?'

'I'm not sure it's worth having imported me, Andrew. Giles doesn't want to drop out — I asked him. But he's very fragile — he loses concentration very easily. Which seems to matter more with a countertenor — you have to concentrate just to stay with a head voice.'

'He drops into a chest voice?'

'No. He stops, having forgotten where he was. He is under serious strain.'

'Oh God.' Andrew Quentin looked away, pale with anxiety. 'It's not — he isn't necessarily . . .'

'I meant only that he must feel he . . . contributed to Catriona's death,' she said, steadily, deciding the words were better spoken.

'I suppose he'll get over that.'

'Not necessarily before tonight, Andrew.'

'What do we do if he can't cope?'

She was ready for this. 'I suggested to Giles that we might announce that he was singing with a cold, so that if it didn't work, he could just stop. I told him that was sometimes done on the professional stage.'

Andrew Quentin considered the point. '*Yes*. Yes, that might work. Of course, usually one would put the understudy in, but—'

'But there isn't one. Look, he needs to know that you would support this device. Will you tell him? I think he would feel less pressurised.'

'I will, I'll do it now.'

He left and Francesca sat, deciding whether to go and listen to the rehearsal or sit, guiltily, in the sun when she realised that Roland Willis had arrived and was hovering, looking tired and sombre. She had not seen him since the announcement, so she offered congratulations on his appointment as headmaster. 'Thank you. Thank you. Yes, I was pleased.'

'A great day for you,' she said, hoping to cheer him up. 'The orchestra is going to be spectacular. So is Jamie.'

'Yes. It is good of Sir Andrew, though I could wish he had come before.' This so exactly mirrored her own thought that she laughed and Roland Willis smiled back.

'I felt the same on Giles's behalf. My father died young, but I am convinced he would have been totally attentive all the way through my school career.'

It was meant lightly, but she seemed to have depressed him; he was looking anxious and harassed again.

'Oh, I don't think one ever gets it right. *I* didn't with Catriona. I couldn't make her happy.'

'Perhaps no one could, for the moment,' she said, into the cold silence.

'No.'

Another silence fell which Francesca decided not to try and break. The man was obviously still wretched despite having got the job he wanted and looked as if he might be going to break down and cry. She glanced anxiously round to see that none of the innumerable over-excited pupils were advancing on them.

'Your wife must be very pleased. About the job.'

'Oh, yes. Yes. She's not feeling very well today, so she's getting up late.' He cast a harassed look over at the schoolhouse.

'Oh, I'm sorry.' She saw with relief that Piers Miller was advancing towards them. Roland Willis rose, with a muttered apology, and went while Piers got a coffee and sat beside her. She recognised with a sinking heart that he, too, had come determined to talk to her.

'Is your husband getting anywhere with this case?' She raised her eyebrows at him, and he flushed. 'I wanted the job, you know, and I'd have been good at it. But none of *that* mattered because some of the Trustees thought there was a cloud over me because of Catriona. I can't go on like this. I didn't do anything to or with her, except coach her maths. To no purpose as it turns out.' He visibly replayed his words. 'Oh *shit*, that's not what I mean.'

'It is hard for everyone,' she murmured, wishing not for the first time that she had married someone who worked for the Post Office.

She glanced up to see Amanda Roberts at the next table, hesitating about whether to join them, and smiled at her reluctantly, acknowledging that it was her place after all.

'I suppose you can't tell us anything,' Amanda Roberts said, crossly, by way of greeting. She was displeased with life, that much was clear, but prepared to be civil to Piers, presumably on the grounds that he had been equally disadvantaged. 'I don't know about you, Piers, but I'm looking for another job.'

'I haven't yet decided what to do.'

'You probably need to get term over first.' Francesca knew she was tramping in where any angel might have hesitated, but equally a decision made in the aftermath of an unsolved murder and a long tiring term was plainly going to be wrong. She was not at all surprised when they both left to continue the discussion in more congenial company.

She leaned back against the cushions and sat up again as the baby objected. As she pulled a cushion into a more supportive position she became aware that Vivienne Willis, devoid of make-up and hair barely combed, was sitting herself down, coffee in hand. She smiled at her as welcomingly as she could and declined coffee, remembering guiltily that it was less than two weeks since this woman's daughter had been murdered. She was afraid that any attempt at condolence would also upset her fragile equilibrium, and instead congratulated her on her husband's appointment.

'Yes. Thank you,' she said, lifelessly.

She reminded herself that the woman sitting before her, pale and abstracted, was, in better times, a senior fund manager who had done a good job of looking after Gladstone College's limited resources. Grief for a lost daughter had incapacitated her and nothing anybody could say was going to help.

'I wanted to ask . . .' The voice died away.

'About the . . . about your daughter,' Francesca said, gently. 'I was so sorry . . . I didn't really make much contact with her.'

'None of us did. Or not for the last six months. Or . . . well, she wasn't much interested in women.'

Francesca sat up, cautiously. 'No, the poor child seems to have been struggling with her relationships with young men.'

'Does your husband talk about the case?'

She was about to deny, orthodoxly, all knowledge, but the denial would be false; inevitably she was privy to the case because of Jamie and Giles. And in any case this woman was in pain; if she needed to talk she must not be rebuffed. 'Not normally but, of course, I am involved with two of the boys who were her friends.'

'Jamie was a good friend,' Vivienne Willis acknowledged, gazing into space. 'Do they know who killed her?'

'If they do, no one has told me. I believe they are still searching.' Francesca had not been quite ready for the question direct and hoped this was an adequate response.

'I understand they found the key on the stairs.'

'Sorry?'

'The key to the room. The bathroom where . . .'

Francesca leant forward and took her hand. 'Vivienne, should you be doing this? The police are working on it, you know, a very large team of them. They won't stop until they find out . . .'

'The key was on the stairs, wiped clean, even washed. One of the police told me — not your husband — the next day. So, someone locked her in, then washed and wiped the key,' Vivienne said, in the tones of a teacher explaining something to a person of about six years old.

'Vivienne,' she said, gently, 'let me take you back to the house. Or find your husband for you.'

'No.' She was kneading her hands together, and Francesca put a hand over hers to stop her, trying to decide what to do.

'Vivienne.'

Francesca looked up, startled, and recognised Roland Willis.

'Viv,' he repeated, gently. 'Come on, sweetie, I'll take you back.' He pulled her to her feet and she turned her face into his jacket. 'Come on then, come with me.' He nodded to Francesca, barely acknowledging her existence, and they went off, Vivienne leaning against him, stumbling on the thick grass.

* * *

John McLeish stretched his back; he'd missed lunch and he was starving. 'My feeling is that something else has to happen before we get our arrest.'

'Sir.' It was a promising DC. 'What do you mean, something else needs to happen?'

'We've got six, possibly seven suspects, who had the opportunity. That's Roland Willis, Louis Roberts, Piers Miller, Susie Miller, Giles Quentin and Vivienne Willis, with Sir Andrew Quentin as an outside possibility. All of them are middle-class professional people with no record of violence. If one of them is the murderer he or she isn't just going back to their lives and pick up where they left off.' He looked round the table; they were all waiting on his words. 'It doesn't work like that.' The group continued to wait respectfully for illumination.

'He — or she — could just manage to forget the whole thing.'

Kevin Camberton had been, he saw, less than convinced by his speech.

'Possibly. There *are* people like that. They're the ones you can only crack if they've made a mistake and the evidence nails them. But here the evidence doesn't nail anyone.'

'So either someone's — well, conscience — makes them cough in some way,' Michelle Black said, 'or it'll be like that bloke in — Manchester, wasn't it? — who killed a girl fifty years ago, got clean away with it, was never even charged, then tells us all about it when he was seventy-eight.'

'Told his wife, who made him tell the police,' Camberton said, nodding.

'Sir. John, who do you fancy? Of the six.'

'As you know, I'm not comfortable with Piers Miller. Too light-weight. I'm not saying he couldn't have done it, but — well — what was she threatening?'

'Only his career and his marriage,' Kevin Camberton pointed out.

'True of all the male suspects. Roland Willis, for example.'

'He's too . . . too child-centred,' Michelle Black objected, and he considered her.

'If he were working-class you'd be remembering he's a stepfather.'

'She had several of those,' she objected, blushing. 'Louis Roberts, who she thought was her father, but wasn't. Piers Miller is a stepfather. Well, married to her housemistress, I'm sure that's how she saw him.'

'What about the women, sir?' It was the bright young DC. 'Susie Miller was protecting her whole life — husband and job. I mean, she couldn't go on at the school if her husband had been having it off with a pupil. And he'd never have got another job.'

'True.' He forced himself to consider Susie Miller seriously as a murderer; it was not impossible, he conceded reluctantly, she would protect her own whether it be her husband or her son.

'And Mrs Willis . . .' The DC's voice trailed off as everyone stared at him.

'Her own daughter?' Michelle Black said, shocked.

'Too nervy.' Kevin Camberton cut across her, authoritatively. 'She'd never have managed to do it, or managed to . . . well, to go on.'

Well, she hadn't, had she, McLeish thought, she'd collapsed. Then rallied to help her husband get the head's job. He sat, seeing the school as it had been over the weekend, the children everywhere, frantically busy in the champagne summer air, and the weary staff. The person who had killed Catriona, driven momentarily beyond endurance, was not going to be able to ride through it all. Everything he had learned in twenty years as a policeman told him that this case would resolve itself, but how or when was unpredictable. And meanwhile Francesca was nine days away from having the baby. 'The school breaks up tonight,' he said, pulling on his jacket, 'and they're off on their hols tomorrow. I'm going down there to pick up my wife.' He glanced at the big clock; he would make Faraday's by 8.30 if he went in the next hour. He would miss about half the concert in which Jamie was playing. And Giles singing if Francesca could get him on stage in good order. She had sounded very doubtful when he had talked to her early that morning, but whatever happened, he was going to share her suite tonight and drive her back very slowly to London and blessed UCH where the baby, whatever might be wrong with it, could be safely delivered.

A messenger came in and handed a folded slip of paper to Kevin Camberton, who read it and passed it straight to him.

'Right.' He was on his feet without realising how he had got there and the table rose with him, like flustered birds. 'Where is Havant? Relatively? How far? Forty miles. Well, he's making for the school, isn't he?' He looked round the baffled faces and fought back terror. 'Steven Miles Brett, father of Jamie, on the run from the Halliwick, tried to use a bank debit card in Havant. Two hours ago.'

'Sir, you don't think . . .' Michelle Black's voice faltered in the teeth of his expression.

'Yes, I do.' He drew in a breath and explained the background for the benefit of anyone on the team who had not absorbed it, gratefully observing that Kevin Camberton was phoning the local CID. 'Get a helicopter, will you, Michelle? It's two and a half hours by road and we need to be there quicker than that. I know him well, and the local lads only have photographs. Kevin, I want you, Michelle and two DCs. No, I'll take whatever the helicopter will carry, another two, right.' He looked round the group, slowly adjusting itself for instant action. 'We *know* Mr Miles Brett is violent and dangerous.'

'He may not get there, sir,' Camberton said, cradling the phone. 'Mrs Miles Brett has cleaned out the account like we told her to, so he didn't get any cash. I've called Havant back and told them to watch for him. He's been on the run for what, three days, he'll look a bit rough. Be a bit conspicuous.'

All that ought to be true, McLeish thought, running down the corridor to his office, with Michelle Black on his heels, telling him about the helicopter which by great good fortune was on its way back, expected in five minutes. It would need to refuel, but . . .

'I must speak to someone at the school,' he said, standing over his secretary who applied herself to the phone. He rushed into his own office to stare at the desk and pick up a few bits and pieces that might be useful. Blessedly Nick Lewis himself was on the line in seven minutes and he was able to explain. 'No. Tell them both but keep them where other people are. I don't think he'd tackle a crowd — no, I really don't know what he might not do, or even if he's going to get to you at all. The local lads are on their way and I'll be with you in an hour.'

'Should I alert Jamie?'

'When's his solo?' Whatever the circumstances no one married into the Wilsons could ignore the demands of a solo performance. 'After the interval.' He thought, but his brain seemed to have turned to wool.

'Surely Jamie's mother must be the prime target.'

'Leave it to them to decide.' He put down the phone and ran for the roof, swung himself into the helicopter, five of his staff, breathless, flopping down around him, strapping themselves in and staring out fixedly as the machine clattered off the roof sideways in a sick-making swoop.

* * *

Nick Lewis stood in the shadows at the edge of the hall, reassuring himself that Francesca McLeish, legs planted well apart under a tentlike maternity garment, and her cousin Wendy Miles Brett were in their seats in the front row, flanked by two male teachers. As further reinforcement, Alex Ferguson's substantial young man was sitting in the second row behind Francesca, with Jamie next to him. The dance troupe was arriving at a climax, a fast, twirling finale which was only just within the compass of the participants. Sweat shone on every outflung arm and one girl's hair had come down, but they were moving together and in tune and transported by their performance. From the side he could see Alex's red hair and pale face now white with concentration, calling the beat. The music ended, the dancers stopped, chests heaving, and took their bows, beaming, then dragged Alex on as the applause and shouting intensified. It had been a wonderful effort, he thought affectionately, and his students would always remember it with pride, but you had only to see Alex stalk on to a stage to understand the difference between any of these willing girls and a real dancer. He remembered with a small pang that Catriona Roberts should have been among this sweating, exhausted, beaming gang on stage.

Francesca, applauding, turned her head to shout at Matthew, sitting behind her right ear, but found him unconscious of everything except Alex, hand in hand with her group, taking a final bow. She felt a small sad pang, but good-temperedly returned her attention to the stage, clapping in rough rhythm to the baby's kicks. The dancers filed off and she looked up to see Nick Lewis, pale and serious.

'Headmaster?'

'Your husband rang. May we speak?'

She struggled to her feet and stood with him between the stage and the front row while he told her the news.

'What did he want me to do?' If he were here, she reflected, she would have found herself locked in the headmaster's study with Wendy and their guards, and the footie team posted at every corner outside. In her husband's absence, however, nothing was going to keep her from hearing Jamie play and Giles sing, however badly that went.

'He wanted you to stay in a crowd. He is on his way. In a helicopter.'

'What, just for us?' she asked, startled.

'He thinks that Steve could be very dangerous. I am also to warn Wendy.'

'I'll do that. Quick, before the choir.'

The choir was closing the first half, leaving the senior soloists and the orchestra for the second half.

'I was to let you decide whether to tell Jamie.'

'It will put him off his stroke.' She cast an agonised glance at the audience. 'This show's attracted a lot of attention. Unless Wendy disagrees I think we should take the risk. I'll sit with Jamie in the interval.'

The right decision, she thought, forty minutes later, clapping furiously as Jamie took his bow. Wendy had been naturally inclined to panic but had been soothed by the sight of half a dozen local CID arranging themselves purposefully around the edges of the theatre. Jamie had had two solos, of course, one for the piano, a Mozart sonata, and one for the violin, a duet with piano, which featured stolid, gifted seventeen-year-old Will, who was Jamie's usual accompanist. They had both learned the piece especially, spurred on by Andrew Quentin, who was looking justifiably smug.

Now for Giles; she had been backstage at the interval and had been able to loosen up his voice and keep his father, who was nearly as nervous as his son, from worrying him. The applause died away as the footie team lumbered on to move the piano, then Jamie reappeared with Giles. She waited, as Roland Willis, looking haggard and tired, came on stage to say the words that had been given him, that Giles was singing with a cold and the audience's indulgence was sought. It should of course have been Susie Miller, as head of music, and responsible for the concert, but she and Giles had both thought it wrong for Giles's mother to present his apologies. And moreover, *she* knew it was not a cold that was threatening Giles's performance, whereas Roland Willis had apparently accepted it at face value. He got a round of warm applause for his pains, wholly inappropriate to the words he was saying, which was clearly the school's tribute to his appointment as head. The colour came up in his cheeks, and he managed a tight smile before getting himself clumsily off stage. She returned her attention to Giles; he was looking pinched and nervous and about twelve years old, and he was searching for her over the footlights. She produced resolutely the confident encouraging smile she used for her brothers and Jamie and, inwardly, prayed.

Jamie sorted out the music on the piano while Giles, very pale under the lights, adjusted the stand that had his music on it. It had been agreed that for once both boys would have their music to read. The unearthly voice rose high and clear, though strained. 'Trees where you walk shall crowd in to the shade,' he sang with a perfect couple of trills and she relaxed fractionally. He'd got his mouth open and technique took over; it wasn't a difficult aria for one whose voice placed in that range. And of course he was superbly supported by Jamie, who was a first-class pianist even if the violin was his real love. She watched her godson, the long fingers moving on the piano, and remembered him singing this aria as a treble. She had thought then that he had done it well, but Giles was singing it as Handel had meant it to be sung; an eighteen-year-old countertenor had much more depth and colour and raw power than even the most gifted of trebles as Jamie had been. She saw suddenly why the violin was Jamie's best instrument, the one into which the passion went, it was a substitute for the wonderful clear treble in which he had once addressed an audience.

The second song, a brisk, slightly arch piece of Purcell, passed; Giles had relaxed and the superb voice filled the theatre. He and Jamie nodded to each other approvingly, totally unselfconscious, and got the music for the last song ready. She closed her eyes momentarily in prayer; Giles had decided, after all, to do 'O Gentle Death' despite its uneasy resonances, but she thought the decision risky.

And she was wrong, as it turned out, she thought. Giles was singing with intense, cold passion that held the over-excited kids and adults alike in silence, transported to a different place. She had seen two of her brothers move an audience in the same way, using their superb tenors, but this was different again, the chill clarity of the voice, like a treble but stronger and harsher toned, touched a different place in the brain. The song came to an end, and the audience paid the performers the tribute of thirty seconds' silence while they got themselves back into their skins and started to applaud. She beamed across the lights at Jamie, who had looked for her and his mother, and raised her hands high in applause. Shouting or whistling in the Faraday tradition was beyond her; the baby seemed to be compressing her lungs as well as her bladder, but Jamie and Giles were bowing to her and Wendy and she grinned back, scarlet with pleasure and relief.

The two boys filed off, smiling, and just then, she heard the helicopter, rattling overhead. She and Wendy looked at each other, but the noise died away and the audience returned to its preoccupations. 'I'd like to think he remembered there was a concert in progress,' she whispered, trying to lighten the moment, 'but I doubt it. They probably needed a better spot to land.'

'Can you . . . can you go and see if there's any news?'

'My instructions — *our* instructions — are to sit tight under the eyes of the assorted heavies. In any case we can't miss the orchestra.'

'No, of course not.'

They sat back, Francesca acutely aware that her husband was only a playing field away. She put it resolutely from her mind and watched the orchestra getting itself set up, Jamie as leader, violin dangling from his hand like an extension of his arm, checking the sightline to make sure all the orchestra could see. Strong though the school was musically, they had got in reinforcements for the demanding Mendelssohn symphony. Two of the musical staff, a horn and a clarinettist, were seated among the students and Andrew Quentin, glittering like a peacock, was with his transformed second violins.

She knew suddenly that her husband was close at hand and looked sideways down the row to the entrance. The door opened and a tall figure showed momentarily in the space as the house lights went down. She lifted a hand, remembering suddenly something she needed to tell him, as the door opened again to let him out and the orchestra started up.

* * *

'I don't think he's here, sir, but there's so many people coming and going. We've stopped half a dozen members of the catering staff who are outsiders, but they're all vouched for.

And we've been through the buildings as well as we could. He's likely still in Havant — we're in touch with the CID there.'

John McLeish nodded, totally unreassured. 'Let's do it all again, shall we? In twenty minutes we'll have the whole school and the parents out, and we won't be able to find him.'

They did it again, getting monumentally in the way of a harassed catering organisation but without result, and found themselves gathered outside the magnificent wooden theatre.

'They're on the home stretch,' Kevin Camberton said to McLeish, listening. 'About two minutes to the end.' The man was right of course, the music wound itself up to a climax and stopped, unleashing the usual roars and whistles. A few minutes passed, then a side door opened and his wife, her cousin and two local men came out, and he kissed her, deeply relieved.

'John.'

'Just a minute.' One of the local men had called to him and he set her aside and went over to see.

Francesca, who had been in the theatre for two and a half hours, and whose bladder was protesting, looked round uneasily. 'Ah, Inspector Camberton.'

'Yes, ma'am.'

'Something this morning,' she said, pulling him a little aside from the group. 'About the case — no, not Steve, the murder. *I* knew that you had found a key to the bathroom door, wiped clean of prints. When I think about it, I'm not sure I was supposed to . . . I mean I'm not sure where I heard it. It may have been Jamie, of course, but I've a feeling it was John.' She felt herself blush, but she knew her husband thought highly of his young inspector. She looked at him; his face was narrowed in thought, like her husband's when he was after a lead.

'Who mentioned it to you?'

'Mrs Willis. Vivienne Willis. She was asking me about it.'

His face changed, and he turned to look for her husband.

'I have to get to a lavatory,' she said, anxiously. 'I'll be back.'

He looked at her, and she saw him remember who she was and why they were here, and he summoned two young constables to escort her and Wendy. She glanced back, anxious as she was to reach safety, and saw him in a huddle with her John and the only woman on the team.

'We won't be a minute,' she said reassuringly to her male escort who looked uneasily at the door marked STAFF LADIES and posted themselves outside. It was a small two-cubicle place and with an apologetic look to Wendy she dashed for the open door. She set herself to rights and emerged to find herself looking at the back of an undeniably male person, slightly surprised to find that her escort had found it necessary to follow her in. 'Done,' she said briskly, and the man turned and for a dizzying moment she saw Jamie, thirty years older with the dark curly hair gone grey at the edges. And he had one hand in Wendy's hair, pulling back her head so that the neck was painfully stretched and the other held a knife to her throat. 'Steve,' she said, her voice coming out husky. 'How nice to see you. Did you hear the concert?' He stared at her intently and she saw some recollection settle. He was away, gone, she realised with a clutch at the heart that unsettled the baby. He was dirty and dishevelled and he smelt sour, but he wasn't raving or frothing at the mouth. It was more frightening than that, he was seeing things that she could not. She heard noises outside the door, running feet and shouting, and realised she was staring hypnotically at Steve and Wendy. He had been in here already, she realised, her guards would never have let him by and he had closed the bolt to the outside door.

'Mrs McLeish? Mrs Miles Brett?' an anxious voice called from the corridor. 'Are you all right?'

She hesitated, Steve's hand jerked and a trickle of blood started to run down Wendy's neck. 'Well, Steve,' she said, fighting to make her voice carry through the door, 'what are we going to do now?'

'Jamie.'

'Good idea.' Anything to get them out of this confined space. 'Shall I open the door?' She reached out but his hand jerked again and Wendy made a small terrified noise so she stopped.

'Steve?' It was a deep voice, not her husband's, though she could feel his presence out there. 'Roland Willis here. How are you?' The man's hand relaxed and Wendy gasped for breath. 'Are you coming to see Jamie?'

'Here.'

'That's all right.' The deep voice sounded utterly unperturbed. 'He's just along the corridor.'

'She's going to hell,' Steve said in a tone pitched well above his normal baritone. 'It's evil, everywhere. Except you, you and me, we together.'

'Can we come in?' It was Roland Willis's calm voice again and Francesca, terrified, knees wobbling, reached for the bolt. Steve's eyes slid round to her, and his grip tightened again on his wife who was braced painfully, knees strained straight and shaking to avoid the knife. 'Shall I open?' she asked, trying to imitate Roland Willis's calm, and he nodded. 'I'm opening the door for you,' she called for the benefit of the people in the corridor, expecting her husband, but it was Roland Willis who walked in, and surveyed the scene before him.

'Hello, Steve. Off you go, Francesca,' he said, kindly, and she sidled behind his back not daring to breathe, to be snatched into the arms of her husband who held her briefly. 'Get back and take Jamie away,' he said, thrusting her behind him, as policemen crowded past her.

'I can't leave,' the boy said, pulling away from her, and she looked for help but short of dragging him away and disturbing the delicate balance of whatever was going on there seemed to be nothing to do. They could not see past the police backs but they could hear Roland Willis gently urging Steve to let Wendy go and come and have a cup of tea.

They heard Wendy suck in air, convulsively, and Francesca could just see her husband, tense, waiting, then suddenly Roland Willis, a hand on Steve's arm, was leading the group out, Wendy still held in the vicelike grip, feet slipping on the tiled floor. The police at a snapped order from her husband stood back to let them through, giving Jamie a clear view of his mother, blood streaming down her neck, head braced back, pale as death. He ran forward with a cry before anyone could do anything. Steve Miles Brett, startled, clenched his left arm more tightly round Wendy's throat so that, throttled, her knees sagged and he dropped her and slashed wildly at his son, who stumbled and reeled back, blood spurting from his bare arm.

'No!' Roland Willis shouted and lunged forward. There was a brief scuffle and a cry of pain, then every member of the police team fell on the participants.

* * *

John McLeish, on his knees beside Roland Willis, leaned forward again, straining to hear the husky whisper. They had done what they could, but the wildly stabbing knife must have got the lung and had certainly got the stomach, and even though the helicopter was only a field away he did not dare try move the man without a stretcher and a doctor. Vivienne Willis was crouched, trembling uncontrollably, the other side of her husband. Kevin Camberton knelt behind her, tape recorder running, notebook out, and Nick Lewis, looking ten years older and grey with strain, was waiting by the door behind which Steve Miles Brett was keeping up a high wailing, terrified denunciation of evil.

'I loved her,' Roland Willis said, as he had several times already, the voice a laboured thread. 'But she . . . she turned against me, she was so miserable after Giles Quentin dropped her. I just wanted to comfort her. And then she . . . we . . . Is Jamie all right? And his mother?'

'Yes. You saved them both.'

'He was good to her. I'm glad.' His eyes closed, and Vivienne Willis clutched at his hand.

'Roland, Roland. Come back.'

His eyes opened again, effortfully, without focus. 'I'm sorry, darling.' He moved his hand in hers, and turned his head, restlessly.

'Mr Willis,' McLeish said, gently, 'were you saying that you and Catriona had become lovers?'

'No, no. Not in that sense.' The man's head turned in agitation and he stared at McLeish. 'I wasn't worried about any tests — I never — we . . . we never went that far . . .' The voice trailed off.

'Can't you leave him alone?' Vivienne Willis hit out at McLeish and he edged back out of her way, watching Roland Willis's eyelids close over his eyes.

'Viv, are you there?'

'Yes, yes, darling.' Vivienne Willis bent to put her cheek against his and his eyes opened again, staring past her.

'McLeish?'

'I am here, Mr Willis.'

'I did it.'

McLeish waited, then dared wait no longer. 'You killed Catriona?'

A tiny nod, inadmissible in any known court. The eyes were just open. 'I pushed her under and I locked the door. I'm sorry, sorry. She was going to *tell* you, darling. And Nick . . . it wasn't much . . .' The eyes rolled up definitively, and his wife drew back, then threw herself on him, weeping and stroking his face.

'Kevin.' McLeish had stood up, stiffly, and was looking over his head to where Francesca, pale as death, was kneeling clumsily, holding Jamie's arm aloft while the school nurse struggled to get bandages on two gaping knife cuts. 'Look after Mrs Willis.'

He was not going to try and get her away from her dead husband, Camberton decided, time enough when the ambulance finally got here. He sat beside her on the floor to the sound of Steve Miles Brett's agonised wailings and waited, watching her, receiving on her behalf the cup of tea thrust in his hand which he offered her wordlessly when she turned her head. He held it for her while she sipped, trembling. 'I knew,' she said to the air, 'that something had happened with Trina. But I never . . . not till today when we had a row about the bathroom key — he'd taken it away and I said we all wanted sometimes to lock a door and he went on about the key that . . . that . . .' She started to weep, clutching the mug. 'It was so *silly* — I wouldn't have been that shocked. He's her stepfather, these things happen. Oh Roland.' Hot tea was spilling from the mug and he was still trying to prise it from her fingers when the ambulance crew arrived in a flurry of men and equipment.

It took three of them to get her to leave the body and go to the school sanatorium with the local doctor and DS Black in attendance. He came back just in time to see Roland Willis's body being rolled on to a stretcher. There was blood, darkening as it dried, all over the corridor, and the members of the local force who had come to take Steve Miles Brett to a prison hospital stepped over the worst, awkwardly. John McLeish was there, watching it all. 'You got the tape?'

'Yes, sir. John.' He felt in his pockets. 'I'm not sure about the quality, he was so . . . so soft, but I heard him.'

'So did I.' Nick Lewis had come back to watch the passing of his deputy.

'Did you . . . ?' McLeish asked.

'No. No, I wondered why he wasn't happier about getting my job, but I thought he was still in such grief about Catriona that he could not rejoice . . .' His voice tailed away. 'Did you suspect him?' He was looking at John McLeish, and Camberton waited for the answer.

'He was beginning to look the most likely,' the big man said.

'A panicker,' Nick Lewis said, sadly. 'He needn't have killed her. We would all have forgiven him. I suppose he could not know that.'

'Or couldn't forgive himself,' McLeish said. They stood silent while the men picked up the shrouded stretcher. 'He saved two lives today.'

A noise from outside made them all look anxiously out of the window. The kids and their parents had been carefully kept away from the block and could be seen at the other side of the quadrangle eating supper at long tables.

'No need to hurry, Headmaster,' McLeish said, gently.

'No. No, there isn't, is there?'

EPILOGUE

'Another boy.' Dame Ruth Wallis bobbed up from her station at the foot of the bed and looked over at Francesca professionally. 'Much easier for clothes.'

The audience, John McLeish at the head of the bed and four midwives who had come to watch the great Dame Ruth at work, blinked at her.

'Is he all right?' He felt as if he had been waiting for ever to ask this question. Far from being thrown into labour by shock, Francesca had got back to London in good order after the concert at Faraday's and waited, not at all patiently, for another two weeks to go into hospital.

'He a lovely boy,' the Jamaican one said, indignantly, briskly mopping blood from an incredibly long pink baby, and placing him on Francesca's stomach. 'Look at them big eyes. He gonna have all the girls after him.'

They were all grinning, his wife, Dame Ruth and the four substantial ladies. The birth had been completely without incident; a gloved Dame Ruth had stood, hands held up beside his wife, urging her to push until, at the very last minute, she had moved with the speed of a striking snake to make a cut so the baby had tumbled out. He looked at them, understanding that the baby was normal and healthy, had always been normal and healthy and he could take his wife and son home without the lead weight of anxiety he had been carrying. He laid his head against his wife's, and she soothed him, uncomprehendingly.

'I know you have to go back,' she said, when he had recovered, 'but don't forget to ring our mums.' She was rapt, gazing into the big eyes of the creature who lay so quietly on her tummy, and he drank a cup of tea, thanked Dame Ruth and her supporters and walked out into a summer thunderstorm not even feeling the rain.

He arrived at New Scotland Yard, having rung their mothers. Francesca's had received the news of yet another boy in the family with the slight reserve to be expected from a mother of four difficult sons, but his own had been simply pleased. Kevin Camberton, who was handling two other cases, was waiting for him and offered congratulations.

'The Trustees decided to appoint Piers Miller,' he reported, without expression, and McLeish considered him. The whole thing had been a shock to his talented DI. 'I've been trying to work out why I went so wrong — I suppose I depended too much on previous form.'

'You got the motivation right, but the man wrong.'

'Why did you pick Willis?'

'Oh, I wasn't *that* sure — I would have had to pull him in if I had been. But if you looked at the situation coldly — and with no forensic evidence worth a damn — where does a kid in real distress go for comfort? Not her mother in this case, it was too difficult a relationship. Her little friends were fed up with her — even the good Jamie was deserting her, because his life was preoccupying him. It had to be her stepfather, and she didn't have much idea of what was appropriate, she was just desperate.'

'On that reading she could have done something, well, equally inappropriate, with Piers Miller. Who'd done it before.'

'Could easily have done,' McLeish said, patiently.

'She didn't, that's all. Or he didn't. I just got it wrong.'

'Don't beat yourself up,' McLeish advised. 'You'd have gone over it all again with what Vivienne Willis told Francesca.'

'Yes. Yes, we were just going to do that, weren't we?'

McLeish shivered, involuntarily.

'Sorry, didn't mean to bring back bad memories.'

McLeish nodded. 'Jamie thinks well of Miller,' he said, changing the subject. 'He'll be pleased to hear.'

'Where is Jamie?'

'With Sir Andrew and Giles at a festival in Germany. He'll be OK, he's young and the music will pull him through. His mum is up in Scotland — I think she'll stay.'

'And his dad?'

'In Rampton. Back on the pills, can't remember anything about any of it.' He fell silent; he had been bored by Steve Miles Brett in his right mind, but his fate was the stuff of tragedy; he would not be released from Rampton, the NHS psychiatrists having finally accepted that he wasn't going to act like a conscientious patient. And he would never really understand or accept what he had done. There was another casualty too, in a civilian mental hospital: Vivienne Willis, who unsurprisingly had retreated into a breakdown.

'Mrs Roberts is off; waited to see if they'd pick her as head, but when they didn't she took a job at Roedean. Said it would suit her better to be in a more academic school. To the local paper.'

McLeish laughed. This was familiar territory and he saved it up to tell Francesca, who would be home soon with his boy. He remembered something else. 'Kevin. Michael Harter. Your DC.'

'Oh, yes.'

'Had a talk with him yesterday. Asked that a note be put on his file explaining that he was gay. Sensible man.'

'Me, me and none but me, 'O gentle death . . .'

Matt Sutherland checked, startled. He had thought his ex-client, Giles Quentin, was abroad but this was definitely his voice, unmistakable even to the not particularly musical. He had been directed to the basement of the ramshackle

Covent Garden establishment and was walking through narrow corridors with scuffed linoleum and peeling paint and a pervasive odour of sweat and talcum powder. He stopped at the door labelled '16', the 6 held on at a strange angle by one nail, and peered through the glass panel. The room was empty except for a large cassette player and Alex, in leotard, tights, woolly cardigan and thick leg-warmers, standing on one leg. She extended the other leg, bending forward, and as she did so there was a perfect line from shoe to the crown of the flaming red head, faithfully reflected in the mirrored walls. The muscles of the diaphragm arched as she pulled up and into a turn, and he understood that he was watching the creative process; she was not exercising but designing a set of movements that would complement and extend the song. She revised the turn, wobbled slightly and came down, thought for a minute and walked over to the cassette to turn it off, so he felt it safe to knock. She looked up like a startled animal, the ugly fluorescent lighting making the red hair gleam, then grinned and waved him in.

'Antony wants me to start choreography. He says all dancers should do it. It's terribly difficult.'

He gazed at her; she was glowing with energy and pleasure. 'You've heard from him, then?'

'Only this morning. He doesn't want me for the core company yet. He says I'm not ready.'

'I'm sorry.'

'I never expected. But he wants me for the touring company this summer and he wants me to train with the extended company here after that.' She stretched against the bar, fidgeting her back into the right position.

'And give up university?' I have turned into my father, he thought, horrified.

'No. He doesn't really understand about universities because *he* went to the Royal Ballet school then into the company at eighteen, but he thinks I shouldn't give it up, whatever it is. He does know dancers can have short lives.'

'Durham's a long way to come for rehearsals.'

She sank to the floor, head on arms, flattened a long-extended leg and turned her head to look at him. 'Francesca's got me into UCL to finish off.'

Of course she had, he thought, with a leap of the heart; of all people she would share with his father — and him as it turned out — a deep conviction of the value of higher education. Nor would it have been that difficult with Alex's academic qualifications; Durham was presumably furious.

'You could go on doing part-time with us too,' he said, as casually as he could, as she bent both legs in an impossible position which brought her up on to her feet.

'If I wouldn't be a nuisance.'

He gazed back at her; she was grinning at him and he advanced on her. She melted into his arms and he kissed her, running his hands down the slight but formidably muscled back. 'We'd be very glad to continue to offer you employment,' he said, a little out of breath.

'Oh good,' she said, drawing back, eyes bright. 'Well, what about some dinner then?'

THE END

THE JOFFE BOOKS STORY

We began in 2014 when Jasper agreed to publish his mum's much-rejected romance novel and it became a bestseller.

Since then we've grown into the largest independent publisher in the UK. We're extremely proud to publish some of the very best writers in the world, including Joy Ellis, Faith Martin, Caro Ramsay, Helen Forrester, Simon Brett and Robert Goddard. Everyone at Joffe Books loves reading and we never forget that it all begins with the magic of an author telling a story.

We are proud to publish talented first-time authors, as well as established writers whose books we love introducing to a new generation of readers.

We won Trade Publisher of the Year at the Independent Publishing Awards in 2023. We have been shortlisted for Independent Publisher of the Year at the British Book Awards for the last four years, and were shortlisted for the Diversity and Inclusivity Award at the 2022 Independent Publishing Awards. In 2023 we were shortlisted for Publisher of the Year at the RNA Industry Awards.

We built this company with your help, and we love to hear from you, so please email us about absolutely anything bookish at feedback@joffebooks.com

If you want to receive free books every Friday and hear about all our new releases, join our mailing list: www.joffebooks.com/contact

And when you tell your friends about us, just remember: it's pronounced Joffe as in coffee or toffee!

ALSO BY JANET NEEL

WILSON & McLEISH MYSTERIES

Book 1: A FATAL BLOW
Book 2: A FATAL FALL
Book 3: A FATAL ENCOUNTER
Book 4: A FATAL POINT
Book 5: A FATAL CHOICE
Book 6: A FATAL GASP
Book 7: A FATAL END

Printed in Great Britain
by Amazon

40463651R00169